*if they say
i never loved you*

ALSO BY DAVID PETRY

if they say
i never loved you

A NOVEL

David Petry

THE GREAT GET GONE, SANTA BARBARA, CALIFORNIA

ACKNOWLEDGEMENTS

Thank you to Tom Mueller, Courtney Andelman, Roberta Kramer, and Eric Larson for reading drafts and significantly improving the story.

ISBN 978-1-7336195-0-9 paperback
ISBN 978-1-7336195-1-6 hardcover
ISBN 978-1-7336195-2-3 ebook
ISBN 978-1-7336195-3-0 audio book

First Edition

The Great Get Gone
315 Meigs Road, A114
Santa Barbara, CA 93019

www.TheGreatGetGone.com

To Lara, Samantha, Sarah, and Madison

If they say I never loved you
You know they are a liar

—*The Doors*

if they say
i never loved you

one

Los Angeles, California
September 14, 1967

JUDE TANGIER SLUNG HIS CHAIN LOCK OVER HIS
shoulder. Then he reached out and grasped the green rubber grip
of his handlebar. He closed his eyes a moment and felt it. The grip
was hot and pliant in the afternoon sun. The warmth spread through
his body and, for the first time since they'd moved to Los Angeles,
and definitely for the first time since he'd started school at Le Conte
Junior High, he felt maybe not safe, but at least centered.

Jude looked back at the school. A hundred kids or more were
fanning out from the school's exits. They spilled to the curb where
cars waited—there were no school buses in the big city—or drained
up and down the sidewalks on Bronson Avenue.

What a strange crowd this was. There were kids from all over the
world, wearing clothing Jude had never seen before, and speaking
in other languages. And studded among them like chocolate chips in
ice cream were the hippies.

He shrugged and mounted his green Sting-Ray. Pushing off,
he wove through the kids on the sidewalks. At the curb, he looked
left and hopped the bike down to the street. Hitting his rhythm, he
looked up at the Hollywood sign that loomed on the mountainside
just a couple miles away.

At Sunset Boulevard, Jude hit the dip of the gutter and caught air. Cars sparkled and growled waiting in the hot sun. He lifted his shoulders and put his head down.

He saw himself in his mind. His low metallic-red motorcycle was lofted a foot above the pavement, engine roaring. Rippling gold-flake flames were painted on the gas tank and Jude was leaning into it. He wore the coolest bell-bottoms and flapping peasant shirt, and his hair snapped in the wind behind him. Girls were standing on the corner, agog.

It hardly mattered that he was just a scrawny, short-haired, 15-year-old kid on a Sting-Ray wearing Levi hopsack flares and a short-sleeve plaid shirt.

Jude shot across the street and jumped both tires at once up onto the curb. The whole way up Bronson and for a hundred yards easy the sidewalk was clear. Jude lowered his head and doubled his effort. He stood on the pedals and worked his handlebars in a hard arc from left to right to increase the downward force on each thrust of the pedal.

He was feeling fly. Two weeks in at Le Conte Junior High. Two weeks of utter hell were maybe, or at least partly, over.

He heard a loud squeal ahead and looked up. A vast wall of black metal was swinging to meet him, hinges screaming. The wall was just a few feet away and directly in his path. His legs jerked at the brakes, but before the backward thrust of his feet could catch, he slammed into the black wall.

The next few seconds accordioned out into a painfully slow, jerky, stop-motion movie. He experienced each scene as if from the outside. He saw the metallic green of his bike strike and fold against the dull black metal. He—the lanky, pale boy riding the bike—smacked his face into the metal and then caromed upward, tangled with the bike and still helplessly, mindlessly, peddled. There was a sticky moment when he finally stopped pedaling and everything hung in the air.

Then there was a great disordered clatter and boy and bike crumpled to the pavement. Hands and feet, arms and legs settled. The bike teetered on top of him, a pedal digging painfully into his stomach.

Time continued at a leisurely pace while his mind awaited details.

Was he alive, or conscious, or in excruciating pain? Instead he only knew the pavement was hot and the smells that eddied around him were of oil and cigarette butts and sour, old, rotting garbage. Slowly, as though the fabric of reality had to first reweave itself, sound filtered in. Then the bright blue sky pulled in around him. And then the hard edges and filthy surfaces of Bronson Avenue scuttled in.

Jude blinked hard and let his eyes wander. A large, blue trash dumpster loomed over him. He had slammed into a gate for a large trash enclosure.

He was lying on his back under his bicycle. Up through the bent and broken bike he saw three boys standing over him. All three boys wore dark shirts and blue bandannas folded into headbands. He knew one of them, Hector Elizado. Hector was in Jude's P.E. class at school.

In Jude's absence of thought, he couldn't determine whether these boys were benevolent or dangerous. But he was starting to think they were dangerous.

Hector leaned in and confirmed. "Look, amigos. A piece of fucking honky white trash!" he said. "It's time to go back to fucking Indiana."

The two amigos laughed. One of them stepped closer and kicked Jude in the hip. The boy was desperately trying to grow a moustache. The other amigo, baby-faced and serious, leaned in, popped open a switchblade, and sliced the tire that was in front of Jude's face. A dry, hot rubbery smell flushed out with the air. Babyface sneered and said, "We're putting you out with the trash, motherfucker." He landed a kick to Jude's ribs and yelled, "Pendejo!"

Moustache stepped up and spit on Jude's face as he rifled Jude's pockets. "Fuckin' kike on a bike!" he cursed in a hissing whisper.

Moustache beamed as he tugged a wad of cash and pens and papers from Jude's front pocket. Jude had maybe three dollars and he watched it go with regret. He had planned to stop for an ice cream. But the papers. There was a picture… It was a photo of Betty Brown. Formerly from Texas, and now a resident of Indiana, Jude had fallen for her late last year when she was the new girl in Indiana. She spoke with such a soft, lilting drawl. And her straight blond hair seemed exactly clean and right. He had asked her for a photo the last week of school, and she had crinkled her nose in surprise—he'd never spoken to her—and gave him one.

Now, he saw the familiar face flicker past, dangling from the kid's outstretched hand. "Look at this, 'Zado!"

Hector reached out, the movement slow and looming, his grin smeared over Jude's entire sky. Hector's hand grasped the image and tugged it upward into his face. To Jude, the smile spread and spread and spread.

"You got a little honkey bitch, huh?" Hector said. "Or are you just dating your sister?" He stuffed the image into his shirt pocket.

Jude heard sirens and he let his gaze fall off toward Sunset Boulevard.

When he looked back up, the three boys and his money and photo of Betty were gone.

He didn't move. He was still waiting for information. Maybe pain. Maybe he would see some blood, or maybe a body part a few feet away.

The sirens rushed past on Sunset without stopping. Jude counted three black-and-whites. They bounced on their shocks as they hugged the curbs and shot across the street drains to cut past the slowed cars in the intersection. He listened as their urgent whine ricocheted away into the city. Then he pushed the bike off his chest and rolled to one side. He let his eyes travel.

A gas station attendant was standing at the corner of the building. He wore a dark blue jumpsuit and was holding a push broom, bristles up, like a pitchfork. He stared at Jude, frowning, like Jude was a mess he might have to clean up.

Jude stood slowly and brushed himself off. He looked over his bike. Then he stared down at the smudges of blood on the pavement and wobbled off up the street on foot, pushing his bike.

Jude hobbled up Bronson, but he felt the eyes of other kids from school, riding home in carpools. He turned in at Harold Way. It was a street he knew. He could get home more quietly this way.

The street was lined mostly with apartment buildings. But out near Bronson, an old two-story, shingle-sided, reddish-brown house sat in a gap between two apartments. It sat back from the street with several older cars out front on the asphalt drive and on the lawn.

An American flag hung upside down over the front porch, the stars replaced by a big white peace sign. Jangly, whiny music with nonsense lyrics trickled from the windows and doors.

> *I wrote a letter I mailed in the air,*
> *Mailed it on the air indeed-e*
> *I wrote a letter I mailed in the air.*
> *You may know by that I've got a friend somewhere*

It was this odd house that had drawn Jude down the street the first time. By now he was somewhat acclimated to the residents of the house. They hung out on blankets on the front yard, or on the slanting rooftop over the front porch, or on top of a pink and green Volkswagen bus with sunflowers painted on the sides. They smoked cigarettes, wore bell-bottoms, and a couple of the men had long hair. Today, three of the men were out throwing a Frisbee. One of the men was black.

"Hey, duuude," a blond man with shoulder-length hair and a massive moustache, said to him. He was standing in the street, a red Frisbee in his grip. He wore ragged jean shorts, no shoes, and a torn yellow T-shirt that said MAKE LOVE NOT WAR. "Hey, man. You okay?"

Jude clenched his teeth and lowered his eyes. The front wheel of his bike was bent with broken spokes and both tires were flat. He had to lift the front of his bike to pull it along. His knuckles on his left hand were raw and bleeding. He knew he had a knot on his forehead. Maybe it was bleeding. He shrugged. "I'm fine." He pushed on past the man.

"Hey, dude," the blond man called again, wringing out the last word like a rag.

The black man, with a dark, bouncing orb of hair, called out, "Hey man, he's on his own trip. Let him be."

"He's all fucked up," the blond man said. "I think someone beat on him."

Bouncy hair, holding his hand up impatiently for the Frisbee, said, "The only universal attribute of human life is suffering, man. And you're making me suffer, so throw the fucking Frisbee!"

The blond man whined as though the world were going amiss,

"The kid needs some medical *attention*, man!" But he whipped his hand and the red disk floated silently away.

Jude pressed on. Behind him, the black man was chipping away at the blond man, "Attention does not have to be fucking, like, 'medical,' man. That's like saying military justice when adding military actually makes it, like, you know, *unjust!*"

A few doors down, as Jude approached the next corner, he came to a two-story white plaster apartment building. This building was the reason he came down Harold Way the second time. And all the times after that.

This was one of the older style apartment buildings, built back when Los Angeles defined stylish and modern. It was pure white with raised plaster accents, like a tasteful wedding cake. The narrow end faced Harold Way, and on the wall above a pair of spiky yucca plants, the name THE CRESTVIEW was lined out in raised gold-and-black cursive. Around the corner, the twenty or so apartments all faced out on Canyon Drive.

Between the building and both streets were strips of grass. This late in the afternoon, the Harold Way end of the building was catching direct sun, and clustered there were a few folding chairs, a tall table, an umbrella, and eight or nine women. The women were all wearing robes and bikinis like this little patch of grayish grass was a fancy Las Vegas poolside. They were standing and sitting, drinking iced tea or wine, gabbing like birds at a bird bath, all soaking up the afternoon sun.

This gaggle of women, in one form or another was out here every afternoon when Jude had gone by. They mostly seemed intent on painting toenails and fingernails and had never acknowledged Jude.

Today, Jude lowered his head again, kept to the opposite side of the street, and tugged his bike along.

His effort to be inconspicuous was working. The women seemed perfectly happy to do what they always did, ignore him.

Then, just as he was about to issue a sigh of relief at escaping their attention, one of the women, short, and with the stiff, thrusting bearing of a parrot, came toward the street. She stepped over the wall and hesitated at the curb, looking him over carefully. Then she marched out into the street. Jude dropped his head another notch and poured decisiveness into his gait. His bike, with the front rim bent, literally limped.

"Hey, you, hold up!"

He might have shrugged her off and kept going, but underneath the command there was a tinge of empathy or maybe pity in her voice that made him slow, straighten, and then stop. It was embarrassing, though. The woman wore a bathrobe—a short, pale green terry bathrobe—with slapping red rubber sandals on her feet, and huge round sunglasses with electric blue frames. She held a large bowl-shaped wine glass full of dark red wine in her hand. And now all the women on the lawn were watching.

She stopped a dozen feet away and Jude and the woman stood there, appraising each other. Jude glanced past her to the women. They were odd birds, all gaudy and strangely done up. But he and this parrot woman were the spectacle.

"So, what happened to *you*?" she asked.

Jude opened his mouth but said nothing. He could talk to some girls his age... sort of. And he could talk to his parent's friends and his grandparent's friends... sort of. In both cases they had to be safe, maybe not too young and pretty, and this woman seemed to almost qualify, but maybe behind the sunglasses... And then visible just past her shoulder were seven women who were definitely pretty, only partly dressed, and who seemed wholly unsafe.

"Fall off your bike?" Her eyes traveled over the bike and his clothes and face. He felt the burn and throb of the dent or cut on his face over his left eye. His left hand was chewed up and bleeding. Possibly worst of all, his pants had somehow blown a seam in the crotch. They were extra loose, and he felt the inflow of air. "Or did someone maybe help you?"

He finally lifted his shoulders and let them fall. He leaned toward Van Ness on his handlebars. But, horribly, impossibly, he felt tears start and his lip quivered.

"Hey," her voice was softer, but there was still something of an edge to it.

He made a supreme effort to dry his eyes from the inside and stop his fast, short breathing. He pushed one step toward Van Ness and made a quick swipe at his eyes with his sleeve.

"Hey!" Now her voice carried affront and a command to stop.

He stopped but kept his eyes on the end of the street.

"I don't bite," she said. She laughed. Then she swirled the dark liquid in her glass and he followed it with his eyes, feeling dizzy. She drank. "Not usually, anyway."

Jude remained motionless.

"I'm Penny." She tugged off her sunglasses by way of introduction, and Jude saw that she was, in fact, a very pretty woman.

He spoke.

"Jud?" she said.

He pushed the word out again.

"Okay, Jude," she closed the gap between them, and reached out her free hand. He thought she might touch him, but she pulled at the air just a few inches from his shoulder with her fingers. "Come on."

He lurched and then shifted direction and followed her reluctantly across the street. "Ladies," she said as they reached the curb, "this is Jude. Looks like he's had a rough go of it this afternoon."

"I'll say," a red-haired woman with long, tanned legs and a dangerously small bra top over a plump bosom, pushed up out of her chair. She half-stood and reached out past the wall. She tugged at his pants. Air flooded over his legs and he felt the blood in his face run hot. "He's coming out all over the place!"

He looked down at himself. His bloodied shirt ran down to a flapping pant leg with pale, white flesh driving all the way to his thigh. He felt his face pulse with heat and the very core of him wanted to cry. But the dense wrapping of fearful decorum that was his daily facade held these fresh tears down and back.

The women tittered, watching him like he was a circus act.

The red-haired woman was standing very close to him now, touching his shoulder, and smiling right into his face. She smelled warm and sweet like a strawberry kitten. But a kitten that smoked. He watched her freckles come into focus. The spread of them over her cheeks scattered inside him like a wonderful, warming galaxy. As suddenly as he'd wanted to cry, now he felt flung among the stars. And her warm earthy bosom right there beneath his eyes. He was suddenly a bit giddy.

This was all impossible. He held that word in his head—Impossible!—while he peered out of himself at the redhead. 'Quite impossible,' his mind responded, with a clammy British accent.

Her grin broke through his reverie. It was garish and frightening. She clearly knew something he didn't. He straightened and looked away.

Penny took his arm and said in a voice that pierced the women's sharp noise, "They're a flock of magpies. Don't let 'em bug you." She pulled him from the women and turned to the building.

"Hey, don't steal my candy," the redhead called. There was lipstick smudged on her teeth.

The wedding cake building had staircases climbing up both ends. As they rounded the corner of the building, Jude looked along the apartments. Several had doors or windows thrown open to catch whatever breeze might come along in the still, dry heat. Bright, gritty music tumbled out of more than one apartment, and clusters of limp clothing hung from the upstairs railing and on hangers from hooks and light fixtures along the wall. A woman, a girl really, with long black hair, also wearing a robe, a short silk blue one, leaned on the railing halfway down. She was smoking, watching them. A coffee cup was balanced on the rail in front of her. Her pale legs became the exact length of his attention.

"Frenchie," Penny squinted up at her, "can you do some damage control in a couple minutes?" Penny grasped his pants in front on one side and tugged to show her the issue.

Frenchie pulled her head back and smiled a smile devoid of light. "You're kidding me, right?"

"You've got the sewing machine, Frenchie. And the chops." Penny moved Jude about in a tiny area on the walkway below Frenchie, as though positioning him just so in a shop window. Just past Frenchie's shoulder, Jude could make out someone else's face peering out the window, a pale, almost wraithlike, girl.

Frenchie shook her head. "Shit, Penny, he's a punk kid! He can run on home to his mommy!" She pushed back from the railing in rebellion and disgust. Jude watched the coffee cup rock slightly and then suddenly tip. Its fall was long and silent, a tongue of slippery brown liquid sliding out midair. Then it slapped among the unfurled ferns below. "Fuck! My coffee!" She leaned over the rail and stared down at the cup for a long time.

Penny seemed unimpressed. "Grab her cup, willya?" As Jude bent to retrieve the cup, a large blue and white mug with WORLD'S BEST MOM on the side, Penny said, "We'll be up in sec."

Frenchie threw her hands in the air. "I haven't even had my fucking breakfast!" She spun and stormed into the apartment while the pale face at the window blinked and watched.

Penny called out, "Eat something! Really. You'll see, it's good for you!"

Then Penny turned a rosy, contrived smile on him. "Come on," she grasped his sleeve and tugged him back toward the stairs. They faced the door to the first apartment. A small red-and-white sign on the door read MANAGER. Another sign stuck to the wall above the doorbell said NO SOLICITORS. A dense throb of music came through the door.

"We'll see if Russ is around, okay?" She rang three times, pressing hard and long, then knocked three times loudly, and called out in a boxing arena bark, "Russ! Russell!" Then again, louder, *"Russ!"*

Jude hung back, standing off the small concrete pathway in a tiny median of grass, his bike propped in front of him like a shield.

Penny tapped the NO SOLICITORS sign and looked over her shoulder at him. "That's funny. Right?"

Jude frowned. He said, "Sure." But he didn't know what a solicitor was.

The door sucked inward. A louder, raspier bark of music burst out from the dark interior. "What!" A large black man with bulbous yellow eyes stood behind the screen. Jude felt like a fly confronting a toad. "Ah, Penny," he said, his voice tinged with sarcasm. Music poured out around him like water from a broken dam. Everything about it sounded angry—the instruments, the voices, the beat.

"Hey, Russ, this kid…"

Russ's eyes traveled to him and Russ popped out a laugh. "This kid…" he pushed open the screen, "looks like he fell off a fucking turnip truck from O-fucking-hi-o!"

Penny cocked her wineglass and head in opposite directions but at the same angle, conceding his point.

"Indiana," Jude heard himself say.

"What the fuck you say, boy?" But he'd heard him. "Indi-fucking-ana, Illi-fucking-nois, or O-fucking-hi-o, boy. I don't care if you're from Ken-fucking-tucky. It's all one big Bible belt, honky. And only things on the road out there are turnip trucks." He scowled. "And they all just heading right out here, like there is some promised land around here some-I-don't-know-fucking-where!" Russ gestured with his eyes past the buildings to include, perhaps, all of Los Angeles. Or maybe the entire West Coast.

He grinned at Jude. Now that he'd gotten his digs in, he was willing to engage. He stepped out the door. He was both tall and wide, in a stained yellow T-shirt, stained dark sweatpants held up with a length of cord, and dirty gray slippers. His face was pocked, the pocks white and yellow against his dark, grayish skin, and his brows thick and permanently folded above his eyes. His thick pale lips protruded over gapped teeth and his dense, straight hair had a tinge of red, like he was maybe half-black, half-Irish. He was more menacing than anyone Jude had ever encountered. But Penny, standing small and somehow vulnerable next to him, made the big man seem human somehow.

"Can't fix that shitpile," Russ jutted a chin at the bike. His faded yellow eyes focused on Jude's face. "And I ain't no fuckin' boy-nurse."

"I know, I know," Penny waved her glass, "Frenchie's going to sew up the pants. I'll get him cleaned up and have Lacey look at that eye and the rest of this mess. But, I'm hoping you can give him a ride home in a bit."

Russ's head drew back, and he looked at Penny out from under his brows with disbelief. He shook his large head, shrugged and pursed his lips, smacked the lips, shrugged again and kept on shaking his head.

But he finally said, "All right. All right, sure." His voice was sliced in half. "Gotta be in fifteen minutes or so. I got a fucking life, ya know?" Then, face drawn up into a mask of folds and anger, his voice climbed. "I got to live my *processes*, woman! My *processes*!"

He reached out for Jude's bike. Jude tilted it two inches in his direction. Russ lifted it like a fly by the wing, looked at it analytically, and then grasped the front wheel and the frame and pulled them apart where they had been bent together. Then he turned and set it against the wall by his door.

Russ turned back to them and took a step closer, crowding Jude with his stomach. He lifted his eyebrows and Jude backed up. "I drop you off today, and you and me? We don't…" he stabbed a finger first at his eye, then at Jude's, and then back at his own, "visualize each other again. Not for many, many moons. That right, honky?"

"Ah, um," Jude took a step backward. "Yes, sir."

"Sir!" Russ grinned and took another step toward Jude. Jude moved backward again. "That's pre-zactly it! Sir! You call me Sir and you'll survive another day, you little shit!" Russ swept a gloating grin at Penny.

Jude reached over and touched the railing of the stairs. He felt like he needed to touch something solid and grounded so he wouldn't fall over.

Penny laughed as she pulled him away, "Russ acts like a hard-ass, but he's a pussycat," she said. "He don't bite either. Let's go see Frenchie." As they went up the stairs, Jude glanced down and saw Russ, arms crossed, immobile, watching them.

"Ahhh…," Jude mumbled at Penny's back. "What's a honky?"

"Hah!" she barked out a laugh. "Russ was right about that turnip truck! A honky is a white person. Like a nigger is a black person." She topped the stairs, then looked back and shrugged. "Sorta."

Two women were out along the railing upstairs, but farther down. They sat on chairs against the wall, smoking cigarettes. One had on just a short nightie, the other had on little boy PJs with rockets on them. Coffee cups sat on a small table on the walkway. Penny stopped at an open door and one of the women called out, "Youngsters now? You got a line on a new market?" The women snickered. Penny smiled at him, "You just ignore everything you hear while you're here, and you'll be just fine." She slipped into the apartment.

"Frenchie, thanks for doing this."

Jude couldn't see inside the dark apartment. Penny reached out and pulled him in. He stood blinking, still not really seeing. His eyes adjusted slowly, first to the relative dark, and then to the pall of smoke in the room. Frenchie was sitting at a cluttered kitchen table by the front window. In a small space in front of her, there was a glass bottle of milk that read ADOHR FARMS—the same dairy his family bought their milk and eggs from—and a box of Sugar Pops. She was working her way through a bowl of the Pops with a lit cigarette in the same hand as her spoon. She took a bite, crunching mightily on the cereal, and swallowed. Then she took another bite, chewed and swallowed again. Then she took a deep, eye-squinting drag on her cigarette. She was still in her blue robe with her legs crossed. She looked completely disinterested in her visitors, or in the problem of sewing his pants.

"Okay, Frenchie," Penny let loose of Jude, set her wine glass down, and moved to a closet in a narrow hallway that looked like it went to a bathroom and a bedroom. "I'll prime your pump. Just to show our visitor some manners." After clattering around in the closet for a long moment, she emerged with the sewing machine. It was a beast. It was a heavy, black and metal Singer device, with a frayed black cord. The machine was set on a metal plate in a low, dark wooden box stand. It looked like it had sewn costumes for the circus at the turn of the century.

Penny brought it to the kitchen and pushed it onto the table, forcing the clutter of clothes, magazines, dishes and food back toward the opposite edge.

"I don't even know if this thing still works!" Frenchie mumbled through a mouthful of cereal.

Jude stepped forward and set the blue-and-white mug on a tiny empty space on the table near her. She looked up at him, eyes as flat and dark as the muzzle of a double-barreled shotgun. "Thanks," she said. A shiver of something dark and fundamental raced down his spine. In the midst of a hot, dry afternoon, he felt cold.

He shifted his gaze away from her eyes. Close up, she looked younger than she had from below. She could have been in high school with his brother. Her skin was clear and pale, her features small and gathered close, her mouth a perfect rosebud pout, and her chin sharp and certain. Her legs crossed under the table like something perfect, Grecian, and forbidden. His eye traced the line of her muscles down the side of her thigh. Jude felt cold as ice and hot as melted butter. Her feet were bare and her toes were painted a chipped pink that Jude somehow felt as a warmth in his midriff.

"Sure," he said. He caught movement in the kitchen and looked up. The pale girl who had been watching out the window was there. She had been there all along, leaning against the far counter, watching. She looked younger than even Jude. She wore ragged jean shorts and a blue blouse. She was thinner than the clothes, like a scarecrow. Her eyes were hollow and dark, serious, fearful.

Frenchie followed his gaze and looked over at the girl. But she said nothing.

"Okay, let's get 'em off," Penny said. Her voice was all business. She took him by the arm, but Jude just stared at her.

"You gotta take off your pants, kid. So, Frenchie can fix them."

"Oh," he had somehow overlooked this aspect of getting his pants repaired. "Oh, no. I can't. I mean, that's all right. I mean, it's okay. Everything's okay. My mom…" He leaned away from her, afraid she was going to corner him or pin him or something.

Penny released his arm and stepped back. With the lifting of her hand he felt a lifting of concern. They could talk it through. No need to rush. "Hey," Penny said, "it won't take two minutes and this way your momma won't freak out when you get home."

Then she reached in and deftly popped the snap and unzipped his fly. His pants were falling, and though he attempted to save them, he was shocked to immobility by the suddenness and embarrassment and he stood hunched over grasping nothing but air. His mother's parting words in the mornings scratched through his head. 'Are your underwear clean? You wouldn't want to end up in the hospital with dirty underwear.' He wondered, now, obviously late in the game, what clean meant exactly when it came to underwear. He wore white briefs, and though he didn't dare look down, he felt they must be baggy and gray by this point in the day.

With a light push to his chest, she made him step backward and plop heavily on a chair. She knelt and tugged his shoes off from the heel without untying them. Then she yanked the pants off his ankles. She snapped them up, smiled at him, and thrust them at Frenchie.

Jude leapt to his feet and stood mincing from one foot to the other, covering his underwear with cupped hands.

Frenchie was watching him now with a sleepy grin. "Look at him," she said, "like a little colt prancing around!"

"Let's go!" Penny laughed and slapped him on the butt. He almost leaped through the window. She grabbed her glass and stepped past him, back into the sunlight. His mouth opened but no words came. She said, "Come on, you're not a vampire. The light won't kill you."

Jude shot a confused glance into the kitchen. The pale girl's expression had not changed. She had not moved.

With a jerk, Jude followed Penny robotically. His mouth continued to form words but made no sound. When one of the women down the way hooted, he felt his face and neck burn, but his bare legs felt icy and white as ancient Arctic fish bellies. His crumpled white socks clinging to his feet somehow doubled the pain. He felt like Indiana itself, naive and unzipped and exposed. But he followed Penny. Her matter-of-fact manner seemed to make his complaints half-deflate before they were even up for discussion.

Penny stopped at a door two-down from Frenchie's and knocked. To a muffled response, Penny spoke in at the screened window, "Hey, Lace, you come down to my room in a couple? I want you to look at this one. He's probably fine, but... you know."

There was another muffled response. Penny winked at him, opened the door and put her head in, and said something. Then she closed the door and took him all the way down to the first door at the front, the apartment above Russ's. The music from Russ's apartment rose up through the floor like swamp gas.

Jude looked out the window as if planning an escape. But he was no more than a stick in a river. He had no pants. His bike was mangled. And Los Angeles stretched to the horizon in every direction. There was simply nothing but river.

Again, his eyes worked to see in the near dark, but Penny was already pulling him in through the room. There was a couch, a television, framed prints that danced with vibrant color, and a strange glassy octopus of a device on the coffee table. Then they entered the tiny hall and he was being pushed into a bathroom. Penny guided him to the closed toilet seat.

He sat and looked around at the sparse décor. There were matching blue shag rug, toilet cover, shower mat and towels; a glass with toothpaste and brush; and a little silver tray of small, colored bottles and make-up. Then he found himself in the mirror, and his head jerked back and he squawked.

"Yeah, you'll scare your momma looking like that."

His short hair stood in tufts and his face was dirty in blotches and smears. The effort to wipe away his tears had made matters worse. The tear tracks on his cheeks stood out in the smudges of dirt and grease. But the worst of it was an angry, two-inch cut over his eyebrow that had formed a rivulet of blood that traveled to the line of his jaw. The cut was swollen to a golf-ball-sized welt and all around the cut was a red-and-yellow halo. His gaze shifted from himself to Penny who stood behind him looking at him in the mirror. With nothing but that, his eyes welled and a tear was out and gone before he could even raise a quick wrist.

Penny frowned broadly and roughed his hair. "Hey, getting beat on is no fun. But shit happens, right?" She wet a cloth and gently wiped away some of the dirt. "Like my Daddy used to say, 'The only way to get a thick skin is in the School of Hard Knocks.' I think maybe you got a lesson today."

Jude didn't quite understand. He'd never thought about having a thick skin, or getting your ass kicked in order to get one. But the tears were gone and he watched Penny work. She cleaned his face and neck with cold water and a towel, carefully avoiding the lump over his eye. She wet his hair and finger-combed it. She talked the whole time, but Jude hardly listened. He was wrapped in her warm lemony scent. He was dreaming a dream of her hands and face as they wove a lattice of comfort and care over him, and he didn't even seem to be part of it.

Then Penny was backing from the narrow room saying, "So yeah, a bit of a hen's egg on the eye. Knuckles banged up."

"All right," a new, gruff and muffled voice pushed in. "Lemme see."

The woman who materialized in the mirror behind him wore a red silken robe and had long blonde hair. A tenuous smell of dusky incense traveled with her. He stared at her in the mirror, but her face was a mystery, obscured by her hair and a threaded veil of smoke. Jude could see the glowing orange orb and hear the sharp crackle of burning tobacco as she pulled on her cigarette. Then she lifted a tumbler of amber liquid and ice and drank behind the smokescreen.

She pressed in past Penny and clicked her glass down on the

counter. Then she set her cigarette down, the lit end dangling over the edge of the sink. With a quick toss of her hair over her shoulder, she turned to face Jude.

It was like the climactic unveiling of the last grand act of a magic show. She was breathtaking. Her face was hauntingly perfect. She was buttery tan and the mere layout of her lips, her nose, and her China-blue eyes expressed something exciting and unsettling and simply luscious.

What was it? There was a catch. There was, in the perfection, an imperfection. Maybe a tautness at the bridge of her nose that made her look younger than she was. Almost boyish, mischievous.

Then she bent forward to look at his cuts more closely and suddenly there were her knees and her cleavage and Jude's senses all melted together. She smelled like cinnamon and warm butter. His breath stalled and his heart suddenly raced.

She angled her head to one side, then the other, peering at him. She squinted and said, "Well, he'll live." Then she looked past him at Penny. "Kit?" she asked.

"It's on the counter, Lace."

Lacey spun her head around, eyes unfocused, missing the item once, then finding it on her second, slower, pass. It was a small, zippered blue satchel, splayed open. It contained a surprising array of bandages, ointments, tapes, scissors, needle and thread, and pills.

"Right," she said, smiling inwardly at her own mistake. "Right."

Lacey turned on the tap and felt the water. It wasn't the right temperature and so she fiddled with the knobs and then slumped back against the cabinet. She awkwardly reached over the counter edge to grab her drink. Her gaze slipped on past Jude, but wobbled. She drank and held her drink on her knee. Not smiling now. Just sitting out time.

Jude watched her. Her robe was open still further as she slumped deeper and the flesh between her breasts was visible.

"The water's hot," he told her.

Lacey's head jerked a little and her eyes circled in on his face. Then she frowned, snapped her glass down behind her, took a drag on the cigarette, and pushed off from the cabinet. She adjusted the water temperature and doused a green-and-blue washrag. She pressed the rag to his forehead. It stung, and the dense, rising, oblong shape he could feel beneath the rag was scary big. He winced.

Lacey laughed at this. "Pussy," she said. Her smile loomed and then receded again.

Jude felt himself color.

"I'm kidding," she said. "That's a nasty cut. Probably should get a couple stitches."

She soaked a second washrag and folded it over his battered knuckles. "So, how did you go about getting your ass kicked?" Smoke slid past her words.

"Just some guys from school," he said. "Swung a big metal gate out in front of me when I was riding my bike."

A single laugh bubbled up in her. But then she reassembled her seriousness, piece-by-piece, her lips, her eyes, her jaw, all pulling back into a composed mask. "That's not funny," she said. Her eyes rose to his. "But it's a little funny, right? I mean like, you're just riding along and then..." She took a drag from her cigarette. She blew out the smoke, and then clapped her palms lightly, and said, "Bang!"

"Yeah, I guess so."

He watched her clean his hand. He felt possessive of her, if even for these few moments. He wanted to complete the picture of the incident with the market value of things. "They took my money and..." He let it drop. He didn't want to talk about Betty or her picture.

She squinted up at him. He felt like she was judging whether to find out more. He shrugged.

"People are always taking your shit," she said. And then stretching it out into a sing-song aphorism, she said it again. "All. Ways. Tay. King. Yer. Shit."

Jude had a small, sharp reaction. The things they'd taken from him weren't shit.

"They took a picture..." He looked through the veil of hair for her eyes.

She glanced up, a flicker of awareness.

"Of my girlfriend..."

Lacey's eyes rose again, hung a split second longer.

"Back home."

"Yeah." She reached across the counter and pulled the first aid gear toward her. She plucked scissors and a roll of white adhesive tape out, and with her head hung forward and hair cascading down around her hands, she snipped a few lengths of tape. She studiously stuck each piece to the edge of the sink, just in reach. "Shit is never shit to the shitter."

Jude glowered at her for an instant. And then, to break the tension he was feeling, he flicked his head as if he had long hair and were flipping it out of his eyes. But he caught the motion in the mirror and saw a scrawny, pallid boy with hair high on his forehead with his chin lifted in what was obviously false and misplaced pride.

He slumped over his hand and Lacey's ministrations. "So, do I really need stitches?" he asked.

She shook back her hair and peered at him, as if down a long hall. "Shit," she half-smiled, half-winced. "You're a dude. You don't need stitches. You'll get a bad-ass little battle scar over your eye."

"Oh," he said.

"Besides," she laughed and her eyes found his as she snipped tape. "This is nothing. You should see some of the carnage I've patched up around here."

She concentrated hard on the snipping and had twelve, thirteen, fourteen—Jude counted along—two-inch-long pieces of white tape stuck to the counter edge.

She seemed to realize what she was doing and jerked a little. Then she looked at Jude again, and said, "Anyway, you can tell the girls about it." Then she grabbed a package of gauze and ripped it open. She folded one of the squares and laid it over his knuckles. One-by-one, she tugged the tape from the counter and, as though drawing a tiny bow with a tiny arrow, stretched it over the gauze and pulled it down tight.

"I bet a hundred girls in your life are going to touch that scar and think it says something cool about you."

Jude laughed. He said, "Hah, I'll be lucky to have one girl."

Lacey pulled back and looked at him again. Her eyebrows were lifted as though Jude were sadly misguided.

Jude took it as a false compliment like so many adults laid out on kids. 'That picture you drew is amazing. You'll be the next Picasso.'

'You're so smart, I'll bet you're gonna be a doctor someday. Like your daddy.'

"I thought you said you have a girlfriend."

"She's… I'm…" Jude watched himself redden in the mirror. "I mean I do, or I did. But she's in Indiana."

"Indiana," she said. Then, trying the word out in her mouth again, "In Dee Anna."

She now seemed older and more remote to him. But he continued to watch possessively. Her hair fell from behind her ears and slid, in slender tendrils, across her face. She seemed oblivious until, when her vision appeared to be completely blocked, she would impatiently push it back.

Her lips were dry. Her eyes kept snapping into focus on something she was working on, a knuckle or a piece of tape or her drink, and then they would waver into some middle distance. Her body kept sliding down too far, forcing her hands high up in front of her face. Then, without the use of her hands or arms, she would try to inch back up the cabinet and gain a new balance.

Still, her fingers danced over everything with purpose. Pulling the tape and slicing it. They cleaned the cut on his forehead and piled and aligned squares of gauze to fit the wound even as she was lifting a piece of tape from the counter. And always, like a typist reaching out rotely to clip the carriage back across the page, there was the cigarette and the drink.

Occasionally, she smiled at him as though it were an instruction she had promised to follow and just then remembered to fulfill. The smiles were empty, but each time she found his eyes with hers and locked on, then they came alive. It was nearly instantaneous, but every time it shot through him with a physical shock.

Suddenly, she shoved the gauze wrappers and tape away across the counter and tugged her robe closer around her. Then she stood. Six pieces of tape still poked out expectantly on the counter. She held her glass and wavered over him as though she'd just found him. She took a long drag on her cigarette and stubbed it in the sink. She studied him a long minute.

"You…" she smiled at him and circled a finger over him as though she were stirring a tall drink. "…have a hard-on."

Jude awoke from his reverie, blushed nearly blue, and slammed his hands down over a rising tent pole inside his Jockeys. He barked aloud because he'd forgotten the cuts on his hand.

A dense wedge of silence fell over him as the fact of his erection filled the room... the building... the block... the whole goddamned city... with shame.

Lacey cuffed him on the head. "Hey, take a minute and pull yourself together." She lifted her glass in a silent toast and left the bathroom.

Embarrassment swept over him. Air was suddenly rare and his gut folded over a stabbing pain. He bent down over his knees and gulped air. The situation was impossible! Impossible! He was so embarrassed! He shrieked loudly and wildly, but carefully just inside his head. 'You ass!' he yelled inside. 'You ass! You idiot!'

When he straightened up and found his reflection, it wasn't the crazed person he expected to see. There was no jagged hair, no spittle on the lips, no red eyes, crooked teeth, or translucent skin over pulsing blue veins. That was only what he felt. Instead it was just himself looking impossibly young, small and desperate. And only slightly bruised and bandaged. He wasn't the image of a street hooligan he imagined.

His erection was gone—deflated, painful, and remote.

He stood, making strange, birdlike movements with his hands and arms, enacting an imaginary apology. He glimpsed himself and quit. There was nothing for it. He closed his eyes and grasped the doorknob. He waited for a long beat. Then he was out and in the tiny hallway and stumbling into the living room.

Penny sat on the plush red couch, her wine glass refilled. He swiveled his head quickly. Lacey was gone. Penny said, "Okay, Mr. Jude, how'd the nursing session go?" She stood and, sticking her feet into the red flops again, she raised up on her tiptoes to look at his head. "Hey, it looks good!" She touched the bandage gently and her eyes, as she pulled her hand down, slid down and met his.

"Very sexy," she said. "You're like Steve McQueen, or Brando."

Maybe it *was* like Lacey said: scars were sexy.

Penny turned, "Let's go see how Frenchie's doing with your britches."

He wanted to just run downstairs and grab his bike. He imagined everyone in the building knowing by now that he'd gotten a hard-on. But, of course, he was in his underwear. He couldn't run anywhere.

Instead, he followed Penny down the walkway again, and at Frenchie's he quickly pulled on his repaired pants. Frenchie reached over and tugged at the seams near his crotch to check her work. A cigarette poked from her lips and she squinted through the smoke. He looked down along the curves and smooth surfaces of her and, light-headed, forced his mind to look out the window at the blank curtained windows in the apartment building across the street.

"Looks good to me," she said. "What do you think?"

"Really good," he mumbled. He held his hands up and out like a store window dummy, then let them down with a slap at his hips. "Hey, thanks. That was really, ah," his eyes strayed to Penny who stood aside watching him with a half-smile on her lips. He blurted out, "That was, ah, you know, ah, really cool."

Frenchie sat up straight. "Sure, any time someone beats the pants off you, you just drop on by, Mr. Jude."

"Oh, hey, it won't happen again." He felt the need to proclaim his manhood. But instead he just felt silly and grabbed his shoes. He sat on a chair by the door and awkwardly tugged them back on. He looked down into the kitchen, but the pale girl was gone.

Penny touched Frenchie's hand on the back of the chair, "Thanks French. I owe you one."

Frenchie waved the comment away and lifted her cereal bowl out from beside the sewing machine.

Penny touched Jude's arm just below the elbow. "Let's see if Russ can get you on home. We don't want your momma getting worried."

"Ah, she'll be all right," he said, and felt himself blush. He'd just admitted that he lived with his parents. He could have said... He should have said... Better sentences bumped and crowded in his mind as he descended the stairs after Penny. Better sentences attached to whole better lives. He lived in a commune in the hills. His girlfriend would be worried. Or he lived with his brother up in Griffith Park in a tent back in the trees. Or his parents were dead but he hadn't told the authorities, so he lived in the big old house all alone...

"Russ!" Penny called out halfway down, "You ready to take our street fighter back home?"

She leapt down the last few stairs and spun toward Russ's front door pulling hard on the railing. "Russ!" But the dense music was still raging inside the closed door. She knocked and rang and then yelled again, "Russ!" Jude stood well back this time, caught in a bright shaft of sunlight that reached past the building.

The music stopped abruptly. Then the door opened and Russ was out, locking up after himself before Penny said another word. "Let's motionize, kid." He hoisted Jude's bike with one meaty hand and lumbered out past the stairs to the back of the building. Jude rushed to keep up. Russ turned the corner without stopping, but Jude suddenly pulled up. He looked back at Penny. "Thank you, ma'am."

She laughed. "Ma'am? I'm no ma'am!"

"Oh, sorry." He jerked his head and blinked as though something inside had made the mistake, not him.

She grinned at him. "You're Jude. I'm Penny."

"Okay. Well, thanks." He sought her eyes which danced with amusement. Then he pushed it out, "Penny."

She laughed. "Hey, it was a fun break in the day. Don't worry about it."

Russ barked "Boy!" and Jude startled. He ducked his head, waved, said, "Okay, well, bye," and scuttled after Russ. He hurried along under bathroom windows where a shower was running and bedroom windows were blanked with curtains or blinds. He emerged into an alley where Russ was tugging open a white wooden garage door.

Russ swung the doors wide and tossed the bike into the darkness where it clattered against metal. Then Russ too disappeared into the dark. Jude hung back. He could see the shape of a white Gran Torino sitting in the garage. The springs somewhere in the car squawked and the car sank deeply to one side as Russ got in.

"You wanna ride, honky?" Russ growled.

Jude quickly wedged himself sideways along between the car and the open wooden studs of the wall. He tugged open the door. But the door was nearly as wide as the gap it opened into. Jude didn't think Russ would think that was a problem, so he yanked it a couple inches farther open and squeezed himself in, pressing first one foot in, then his body, and then hauling the other foot up into the car.

Russ fired up the car. A deep rumble filled the garage. Then Russ bent forward and shoved a tape into an eight-track player beneath the dash by Jude's knees. A warped noise arose and then the same dense sounds like those in the apartment crackled. The crinkled label on the cassette that stuck out said *The Seeds*.

Russ backed out and, leaving the doors standing open, and pulled out to Canyon Drive. But then he stopped and they just sat there, the car idling.

Jude looked over at the man. Russ was shaking his head in obvious anger or disgust.

He sneered at Jude. "You hear that, boy?"

Jude could only hear the nerve-stretching jangle of music. But then, as he listened, a dark thunder rose and then quickly filled the air. A gleaming silver-and-black motorcycle turned in from Harold Way. With the knotted pulse of the engine and the sheer size of the thing, it seemed ominous and evil.

The man riding it wore black hair down over his shoulders, held in place with a dirty red bandanna. The sleeves were ripped from his jean jacket. His jeans were nearly black with grease. His boots, his pants tucked into them, were dull black beasts with a gold harness ring at the ankle as though each were itself a small angry bull.

He pulled the bike to the curb and sat for a few moments, revving the engine in short, window-rattling bursts. Then he shut the bike down, tilted it onto a massive kickstand, and dismounted. He wore black shades and a long, thick moustache. Under his jean vest, he wore a filthy T-shirt with a blue background with five white stars up top and vertical red-and-white stripes below.

He looked back the way he'd come. Another bike, just as big, but not as shiny, rolled around the corner. This was ridden by a tall, skinny blond man with a dense handlebar moustache. This one was dressed in bell-bottom jeans and a suede vest. Nothing more. His feet were filthy and bare, his chest a fuzzy cloud of reddish hair.

Russ sat in the Torino and watched the scene unfold.

The first man spoke to the blond one, then looked up and down the street and then headed for the apartment's backstairs. On the back of his vest was an emblem of a skull topped with a great red and yellow trailing wing. It read HELL'S ANGELS in an arc above the symbol, BERDOO beneath it.

The blond man stayed on his motorcycle, the engine rattling out an idle.

Russ watched the dark man's progress and grumbled over the music, "Fuckin' trouble in spades, hearts, diamonds and clubs." He shot the Torino onto the street and drove past the second biker. Jude looked up to the balcony. The dark man had stopped at Lacey's door. He knocked once, looked out at the street to watch Russ's Gran Torino squeal away, then he opened the door and went inside.

Russ turned toward Bronson and then turned north without asking, knowing Jude had come from the junior high two blocks south. He turned the music down, but it remained a turgid, violent undercurrent in the car. "Where you live, boy?"

Jude gave him the address and registered, from the corner of his eye, Russ's low-wattage surprise. "I shoulda al-fucking-ready known. A fuckin' rich white kid." He shook his large head and then bent to the console and lit himself a cigarette.

two

A RICH KID. JUDE HAD NEVER THOUGHT OF HIMSELF in that way before.

He stood in the street with his battered bike and looked up the hill. The green-and-gray that was the landscape of Los Angeles rose into Griffith Park. The rounded front of the Griffith Observatory was directly above him, a mile or so away. Somewhere to the west, beyond the ridgeline, was the Hollywood sign. Studded into the drab chaparral were glinting white-and-tan-and-glass boxes where people lived. He knew many of the roads that laced those homes together up there. Riding his bike along those roads, sometimes you could see the view as you passed between the boxes or rounded a curve. Los Angeles lay below like a spray of shattered glass, plastic and metal that had been raked into neat rows. It was so dense and complete, it felt like you could reach down and run your fingers through it.

The houses on the hills were amazing. Some of them were literally breathtaking, cantilevered out over the city as though you would take your life in your hands just walking into them. But in the short two miles of flatlands between school and his family's house there were twice as many dwellings as on the entire slope above. In the lowlands, the buildings were plaster and stucco rectangles, grafted with external stairways, mailboxes that bulged with facets like flies' eyes, and long rows of covered parking spots. Shopping carts sat on the bare brown lawns. Pizza delivery and porn theater flyers were hung over exterior doorknobs and shoved under mats. The sidewalks were stained, dusty and grimy. The plants were either dead or gruelingly hardy. It all felt stolid and permanent, but like round, dry stones in a riverbed, the result of some unseen, constant drumming. In Los Angeles, to Jude, the drumming was cars and people, cars and people, cars and people. Then throw in a few thousand buses and trucks. And a relentless sun. And smog.

The city felt like a science fiction story out of "The Twilight Zone."

Jude unlocked the garage and limped his bike in. He set it just so. The garage was narrow and barely fit his father's car. His father had a thing about his car, a shiny red Triumph TR-4, very strange and English. The bikes were not to fall or tip, ever.

He locked back up and started up the stairs. The house had been a palace to Jude when they had moved in. It was a white stucco box 37 stairs above the street and was, with dark green trim and red tile roof, imposing. It stood two stories with a balcony running two-thirds of the way across the upstairs front. The other window on the front had a dark green, wrought-iron planter cage. The cage rose seven feet high—higher than Jude could quite reach—and had a platform bottom that was large enough for him to curl up on.

That cage was outside Jude's room and he loved it. He sat in the cage in the evenings and on weekend mornings, feeling as though he were adrift on the wind itself. He would read a book or, lately, do his homework. He especially liked watching the city sink into darkness and, at the same time, light itself as though from the inside out. Whole networks of streetlamps came alight at once. Other lights clicked on and off like love, ideas, hopes… life.

He closed the front door after him and stood in the entry hall, listening. His mother was, now and eternally, on the phone. He didn't even have to see her. She was sitting on her high stool in the kitchen, a cigarette throwing a trail of smoke and an iced tea sweating on the counter, her voice and laugh piercing through the downstairs rooms. At a lull, Jude called out, "I'm home!"

She called out, projecting around corners, "Do your homework!"

Jude went upstairs and changed and washed his face and hands and arms. His forehead was blooming into yellows and light blues. A dense thread of purpled red showed at the outside of his left eye. As he wetted and washed the area, he carefully removed all traces of the white adhesive bandages and gauze from Lacey and replaced them with the familiar tan bandages in the bathroom cabinet. He balled the other bandages up and flushed them down the toilet.

He lay on his bed and felt the odd workings of pain. His hand returned sharp, stinging alerts, but only when he moved it. Each state of pain in his knuckles seemed to package up a vivid image of the raw little cups of flesh beneath the flaps of skin.

He could map where he'd been kicked by tracing a different sort of pain. This was a persistent, smoldering ache. It emanated from his left thigh, his ribs on his right side and his right shoulder blade. The last of these sources of pain occasionally added a pinprick of pain when he moved. Maybe the skin was broken.

Then there was his face. This pain concerned him. It felt like a golf ball, or maybe a hockey puck, was blasting into his skull in very slow motion. The pain was continuous and growing. It traveled along the nerves in sharp bursts, but it also seeped through the bones of his skull, like dark sewage. If he closed his eyes, the light that pressed through his eyelids on the left side was a nauseous swirl of purple and green.

Two hours after Jude had gotten home, his father stood at the bottom of the stairs and yelled, "Boys!" A pause and then, "Dinner!"

Jude held back until he heard his brother Mark's door open and the thud of his feet on the stairs. Then he followed.

At the table, Jude sidled to his seat and kept his head down.

"Jude!" his mother almost dropped the platter of asparagus.

His father snapped his attention to Jude, first the eye and then the knuckles. His face darkened. "What happened to your face?"

"I crashed my bike on the way home."

His mother had a hand to her mouth. "Why didn't you say something when you came home?"

"I did."

"You did not! I didn't even see you!" his mother was still standing over the table and she was holding the asparagus at a precipitous angle.

"I said, 'I'm home.'"

She rolled her eyes, thrust the asparagus dish on the table with a loud clunk, and stabbed her hands on her hips. A smirk tripped her mouth. His father smiled and shook his head. The humor pushed the foundering conversation off the shoals. His mother uttered, "Honestly!" Shaking her head, she went back to the kitchen.

"I'm fine," Jude said after her. "My bike's kinda messed up. But I'm fine."

"That's gonna be a groovy shiner," Mark said.

"Mark!" Their mother censored him as she came back out with a platter of meatloaf. "What exactly happened?" she asked, sitting.

Jude made up a story about a big old car stopping suddenly in front of him. Jude had slammed into the bumper. The guy had gotten out and checked on Jude. But Jude hadn't even scratched the car, and so the man just took off. Jude made it a Chrysler Imperial, dark blue, with big fins.

"Did you get his license plate?" Jude's father wanted justice.

"I didn't even think about it. Sorry."

That night, after he finished with the dishes, he walked down to look at the bike with his father. They brought it out to the street where a late summer sun was still pulsing west. His father bent and fingered the slashed tire, looking up at Jude. Jude could tell he was wondering if he'd just caught Jude in a lie. Jude just shrugged. "I don't know how that happened," he said. "Maybe it caught the license plate."

His father let it go. But after looking over the bike in the street he was of the opinion that with two fresh tires and innertubes, the bike would work just fine.

He drove Jude to Pep Boys for the necessary supplies. Then Jude spent a frustrating hour out in front of the house on the little postage stamp lawn that spread out in between beds of ivy halfway up the stairs. While dusk settled over him, he pulled the tires off the rims and replaced the innertubes and tires and painstakingly blew them up using the T-handled bicycle pump.

When he was done, with the bike still upside down on seat and handlebars, he spun the wheels. They wobbled and rubbed unevenly on the brakes. He shoved and twisted the wheel until it was mostly better. Then he flipped the bike over, and in the dark, took it down to the street and rode it to the end of the block and back. The brakes still worked, but intermittently. The bike rolled along with one large and one small lump for every turn of the tire.

He took the bike back and locked it up in the garage. Going up the stairs, he realized he forgotten the tools he'd used on the lawn. He spit the word, "Fuck!", under his breath. Then he stood with his eyebrows raised and his mouth pursed and open. He had never said that word before. He knew the white trash kids in Indiana used it. But ever since moving to Los Angeles, he'd been hearing it everywhere. Especially today from Hector, the hippies, the women, and Russ.

He put the tools away and climbed the stairs.

"Shower before you finish your homework," his mother called from her perch in the living room where the television winked across the room at them.

Jude slowed as he started up the stairs. On the arm of her chair was a tumbler of ice and clear liquid. On the table by his father, the tumbler was larger, the liquid also clear. Dual columns of cigarette smoke coiled from an ashtray between them, and met, mingled, and disappeared.

KEVIN LONG was waiting for Jude on the sidewalk in front of the house in the morning. He sat astride his red three-speed, hunched and smiling.

"Hey, sleepyhead," Kevin called. "You're practically..." he gave his watch a dramatic wave in front of his face, "...wow, a minute late!"

The day was warm and the view was already truncated by the sluggish brown haze that Los Angeles called smog, but Jude wore a hooded blue sweatshirt and a baseball cap and hid his eye. But as soon as he joined Kevin at the curb with his lumping bike, Kevin peered under the hood and recoiled.

"Whoa! What happened to you?"

Jude glanced back at the house, acknowledging the secrecy of what he was going to say. "I kind of ran into Hector Elizado and his friends after school."

"No way! What happened?"

They set off down the steep street. "I'll tell you when we get down the hill," Jude said and tentatively released his dubious brakes, wobbling ahead.

He told the story as they rode down the wide, flat streets filled with shouldering cars. Kevin inserted his exclamations of surprise and anger as they rode.

"What's a pendejo?" Jude asked.

"Fuck if I know," Kevin said. "I've heard the Spics say it."

"Okay, so, what's a kike?" Jude asked.

"That's what he called you?"

"His buddy did. When he was kicking me."

"Damn." Kevin shook his head and pedaled in silence.

"What is it?" Jude demanded.

"It's me."

"You? What do you mean, 'It's you'?"

"It's a Jew. It's like a Spic or a Mic or a Nigger. But it's Jewish people."

"Oh."

As they turned down Bronson, Jude said, "They took my money," he said. "And my picture of Betty." He'd shown Kevin the picture and lied about her. That she had been his girlfriend. Cried when he left. Promised to write.

"No way," Kevin caught on immediately. "They took the picture of your girlfriend?"

"Yep."

They slipped in and out of traffic for another block. At the next light, Jude rolled up beside Kevin. Kevin asked, "Your parents know? About Hector?"

"No. Nothing. I told them I hit a car at an intersection." The light changed and they pushed ahead.

"Yeah," Kevin agreed. "Probably a good idea." He was shaking his head sadly at a world where a boy had to tell such lies to his parents. "Did they buy it?"

"Yeah," Jude swerved his bike through a scattered splay of trash. "I think so."

They arrived at LeConte Junior High School and locked their bikes in the racks among many other bikes. "I shoulda been there, man," Kevin said.

"Hell, I was just being stupid," Jude replied. "But, as for helping out, you're not exactly Muhammad Ali."

Kevin raised his fists in the old-fashioned boxer's stance. "I can kick some butt," he grinned. "...if they're elementary school kids."

They laughed. That was Kevin. He was short and scrawny, but quick to smile, always upbeat, always friendly. Jude appreciated that. It had made meeting him and forging a friendship at the new school easy.

Easy. But so different from Indiana.

In Indiana, for one, Jude didn't remember 'making' friends. There were kids in his neighborhood, and then there were kids at his school. And he hung out with them.

In Los Angeles, he had yet to see a kid in his immediate neighborhood. And at the school, there were a whole lot of kids he didn't feel like he would ever get to know. They didn't look like him. Or dress like him. School looked like a movie set from the United Nations. There were kids of every color. But even most of the white kids there seemed aloof and strange. And of course there were the strange creatures called hippies.

Jude and Kevin pushed through the LeConte crowds to get to their lockers. It hadn't really struck Jude what was going on until Mr. Diaz had laid it out in social studies. Mr. Diaz, a dark-skinned, fireplug of a man, was committed, he told the students, to teaching them "where they were, why they were, and when." It had seemed like a strange statement to make. It was all pretty obvious. But Mr. Diaz spent some portion of every class period 'peeling the onion,' as he called it.

"Los Angeles," he said, "was a reasonably safe and homogenous city until recently. Most neighborhoods," he explained, "had legal covenants—rules—that excluded anyone that was ethnic. That's usually anyone who's black or Hispanic, but it was also the Chinese and Japanese, the Thais and the Turks, the Indians and the Armenians. These covenants have been illegal now for many years, but the practices and habits didn't go away.

"I grew up in Hacienda Heights when the streets there were safe," he told them. "Where even strangers would look out for you if you were lost or maybe were thinking about causing some trouble.

"A decade ago, Los Angeles had the highest percentage of church-goers for any big city in the United States. Los Angeles had so few conflicts in their neighborhoods because the neighborhoods were so homogenous. And because a vast majority of residents owned their homes. The place was basically an ever-expanding pool of cheap housing.

"So people came." He walked to the windows as if to watch them arrive. "From everywhere." He lifted one hand to gesture toward the outside world.

"You have no idea what this means. In terms of stability. Law. Safety. All of it." He spun back to the room. He let his eyes travel over the students slowly, as though recording history. "I'll bet a lot of your families probably rent now." He started pacing. He bobbed his head, agreeing with his ideas as he spoke them.

"So, let me ask you this," he strode to the colorful world map stuck to the chalkboard behind his desk. "Where were your parents born? And where were you born?"

Mr. Diaz lifted a long wooden pointer from the chalk tray and anchored himself at one corner of his desk, one leg swinging, his shoe making a soft resonant bump, bump, bump as it hit the wood. "I'm serious now," he said, and gestured to the first kid in the first row.

The kids and their parents came from Thailand, Israel, South Africa, India, Armenia, Australia, Syria. With each kid, Mr. Diaz reached back and poked locations on the map. For a lot of the kids, he poked three locations, one for the father, one for the mother, and one for the kid.

There were three kids from Mexico. Four from Japan and four from Armenia. There were also kids from Chicago, Philadelphia, Fresno, Houston, and of course, Jude from Indianapolis. Jude was one of four kids where all three family members under discussion were born in the same city. The other three whose family were all from the same place were from Los Angeles. Mr. Diaz called those three "the old guard."

Jude was surprised. He thought he was observant. But hearing these kids talk about where they'd come from, he realized that he'd barely even seen the other kids in the classroom. In Indiana, if you had asked the same question, out of thirty kids, you might get two or three kids from somewhere else. And you already knew which kids, because they had arrived over the years in his kindergarten or elementary school classes one by one, as strange and new as solar eclipses.

But it was considered impolite to ask them where they came from, so Jude usually never found out.

One kid who sat in the back, a black kid from Los Angeles, raised his hand. Mr. Diaz called on him, "Frank?"

"What you mean by homogenous is white?"

Mr. Diaz waved a dismissive hand, "Race actually doesn't always come into the equation. Homogeneity simply means that people who are similar to each other live in the same neighborhoods."

"But in Los Angeles, the neighborhoods are white."

"Mostly were white," Mr. Diaz said. "But not everywhere. Hacienda Heights has been mostly Hispanic for decades. Watts is a black community. Always has been."

Mr. Diaz immediately cocked his head. "Well, that's not quite true. Watts was a farming community first, mostly white, up to maybe 1920. Negroes started moving in after World War I and started to dominate. They increased in numbers until sometime in the twenties. Then, when it looked like they were going to elect a Negro mayor, the political powers in Los Angeles didn't want that. So L.A. annexed Watts."

He shrugged, "Now Watts is a black community." He tapped the map in the area of Southern California. "One of the most vital black communities in the United States. The largest in California."

"Yeah," Frank muttered sourly, "home of the Watts riots."

"I'm sorry Frank, I didn't hear you."

"I said…" Frank raised his head, his eyes fiery. But no more words came. He shrugged and lowered his eyes.

Mr. Diaz pursed his lips and nodded. His foot kept the bump at a steady rate. "The Watts riots," he said, nodding, connecting the dots. "Does your family live in Watts?"

Frank pulled back into himself, his eyes half-closed. But he spoke, his voice edged, "My family got out, because we could."

"This," Mr. Diaz raised his pointer, "is exactly my point. The homogeneity is breaking down. Many neighborhoods in Los Angeles are now some of the most diverse in this entire country. More so even than New York City or San Francisco. We're seeing it, obviously, right here in this classroom. Los Angeles is being called the great melting pot of America."

Mr. Diaz paced again, wearing the silence down. The bell jangled in the hall and he stopped. No one moved to leave.

"Mr. Taylor," he addressed Frank, eyes locked on him. "I'm not saying anything about right or wrong here. I'm not saying Watts, or anywhere on the south end, or East L.A. for that matter, are safe places to live."

Mr. Diaz paced again, to the windows and then back.

"What I'm saying is, if people are going to get along together, maybe L.A. has a chance at that. Maybe..." he stared out at the classroom as though daring anyone to move. "Maybe L.A. has a chance, and maybe it will be because of young people like you. Because you're growing up together. As neighbors."

He squared off looking out on the school's front lawn and waved a hand to dismiss them. Jude rolled his eyes as he left. He thought, 'What about Hector Elizado?'

JUDE followed Kevin out the door of social studies. He stayed close, hoping to be invited again, like yesterday, to come to lunch with Kevin and his friends.

Jude knew it had been a mixed bag the day before. Kevin and Robby welcomed and included Jude at once. A new kid from Indiana seemed to amuse them. Henry was so quiet, Jude was unsure what he felt, but at least Henry wasn't impolite or mean. James was another story. He was the leader of this pack, and as far as Jude could tell, Kevin bringing Jude in was an unwelcome breach of protocol for James.

Jude knew he didn't help matters. He wanted to fit in, but he'd found himself bragging about things he'd done in Indiana—the tree forts forty feet up in the cottonwoods, the farmers who shot at them with rock salt from their biplanes when they trespassed in the cornfields, the afternoons spent in Gasoline Alley at the Indy 500 meeting the likes of A. J. Foyt and Parnelli Jones.

James had scoffed at his stories. Jude had photos today. Proof.

There was one of him standing next to Parnelli Jones and his winning number 40 car of that year, one of his brother sitting in Mario Andretti's car while Andretti leaned on his knee, his foot propped on the big black front left mag tire. Another showed he and Mark and a couple of friends peering out of a tree fort that was obviously very far from the packed dirt below.

But Jude was unsure whether he'd have a chance to show them.

Then, as Kevin peeled away from Jude to go to his locker, he turned to Jude, "Hey, meet you back here? The guys are gonna totally want to hear what happened, man."

"Sure, man," Jude let it ooze out like he was reluctant. But, if he could do Kevin a favor…

Kevin gathered him on his way back and they navigated the dense, turgid flow of kids in the halls. At the north end of the hall, Kevin pushed through the steel doors and they emerged into heat, heat, heat and bright, stinging sunlight.

Jude and Kevin approached from the main building. The boys sat in the dark crevasse that lay between two older brick buildings. It was cooler there than most places.

Benches were arranged in three-sided squares, five of them, one after another, along the wall. They sat in the middle square. The one where the word FUCK was carved in capital letters in the bench against the wall. It had been filled in with putty and painted over, but every few days, someone came by and recarved it, and a day or two later, the putty and paint crew came back through.

Kevin's cadre of lunch friends included blond and fuzzy-headed James Hinkle, black-haired and freckled Robby Black, and the curly-headed and quiet Henry Shaver. They were a bit like the friends Jude had had in Indiana. They were all born and raised in Los Angeles. They'd known each other since kindergarten. The only difference was their hair was longer than Indiana kids' and they were all Jewish—Jude didn't have a clue what being Jewish meant, except that it was a religious thing—and they all lived within a couple blocks of each other. They all lived within a couple blocks of Jude as well, but up the hill across Los Feliz Boulevard.

As Jude rounded the bench and entered the square, James greeted Jude's shiner with disdain, "What'd ya do? Kiss a door?" By now the bruise had become a blue-and-purple flower the size of his hand with fully outstretched fingers.

Kevin answered for Jude, "Hector Elizado and probably Juan Grigio and Ruben Valdez jumped him after school."

"Well," Jude slowed him down. "They swung a metal gate out in front of me when I was riding my bike."

James laughed outright at him. "A metal gate?"

"Like a big trash enclosure gate. The size of a garage door," he said. "The one right across Sunset on Bronson."

James nodded as if he knew the very gate. "And you tried to ride through it?"

"I was looking down," Jude admitted. "I didn't see it until it was too late."

James didn't like Hector. "Yeah, well, we've been dealing with Hector ever since last year. He's a dick."

"A Spic dick," Robby said. And the boys laughed.

Their comment reminded Jude of what the kid had said to him the day before. Kevin met Jude's gaze and spoke up. "They called Jude a kike."

"He called me 'A fucking kike on a bike,'" Jude said.

"No fucking way," James was pissed. "Who?"

"One of the kids," Jude said. "When he was kicking me."

"Which one?"

"I don't know. I've never seen the other two." Their conversation was punctuated with the rustle of lunch bags.

Kevin remembered something and sat up, his face brightening. "After Hector kicked Jude's butt, a hot blonde in a silky red robe fixed him up," he said.

"Right," James sneered, "a hot blonde." The sarcasm was back.

Jude looked across the lunch table at him. "Sorry, I didn't have my camera." He awkwardly reached into his back pocket and pulled out the envelop he'd brought with photos from Indiana. He pulled the three photos out and fanned them.

James waved them off, but his eyes were glued to them out of curiosity. "Nah, I believed you yesterday."

But Kevin and Robby leaned in. And then Henry. They each took a photo and stared down at it and then passed them back and forth. James stole glances but could not bring himself to touch them.

Henry handed the photos back to Jude. "Cool."

Then Kevin returned to the story. "Another hotty sewed his pants."

"But her hair was black," Jude said sarcastically. "And her robe was blue."

James scowled at Jude and looked away.

Then lunch was over and Jude was on his own again, navigating through strange seas of strange people.

Mostly the strange kids—exemplars of skin colors and accents and clothing Jude had never seen—simply saw past or through Jude and so there was no effort or thought about it. Jude simply didn't mix with them. The only kids Jude had consciously avoided around school, at least before Hector, were the hippies.

Hippies, Jude was coming to see, came in all shapes and sizes. Riding his bike around Hollywood, he saw them.

At first he only saw the flamboyant ones. The ones who stood out like flowers growing out of the dirty sidewalks. They wore flouncy bright clothing, man or woman, and many of the men grew beards and had their hair as big and long as they could get it. He'd seen men with hair over their shoulders, big afros, and even ponytails. The hippies wore vests and torn jeans. It seemed like they were all wearing bell-bottoms, and they all had headbands and bracelets and necklaces. Many of them, including the men, wore knit or leather bags over their shoulders.

They all smoked.

But, as Jude ground mile after mile, and street after street, under his bicycle tires, he began to see beyond the flamboyant ones.

There were other people he hadn't thought of as hippies at first. Some of these were well-dressed, maybe business people, but their clothes, otherwise normal, showed flares and floppy sleeves. There were men in business suits with wide collars, paisley shirts under jackets, snakeskin boots, and tufts of facial hair. Women slipped among the crowds like beings out of magazines with tight dresses, stacked hair, and big blue basins of mascara painted around their eyes.

It was a subtle upward gradation into the world Jude least expected to see.

It went the other way too.

Jude began to see, more and more, the still or slowly moving characters in the backgrounds of the scenes he passed through. There were people he'd thought of as bums, but mingled among them were so many who were so young, barely older than he was. They clustered near alleyways, in front of closed-down shops, or sauntered alone or in pairs.

He could see that some of these were hippies, too. True, they begged as pedestrians cut past, but leaning on their bedrolls or backpacks, they laughed and smoked and gazed at the sky, or played guitars and sang.

Then there were the Hare Krishna, men and women both, in their pale orange robes, their heads shaved except some kept a pony-tail high on the back of their heads. They moved down the sidewalks in packs of five or ten or more, singing unintelligible words, clashing cymbals and playing skin drums. They handed out brightly printed leaflets and flowers and held out cans for coins that they rattled to the beat like tambourines.

Even the normal people in Los Angeles could be strange. Men who were clearly not hippies wore jeans and tight shirts, open jackets. The women wore surprisingly short dresses and colorful pants suits. Their hair was piled high. Their makeup was thick and, to Jude, a bit thrilling. Los Angeles, and especially Hollywood, felt a bit like The Jetson's gone awry.

And through it all, Jude moved like a pinball in a Pachinko game. Just traveling. Just seeing. Just bouncing along.

The hippies were definitely worth a wide berth. Just too damned strange.

JUDE rode home that afternoon with Kevin. It had been decided at the end of lunch—James conducted the decision-making with great authority, his head held high and his eyes squinting and filled with incisive wisdom—that Jude would show Kevin the Crestview. Then Kevin would report the results at Jewish Temple to the other guys over the weekend.

Jude had seen the women when he'd ridden by before, but now that there was a plan to go by, he couldn't remember if they were there every day or not. Maybe the day before had just been a fluke.

But, as soon as they turned the corner off Bronson, Jude could see he was in luck. The hippies were out in front of the house on the near corner, the red Frisbee skittering over the pavement ahead. And, more importantly, there were women in front of the apartment on the far corner.

But a sudden icy wind inside him blew fear into every inch of his flesh. What if none of the women recognized him, or if they just ignored him.

As they rode past the hippies, the black guy with the bouncy afro lifted his chin, "Hey duuuuude!" He pulled the 'dude' out like warm caramel until it was no longer a word. Behind him, Jude could see the blond hippy, the stressed-out one, coming out onto the porch, peering.

"Hey," Jude responded, surprised.

Afro called out, "Keep it cool, man!"

Jude lifted his chin, cementing, at least in his own mind, his coolness with Kevin. "Yeah, man," he said. "You too."

Jude tried to be nonchalant about their approach to the women. He pulled a conversation with Kevin up from the pits of his fear. "So, have you seen *Bonnie and Clyde*?"

"Can't. My mom says it's too violent." Kevin's eyes were shooting back-and-forth across the street ahead, like an animal approaching a trap.

"My brother got to go. He said it was really cool."

"Yeah, I want to see it, but there's no way." Kevin rode on Jude's right, away from where he could see the women ahead, and a couple feet behind him. "Maybe when I turn forty."

They both laughed too loudly.

Jude curved a little toward the apartment and peered closely at the women. The day was hot like it had been yesterday, and there were seven or eight women wearing bikinis and hats on the lawn. They held big colorful glasses with straws protruding, and lay on chaises or towels. It was all bare legs and midriffs to Jude. He couldn't identify any of them.

He was about to slow and ask about Penny when he saw her laying back in a bright yellow bikini with her massive blue sunglasses and red flip-flops in the last chaise in the line.

He pulled to the curb five feet away from her, and said, "Hey, Penny."

The other women watched him and glanced over at Penny. He

didn't recognize any of them except Penny. The red-haired girl wasn't here, and neither were Frenchie or Lacey. Penny didn't move.

"Hey, Penny," he called again, "It's Jude."

"She's getting her beauty rest," one of the women said dismissively. She was a magnetic-looking, dark-haired beauty. Her skin was deeply tanned, her legs long and alluring, and her lips painted a thin pallor like glaze on a donut.

But Penny stirred and shaded her eyes with her hand. She stared at Jude and Kevin, who was stopped a few feet behind him, for a long moment. The dark-haired woman said, "You've got visitors."

Penny propped herself on an elbow. Music crackled from a transistor radio on the lawn. The Byrds sang, "Run by, don't turn back, Can't hide from that look in her eyes…"

Penny finally spoke. "Hey. So, it's Mr. Jude. Who's your friend?"

"Oh, hey, Penny," relieved she was finally addressing him. "This is Kevin."

"Kevin," she said flatly.

She sat up and set her feet on either side of the chaise. "How's the eye, Jude?"

"My eye is okay, I guess," Jude told Penny. "Is… ah…"

Penny groaned and rubbed her face. She had been asleep. "You want to see Lacey," she prophesied.

The black-haired woman said, "Another one. The Lacey fan club." Then she turned away from the conversation and said something to the blonde next to her.

Jude felt guilt trickle through his veins. "I'm sorry if I woke you, and I didn't mean…"

"It's okay, Mr. Jude." She stood, and Jude drank her in. She hadn't been in a bikini yesterday. Today, he slid his gaze along her thighs and up her trim belly. His eyes lingered over her breasts and then traveled, slowly, to her eyes.

She had stopped and even struck a pose while he looked her over. She took off her sunglasses and peered at him a moment. She smiled at him and then put the sunglasses back on. Jude felt like he was a candy being dipped, again and again, into chocolaty embarrassment. He looked pointedly at the grass and said nothing while his face burned.

"Come on boys, let's go find Lacey." Penny headed for the building.

"Hey," Kevin clutched at Jude's elbow. "I prob'ly better go!"

When Jude looked at him, his eyes were like his own had probably been the day before—like a frightened colt's. They rolled and bolted, jumped and started.

"It's cool," Jude said. "It's cool. Five minutes and we're good." He touched Kevin's shoulder. "Okay?"

Jude was having his own doubts though. Penny didn't seem all that thrilled to see him, or be woken up either. And the thought of coming across Russ seemed far more real now that they were here on the curb.

Kevin looked down the street as if seeing the way out would somehow transport him there. Then he slowly laid his bike on the lawn and straightened up. A petite, dark-skinned woman on one of the chaises circled her finger in the air toward Kevin. She blew a smoke ring and said, "Such a creamy center on this one."

The women laughed as Kevin bolted across the grass to Jude's side and ducked his head as if she'd thrown something at him.

They went up the stairs and traveled down the walkway. At Lacey's door, Penny knocked once and pushed the door open without waiting for an answer. "Lace, your new boyfriend is here!"

Jude peered into the dark rooms inside. He could see nothing. Music was playing. He recognized The Mamas and the Papas, "California Dreamin'."

"Come on," Penny said.

Jude and Kevin followed. The room was dark and threaded with a sour smell.

"Lace?" Penny pushed deeper. She opened the bedroom door and peered inside.

Jude drank in the decor. Rather than the tapestries and bright prints he'd seen on the walls of Penny's apartment, in Lacey's small living room there were black-and-white photos. There were portraits of men and women and children, people of all ages. They were all out in the streets, with signs, buildings, crowds, and shopping carts around and behind them. They were smiling, some of them, but some not. In each there was something immediate and electric, as though the person had just at that moment turned and connected with the camera.

In one, an elderly black woman dressed in white lace with pale, translucent glasses and a wide-sweeping black hat, was leading a small pack of kids along a sidewalk. She was brandishing a Bible and looking up into the camera as though she were dragging the photographer and the kids all along to the church. She was beaming, and missing some teeth.

In another, a pretty young woman just stared out. She was wearing worn overalls and had blonde hair and scattershot freckles. She was sitting on a high-backed chair on a porch. But her pale hands were bloody to the wrists, and to one side was a small froth of blood and feathers that had been a chicken. The portrait disconcerted Jude because the pretty girl was so unpretty to him. Not smiling. Not engaging. And bloodied.

He wanted to keep looking, going from one portrait to the next, but Penny turned aside from the bedroom and pushed open the bathroom door and he heard her call out.

"Oh, baby," Penny's voice was disappointed and soft. She disappeared into the bathroom. The toilet flushed. Then Jude and Kevin listened to grunts from Penny and groans from Lacey. Jude was on the verge of giving Kevin a shove toward the door and getting them out of there when Penny called out.

"Jude! Get in here and give me a hand!"

He looked at Kevin. "It'll just be a sec," he said. And he went.

He stepped into the bathroom and his breath slid out of him. A slow seeping chill filled the places it escaped. Penny was seated on the edge of the tub. She was bent over, struggling to hold Lacey up from under her arms.

Lacey was sprawled on the floor, her legs askew as if she'd fallen. Her head hung down and her hair fell over her torso. But Lacey wore only a pair of white panties with little yellow flowers, and one naked breast, the size and shape of heaven, pushed through the veil of her blonde hair. There was vomit on her hands and legs and on the floor. The whole scene, even the perfect orb of her breast, looked sordid and messy.

"Let's get her in the tub," Penny said.

Jude met Penny's eyes, then quickly reached down and grasped Lacey under her knees. The taut warm smoothness of her flesh traveled through him. Penny stood and stepped back into the tub. They lifted Lacey awkwardly and laid her gently down in the tub.

Penny stood, relieved. She climbed out of the tub and reached across and turned on the water. She stayed bent across the tub waiting for the water to warm. Lacey pulling her feet away from the cold splash of water, moaning.

Jude stared down at her. Her lips were pale, almost white, and her eyes closed and calm. Both her breasts were naked and exposed now, her hair falling around her shoulders. He traced the narrowing of her waist and the rounding of her hips with his eyes as if he were discovering some fundamental principle of existence. He floated over her as if in a dream.

Then Penny plugged the drain, turned the water on high, checked the temperature again, and stood up.

Jude looked into her face and encountered her frank gaze. It was some large truth she was telling. About Lacey maybe. About life. But it sat there inches away from him and he could not grasp it.

He felt rattled. He turned to the sink and tugged a handful of tissues from the box there and knelt down to clean up after Lacey.

Penny touched his shoulder. "Thanks, Jude, but you and your pal better go."

"All right," he held the soiled tissues a moment, frowned at them, and then lifted the seat and dropped them in the toilet.

From the living room he heard voices. One was a gruff male's voice, angry and dark, and Jude felt a chill slide through him. Penny stepped past him, touched his shoulder, and said, "You better head on out, Jude."

When Jude came out into the living room behind Penny, however, she was standing her ground and blocking his way. Beyond her, Kevin was gone, and in the front doorway stood the tall, dark-haired man that he had seen on the motorcycle the day before.

"Hi, Paulo," Penny said, her voice low and even. "Lacey's not feeling so good."

"What the fuck is this? A bar mitzvah?" Paulo took a stride deeper into the living room and closer to Penny and Jude, his eyes restless and sweeping. He stopped and gestured around him. "What the fuck with all the kids, Penny?"

"Paulo," she let it hang there, a warning.

"Fuck you!" he yelled.

There was a smell of the man in the room. It was a cologne of some sort, but undercut with a sharp, near-rancid odor of sweat and grease.

"Paulo," Penny was quiet now. "You're gonna have Russ up here in a second."

"You!" Paulo stabbed a finger at Jude past Penny's shoulder. "You get the fuck out of here along with your fucking twerp friend." His finger made three quick silent stabs. Then he said, "And then you *stay* the fuck outta here!"

Penny's hands lifted slightly beside her, creating a small, human wall between Paulo and Jude. "He's helping me out, Paulo. You can leave him alone. And in the meantime, you're the one that needs to get out of here." Her voice was calm, but icy.

Paulo rolled his jaw. It looked to Jude like he was chewing his dense, floppy moustache. The air in the room felt cemented in place.

"No, I'm gonna talk to her. Right, fucking, now!" His jaw jutted and his eyes, mottled green-and-brown orbs, bulged. He took a step toward them, but then stopped.

Penny did not retreat. She shrugged, "Sorry Paulo, she's not feeling so hot."

Paulo's eyes scoured the room as though he would find the obstacle to his seeing her and would smash it right there. Then he swung his gaze back at Penny, scowling. "You tell her," Paulo stabbed his finger at Penny now, "I'll be back." Then he spun and was gone. They could hear the angry beat of his boots down the walkway.

Penny stood stock still long enough to hear Paulo clump down the stairs and, a few beats later, start the huge motorcycle. It sputtered, roared and crackled. Then they heard the sound of the second bike rip through the music. They listened as both motorcycles roared down the block, shifting through the gears, and were slowly wicked away into the city.

When the tear of the engines finally faded, Penny dropped her hands and took a deep breath. She turned, looked at Jude, her eyes pinched with stress, and slipped past him into the bathroom. She shut off the water tap and crouched down by the tub.

Jude could hear Lacey say something and he came in behind Penny, closed the toilet seat, and sat.

Lacey's eyes were swollen, but they were open to slits, and she was saying, "Hey, it's my pretty Penny." A tight smile formed and she raised a hand a couple inches above the water level. "Guess it was time for a bath, huh?" Each word she spoke emerged spongy and oddly distinct from each other.

Jude's eyes ran over every inch of her. Her sore and tired face, small like a child's under her wet hair. Her slender arms with reddish knuckles rising from the warm water. The curve of her thighs. The dark patch of hair now apparent beneath her wet underwear. The swell of her breasts and the magnetic grip of her nipples on his eyes.

He caressed her with his gaze. He moved his eyes along her, feeling the forms and transitions inside himself. It was an exquisite, heady experience.

Penny pulled a washrag from a rack inside the enclosure. She wet the rag and wiped Lacey's face.

Lacey squinted and slurred, "Who's zat?"

"That's Jude," Penny said.

Lacey frowned, confused. "Juuuude?"

"You patched up his eye and his hand yesterday."

"Oh, right. Juuuude." She arched her back, her breasts breaking the surface and gleaming with wet. Jude felt faint. Lacey rolled her head on her shoulders and then slumped back in the water.

She frowned again. "Penny?"

"Yeah, Lace?" Penny sounded sad to Jude.

"But what's he here... doing... there?" Her own words confused her.

"He came by to..." Penny looked at him, and then back at Lacey, "to say thank you. That's all."

"Bah Penny," she laughed and smirked.

"Yeah, Lace?"

"I'm..." she splashed her hands at the surface. "I'm naked!"

"Yeah, well," Penny looked back at Jude. Her lips were pursed and Jude suddenly realized he wasn't supposed to be there any longer. "He was just leaving," Penny said.

It was Jude's turn to frown. "Okay." He waved at Lacey. "Bye, ah, Lacey."

"Yeah, bye, ah... ah... Ju... Juu." She lifted a hand. "Juude. Bye Jude."

"Bye, Penny," he said.

"Yeah, thanks for the help. See you."

"Right."

He careened through the living room and out.

JUDE grabbed his bike, barely hearing the catcalls from the women behind him. He rode east toward home, and was surprised when he encountered Kevin at the end of the next block. He'd forgotten Kevin was even there. Kevin leapt on his bike and arced out to join Jude on the ride.

Jude waved back and turned into Van Ness. Kevin called out as he caught up, "Hey, we can't go this way!"

But Jude, always looking for new ways to ride—side streets, alleys, between buildings, across parking lots—had stumbled onto a back way. Harold Way ended at Van Ness, right where the 101 freeway flowed through Hollywood. If you stopped at the fence and looked down, cars and trucks pulsed past thirty feet below in an impatient river of concrete, steel and glass. An offramp from the southbound side of the freeway surfaced here on Van Ness Avenue. Cars popped up out of the opening, and without a stop, filed down to Sunset Boulevard where they waited for the light.

The intersection at Van Ness and Howard was inhospitable. Trash and spiky green-and-brown weeds lined the fences. A shopping cart was wedged between the guardrail and the chain link. Inside the cart were a dusty, stained, bedroll and a bag of ragged clothing. On the ground beneath the cart were three empty green Thunderbird wine bottles, all different vintages to judge by their patinas. The nearby apartments all had their curtains drawn and the buildings looked tired and dirty. The entire intersection looked dirty, with even the sidewalks pooling black, sooty dirt.

Jude ignored Kevin's warning, and without slowing, rode his bike straight into the mouth of the off-ramp. He kept tight to the left side as he descended toward the freeway. But when there was a gap in the cars, he switched over to the right side so that he was riding down on the driver side of the oncoming cars.

He glanced back. Kevin was still with him, a ways back, and riding hesitantly.

Halfway down the offramp, Jude slowed and hopped off. He hopped his bike up and over the guardrails, and he was now standing on the onramp that descended from Hollywood Boulevard. He jumped on his bike and rode up to the light.

"How did you find that?" Kevin asked when he caught up.

Jude shrugged, "I think I was just late for school and thought it might work."

Jude rode ahead, skirting the parked cars along the boulevard, slipstreaming along behind the massive RTD buses and then jetting past as they sidled for a bus stop at the curb. He had mastered the lights along the boulevard, setting his speed to hit greens all the way along.

As the blocks clicked smoothly past, Kevin kept a steady patter going about the women. They were "definitely real." They were "cool and groovy and beautiful. And I mean all of them." They knew Jude by name. They "weren't wearing hardly anything."

Kevin started asking questions about what was happening in the bathroom. But Jude gave only brief answers, bleached of all information. Kevin went right on, talking about Paulo. "He was an asshole, man. Was he like a Hell's Angel or something?"

Jude nodded and pedaled. The Hell's Angels were getting all sorts of press recently with their big holiday rides, going out en masse to terrorize small towns. His mother talked about these things on the phone to her friends as one of the downsides of living in Southern California.

At Normandie, Jude's street, they turned left. Jude brought them out into traffic and slipped into the left turn lane just as the light snapped from yellow to red. They cleared the intersection and headed, literally, for the hills.

Kevin was talking again, almost manic, about the women. He wanted to go back next week. He wanted to take James and Henry and Bobby. "Just ride by, you know." But Jude knew this wasn't true. Kevin didn't want to go back. He could hear it in Kevin's voice. More importantly, Jude knew he would never take anyone there again.

They pushed up the brutally steep last block of Normandie and stopped in front of Jude's house. "Hey," Kevin said, "You around tomorrow?"

"I don't think so," Jude said, surprising himself for letting this chance to hang with a new friend slip past. "My cousins are in town."

They said goodbye and Kevin rode off. He lived a few blocks away, on Nottingham, above Los Feliz Boulevard.

Jude locked up the garage and mounted the steps two and three at a time. His mother, as usual, was on the phone. She laughed aloud, "Oh, Mary Ellen *would* do that!" Jude went in the kitchen and opened the fridge. From inside, he grabbed a quart-size cottage cheese container, then a spoon from the drawer.

His mother snapped her fingers at him and shook her head vehemently. "Dinner," she hissed.

Jude just flopped the spoon around in air and said, "Hungry."

She pursed her lips, fuming, and started to speak, "Just… just…" Then she flipped her fingers at him in the universal sign language, useful for underlings, children, and dogs. 'Scoot!'

He took the cottage cheese and went out the side door, climbing the steps to the back yard. After he ate, he lay on his back on the flagstone patio and stared at the clouds that staggered across the sky. He was a shell of silence and dry watchfulness on the outside. Inside, his heart felt like a float in a turbulent sea, swaggering and banging against the walls of his chest. He was certain of one thing: he was in love with Lacey.

This certainty made everything else in his life, everything in his world—just everything—suddenly uncertain.

three

IT WAS THE LONGEST WEEKEND OF HIS LIFE, MADE up of the longest days, and then diced and sliced into long, stale and painfully slow hours and minutes.

On Saturday, Jude woke early, or rather got up early because he hadn't really been asleep, and padded to the window. Los Angeles, an Impressionist painting in softly dawning pastels, lay under the pervasive tinge of purplish-brown. It was sunrise over smog. It was six-fifteen.

He got dressed and opened his door quietly. His room was on the front of the house. His parents' room, down a hall that accessed a master bath and a dressing room, was also on the front. At the back of the house were a sunroom and Mark's bedroom. Jude crept through the upstairs hall past the entry to his parent's room and then past Mark's door and down the stairs.

The last time he'd been up this early on a Saturday had been... He pried at the question a moment and gave up. The answer was plausibly never.

He stood at the verge of the living room a moment, and peered in. His father had been in the military, serving a post-war stint in Japan. While there, his mother had acquired a houseful of Japanese art and furniture. There were ink scrolls on the walls, a bamboo couch and chairs, a lacquered black table with an ornate red mandala, carved jade statues, a three-stringed samisen. He found these items notable for the first time. His first memories were in the house on Melbourne Drive in Indiana. These objects had been there from the beginning. From his beginning. Now, the artifacts were scattered around a very different house in Los Angeles, and they seemed suddenly very Japanese in a very American household. They felt borrowed or accidental. Definitely strange.

Passing the den, and on into the kitchen, no one else was awake.

It was too early to eat. But he was too agitated to sit down. He was worried about Lacey. She wasn't just sick, but troubled. And in some complicated way that emerged as tangled sheets in his semi-waking dreams, he felt he could help her. He was sure, if he could just see her, if he could just ask her how she was doing, then she would know he cared. She would know, and this would make a difference. An important one.

And if she told him what was wrong, he was also sure he could fix it. It was as if, Jude thought, he had a lurking superpower that he'd never had to use before. One that maybe no one knew he had.

Somehow, he had to let Lacey know—maybe Penny too—that he could help.

He wrote a note to his mother and slid it under the plastic foot of the coffee urn. It read simply, "Went for a bike ride. Jude."

He slid down the hill in the cool morning mists like he was parting a veil. He rode an obstacle course down back alleys and narrow side streets where trucks were unloading, the pavements were broken and wet, and men shouted gruffly at one another. In a few minutes, he rode past the apartment on Harold. There wasn't a soul about. There were no doors open, no music, not even curtains open to the breezeless morning.

He lingered across the street, sitting on a low concrete block wall, and pretended to examine a technical problem with his bike. At the Crestview a door downstairs opened and a man stepped out. He wore a steely gray suit. He was cinching his tie and his eyes were inclined into the morning sun, blinking like a lizard greeting the day. He leaned back in the door, said something, and strode out to a sleek black Jaguar. He saw Jude as he unlocked the car door. He nodded at Jude. Then he slid down into the car and clicked the engine over to a soft purr. The car passed down the street as smooth as a new zipper.

The apartment was still as a photo again. Jude watched for a long while, carefully placing and naming the four apartments he knew—Lacey, Frenchie, Penny, and of course, Russ.

Then, feeling exposed—anyone looking out from the Crestview could see him—he climbed on his bike and left. Trying to distract himself, he rode all the way down to Santa Monica. He rode into the dawning heat and noise for a long time until he was traversing the palisades high above the beach. When he got to Colorado Avenue, he cut right and rode down onto the pier. Cars and people were filtering in, like water from drainpipes after a rain.

It was kind of exciting to have ridden all the way to the beach. He'd arrived in time to watch clusters of people arriving on the pier and the beach, and in the stores and restaurants on the palisades above. But he felt Lacey inside him like a clock or a bomb, ticking, ticking, ticking.

So almost at once, he turned around and rode back toward Hollywood. It was uphill and by now he was terribly hungry.

Finally, he rode past the apartment again. It was just after noon.

Again, the place was silent with one exception. Russ stood on the sidewalk just outside his door. He held the newspaper and a cigarette, was dressed in a stained, blue T-shirt and black pants with suspenders. Every once in a while he raised his eye and peered out at the world. He was a guardian toad.

Jude slipped on past, his eyes hanging on Lacey's door.

When he got home, he ate and went upstairs. He lay on his bed, listened to music, and moped. But his father pushed open his door without knocking and said, "Have you finished the yardwork?" Jude tried to wriggle out of the work by feigning tiredness and maybe even a little sickness, but his father's expression never changed. He stood like a warden, waiting, his mouth pursed and tight. So Jude worked in the yard the rest of the day, mowing, trimming, raking and bagging.

That night, he tossed and turned, and finally slipped out his open window to sit in the iron planter cage. Looking southeast, he had a view of downtown. North, above the house, the Griffith Observatory loomed. Lacey and the Crestview were southwest, out of his view.

Sunday, he told his mother he wanted to try coffee and, with a heavy dose of cream, he worked through his first cup. After church, he rode past the apartment again. Only Russ was out again, smoking in the sunlight with his newspaper in hand. Jude felt a physical tugging in his chest as he pedaled by. An urgent, reedy little voice in him told him he needed to see Lacey. That Lacey needed to see him.

He rode down to the Wilshire District, which turned out to be a boring inflammation of skyscrapers a mile past his junior high. He circled the La Brea Tar Pits where he could see a display of a standing skeleton of a mastodon. It seemed like it should be really cool, but it wasn't.

But mostly he rode aimlessly, waiting. He was determined: when he came back by the Crestview, he would stop. It was Sunday. He had to see Lacey.

On the way back, it was early afternoon, hot and still with the needling jangle of car horns and sirens. Doors and windows were open at the apartment. Penny was out on the upper walkway, moving between doors. Lacey's door and curtains were still closed. And Russ was driving a stake into the flowerbeds where a tall plant had been knocked over. A cigarette dangled from his lip.

Jude felt like a fly battering against the glass. He couldn't tell if the glass he was up against was Lacey's closed door, Russ's rules, the threat of Paulo, or his own fears. Whatever it was, it was overwhelming and bleak. He felt small and unequal, and he rode on past.

He biked in the area for another hour, trying at first to talk himself back into the aura of his unique necessity to the situation, but he finally just rode around while he waited for things in his mind to change. Then, riding past Frederick's of Hollywood on Hollywood Boulevard, a flamboyant lingerie store with buxom manikins in scant fabrics in the display window, he felt horribly young and naive. He stopped at the curb a block away, pretending to examine a bookstore window display, and almost cried. He was useless. Just a fucking kid on a fucking bicycle. He rode home without going by the apartment again.

JUDE'S brother Mark, like Jude, played a brass instrument that had been chosen for him by their father. There had been a field trip of sorts to the Golden Calf Pawn Shop in downtown Indianapolis.

The trip had been memorable to Jude. For one thing, Jude couldn't remember another time he and Mark had done anything with just their father. But the significance of the three of them alone was overshadowed by other aspects of the event.

There was the fact that thirty minutes from their house in Marion County was a metropolis of skyscrapers and taxis, a place so dense with people and traffic he felt like he'd visited another planet. Then there were the Negroes. There were scores of them on the streets, people he'd only seen on TV, in National Geographic magazine, and rarely out in the world. There were exactly three at his Indiana middle school.

While they'd waited at one stoplight Jude had watched three Negro men sitting on crates. They were all smoking. Their clothes were clean but worn. They each wore a hat, little pork pies. One of the men had a small rifle lying across his lap. While Jude was watching, a flock of pigeons swirled overhead and landed above on the telephone wires. The man with the gun raised it, and squinting along the sites, squeezed off two loud pops. The flock burst into flight while a bird, a small cloud of feathers lifting away from it, tumbled downward.

As his father pulled away with the light, Jude strained over the back seat to watch a young boy, younger than Jude by a couple years at least, leap up, run across the street, and snatch up the dead bird. He immediately was running back, the bird held upside down by its yellow-tinged scaly feet. The bird's yellow eyes were already reflective as glass balls.

Another surprise to Jude had been his father. In the Golden Calf, an older Negro man had shown them the musical instruments. He was slow and patient and very tall and thin. He wore a blue suit and a yellow dress shirt open at the neck. But on his feet he wore ragged green bedroom slippers. He smelled sweet, like caramel left in the sun. His skin was a deep, dark black that made his features indistinct in the dead light of the shop. He watched them cautiously with black pits encased in bloodshot, yellowed eyes. He stood by while their father had taken down one brass instrument after another, carefully wiped the mouthpiece on a handkerchief, and then had blown through the instrument. He didn't know how to play, but he got a blaring squawk out of some, a fitful gusting out of others, and finally a wavering tone out of a couple.

Perhaps based on the success of his efforts, a trombone was laid in a case with purple crushed velvet inside, and then a trumpet in a case with blue crushed velvet. Their father lifted the cases onto the counter and said he thought the prices were too high. The two men, their father and the shop owner, entered an argument about payment. Jude had never seen such a thing.

At one point, their father had grasped their shoulders and said, "Well, let's go boys. We'll try down the street."

The three of them awkwardly navigated the long passage between fishing poles, display cases, and a pair of large brass diving helmets. They moved toward the dirty front windows and the wash of light that crept reluctantly in.

The shop owner let their father touch the door handle, and said quietly, "I can do a hundred for the two." This was more than their father's "final offer" of ninety, but below the shop-owner's low of one-twenty-five.

His father stopped, considering the offer as he stared out through the dingy glass. Then he steered them back. A small stack of bills crossed the counter, and their father apportioned the instruments by size, the trombone to Mark, the trumpet to Jude. The two boys hefted the cases and the three of them walked out.

That had been two or three years ago. Mark had stopped playing trombone several months before the move to Los Angeles. Jude kept at the trumpet, mostly because he didn't think he would be allowed to quit.

The week before school started in Los Angeles, Mrs. Wallette, their new next door neighbor, had asked Mark and Jude to help her move some boxes down from her attic. While doing this, Mark had seen an old red-and-gold Prairie Ramblers Cowboy Guitar propped against a wall coated with dust. Before he'd so much as recognized his desire for the thing, Mrs. Wallette had said, "Would you like that old guitar, Mark? That used to be our daughter, Susan's. But we have no use for it now, I can assure you!"

That old guitar had dropped like a coin in a slot. Mark went from being any old geeky kid to being a guitar player in mere weeks. He used his years of untouched allowances to get a stack of guitar books and he hunkered over the body of the instrument as though it were a tumor in his side. His musical diet changed—suddenly he was listening to rock n' roll—and soon he was playing recognizable sequences of notes and chords that matched the music he was listening to. To Jude, his brother's accomplishments on the guitar were on the verge of magic.

Now Mark was mining records for guitar licks and would set six records on his record player's turntable and then play along on guitar with reverence and zeal, and quickly improving verisimilitude, for hours on end.

Their father made noises about the guitar the moment it arrived. At first, he tried to be funny about it. He ventured one night at dinner, "It's hardly even an instrument. Folk singers use them so they won't look silly reading poetry."

But Mark's dedication, and then his skill, and finally his choice of music, heightened their father's alarm. Two weeks later, their father was saying, "That guitar is a devil's instrument. That music you're learning is the way into a destructive lifestyle. Drugs and crime and an early death are the best a rock musician can hope for."

Mark seemed confused rather than angry, and uninterested rather than alarmed. Their father had a guitar on which he would play old folk songs: "Frog Went A-Courtin'" and "Red River Valley" had haunted their bedsides at night for many years. In Jude's opinion, he still looked silly.

That Sunday night, after Jude's failed attempts at seeing Lacey again, their father launched another attack on the guitar. As Mark was getting up from dinner, obviously avid about getting back to his guitar, their father said, "This has gone far enough. No more guitar until we get your grades."

Mark stopped in his tracks, stunned. Jude watched him as closely as someone discerning their own possible future would. Mark's face worked, his hands convulsively wrapped into fists and then released. Their father's eyes flickered, surprised by the fury Mark showed. He said, "You have a trombone."

Mark lifted his lips into a remote smile and said, very quietly, "Fuck you," as he left the room.

"You will *not* use that language in *this house!*" their father bellowed. He slammed his fork down on the table with a crack and seethed, "Get back in here, young man!"

Mark returned. He stood just inside the door, sullen and angry.

"You can put the guitar in my bedroom. Right now."

Mark spun and left.

The breakfast nook where they ate their dinners looked the same, but it felt so packed with tension and energy that Jude felt like it might explode. Jude's mother stared across the table at her husband as though she might say something. Then she pulled her eyes away from him and asked Jude, "Do you want any more dessert, Jude?"

"No thanks." Jude wanted to be out of that room as soon as he could possibly be.

"Lyle?" she asked his father.

His eyes swept to Jude. His lips were pinched shut and his eyes were molten. "Yes, I'll have some more."

Officially, no one was allowed to leave the dinner table until everyone was finished. Mark had somehow slipped out through a loophole. So now, they all sat there as stiff and cold as the near-naked manikins at Frederick's while his father methodically clinked his spoon through a second scoop of ice cream.

When the puzzle of dinner and his father's anger and getting to leave the table was finally disentangled, Jude slipped quickly up the stairs. In the hall outside Mark's room were carefully stacked all his records, all his guitar books and the guitar. Next to these was the trombone case.

Jude went to his room and as soon as he'd sat down on his bed, Mark knocked lightly on the bathroom door. The bathroom, appropriately a Hollywood bath in Hollywood, connected to both their rooms. "Well, that's it," Mark said. "I'm gone."

"Gone? Because of the guitar?" Jude was surprised.

"Because he's a motherfucker!" Mark spit out in a hoarse whisper.

Jude had been aware that Mark and his father were struggling. Until this night Jude had assumed it was about Mark's new friends. Mark was going to two different kids' houses after school a couple days a week now. One of the kids, Emilio, was a tall, Salvadoran kid with one arm. He scared Jude.

The scariest aspects of Emilio were his long sideburns, his fierce but sporadic moustache, his bottomless black eyes, his leather-dark skin, and his bullwhip. Every time Jude had seen him, he had a twenty-foot leather bullwhip coiled over his shoulder and under his missing arm. The wooden grip handle always faced forward. Like a gunslinger in the old West, Emilio could grasp the handle, unfurl the whip, and crack it with impressive precision on tiny moving targets fifteen or more feet away, all in split seconds.

Curious about this big brooding kid, Jude had followed his brother and Emilio out into the backyard one afternoon. At first, the swift crack of the whip had been exhilarating to Jude. Emilio monosyllabically identified what he would hit and Jude's eyes leapt to the hapless bee or dragonfly and, a millisecond later, saw a sort of double exposure of the whip's ragged tip and the insect, and then there was nothing, unless perhaps there were a wing or two, or maybe a puff of pollen dust, floating on the air.

But as Emilio continued to surgically remove bees from above flowers, Jude's attention traveled up the whip to Emilio himself. It unsettled him. Emilio spoke little—"Bee." *Crack!* "Spider." *Crack!*— and his expression never shifted from a deadly machinelike focus.

Then he'd said, "Bird." Three sparrows darted from among the trees and traversed the yard. Suddenly there were two, and hanging in the air over them was a cloud of feathers and a mist of blood. Mark hooted in appreciation. Jude felt sick and went inside.

But apparently it wasn't the friends their father hated, but what they did.

"He hates rock music and modern jazz," Mark said. "He keeps making snide comments about how regressive rock is, played by Neanderthals for Neanderthals. But he can't play an instrument. He scrubs at that guitar of his. He can play three chords. He doesn't have a fucking clue."

Mark strode to the window and looked out. It was dusk and the city was half lit under blue-brown skies. Mark leaned his head out and peered out over the city.

"Anyway," he straightened up. "Just tell em you don't know anything."

"Anything about what? You're not really leaving?"

"I am. I'm fed up."

"Where will you go?"

"Hell, I don't know."

Jude heard him, ten minutes later, slip out his window. The house was poked into the front of a hillside, and the backyard sat level with the upstairs bedrooms.

An hour later, he heard his mother's tentative tapping at Mark's door. "Mark?"

A minute after that, she burst into Jude's room from the bathroom. "Where's Mark?"

Jude blinked and shrugged. "I don't know. Isn't he in his room?"

"No!" Her hand slowly lifted and settled, fingers spread, on her chest.

"Maybe he's in the back yard."

She nodded, looking past him, and then spun and was gone.

A few minutes later, he could hear his father at Mark's door, addressing his mother. "Relax, he's not going anywhere far."

Jude heard it. Curled up inside that sentence was an insult. Mark was just a little boy still, a little boy who would come home after an hour because he was scared of the dark.

Jude left his doors standing open just as his mother had left them. It gave him ears on the house. He listened while his mother called Mark's friends' parents. And then while she reported out to his father. She had learned that Emilio lived only with his uncle, and that Mark's other good friend, Jimmy, who played bass, was away for the weekend.

That night, Jude could feel the wakeful attention in the house. He felt like he was lying in a loaded mousetrap. But the trap never tripped.

Where on earth was his brother?

Who was this lurking, angry man in the house? True, he'd always been there, but now he seemed like an enemy. And Indiana… Well, Indiana seemed another country.

BY MONDAY morning, Jude felt like that mousetrap all by himself, not just a spring-loaded slab lying in bed waiting, but a spring-loaded slab swinging about the world, among people.

School, which had been a rich and vibrant tapestry of strange people and events only last week, lay over Monday like a black-out curtain. There was no light, no luster. He stood at his locker in the deep shadows of the morning hallway and looked down the tunnel of his day: homeroom, math, wood shop, and then social studies. After social studies, lunch. Then Jude went to English, band, and P.E.

In Indiana, Jude's elementary and middle schools were low-slung, modern buildings spread over acres of pavement and grass. They seemed, at least in his memory, to hum with simple purpose and intention. At the elementary school in Indiana, you entered green-painted steel-and-glass front doors and exited through the back and sides to an extensive patchwork of playgrounds. The buildings were self-contained and utterly polite and sensible. The middle school was similar. It just lacked the childish jungle gyms and swings.

More than even his first day at Le Conte, Jude felt like a stranger. He sat in homeroom listening to Ms. Mantle grind out the school announcements. To each one she added her gloss—whether it was worth going, where it was, who the teachers involved were. They were supposed to catch up on homework in her class, but she held the front of the class like a jaybird, ready to peck anyone who didn't "pay proper attention" while she droned on.

Today, Jude worked at arranging his torso in the desk in a way that kept his head upright and his face turned toward the front, while his eyes closed for brief moments and his brain slithered through avenues of sleep.

She caught him only once. "Jude Tangier! Are you with us this morning?"

The comment registered, but he remained mired in dreams.

The kid behind him poked him in the back and he opened his eyes wide and looked at her. Ms. Mantle always wore flouncy white or pale pastel sweaters with pearlescent round buttons, over blue or yellow flowered dresses, with small blue-edged horn-rim glasses. It was the outfit of a youthful new teacher, but it was hung over the carcass of a woman older than his grandmother. Her face was a network of wrinkles and the occasional jutting white hair, all shrouded with a peachy dust that must have been some kind of make-up.

"I'm here," he said. "I'm listening."

She relented reluctantly, her eyes quickly cast over the rest of the room to see if anyone else was daring to drift.

Between classes, he learned that neither the snack counter or vending machines offered coffee. Now that he had had coffee, he wanted it again to wake himself up.

He sat next to Kevin in social studies. Kevin wanted to talk, but Mr. Diaz wasn't one to allow talk in his classroom. Mr. Diaz immediately dove into how the state of California, along with the entire modern Southwestern United States, had been wrested from the Mexican government by a "handful of gringos" as he called them.

"The independent Mexican government was literally twenty-five years old," he explained. "And in a few short years, United States military actions, which culminated in the Mexican-American War of eighteen forty-six, defeated the much smaller Mexican forces and enabled the United States to steal over half the new country's territory." He dragged his pointer over the map. "Texas," he pronounced it *TE-haas*, "Arizona, New Mexico," *MEH-hee-co*, "Nevada, Utah, and parts of California, Colorado and Oklahoma."

Mexico had ceded the territory in the 1848 Treaty of Guadalupe-Hidalgo. Mr. Diaz sounded disbelieving that such a vast injustice could continue to stand. He snapped the pointer against his open palm and stood in a spread stance as though speaking to troops. "They say history is written by the victors. So far this is true. But I'm sure some of you have dealt with bullies, and, you know what…" he glared at the class, chin thrust forward, "sometimes bullies get their just reward."

Jude literally sat in his desk and shook his head, as if to dislodge a clutter of thoughts, or maybe allow something through. What Mr. Diaz was saying was colliding with something in his waking dream.

"Mr. Tangier, you got something you want to say?" Mr. Diaz was standing at the head of his row of desks.

"No, sir, I just…"

"You just what, Mr. Tangier?"

"It's just that," He let his mind jump into the dream. "I mean, we—my family—drove through all of that area when we came out here. And now, like, here we are in Los Angeles."

"Yeah, your point?"

"I guess eighteen forty-eight seems like a really long time ago, and the United States seems... I don't know..."

"Yeah," Mr. Diaz smiled and pulled back a little. "Permanent?"

"Okay."

"Ms. Richter," he flagged another white student, a girl who often resisted Mr. Diaz' take on things. "Do you feel America is a moral country? A Christian country? That they govern themselves and deal with other countries as a morally legitimate entity?"

"Ah, un-titty?" she asked. A few students snickered.

"En-tity," he enunciated. More snickering.

He frowned at the class. "Government," he snapped out.

Ms. Richter, Molly was her name, blinked and crinkled her nose. "Yes. This is a Christian country." She sat up when she spoke, as though separating herself from any immigrants in the room.

"Well, Christians do make up a majority still," he said, "but that majority is eroding quickly. And as for morality... Later in this class we'll talk about Vietnam and the Red Scare. Some of the events that have evidenced our national immoralities. And we'll certainly talk more about Watts and the Zoot Suit riots that took place right here in Los Angeles."

He slapped his pointer into his palm again, once, twice, and then held it. "I will say this: the morals of this country have been doubtful from the start. The Louisiana Purchase, that was a valid purchase when Napoleon Bonaparte needed cash to pay for his wars of conquest. But most of the land before and after that..." he lifted his hands, unable to answer for the country's behavior.

The bell rang and students began pulling their books and papers together and standing to leave. Mr. Diaz said, "Let's just say, calling something a treaty or a law doesn't mean you didn't commit illegal and immoral acts.

"In fact..." Diaz was stepping back, wading through the passing, hurried students. "Get outta here," he said. Then returned to his thought. "In fact, maybe it's axiomatically the opposite."

Jude slipped past Mr. Diaz at the front of the room, the word axiomatically bouncing around his head, looking for a place to land.

Jude and Kevin stepped into the hall together, and then Jude peeled off and turned right toward his locker. In the riverine flow of kids and the occasional adult, only kids at lockers stopped, and they were purposeful and temporary, bees over flowers.

So the point of stillness across the hall was out of place.

Jude shot a glance over and saw Hector standing there, leaning against the small gap of wall that stood between two large banks of lockers. He had one knee cocked, the foot flat against the wall. He wore the standard issue large black slacks, white T-shirt, and dark gray overshirt. His shoes were dark blue Keds. His eyes were following Jude.

Jude pulled his gaze away and hurried along the wall.

But the image of Hector was embedded. He had been holding a photograph by the corner. Twitching it rhythmically back and forth. Jude's photo. Of Betty Brown.

AT LUNCH, Kevin, James, Robby and Henry gathered together closer than ever and Kevin retold the events of Friday. Jude knew Kevin had already told the others at Temple over the weekend, but a retelling while Jude was there to fill in the gaps was required.

But he didn't fill in any gaps. He listened and nodded. Kevin's story was like his story had been last week. Some pretty women had helped Jude out after he got beat up. They all lived in the same building. They wore bikinis and robes. It was awesome.

When Kevin was done with his telling, he punched Jude in the shoulder. "But what the freak happened in the bathroom, man?"

Jude was surprised by the question. Taking Kevin there seemed so distant now, so juvenile. And what had happened since slewed sharply into a realm more personal and adult and private. He hunted for what to say. "Well, Lacey, the blonde one that bandaged my head and hand, she was sick. And I just helped Penny, the friendly one, I helped her get her cleaned up a little, and put her into the bath."

"Sick, like what kind of sick?" Henry asked.

"I don't know. She was throwing up."

"Did she stink?" James asked.

"No…" Jude scrunched his nose, pulling back the odors from memory. The sickly-sweet smell lurched into his memory. "Well, yes. I mean, she'd thrown up. And that didn't smell too good."

"Well, if she was drunk, you'd know it," James said.

"His sister," Bobby pointed a thumb at James. They all laughed.

James said, "Leave my sister out of this. Anyway, maybe your blonde was on drugs."

"I don't think so," Jude said. He felt deeply defensive, as though a bullet-proof, iron plate were hardening in his chest: Lacey wasn't well. She was weak. She needed his help.

"Yeah, then that dude that came in. He was creepy," Kevin said.

"Yeah," Jude allowed. Another reason for Jude's presence in Lacey's life, she needed protection.

"Who was that guy?" Kevin asked.

"I don't know. They called him Paulo."

"He didn't look Mexican," Kevin said.

"What did he say to you?" Jude asked him.

"He said," Kevin squinted the event back into memory. "Ah, he said… 'Boy, whatever the fuck you're doing here ends now. Leave, motherfucker.' So I left."

"Whoa, that's a badass dude," Bobby said.

"He acted like he was going to kick my ass," Kevin said. "I was just glad to get out of there."

"So, Jude," a sly smile flitted across James's face. "What was the chick wearing when you, you know, put her in the tub."

Jude shrugged. "You know," he tried to deflect.

"No, not really," he said. "We don't."

"Panties," he said.

"Panties?" James was pleased with this information. "So, no bra? No top? No PJs? No robe? No…"

"Slippers?" Henry filled in. The boys all laughed.

"No."

James leaned all the way in, "So you totally saw her tits!"

Jude shrugged. "Yeah, I guess so."

"Holy shit," Kevin said. "Were they… Were they…"

"Nice?" It was Henry again.

Jude shrugged again. Though it was just words, he felt like his friends were enjoying Lacey in some illicit way. But, at the same time, he certainly didn't want to misrepresent her breasts. They loomed in his mind, two perfect orbs breaking the surface of the water, like nothing in his life so far. But he really didn't want to go there with these guys.

"So…" Jude looked at their faces, almost joyfully expectant. "My brother ran away from home last night."

Only Kevin had ever seen Jude's house or its inhabitants. He looked shocked. "Whoa, he's like in eleventh grade!" Kevin said. "Like Janey and Krissy," he said this to James. Janey was Kevin's sister who was Mark's age. Krissy, Jude filled in the blanks, was James's sister who must have been the same age.

James nodded his head, acknowledging the seriousness of this. "Where'd he go?"

"No one knows. My mom called his friends. They didn't know."

"Wow, man, in Los Angeles…" Henry was duly impressed.

"Why'd he leave?" James asked.

"My dad took his guitar away."

"He plays guitar?" Robby asked. There was reverence in his voice. "Is he any good?"

"Yeah, he's getting real good," Jude said.

The bell jangled over them. James stood and fired his crumpled lunch bag in an arc that ended in a trashcan twenty feet away. "Jeez," he said, "and just a minute ago, we were all thinking about Lacey's tits!" James turned to Jude and his face widened into a lascivious grin.

IN ENGLISH class, the seats were arranged in an L-shape to accommodate the long narrow room where the class was held. There were five rows of desks that went three-deep on the left as you entered, and three rows four deep at the back of the room. Ms. Loral's desk sat to the right in front of the chalkboard.

The desks at the back on the left were in relative darkness with just one fluorescent light fixture above the front desks. The back on the left is where Jude sat. It gave him the perfect, secretive vantage of the girl who sat in the back of the other section, a hippy girl, Melinda Eastman.

He hadn't admitted to himself that he'd chosen his seat for this reason. But this day, worn and pulling himself along solely within the lower, animal portion of his brain, he could admit to and enjoy the fact.

Melinda Eastman was… Jude allowed his slow mind to slow even further, as though he were passing a compelling painting. He wanted to get his description of Melinda right. He felt, in getting it right, he would learn something about himself, about Melinda, and maybe even about girls in general. Words sang silently in his head, "She's like a rainbow. She comes in colors in the air…" That, he realized, as a tune emerged from the words, was the Rolling Stones.

She was, first and foremost, a hippy. For being in the middle of Hollywood where the streets thrived with a multitude of hippies of every brand and style, their heads wreathed with smoke and floppy hats and long hair, LeConte had few. Melinda and her boyfriend Greg Oberst were the most noticeable and the most authentic.

There were other kids that tried to be hippies, but the only true hippies that Jude had seen were Greg and Melinda and a couple of kids in their small circle of friends.

Jude was pretty sure he hated hippies. They were everything un-American. They were anti-war. They didn't bathe. They wore weird clothing.

But Jude remembered Melinda's entrance the second day of school—she hadn't attended the first day. She swept in barefooted, wearing faded blue jean bell-bottoms and a white, gauzy blouse with blue embroidery at the neckline. The bell-bottoms were homemade with the side seams of her regular blue jeans ripped out and large triangles of flowered yellow-and-blue cotton sewn in. Her blonde hair sailed off her shoulders behind her, and flopped forcibly to the middle of her back with every stride. A braided leather headband circled her head, and her wrists and fingers were studded with rings and bracelets.

Her face—this was when Jude had conspired to move his seat so he could more closely observe the enemy—was serene and stunningly beautiful. Her skin was a buttery tan. She appeared to wear no make-up. Her entire being, her package, her self, Jude reflected, was so confident and assured. He wasn't used to girls his age being so centered. They'd always seemed a bit giddy to him, as though they were tipped forward and rushing downhill. He had to admit, hippy or not, she was some kind of royalty, at least in the tiny world of LeConte.

Jude learned that she was a year older than he was, a tenth grader, held back for "behavior problems." But this just made her somehow more remote and more compelling.

Greg Oberst, her boyfriend, had been in band with Jude, the class Jude went to after English, for all of two days. He, too, was a hippy. He too entered barefooted and also on the second day of classes. His bell-bottoms, also homemade, were striped vertically in tans and browns with bright red paisley inserts to create the bells. The pants were frayed from wear on the bottom. He wore a white T-shirt with a green KEEP ON TRUCKIN' emblem, and a fringed leather vest. His hair was darker and shorter than Melinda's, but still reached his shoulders.

Greg engaged with the world on his own terms. He'd said loudly, "Good afternoon, Mr. Denny," when he entered the band room. Mr. Denny snapped his head up from where he was moving sheet music about on his desk. He glowered at Greg as he crossed the room to the drum area. Jude sat with his trumpet in his lap, waiting in silence for acknowledgement or instruction.

Finally, when Mr. Denny stood, picking up a cork-handled and sharply-pointed baton, he said, "Welcome to the band room, Mr. Oberst. Sorry you couldn't find time in your busy schedule to join us yesterday." He strode across the front of the room. "We have rules in this room that will be obeyed."

Greg echoed, "Obey!" and fired off a short burst of a drum roll.

"Silence!" Denny burst out, spinning to face Greg. Denny was a short, squat man with a squarish mass of dark curls on top of his head. He leaned aggressively toward the offender with a mighty frown.

"That!" Denny stabbed the air, "is rule one." He strode across the front of the room, glared down at the flautists, and spun back. "Absolutely *no* playing of *any* instrument while I am *speaking*!" He shook the baton wrapped tightly in a meaty fist at Greg.

Jude had looked back. Greg was grinning happily. He saw Jude watching him and snapped out a silent drum roll in the air above the drums with his sticks.

They hadn't played another note that day. The next day, Greg had again greeted Mr. Denny with a wave and a "Good afternoon, Mr. Denny," at the start of class. Then Denny had passed out a page of sheet music. It was "Twinkle, Twinkle Little Star." Mr. Denny paced back-and-forth, his caged energy making Jude nervous. He said, "Do the best you can. Play it. Every note. If you fall behind, just jump ahead and catch up. We need to know what you can do."

Jude felt the 'We' in his statement. He was gathering the better musicians in the room into his inner circle and, as a group, passing judgment on the rest.

Mr. Denny raised his baton theatrically and counted off a convincing "One-and, two-and, three-and…" The students scratched and blew and banged into the piece. As it was coming to the end and Mr. Denny's arms were raised to command a decisive ending, Greg Oberst called out loudly, "Drum solo!" and head down and hair flying, had taken off in a run of drumming that lasted one or two very long minutes.

He closed it off with a slowing *Bam! Bam!… Bam!… Bam!* with both sticks on the snare.

When he raised his head, pushing his wild hair back out of his eyes, he found Mr. Denny at the front of the room pointing to the door. Greg shrugged and slid his drumsticks into his back pocket. He said, "Everyone loves a drum solo. Right?"

He made his way across the back of the room, ducking past the bassoon and the trombones. Waving at the door, he said, "All right, have yourself a great afternoon, Mr. Denny!"

Mr. Denny didn't say another word until Greg had been gone for a full minute. Jude felt in accord with Mr. Denny just then. Rid the school of hippies, he thought.

Then Mr. Denny rapped his baton crisply on his black steel music stand. "Start again! One-and. Two-and. Three-and!" The baton sliced down through the air.

⸺

AT THE END of English class on Monday, Ms. Loral wrote an assignment on the board. "When have you been an outsider?" Three pages. Due Friday. They were finishing reading S. E. Hinton's *The Outsiders*.

Jude left and watched Melinda meet up with Greg in the hallway. He realized that Greg had been doing this every day since she'd first come to class. The two of them were perfectly cool. Greg called out dramatically when he was close, "Melinda! Oh, baby, I'm here!" He made her laugh. He made everyone around them laugh or smile.

They kissed on the lips. It wasn't a tilting in, but lips and jaws, hands raised to their faces, their eyes closed. Jude realized the shocking thing about it was that it looked absolutely real. No one else on campus that he'd seen kissed like this. No one anywhere in fact. Certainly not his parents. Maybe, but only maybe, in movies did they kiss like this. And that was pretending.

Then the two of them set off like a king and queen with an entourage. Greg was a couple inches shorter than Melinda, but he made up for it with confidence. He pushed his chest out, threw his head back, and walked a half-foot ahead. He was the perfect image of a hippy. On a campus where there were maybe ten true hippies out of twelve hundred kids, Greg Oberst had condensed the vibe and represented it absolutely. It was this perfect fit, Jude thought, that gave Greg his immense confidence. Either that, or having someone like Melinda be in love with him.

Jude sweltered through band. Mr. Denny wanted the doors closed at all times, saying, "You people are like flies. Turn your back and one flies in and three fly out!"

They were working their way through three pieces now, a Bach, a Sousa, and something by Donald Smith that was as boring as the man's name. Two of the pieces were recognizable and the trumpet parts were hard for Jude. Not to play, but to play on time, in time, and in a way that Mr. Denny approved of. Jude had received several scowls from him, and one incident of pretty complete humiliation.

In the middle of playing the Sousa piece, a march, Denny snatched Jude's music from the stand in front of him. The music in the room faltered, and then stopped. All eyes moved from Jude to Denny and back again. Mr. Denny shoved his thick-framed glasses up on top of his head and held the music up close in front of his face. He acted as though he were reading it very carefully.

Then he slapped it back in place. "I thought I must have given you the wrong music. But no, that's the right piece." Then he threw his hands up to tell the room that Jude was a hopeless case.

Before this incident, Jude had felt like he was on a craft rolling in the wide sea. The craft was sturdy, constructed of the boisterous and robust music of Sousa, but after that incident, all the music in that room—present, past and future—just seemed to float away over the horizon from anything of any interest or use to him, now or ever.

He scowled at Mr. Denny and mostly only pretended to play, studiously fingering the valves to the music.

He slogged through the hot afternoon. In wood shop, at least the doors were kept wide open and a breeze faltered through. But in P.E., Mr. Hill made them run a mile in the dire heat over the circular track painted onto the black pavement. Then they climbed ropes. This, at least, was something Jude did well. He was the fastest in his class, climbing the twenty-five-foot rope in under ten seconds. The closest kid to him took 11.2 seconds. And all the other kids used their legs. Jude thought the legs were a waste of time and effort and just yanked himself up hand-over-hand. This was how they'd gotten in and out of their tree forts in Indiana. Mr. Hill seemed impressed.

Jude showered, muttering to himself about the heated activities forced upon them on a hot and smoggy day. Then he escaped out onto the paved yard again and crossed the entire campus back to his bike.

As he rode up from the school, he tried to unfurl the thoughts and emotions that were knotted in him. He still didn't feel like he deserved to be worried about Lacey, as though he simply wasn't old enough. He puzzled over Penny and Frenchie and Russ and the rest of the women. Were they taking care of Lacey? Could they?

But as he reached Harold Way, as always on the alert for Hector and his friends, he pedaled past. He was surprised to find that he was more worried about Mark. That single thing tugged him toward home like a fishhook in his breast. Was Mark home? Where was he? When would he see his brother again? But almost more than all of that, it was a nagging undercurrent in his thoughts: Where do I live now? And, who the hell am I living with? Nothing was stable. Nothing was expected. Nothing was itself anymore.

four

JUDE STOOD OVER HIS BIKE AT THE CORNER OF Van Ness and Harold. He stared down the street at the apartment building. It was Tuesday afternoon and the women were once again out in the sun. But they were too far away for Jude to identify any of them.

He held his hand up in front of himself. It was shaking. Exhaustion, he decided. It had been two nights now with no word and no sign of Mark. His mother was a wreck. She was at the front windows staring out, or in the kitchen calling Mark's friends again, and waiting until the moment—later today—when she could officially report her oldest son missing in Los Angeles.

She'd called the LAPD but had been rebuffed by their switchboard. "Is he a minor? Yes? Well, has he been gone forty-eight hours? No? Well, we cannot take a report from you. Call back if he's still missing after forty-eight hours."

Their response had given his mother a prism through which to focus her unstated worries about Los Angeles. "Of course children would go missing in a city like this," she said. "Of course the police would be focused on bigger things like murder and drugs and... and riots of course." And, of course, "None of this would have happened in Indiana." But that last statement she only made on the phone when his father wasn't around.

To Jude, his father seemed completely satisfied with the situation. First of all, there was no rock guitar being played in the house. And, Jude inferred from his weird soliloquy as he walked through the house, no one playing rock n' roll guitar could be trusted to be in communication, to be logical and sane, to be a good son or turn out to be a good person. So his father went through his evenings doing exactly what he did on other evenings: he read the paper, watched Cronkite, smoked a couple cigarettes, and drank large glasses of vodka. Then he ate dinner, excused himself, and went into his den to read journals or a book and listen to Louis Armstrong or Al Hirt pump out New Orleans jazz.

Jude felt like he alone was swimming upstream against the dense air inside the house. He alone seemed to be aware that his brother was loose in Los Angeles and that his parent's responses were entirely selfish and useless. His brother could be dead, stoned out of his mind, traveling with some strangers to Oregon or Mexico or where-the-fuck-ever and his mother and father were worried about the problems of Los Angeles and what was 'sane.'

He needed to escape.

He climbed on his bike and rode toward the women. When he approached, he waved, but turned the corner and rode up past the building. He pulled into the alley and parked his bike out of sight behind the trash cans. Then he rounded the side of the building and approached from the opposite end, away from Russ and Penny on the southern end of the building. He ascended the stairs at the north end.

Jude wasn't certain of the factors that enabled him to now be here, to now walk up the stairs, but he felt oddly unconcerned with his course as though he were impelled. His fear of Russ and of Paulo, his shyness around women, and his usual sense of apology for treading among adults, ever—all these were missing, or at least they were momentarily at bay. It made his feet and hips, his shoulders and chest, and his face, all seem relaxed and, oddly to his ragged thinking, almost like they were his own.

A slender black woman he didn't recognize was coming up the front stairs. He stopped and knocked on Lacey's door, waited two beats, and before the woman could say anything to him, he opened the door and stepped inside. "Lacey?" he called out. He shut the door behind him.

The shower was running and Jude felt a wash of embarrassed heat pass through his face and neck. It was Lacey. He could tell from the voice. She was singing, her voice almost lazy.

Once I was livin' in fortune and fame
Had all that I dreamed of to get a start in life's game
Then suddenly it happened, I lost every dime
But I'm richer by far, with a satisfied mind.

Jude wanted to listen to her sing—the song was sweet and lazy—but he felt the need to let her know he was in her apartment. He stepped lightly to the open bathroom door and, without leaning in, called out, "Hi Lacey?" Her singing halted and he grasped the doorframe, as if holding on against her anger. "It's Jude. I had something I wanted to ask you about. Should I come back later?"

"Jude?"

"Yeah, Jude with the black eye?"

"Juuuude," she enunciated with a thread of enjoyment that thrilled Jude. "No, stick around. But make some coffee!"

Jude had never made coffee, but he had seen his mother make it, maybe a thousand times. He let the memory play. He could see his mother filling the percolator with tap water and plugging it in on the counter. Then she was scooping coffee grounds from a brown Yuban can with a black plastic measuring cup and pouring them—one, two, three, four—into the aluminum basket in the top of the percolator. It was weird. The memory rose right out of his bones, as though, because it was unvarying and absolute, it was more sharply ingrained than any family rituals around meals, or holidays, or television.

But Lacey's kitchen didn't have a percolator sitting on the counter. Instead there was a glass carafe on the back burner of the stove with a hard black rind of old coffee inside. In the clutter of the sink he found a black plastic funnel with a discolored paper towel filled with old dried coffee grounds. He stared at the two artifacts for a while and finally decided that he should pour hot water over coffee grounds and it would drip into the glass carafe. Having worked this out, he turned and found a pan sitting on the stove with a half-inch of water in it.

Then he rummaged for coffee in every cupboard, each cupboard door opening on an aspect of Lacey's existence that felt intimate and strange. In the cupboard to the left of the sink where he expected the coffee, she had two plates and one bowl. There were two plates and two bowls dirty in the sink.

On the shelf above these were a jumble of mismatched coffee cups, water glasses, and wine glasses. In the cupboard on the right of the sink, three boxes of sugary cereals—Cap'n Crunch, Cocoa Puffs and Frosted Flakes—sat among bottles of liquor. There were clear bottles and dark green and caramel brown ones. On the shelf above these were cans of Spaghetti-Os, Campbell's soups, and Dinty Moore beef stew.

He saw the box of the coffee filters on top of the refrigerator, and this inspired him to open the refrigerator itself, and then as an after-thought, the freezer. There in the freezer was a blue can of Maxwell House coffee.

Now Jude was ready and he looked up to find Lacey smiling at him. She was wearing a pale blue robe that halted a good six inches above her knees, and she was wrapping her hair in a yellow towel. She looked like a perfect summer day, stretched end-to-end and filling every crevice of his experience with bird song and a warm breeze.

"Wow," he said.

""Wow?" She tucked in the end of the towel.

"You're... here."

"And there's no coffee!" She lifted her hands as though his incom-petence was unbelievable. But there was a laugh in her voice and Jude smiled.

"I've never made coffee before, but I have it figured out now."

"Yeah, right. We'll see. I'm going to get dressed, and then..." she pointed at a coffee cup on the kitchen table. "I want to see steam coming up out of that mug!"

She spun, her robe rising on the air, and Jude drank in the lovely tight warm skin, high on the backs of her thighs.

He filled the pan with water and set it on the stove, and then built out the sequence of events that would have to follow—the paper filter, like the one he tossed in the trash, filled with four scoops of coffee—five to be sure—and the carafe scrubbed clean of the dark rind of dried coffee, awaiting the pour.

When the water boiled, he poured. The water was uncooperative and nearly as much spilled as poured. It took Jude four pours to get enough water down into the carafe.

After a quick wash of the cup, he had it waiting, steaming, black as a cave when Lacey walked back in. He reached up in the cabinet and pulled out a blue cup that read MAINE IS FOR LOVERS, and poured himself a cup.

Lacey was wearing blue jean shorts and a white blouse. The blouse was a bit translucent and Jude established without a reasonable doubt that she wasn't wearing a bra. Her legs were excitingly beautiful and perfectly tan. Her bare feet were tipped now with dark red polish, already chipped, but to Jude, luscious as candies.

She took her coffee, pulled a cinnamon roll out of a plastic-wrapped tray of them on the table, and crossed to the couch. She sat, curling her legs up beneath her. "So, Mr. Jude with the black eye, what's up?"

Jude carried his coffee with caution to the kitchen chair that sat across from Lacey. He sipped the coffee, found it foul as hot muddy water that had gone sour, and set it down on the coffee table. He looked at her and tried to find some single thing he could say from inside his mental disorder.

So he picked up the cup again and sipped again. It was better this time. Something more of a flavor, more solid. It seemed to rattle through him and pull things into order.

"My brother," he said. "He's older. He's seventeen. He…" Jude was uncertain how much to say. He peered down into the coffee. He couldn't find a way to shape what he wanted to say, so he just started. "We're from Indiana. We just moved here a couple of months ago. And in Indiana, Mark, my brother, sort of played trombone and I played trumpet. But our neighbors here gave Mark a guitar, and he's gotten really good really fast. It's all he does. And on Sunday my dad took his guitar away. So…" Jude looked up at Lacey and felt tears lurking behind his words. He took a deep breath and spit it out. "He left home and he hasn't been back since."

Lacey nodded. Sipped her coffee. "Well," she said, "you're a hell of a long way from Indiana."

Jude nodded.

"So, two nights?" She bit into the roll. "He's been gone two nights?"

"Yeah."

"Not at a friend's? Not that you knew of?"

"No."

"Well, Jude, I don't know…" She set her coffee and the roll on a dishtowel on the coffee table and reached up and rubbed her hair vigorously with the towel before letting her damp hair fall over her shoulders. "I'm no one to be asking for advice."

Jude shrugged. He had sort of thought that that's what he was doing, seeking her advice, but when she said it, he knew he wasn't asking for that. He wanted something else.

"Look," she said, "I left home. We lived in Atlanta. I was fifteen. I'm not saying I turned out okay. But home…" she let the idea travel out on its own thin string. It hung there between them like a wilting balloon.

"Well, yeah, I mean, I don't want to live at home anymore," Jude said, edging his voice with disgust. "But, I don't know. I feel like waiting a couple years is, I mean, it's not that long."

"Depends," she said.

"Why did you leave home," Jude asked her.

"It was time."

"Have you talked to your parents? I mean, since you left?"

"No." She offered Jude a wry, sad smile. "Well, my mom once. And I call my sister sometimes."

"Yeah?"

"Yeah."

"How did you… you know, call her?"

"She would go to her friend's house after school and we could talk on the phone."

"Where did you go, when you ran away?"

"I came pretty much straight here."

"How did you get here?"

"I had a little money," she drank off her coffee. "Took the good old Greyhound." Her eyes traveled past him to the photographs on her wall. He thought that maybe these photos had been taken on that trip.

"Did you take these pictures on that trip?"

"Most of them," she said. "I thought I was going to be an actress and a photographer," she laughed.

"They're really good."

"She laughed again. "Yeah, not so much. But thank you."

Jude sipped at his coffee, the flavor slowly coming around the bend to him, and dreamed a dream of his brother. Mark was floating farther and farther away. He didn't even have the thread that Lacey had to her sister. Mark didn't know Jude's friends. There was no one to call.

She asked, "You don't think he'd go back to Indiana, do you?"

"No. He likes L.A.. He calls Indiana 'Hicksville.'"

"Well, I'm guessing," she pushed up off the couch. "That he'll either be back in a day or two, or it was time for him to move on and you'll hear from him when he's ready."

Jude sank back. This was new information—that Mark could be gone for good—and stated so matter-of-factly. A well of blackness opened up in him as though a vast veil had simply evaporated. He was swept into it, experiencing the state of no more Mark.

Lacey was talking, but he couldn't hear her.

Then she got up and poured herself another cup of coffee. He clicked back into the room, clinging to the pleasure of watching her move. "Coffee's a little strong," she said. "But not bad for your first try."

But Jude found this unexpected and spectacular moment—gorgeous blonde Lacey leaning over the sink and pouring coffee in her kitchen with no one there but Jude himself—even this was faded and dry somehow. Distant.

Where the ever-loving fuck was Mark?

"Your eye's a lot better," she said, looking closely at his brow.

"Yeah."

"So," she straightened up, "I got stuff I gotta do…" She stood in front of the couch, the steam from her cup rising past her eyes.

"Oh, yeah, sorry," Jude stood quickly, holding the coffee cup out in front of himself.

"I don't mean to kick you out, I mean, I just need to get my day rolling, you know?"

"Oh, sure," Jude carried the mug to the kitchen, lifted it and drained the lukewarm contents in a single gulp.

Lacey bent, set her cup on the table. "Do you usually drink coffee?" she asked him.

"No," Jude shrugged. "This is like my third cup. Ever."

She laughed and her eyes twinkled. To Jude, her smile was physical. It felt like she was pelting him with little warm feathers. "Well, you may have a little trouble sleeping tonight."

"Oh, okay." Jude made to leave, moving between Lacey and the door.

"And hey," Lacey touched his wrist. Her voice fell almost quiet. "Penny told me you came by when I wasn't feeling too hot last week."

"Oh, yeah, well, I just wanted to thank you, you know, for," his bandaged hand rose to point to his eye.

"Hey, I'm glad I could help out."

Jude moved another step toward the door. But his body didn't want to go. He took another step and then stopped. It felt like some sort of payment had just occurred, like Lacey had admitted him, had given him coffee, and had listened to him because he'd come by when she was out of it. And now something final was happening. And that was all wrong.

"Was this a bad thing?" he asked. "That I came by?"

Now it was Lacey who shrugged but with just one shoulder. Her face scrunched a bit into a 'Yes' while she said, "No, Jude, not at all. It was fine. Really."

The 'fine' hung in the air like something bright and false and Jude looked past her at the bathroom door where just a couple days ago he'd seen her almost completely naked.

He felt stalled, sad. The light on the bathroom door was hauntingly beautiful, fleeting, precious.

"You know, it's definitely a little weird," she finally said. "I mean, kids don't come around here. You know?"

Jude felt his skin get hot. He hadn't been seeing himself as a kid, not with Lacey. He found himself staring down at the carpet under his feet.

"It's fine, really, but, you know…" Her eyes were darkened and hollowed.

Jude felt her pushing him out with her words. He took a deep breath and just asked the question that kept battering away inside him. "So, who is that guy that comes by all the time?"

Lacey pulled her head back and threw him a half-smile, empty as her eyes now. "Guy?"

"He's been here both times I was here. Pauly or something like that. The Hell's Angel dude."

Lacey shook her head at him, sharply enough to send her hair in a quick dance across her shoulders. "Paulo! He's nobody." She let out a quick stab of laughter and then pulled her hair back into a ponytail with one hand. "Why do you want to know about Paulo?"

"He's pretty scary, that's all," Jude said.

She executed the one-shoulder shrug again, but her eyes kept traveling inward and sank downward. "He's… I don't know, he's sort of helping me, I guess." Her reflections hit some level inside her and stopped. Her eyes came back and she centered a smile on Jude that he couldn't read. "And he's not scary, really. He's like a lapdog. His bark is really all he's got. He's not dangerous."

Jude kept his eyes on hers as she spoke.

She took a step toward him, just enough that she could reach out and touch his wrist again. "Really, it's fine." She watched his eyes. Her own eyes seemed to come closer to the surface again. "I'm fine," she emphasized.

There was that word again. He wanted to shout it back at her, 'Fine! Fine! Fine! I'm fine! You're fine! Even Paulo is fine! We're all fucking *fine!*

But when Jude looked at Lacey, he felt as though her eyes were draining into his. He felt fear and sadness in her, and… What was it? He experienced her as a little girl. Down inside her eyes she was just a kid, six or seven years old. It was like she was trying to say something, but as a kid. His being was swamped with hers. He was awash with Lacey. Not the sexy and beautiful blonde Lacey, but this other frightened and lonely one, the one who tipped so easily into the darkness.

Her smile broke a little and she moved another step closer to him. "You're sweet, Jude." She put a hand on his face and, pushing up on tiptoes, pressed her lips to his cheek. Her felt her lips and nose against him, her breasts and belly, her hand on his face. It was a universe of sensory experience outside of any universe he'd ever inhabited, and a million times the size.

He let himself fall into it, and even luxuriated in the sensations as she lightened her kiss, and then inch-by-inch, molecule-by-molecule, pulled herself away.

She took his elbow and led him to the door. He opened the door, she let loose of his elbow, and he stepped out. He turned to meet her eyes again. She smiled at him. He felt wistfulness in it. "I'll be fine, Jude." A sad smile. "I *am* fine," she affirmed.

Jude searched her eyes but found no truth in her claim.

"Okay," he said.

"Bye, Jude," she raised one hand and started closing the door.

"Bye," he said. He listened to the door click shut. He looked down the walkway. The pale girl who'd been in Frenchie's apartment was leaning back against the wall watching him. She was almost lost in the shadows. She did not smile, nod, wave. Jude turned and retreated down the stairs.

five

WHEN JUDE GOT HOME, THERE WAS STILL NO WORD from Mark. His mother wasn't a crier, not at least in front of Jude. But she looked thinner, wrung out. Her voice and words were scratchy and filled with false optimism.

"He'll call tonight, I expect."

"He's with some friend we just haven't met yet."

"He's probably on his way home right now."

As she said these things, she moved about the house, cleaning and cooking and turning the TV or stereo console on or off and, for long minutes, going to the living room or dining room window where she weakly squared off against her new-found enemy, Los Angeles.

Jude's father went to the hospital in the mornings and came home in the evenings, same as always. He never talked about what he did, but Jude knew he was a heart doctor for little kids. Little-little kids. Infants.

After dinner, his father got up from the table and then stopped in the doorway. "When you're through with the dishes," he said to Jude, "come to the den."

Jude nodded, cringing inside, and said, "Okay."

When he got there, his father had changed into his running clothes and there was an assortment of LPs from Mark's collection spread out on his father's desk.

"Those are Mark's," Jude said.

"Yes." A smug flicker ran across his father's face, a victor pawing over the spoils of war. "Sit down."

Jude moved past the coffee table and sat on the couch. Across from him, his father sat, a good foot higher up in his desk chair.

His father's den, here and in Indianapolis, was pretty much off limits to Mark and himself. Jude always found it an odd space. Both places, Indiana and here, were painted a darkish green and furnished with dark wooden bookshelves and a big glass-topped desk. The couch was a brown and red weave. On the walls were drawings of cars.

"There are things you need to know," his father opened. "Your brother left home because he was doing drugs."

Jude's eyes widened in surprise. He was pretty sure this wasn't true. Mark would have told him.

"He started listening to these records and they carry very strong pro-drug messages. Many of these messages are subliminal, like this one." He held up the Beatles' *Yellow Submarine* album, and then, pulling the slipcase from the sleeve, started reading. His voice was laced with sarcasm.

So we sailed up to the sun
Till we found the sea of green
And we lived beneath the waves
In our yellow submarine

"These are references to pills," he said.

He read lyrics from "Lucy in the Sky with Diamonds," "White Rabbit," "Purple Haze," and "Eight Miles High."

Finally, he leaned forward and tapped a large plastic container on the coffee table. Jude hadn't paid attention to these, but there were three of them. Each was a bottle with a screw-top lid, maybe a gallon in size. The plastic was whitish, nearly opaque, but he could make out what was inside. One contained yellow and red capsules, another small white pills, and the last contained small blue pills.

"This one," his tapping was uneven, almost disordered, like he was communicating his real message in Morse code. "This one is seconal barbital. Do you know what that does?"

"No," Jude shook his head. He'd never heard of seconal barbital.

"This medication depresses the central nervous system. It is used by doctors to relax patients before a major surgery, or to help people sleep if they suffer from insomnia."

Jude nodded. "Okay." His father complained of insomnia all the time but Jude had never even wondered what it was.

"Do you know what young people are using seconal for?" He spit the words 'young people' out as though they were people who had farted in an elevator.

"No."

"To get high."

"Okay." Jude wondered how you got high if you were asleep.

His father tapped out new messages on the tops of the next two jars. The white tablets were amphetamines. They, according to his father, were used to wake up patients who were dangerously lethargic. "It stimulates the central nervous system," his father lifted his fingers letting the message sink in. "It's like drinking twenty cups of coffee."

His father sat back in his chair, smug and regal, looking down at Jude from his higher perch.

"This one," the blue tablets, "is Valium." It was used to treat seizures. Jude could see the label. There were 10000 pills in the bottle.

"Young people are using these drugs—they mix them with other drugs like heroin, LSD, and marijuana—simply to get high. Do you know how dangerous that is?"

Jude found himself following a line of thought, and he had some trouble hearing his father for a moment.

"Are you listening, young man?"

"Yeah, sure," he said.

"Young people are dying from using these drugs and from mixing them together. Or they are ending up unable to use their brains, or their hands and arms and feet and legs in normal ways. They are almost invariably addicted to these drug concoctions, and because these drugs are illegal, they are hard to get and expensive.

"That means that young addicts commit crimes when they take the drugs and then commit more crimes to get money to buy more drugs."

His father spent some time restacking and reordering Mark's LPs, occasionally holding one up to stare at the cover a moment. When all was in order, he turned back to Jude.

"Your mother and I believe your brother ingested drugs that he acquired from a friend and may even be comatose somewhere." He leaned back and watched Jude. Jude watched him back.

"If you think I'm wrong, listen to this." He plucked up an LP cover from the top of the stack and read from the lyric sheet.

> *Well, they'll stone you when you walk all alone*
> *They'll stone you when you are walking home*
> *They'll stone you and then say you are brave*
> *They'll stone you when you are set down in your grave*
> *But I would not feel so all alone*
> *Everybody must get stoned*

"Have you heard this song on the radio?" his father asked, leaning forward.

"Yeah, sure."

"Did you know it was about drugs?"

"I guess not really," Jude said.

"Read this," his father handed him the next record in the stack. It was a new one that Jude knew Mark loved—*Are You Experienced?* by Jimi Hendrix. His father tapped the lyrics to the title song and Jude read them.

> *If you can just get your mind together*
> *Then come on across to me*
> *We'll hold hands an' then we'll watch the sun rise*
> *from the bottom of the sea*
> *But first, are you experienced?*
> *Have you ever been experienced?*
> *Well, I have…*

He read through to the last line:

> *Not necessarily stoned, but beautiful…*

"Once you're in," his father said, "then you're in. But by then, it's too late. The addiction has taken over and your life is just a series of hits and crimes to pay for hits. In between, you sleep in places they call 'crash pads.' These are dens where scores of kids too high to take care of themselves sleep. They indiscriminately communicate sexual diseases. They don't even sleep in beds.

"Disgusting, really."

Jude let his eyes travel over the scene, one piece at a time. The records atop the glass-topped desk, the three pill bottles, and then his father wearing his running clothes.

"I'm a physician," his father reminded him. "I can see when someone uses drugs. I can tell just by looking at them."

Jude's eyes crossed paths with his father's. His father said, "Do you understand?"

Jude nodded.

"All right, you probably have homework."

Jude stood. Blinked three times. Then he left.

He heard the front door slam after his father a moment later. The health nut was off on his run.

AT LUNCH the next day, Jude asked Kevin, James, Robby and Henry if they knew kids that took drugs.

"Why do you want to know that?" James asked scornfully. "You planning to be a druggie?"

"No," Jude said, "my parents think my brother might have left because he's on drugs."

"My sister knows people," Kevin said.

"Yeah, at the high school there are some people," James agreed.

Henry laughed, "And we have Greg and Melinda and their crew."

"Too true," James said. "Yeah, have you met the LeConte hippies?"

"Yeah," Jude said. "Greg was in my band class for a couple days until he got kicked out. And Melinda's in my English class."

"Well, at least she's hot," James said.

"But they take drugs?" Jude asked.

"They smoke pot after school right on campus," Robby was as clouded and serious as marble.

"No way!" James said, disbelieving and disapproving at once.

"Yeah, you can check it out," Henry backed Robby up. "They meet by the side gate behind the auditorium and then go down between the auditorium and the school fence."

"No way!" Kevin and James were in unison, almost in harmony. Kevin continued the thought, "Don't people smell it?"

"They smoke regular cigarettes at the same time," Robby said. "And hardly anyone is ever over there."

"We gotta check this out," James was avid.

After school, the five of them met out by the back gate near the gym and lockers. The school faced west. They were at the eastern gate. When they had all gathered, they circled down toward the southern fence and traveled along it, nonchalant as if some external circumstance had sent them on this course.

Jude was thrilled. He was being included in an adventure, which so far, he hadn't been. And he was going to see Greg and Melinda in their 'natural habitat,' kind of like going to a hippy museum or zoo.

The buildings on the back quadrant of the campus were small, tan-colored wooden buildings. Some were classrooms with glass and doors and desks. Jude had band over here in one of the larger, windowless buildings.

The other boys kept up a studied patter about Robby's cousin who might be able to get them tickets to the Turtles when they came through L.A. the next time because his father, Robby's uncle, was one of the founders of White Whale Records, the Turtles record company.

Jude kept to himself and scanned the narrow gap of fence and pavement he could see between the buildings as they approached. An occasional student passed through the gate, but he saw no one else.

When they emerged from behind the last building, Jude saw them. Greg Oberst was leaning against the side of the auditorium. He was well past the gate. Leaning with their backs against the wall beyond him were Greg's whole crew—Melinda, Theo Hatling, Steven Neely, Carissa Long, and Serena Villaba. A puff of smoke rose from among them and drifted away.

"Holy shit," James said, and almost ducked away. But then he remembered the strategy of nonchalance and guided the crew of them out through the gate. On the sidewalk, he turned to the right.

They would walk right past Greg and his friends, but outside the fence. The two groups were hidden from each other by a thicket of bougainvillea.

Just as they reached where Greg was standing, James speared into the conversation more loudly than was necessary. "Man, I'd rather see Jefferson Airplane than the Turtles any day."

"Ohhhh yeah," Henry agreed. "I love the Airplane." He busted out singing, "One pill makes you larger, and one pill makes you small, and the ones that mother gives you, don't do anything at all!"

Smoke rose and carried to and through their pack on the sidewalk. Jude was surprised by the pungency of the smoke.

"Whoa, that's totally pot, man," James turned back to face them and swiveled on ahead again. "Druggies! And right on campus! Unbelievable!" He smacked a fist into an open palm and said it again. "Un-fucking-believable!"

On the other side of the bougainvillea, they'd been heard. They could hear Theo and Steve slapping the wall like drums and calling out name after name for marijuana, "Pot!" "Smoke." "Toke!" "Weed." "Mary Jane." "Dope!" "Grass." "Reeeeefer!" "Bush." "Boo!"

Far behind them now, Jude heard Greg call out in a heavily weighted accent, "Ganja, maaahn!"

Jude looked back down the street to see if he could see Greg or his friends. A battered red truck was pulling up outside the school gate. The man who stepped out of the cab wore a jean jacket with the sleeves torn off, denim bell-bottoms, a monkey-shit brown cowboy hat, and cowboy boots. His black moustache drooped over a threatening scowl. Even from this distance Jude knew who it was immediately. Paulo.

Greg, flipping his hair back from his shoulders, emerged from the gate. He talked to Paulo. Melinda joined him. Then Greg and Melinda ducked their heads and climbed into the cab of the pickup truck.

As the truck rolled past them, Greg waggled a hand sign to them, his pinky and index finger raised like a bull's horns.

"Ugly fucking truck, man," Robby said.

"Yeah," James agreed.

"Wasn't that the guy from the apartment?" Kevin asked Jude.

Jude looked into the sky past the buildings across the street and said, "I don't think so."

⌒

ENTIRE DAYS passed with a bleak sense of near motionless grinding. There was only one thing, Mark. Everything else was a distraction.

Jude could do his math homework, but reading was nearly impossible. He could ride his bike, but the act of thinking felt futile. He let the blather of Kevin and his buddies wash over him. He passed through school like flotsam on a slow tide. He rode past the Crestview feeling like a shunned puppy, rolling his eyes and pressing harder on the pedals.

And home... Home felt like warfare. The two sides, his mother and father, were entrenched and mostly laid low. But when the guns came out, bright tracers and shrieking mortars had nothing on them. His mother's litany was sliding into a hard line, "Mark left because you are forcing him out. You don't like a thing about him!"

His father, more of an assassin actually than a field soldier, sneered and said, "What's to like?"

In the meantime, Jude wanted to shout at them, 'Where the fuck is Mark?'

On Monday after school, he turned his bike to the hills.

When he got where he was going, he turned into a driveway, rolled down the slight slope and stashed his bike inside the white stucco carport. It was empty except for a desk that had been laid on one end and pushed to the back beneath two cabinets that hung from the ceiling. Out the back of the carport, standing to one side of the cabinets, Jude could see all of Los Angeles. It started a few hundred feet below where he stood and traveled out toward the Pacific. It was dirty, smoggy and half-hidden. But Jude knew it was there. Catalina Island split the smoggy horizon many miles out to sea.

Jude was sweating. The day was hot and he'd ridden uphill from the school for a mile or more. His chest felt constricted as though he'd smoked a cigarette. Though he'd never smoked one, so he didn't know for sure.

Jude left the carport and crossed the driveway to the front door. The house loomed over him. It was a two-story, high white box with rectangular black windows. The front of the house seemed to run from the planting beds right into the sky. A balcony ran along one side of the house, the side facing toward the ocean, and the balcony seemed a long way up to Jude.

Jimmy lived here. He was a bass player Mark had met at school. Jude had come up here with Mark once before. He'd gotten bored stiff while Mark and Jimmy worked endlessly on playing "Sunshine of Your Love." The music they got down quickly—Mark had done the figuring out—but the vocals, all done by Jimmy, sounded high and scratchy like a cat caught in a vacuum cleaner.

Jude rang the bell and heard the tone wander vaguely back into the house. He waited, looking at the high, blank, black doors for a minute or so, then rang again and turned to face out. He looked out over the driveway and street. There was a small, dirty pile of newspapers scattered at the driveway entrance.

He was about to ring again when the door sucked inward.

"Yeah! Whaddya want?" It was Jimmy, looking out of sorts. He was a tall, chubby kid with a mass of longish black hair. The hair half covered his eyes and reached his shoulders, which to Jude made him an official hippy. But his clothes were plain. He wore regular old blue jeans, no bells, a blue-and-white striped T-shirt, and white PF Flyers.

"Hey," Jude said.

"Hey," his affront fell away when he recognized Jude. "Wow, man, did you ride all the way up here?"

"Yeah."

"That's a fucking long way in this heat."

"Yeah," Jude plucked at his shirt, pulling the damp cloth away from his skin to signify agreement.

"Fuck, man. I've lived here since I was like six and I've never ridden a bike up that hill."

"Yeah," Jude nodded.

"You're looking for Mark."

"Just thought... I don't know." Jude felt like he was dealing in realms he not only didn't know about but were somehow illicit. He understood that coming here meant that he didn't trust his mother to get the full story over the phone—who did she talk to at Jimmy's house anyway? And he certainly didn't trust his father to do what was needed to find Mark.

"Yeah, well, I get it, man." He shook his head at the lousy way of all things. Then he stepped back, "Hey, come on in."

Jude came inside, and again swiveled his head to take in the vast, echoing front hall. It was a huge box, really. The floors were tiled in gleaming black. White carpeted stairs, seemingly hung in the air by tiny steel threads, rose up into near darkness. The living room, down two steps, was carpeted in white and ran several yards among black and white furniture to the windows. Beyond the windows was the mottled brown blanket of Los Angeles.

"Yeah, sorry to just show up," Jude said.

"Man, it's cool. I totally get it, dude." Jimmy lifted a hand in a sloppy and vague rendition of 'Follow me' and climbed the stairs.

Jude followed, feeling the living room fall away beneath him viscerally.

"Cool house," Jude said.

"Yeah, man, it's groovy if you're into that kind of thing." Words fell from Jimmy in a lazy drawl, and yet it was the laziness that made the lingo seem so real. It felt like Jimmy, and people like him, knew how to say things in a way that made even the new and strange seem worn-in and soft. Almost normal.

Jimmy led them down a dark hallway. They passed Jimmy's sister's room and Jimmy stopped and poked his head in. "Hey, Bella, it was just Jude, Mark's brother." He opened the door another few inches to let her see Jude from her perch on the bed.

Jude got a glimpse of the dark-haired girl sitting on her bed, legs crossed and a book propped in her lap. The scene was per-fectly frozen, not a whiff of motion. The room was unexpectedly almost wholly black-and-white. No reds, pinks or yellows in this girl's room.

Then Jimmy closed the door and they continued on.

Jude remembered the house. The rooms upstairs were like tract house rooms with the standard white boxy shapes and aluminum window frames. Jimmy's room, he remembered, was different.

Jimmy pushed open his door and went in. Jude followed.

This time the room was dark except for vivid purple and green images and letters on the walls. The room was lit solely by black lights. The colors were dense, soft, oozing and so was the room. Much of this was due to the sour sweet smell of the room. Like cigars but not. Like cigarettes, but not. Like pipe tobacco, but not. Jude felt like he was slipping inside one of the velvet paintings.

He knew the room because he'd seen it in the light the last time he'd been there. He assumed Jimmy would turn on a light, but in the meantime, Jude crossed to where he knew Jimmy had a couch pushed up under the heavily curtained window. He slumped down and waited for either light or for his eyes to adjust.

Jimmy ignored the lights and went across to where a red light glowed. This, Jude knew, was the amp for his bass. Jimmy launched himself up the few inches to sit on top of the amp.

"So how are your mom and dad doing?" Jimmy asked him.

"My mom's freaking out," he said.

"Your dad?"

"He's…" Jude wavered. Then he just said it, the thought that had perched there for the last few days. "He's an asshole."

"Hah, that's for sure!"

Jude leapt up. The voice had come from the other side of the room, and it was Mark's.

"You bastard!" Jude yelled at him, but it was a happy yell. He had found his brother.

"I figured you would either find me, or you wouldn't," Mark said, laughing.

"Have you been here the whole time?" Jude felt like he should cross the room and hug his brother, but in the dim light, his brother sat deep in a bean bag chair, wore an electric guitar, and he hadn't moved.

"Yep." He plucked out a lick on the guitar. "Hey, Jimmy, you should light him up."

A lighter flared in front of Jimmy's face and a caricature of a long-nosed, hollow-eyed Jimmy with a stout glass pipe glowed in the dark room. Jimmy studiously drew in a long, sucking breath. The bowl of the pipe knotted red and urgent. Then the lighter out, Jimmy faded back into shadows and all that was left was a pale cloud of smoke and the tiny knuckle of red light in the pipe.

Jimmy slid off the amp and walked the pipe and lighter to Jude.

Jude took them like he might accept a calling card from Mars. These were foreign materials to him. But this was something Jude was curious about. This was Greg Oberst's "ganja."

The pipe was short, surprisingly heavy, warm, and smooth. He carefully arranged it in his left hand, then thought maybe he should wipe the mouthpiece off. Jimmy had just used it. He did this, wiping it on his shirttail. In doing this, he dropped the lighter. Finding it on the couch, he reoriented the pipe in his hand and mouth, and with his right hand held the lighter up near the pipe.

But the slender plastic lighter consisted of more small moving parts than Jude expected. He got his thumb aligned over the flame opening. Then fixed that, and got it centered on the thumb tab. He practiced getting a flame to leap up, having crisp memories of getting his father's heavy old silver flint lighter to spark, the weight of it, the shape.

Now he joined the two mysteries together, snapping the flame to life and brought it close to the pipe. He burned his thumb. He jerked his hand away, waving it. Then he adjusted and tried again.

Jimmy was back on the amp laughing, but the only sounds were snicks and churs. His face was down in his hand. Mark said, patient, "You gotta suck the fire down inside the pipe." He played a long, bending guitar lick. "And then hold it in."

Jude sucked harder at the pipe and the flame obeyed. It felt like the fire entered his lungs. He barked out the smoke, coughing.

"Holy shit," Jimmy spewed out, "another Indiana greenhorn!" He pulled his bass to his lap and started thumping out notes. Mark slipped in with chords and Jimmy started singing.

> *If you can just get your mind together then come across to me*
> *We'll hold hands and then we'll watch the sun rise*
> *from the bottom of the sea… But first…*
> *Are You Experienced? Ah! Have you ever been experienced?*
> *Well, I have…*

It was that last song Jude's father had made him read. The song petered out as Jimmy dissolved into silent laughter again.

Jude shrugged. "Well, nice to have a soundtrack at least."

"Woooo!" Jimmy loved this and folded over his bass, nearly in tears.

"So mom's freaking out, huh?" Mark said.

Jude studiously relit the lighter and sucked more gently at the pipe. Then he tried to hold the grinding steel wool of the smoke in his lungs. It wouldn't stay. It burst from him with coughing again.

"Yeah," Jude finally answered. "She walks around the house saying that you're on your way home. You're staying with a new friend they haven't met. You're warm and fed. Stuff like that."

He stood to give the pipe and lighter to Mark.

"Try it one more time," Mark said.

Jude sat and lit the pipe again. He coughed the smoke out again, this time after a slightly longer incubation period. This time Mark took the pipe and expertly drew in a long measured toke and held it, snipping it off with a suck and purse of his lips. Then he reached the pipe across to Jimmy, and then he tossed the lighter.

"So, Mom called here," Jude said. "Who did she talk to?"

Jimmy pointed at his own head while he made another pull at the pipe. He held the smoke in and walked the pipe and lighter to Jude.

After he released the smoke, he said, "She talked to me, man. And then later that night, she talked to Nina, my step-mother."

Jude was unclear on what a step-mother was. His only experience was from stories like Cinderella. "So what did she say?" Jude asked.

"She said Mark wasn't here. She hadn't seen him."

"Had she?"

"She was looking right at him when she was talking to your mom."

"So, she's okay with…" Jude let it hang. It was Mark, Jimmy, lying. It was a situation.

"Yeah, she's cool. She's where we got this pot," Jimmy slid a long note down the neck of his bass. "She's like, I don't know, twenty?"

"Twenty?" Jude was disbelieving.

"More like twenty-five," Mark said.

"Are you coming home?" Jude asked Mark. "Like soon, or… ever?"

"Probably," Mark said. "Maybe in a day or two. Maybe at Thanksgiving. I don't know yet."

"Thanksgiving is, like, over a month away," Jude said.

Mark shrugged.

"Should I tell Mom I saw you?" Jude asked.

"No way," Mark's voice hardened. "She'll tell Dad. And he'll call the cops."

The three of them sat there for a long time, just smoking, Mark occasionally playing quick, evocative strings of notes.

Then Jude asked, "So, what do you know about Dad's pills?"

"His pills?"

Jude told the tale of the Yellow Submarine. Reese and Mark were both impressed, laughing, joyful. Jude was feeling oddly sluggish and happy too. His eyes felt sleepy but the room seemed to sing a little. When Mark or Jimmy or both played or sang, the music sounded richer, better.

Then he was standing and peering out past the drapes. "Shit, I gotta go! It's late!"

Jimmy and Mark caved into laughter. "Woooo, he's gotta go!" Jimmy called out.

"I'm serious," Jude said, turning on Jimmy and facing off. "It's really late. If I don't get home before Dad, they're going to be asking where I was."

Mark and Jimmy laughed harder.

Through the laughter, Jude felt his perspective shift, almost physically. Suddenly, he was looking into the experience he'd just been having a moment before. He saw a strident boy with a fierce argument. But the fierceness was driven by a rippling fabric of fear inside him that worked itself even when he watched it from outside. Only thing was, the fabric was empty of anything to be afraid of—it was just moving, working inside him. And the strident part was driven by the odd idea of "late" and even "time." It just all seemed so... conceptual, and he seemed to be the one who was making the whole thing up.

"Oh, okay, I get it," he announced. "I'm making this shit up like little mouse turds of words."

"Ooooh, Little Mouse Turds of Words!" Jimmy sang and played. Mark punctuated with a guitar riff that climbed the neck. It all gave Jude the chills.

"That was awesome," he said.

"Hey, welcome to nineteen sixty-seven, Puke," Jimmy called out.

"Glad I could make it," Jude said. But he was worried. Would it get worse? Could he ride his bike?

Jude rubbed his hands on his pockets and looked out the window again. He really would have to leave soon. Then he turned back to the room. "I'm hungry."

Mark and Jimmy fell apart all over again. *"Munchies!"*

AT HOME, he went into the kitchen for a snack and his mother was there on the phone. She surprised Jude by covering the mouthpiece, "Young man, it's late. Where have you been?"

Jude dished out large lumps of cottage cheese into a bowl. He shrugged. He said, "I just took a long way home."

She shook her head and returned to the phone.

Jude leaned against the counter eating, listening to his mother's conversation. "...no idea where he is. This city is so dangerous..." She seemed so brittle. Jude felt sorry for her and he wanted to say something. Maybe he could give her a clue.

He finished his snack and set the bowl in the sink. Then, in a lull in her phone conversation, he said to his mother, "Hey, mom, I saw a friend of Mark's today."

"You did?" She turned her chin to the mouthpiece. "Irene," she said, "just a sec." She put a hand over the mouthpiece again, this time lowering it to her lap.

He decided he couldn't do it. Not what he'd thought of, telling her he'd seen someone that had actually seen Mark. Instead he spun a white lie about seeing Emilio and Emilio saying 'I haven't seen him. I thought he left school, I guess.'

His mother's face was pinched, unrelieved by or maybe even discerning the lie, but she thanked him for telling her.

Not much later, he could hear her in the downstairs hall telling his father as he came in the front door, "Jude saw Mark's friend Emilio today." She ran through everything Jude had said.

When she was finished, he didn't ask any questions. He just said, "Well, that tells us exactly nothing."

"It tells us," his mother said, "that Mark is probably okay."

"Well, obviously he's not okay," his father snapped. "He ran away.

He's let himself be swept up by the drug culture and psychedelic rock music."

At school, Jude told a different lie to Kevin and the gang. He was tired of their endless discussion of Mark's possible paths and chances out in the world. So Jude said that Emilio had seen Mark and he was okay.

An hour after he got home that afternoon, his mother pushed into his room without knocking. He had the radio on to KHJ's "The Real Don Steele" show. He liked this radio show. It played a grittier, and to his ear, more authentic, music. The station played the Doors, the Rolling Stones, Jefferson Airplane, and Jude had even started to like Bob Dylan as his lyrics started to make sense. To the backdrop of Hendrix's "Purple Haze," Jude was propped on the bed reading his English assignment, *The Outsiders*.

"What's this about Emilio seeing Mark?" she melded desperation and anger in her voice and in her stiff, unrelenting stance.

"Who told you that?" he asked her.

"Sonya, Kevin's mother."

Jude could feel the chill of fear slide into him—the old fear of being caught in a lie—but it passed. It all felt so pragmatic. He said, "I kinda lied to the guys. Kevin must have told his mom."

"Why on earth would you tell a lie? And why…" she shook her head and leaned back heavily against his dresser.

Jude set his book down on his lap. "They just keep making stuff up and I was tired of it."

"Making stuff up? What do you mean? Like what?" His mother pushed off the dresser and hovered uncertainly for a moment. She was wearing the Capri pants she favored, today in a sort of turtle green, and a white blouse with a wispy vine pattern over it in the same green. She shook her head to clear it and came and sat on the end of his bed.

"Oh, you don't want to hear it, Mom."

"No, I do. What stuff?"

"It's just like you, Mom, but opposite. You're like, 'Oh, he's on his way home right now.' Or, 'He's staying with a friend we don't know.'"

She lifted her chin, silently asserting to him and to herself that she had a right to such fantasies. But it was only momentary. Her head came down and she placed a hand on the side of his foot. "Tell me what they say."

"Mom," he shrugged. He didn't have to make this one up, because they did say these things. "They say stuff like 'Oh, he hitchhiked to San Francisco and he's up in the Haight.' Or, 'He discovered heroin and he's in a crash pad stoned out of his mind.'"

"The Haight? What's that?"

"Haight-Ashbury. It's a place in San Francisco where the hippies and run-aways all go."

"Oh," the word climbed as she said it. Maybe she hadn't thought about Mark leaving town, or there being a 'destination' for runaways. But her mind ran back along the words she'd heard. "Heroin?" she frowned. "That's terrible."

"Dad said you guys think Mark left because he's taking drugs."

"We never…" she held her hand up against her chest and her gaze reached some middle distance. "Well, I never said that. I don't think he was…" Then her head snapped around to peer at Jude. "You don't think…"

"I don't," he said. "I think he would have told me."

"Exactly," she nodded vigorously. "That's exactly right."

She retreated to someplace where she seemed to be processing the new information. A warm breeze pushed at the curtains, and the city rummaged and banged below, muffled by the blanket of smog. Jude lay there experiencing the moment. Mark had been gone four nights and the house had become morgue-like. But it was also weirdly intimate when two of the inhabitants sat together like this. As though there were secrets to be told and they were finally telling them.

His mother's ride down her interior avenue over, she looked back at Jude. "What else do they say?"

"Well, they say worse, but, you know, it's just kids."

"Worse?"

"You know, the obvious. 'He took LSD and jumped off a roof,' or 'He's a drug mule for a cartel.'"

"A what?" She lifted her hand again, this time all the way to her throat. "A mule? A what?"

"Drug mule, Mom," he dipped his voice in world-weariness. "They go to Mexico, swallow drugs in sealed plastic bags, cross back into the States, and poop the bags out." It was a scenario straight out of his social studies class. Another piece of Mr. Diaz's 'honest and functional portrait' of where they lived. Jude found it mostly depressing and frightening, but at this moment it was turning out to be useful.

"Oh," the hand rose to her mouth. "That's disgusting. Do people do that?"

"Yeah, but most kids that run away turn up and they're fine."

"How do you know this?"

"I asked Mr. Diaz, my social studies teacher."

"He's the Mexican man?"

"He's from Honduras, Mom. But he grew up in L.A."

"Oh, where's Honduras?"

Jude knew because Mr. Diaz had tapped it on the map, but he just shrugged.

"What did he say?" She folded her hands in her lap.

Jude marked his spot and set the book aside. "He just said not to worry. Kids take off. Especially Mark's age. And especially now."

"Why especially now?"

"Well, he said because kids are inheriting stuff from their parents they don't want, like racism and ingrained poverty and Vietnam, and to cap it off adults all act like they're moral and right and the kids that complain are stupid and immature."

"Oh," she frowned. Her eyes winked with wetness behind her glasses. The radio was playing "Take Another Little Piece of My Heart" by Janis Joplin.

She sat for a long moment. Then she turned a bit toward Jude. "What do you think? I mean, about what your teacher said?"

Jude shrugged. "What he said is pretty obvious, Mom. The news is full of it. You don't really need to check the facts on that one."

"I guess." She stood and held the fingers of her left hand tightly in the fingers of her right. "Your father will be home soon."

"Yeah," Jude lifted his book, opened it and tugged the bookmark out.

When the front door slammed after his father, he could hear his mother down there spouting their entire conversation. Jude set his book down and listened. Between the moments when he rolled his eyes at her weakness, he felt little daggers of betrayal. Why couldn't the truths they'd shared just be theirs? His father was like a warden, warping and using every piece of information against Mark, and ultimately against Jude.

⌐⌐

THE NEXT day at school, he listened while Kevin and his friends talked about Lacey and Penny and how sexy they were. All based on Kevin's now ancient descriptions.

That night, when he sat down to do his English homework, he found his English essay bleeding down multiple pages, spilling into tangents and loosing a surprising quantity of venom in his blood. He stopped when the momentum slowed and stared down at the pages and words. They boiled. He could read a passage and it would cause his blood to race all over again, setting him off in new directions.

He threw himself on the bed and listened to "Volunteers" by Jefferson Airplane on the radio. Then it was the Byrds singing "My Back Pages." Then a loud, brash ad for Twiggy Lashes makeup.

The English assignment was to write about a time when he felt outside and to compare that time to Ponyboy's experience in *The Outsiders*.

He returned to the desk, tore the old pages away from the writing pad and started fresh.

⌐⌐

IN CLASS that Friday, Ms. Loral talked about their next book, *Catcher in the Rye*. Then she said, "Before we turn our homework in, let's hear a couple of your essays."

They listened to a girl named Vivian whose writing was clear and crisp, but as colorless and empty as a plastic bag.

"Ponyboy wanted to be inside," she read. "I, too, wanted to be inside. My sister and her friend were always leaving me out when they played together."

When Vivian finished, Jude did not join in the obligatory applause. Then Ms. Loral poked her finger out and swept it over the room. It felt like a gun primed to go off randomly.

It did. "Jude, how about you?" He felt the bullet lodge with a quickening of his breath.

Jude looked quickly around the room as though there might be an escape route, then lowered his head and tapped his pages into alignment on his desktop. He read.

THE INSIDER

The book is called The Outsiders, but they're not. Ponyboy is a Greaser and he wanks about the Socs. The Socs have money and better clothes and houses and cars. They've got girlfriends. They live on the other side of the tracks—the right side.

But that's the only thing Ponyboy is outside of—rich people's houses.

Ponyboy has two brothers and a bunch of friends. His parents are dead. His older brother has to work and raise him. But he has a house to live in. Food to eat. Friends. Cigarettes. They live on the other side of the tracks and they decide that means they have to smoke cigarettes and get in fights.

Even when he runs away because his buddy murdered some Soc kid, he's still got family and brothers watching out for him. He's got a safe place to hide. Food.

The whole outside thing is his idea.

Me, I'm on the inside.

My parents are home every night. I live in one of those houses Ponyboy hated. Even though I moved here just a couple months ago, I have friends. They live in other houses on the 'right' side of the tracks. I eat lunch with them.

I think all my life so far, I've been inside. But it's pretty much all I've had, so there was no outside to go to. But now, the inside seems rotten.

My brother ran away from home a few days ago. It started when my dad took his guitar away. He said it was going to ruin him, turn him into a druggie. My mom seems to care, but my dad just wants to punish him. And tell him how stupid he is.

I asked a teacher about it. He grew up in L.A. and had

talked in class about the runaway problem. He said my
brother would probably come home soon. Because running
away isn't easy. And most kids can't take it. I think he meant
white kids. Because we're insiders. Sissies.

I don't have a neighbor, or minister, no uncle, no school
counselor. But I don't want anyone. You can't trust people.
They don't care. They just want a juicy story. So they can
gossip. I don't know anyone. Even the people I've known
my whole life.

Maybe my outside is just an idea, too. But I don't think
so. I'm beginning to think that inside is an illusion.

A rotten one.

Jude felt heat swirl around his neck and face. He pulled the front
page out and settled it back on top of the second page. Then he
glanced up. Ms. Loral stood looking at him with raised eyebrows,
almost expectantly.

She said, "Well, Jude, that was quite interesting." She addressed
the room, "Wouldn't you agree?" A ragged round of murmuring and
half-hearted clapping rose up and then quickly died.

"All right," she looked at the wall clock. Two minutes to go. "Turn
in your papers!"

As the papers shushered forward, Ms. Loral stood and wrote the
assignment on the board. "*Catcher in the Rye*. Chapters one through
five."

As soon as the bell rang, Jude was up and heading for the door.
Kids were looking at him as he shouldered past them. Then, at the
door, he let the Vivian girl go out in front of him and as he sidled
out—she looked at him blankly as though maybe being upstaged by
a boy was a surprise—and he found Melinda walking out beside him.

"Jude, isn't it?" She grasped his upper arm and the warmth of
her touch shuddered through him. "That was good. I mean, really
good, man."

"Oh hey, thanks," he felt himself color all over again. He nodded
once and tried to peel away.

Melinda didn't let loose. "Hey."

Jude stopped and met her gaze. She was smiling and her eyes

were so green and sharp. She was taller than he was by an inch or so. He dropped his eyes, blushing.

"Hey, what are you doing after school?"

"Oh, ah," he looked down the hall at Greg's approach and felt guilty for talking to his girl. "I don't know. Goin' home."

"Come out behind the auditorium, out by the gate. You'll see us when you get there." She released him. Before he turned to escape she said, "I'll tell Greg you're coming. He'll be stoked."

She watched the doubt in his eyes. She said, "Really. He'll be stoked."

Jude couldn't speak. He felt like a bunny in the headlights.

Melinda reached out and touched his forehead. "Cool scar, dude. It's real 'street.'"

Jude touched the lump over his eye and shrugged.

six

JUDE DIDN'T GO TO THE AUDITORIUM AFTER school. He wanted to, but he couldn't see himself among the people he knew would be there. He stopped after all the other kids were done at PE and stared at himself in the mirror in the locker rooms. He was pale as fish bellies and his hair... His father cut his hair. He could see it now. This, like everything his father did to or with his sons, was a form of punishment. His hair, for as long as he could remember, had been trimmed short on the sides with slanted bangs on the front. It was growing out now, but it was ridiculous neverthe-less. He looked like a Kewpie doll. He rolled his eyes at himself. How was it he had any friends at all?

It was Friday. He was sure that by Monday, Melinda would forget she'd ever invited him to hang out with them after school. It would be a non-issue. He would forget. She would forget.

He went home.

He lay on his bed and tried to find some way out of himself. What possible plan or hope or dream could pull him out and away from this hopelessly childish and naive life? His thoughts were sluggish, sticky and enervating.

When he heard his mother call dinner, he rolled over and sat up. He felt drugged and tired. His father called up to him as he was going in to dinner, "Juuude!"

Jude rose and went out. As he passed his parents' bedroom, he heard them talking downstairs. He hesitated and then ducked in. He went straight into the bathroom, popped open the linens cabinet above the toilet and there they sat like three fat Buddhas: the bottles of pills.

One-by-one, Jude unscrewed the tops and pulled a small handful of pills from each, thrusting them into his pocket. Then he screwed the tops back on, closed the cabinet, and hustled out.

"Juuude!"

"Coming!"

MONDAY, before Jude even got to homeroom, Melinda was walking next to him from out of nowhere. "So, make me look crazy," she said.

"What? Who? What?"

"You said you'd be there after school," she said.

"I didn't, actually. I didn't say anything."

"So, what's the deal? Why not?"

Jude shrugged. "Maybe I'm not the type." He flicked his head self-consciously, as though there were hair—long tresses of hippy hair—in his eyes. "Maybe."

She laughed. "What's 'the type?'" She angled away from him to get a better look at him. "No really, Jude. What's 'the type,' exactly? Like," she swept her hair back from her face, "who do you think *I* am?"

Jude shrugged again. He was confused. She was taking his fear personally. But there was no argument, really. He wanted to go there. He wanted to go today. "I'll come by today, okay?"

"Right, if you say so." She sounded miffed. Melinda peeled away and he watched her move with certainty through the crowds of students, her hair lifting and falling, her bell-bottoms billowing like sails. Her ass, rolling side-to-side, tight and round. Why was an ass so… important? She was breathtakingly beautiful. She did not look back.

In social studies, Mr. Diaz returned their homework. Jude looked at the big red 'B' on his paper. He had thought he would do better. He took the assignment seriously. Mr. Diaz had asked them to write about their experience with races other than their own. Jude had titled his paper, "White Side of the Tracks," and had explained how his old school had had less than ten black kids, and no Mexicans that he was aware of. But that here, he attended classes and rode through streets where a lot of people were from somewhere else.

"Well done," Mr. Diaz had written below the grade.

In class he said, "A lot of you dropped a grade, or even two, on this homework, because you were just feeding back the stuff we talked about in class." He strode to the windows and leaned with his fingertips against the sill. Speaking out the glass, he said, "I want you to *connect*," he spun and faced them. "To really *engage*." He locked a fist firmly inside his other palm.

"Look, I know. Most of you just *do not live it*." His hand chopped down through the air with each word. "Most of you," his voice softened, "most of you. You don't live it."

He went to his desk and hoisted the copy of the newspaper that lay there. "How many of you get the *Times* at home?"

Jude and about half the rest of the class raised their hands.

"*Look* at it," Diaz pleaded. "I am not telling you to *read* it. I am not going to test you on it. But *this*," he snapped the front page. The headline blared, VIET PEASANTS TOLD TO RETREAT TO DMZ. For Jude, it was actually more a yawn than a blare. "This," he snapped the page again, "is your connection to the rest of the city, and the country." He tossed the paper to the desktop in front of himself. "The world!"

Then he hefted a brown paper grocery bag onto his desk and spilled its contents. Paperback books tumbled out. "I'm also not going to assign you any extra reading. But these," he waved a hand over the books, "are also ways to connect." His vehemence had all but died out. "I can't guarantee you a better grade on your assignments if you read these, but I'm here to tell you, it would be a good bet to make. A bet that will pay off in your life, long-term."

On the way out of the classroom, Jude sidled past Diaz's desk. Kids were either plucking up a book without looking at the cover— they would never read them, Jude thought—or they were just pushing past, ignoring the books. But Jude decided he would at least look at them.

He lifted one and looked at the cover. It showed a man painting his face black and was titled *Black Like Me*.

Mr. Diaz pushed a different book toward him. It was *The Autobiography of Malcolm X*. There was a picture on the cover of a Negro man with glasses, in a shirt and loosened tie, talking at a microphone. Jude stifled a yawn.

"Okay, Mr. Tangier," Mr. Diaz practically winced at him, "this book for you, maybe, okay?"

Jude puzzled, flipped the book over. The back cover was a sprawl of text. He read snippets, but none of them held him. They all made the book sound important and serious. Not interesting. Not to Jude.

Mr. Diaz kept at him, "Malcolm X was assassinated in New York just two years ago. For some people, his assassination was as important, maybe more important, than John F. Kennedy's. And this book," he gestured at the book in Jude's hand, "has become a Bible of sorts for a lot of people."

Jude shrugged. He didn't like the Bible much. But he accepted the book from Mr. Diaz. He slid it into his pack, deciding he would at least skim it.

"Hey," Mr. Diaz said. "It would be better, I think, if you didn't mention the book to anyone until maybe after you're done. I mean, like your mom and dad. And maybe other students."

Jude's eyebrows arched. "Okay," he said.

In English, Jude looked for Melinda. She was in her usual chair, but she didn't look at him. He'd never dated in his life, but he felt like they'd broken up. He felt like he'd hurt her feelings, but that was impossible. He was a hick, a nerd, an Indiana kid.

He angled for her as they started to leave, but Ms. Loral called his name and asked him to stay after class, so he didn't see Melinda leaving, or Greg arriving.

"Jude Tangier," Ms. Loral said when she saw him in front of her desk. "That was quite a paper you wrote."

"Was there a problem with it?" he asked.

"No, no, not at all." She fluffed and stacked papers, moved a stapler and an apple. Set his paper in the empty space. "I think, if you don't mind me saying so, that the paper is true."

Jude shrugged. "You didn't tell us to write a story."

She laughed. "Right, I just wanted to check." She smiled up at him. "Do you want to sit?"

He shrugged and came around the side of her desk. He sat in the hard plastic chair stationed there and slouched down, wary and wondering.

"Look, I don't want to intrude, but is there anything going on at home you want to talk about?" She spoke quietly, almost in a whisper as her next class started to file in.

"I don't think so, ma'am."

"You can call me Kathy," she said.

Jude's eyes leapt to hers. She wasn't serious. But she seemed to be. He had never heard anyone call her Kathy before. And he had never called a teacher by their first name.

She said, "I'm glad to see your black eye is healing up nicely."

"Yes, Ma'am."

Her hand came up and stopped a foot from his face. "That's going to be quite a scar, isn't it?"

"I guess so." But he thought, 'Wow, even Ms. Loral?'

"How is your brother, do you know?"

"I'm pretty sure he's okay." Jude straightened. He tugged his books higher on his lap. He was trying to signal the racing of time. He shouldn't be late for band.

She read him. "I'll give you a note for your next class. You don't need to worry about that."

He nodded. But, she didn't know Mr. Denny.

"Look, here's what I'm thinking. It helps when you're going through things that are difficult, or confusing, or whatever. It helps to write." She cocked her head to one side to see if he had a reaction. He didn't.

"Do you write now? Like a journal? Or a diary?"

He shook his head.

"Would you be willing to write a page or two each night for extra credit?" she asked. "Turn it in maybe on Mondays?"

He looked at her. He had observed her closely, as he did all his teachers as he sat out there in the classroom, a member of the audience. But he felt he was seeing this woman for the first time. She was a small woman with dense brown hair that fell to her shoulders. Where it grew from her forehead was sharply distinct and drew down to a widow's peak. Her eyes were a brown so dark and chocolatey that they looked tasty.

But what he was seeing now for the first time was the scrimshaw of lines around her mouth and eyes. Maybe they were crow's feet. He didn't know. She was older, more earnest than he'd thought. And yet, she was closer to his age than he'd thought, too. Her face read of something he wasn't used to. She was an adult, taking him seriously. Listening.

"Okay," he said.

"Okay," she responded. "Next Monday? Okay?"

He nodded.

"Here, let me write you a note."

Two periods later, Jude walked to the south campus gate by the auditorium instead of out front to the bike racks.

"THIS is precisely what's happening," Greg was saying. He was standing on one leg, the other leg crooked with a foot flat to the standing knee. His hands were held out palms together like he was praying. He appeared perfectly balanced, his face raised to the sun.

He turned his head slightly as Jude approached and watched him with open curiosity. He kept talking. "This and what's happening are identical. There is no overlap. There is only this." He spread his hands above him, still holding the single-leg stance. His feet were dirty and bare.

"Which is why," he said, now to Jude, "the swamis like to say, 'This is that.'"

Jude sidled close to the group sitting and standing around Greg and set himself against the low wall by the fence. He faced Greg, standing, and Theo Hatling and Melinda sitting against the auditorium wall. Steven Neely, Carissa Long, and Mike Pulec also sat in front of the fence. Standing at the far end was Cindy Yang. And walking up and sidling quietly past Jude was Serena Villaba. She cleared him and looked back at him with flat dark eyes.

"Tupperware," Greg said. "It's not like the sky could cover just part of the sky, or the earth could only go so far. We're sealed in, end-to-fucking-end, like Tupperware. Sealed," he opened his hands out to include them all, and everything beyond, "perfectly in this exact now."

"Man," Theo said. "That's completely spelled, man." He stressed the word spelled, like it carried a specific meaning.

"Isn't it?" Greg said. "Everything is exactly itself. And everything is *spelled*, man!"

Greg came down out of his stance. "Like," he spun once on his toes and came down on both feet facing Jude, "do you *dig*?"

Jude looked at the boy's face. Greg had wisps of sideburns. A struggling moustache. But he was asking, Jude felt, a serious question.

"Sure."

"Like Tupperware, right?"

Jude was following, or at least thought he was, the word game Greg was playing. "I don't know," Jude shrugged. "I thought you were saying everything is what it is. And then we add words to it. Like, spell it." Jude scanned the faces watching him. They were expectant, a little confused. He finished the thought. "Like we break everything into pieces. Or at least we try. You know. And then it's not now any-more. Not really real."

Greg's head tipped to one side, like an inquisitive dog's. His brown eyes squinted and mouth pursed. Then he shook his long hair and gestured over his head, hands exploding outward. *"Fucking A!"* Greg took two paces to Jude and grasped his shoulders, and then embraced him. He released Jude and grinned at him. "Deeply groovy! We are naming the names of names!"

He turned to Theo. "Digging?"

"Dug, man." He was nodding his agreement.

Greg patted Jude on the shoulder, "My brother, dude. Welcome!" He started to spin again, lifted one leg to do it, but stopped. He drew close to Jude and said, "Insanely cool shiner, dude." Then he spun, his toes dirty and splayed on the pavement.

Jude looked across at Melinda. She smiled at him. Winked. The break-up was maybe over.

Greg spread his hands out above his shoulders and sang softly to the sky. "'Turn off your mind, relax, and float downstream. This is not dying.'"

Jude recognized the lyrics from the Beatles *Revolver*.

Theo, from his roost against the wall, held up a hand-rolled ciga-rette and lighter in Jude's direction. He spoke through tightly knitted lips where tendrils of smoke escaped. "Toke?"

Jude looked over the group and then around him, scanning the paths and buildings, the windows and street.

"It's cool, man," Greg took the gear and passed it to Jude. "No one ever comes over here." Then he smiled broadly and ducked his head secretively. "It kinda hurts, ya know, but I think they're avoiding us."

Jude took the joint and lighter and with only one misfire of the flame, was able to pull the flames into the end of the joint. The red ember of fire flared, crackling, perfectly displaying his consumption for all to see.

He drew in, let up and held the smoke. He passed the lighter and joint back to Greg. Melinda was nodding at him. He was sure he looked like a freshly-groomed Pekingese standing amidst a pack of working Huskies. He could feel his bouncy little Indiana haircut and his yellow-plaid short-sleeved shirt hung on his flesh like an itchy husk. Embarrassment mounted through him. It began as a wet weak-ness somewhere around his knees, but it rose and struck his hips like bagged wet sand. He could feel his whole being shrinking and fearing and running.

Greg tottered back over and swung around Jude with immense curiosity. He was examining the cut above Jude's eye. He said, "This is truly…" His eyes danced over Jude's wound. "…Cool, man. Are you like a fighter?"

The bandage was off. The bruising was mostly gone.

"I ran into some trouble," Jude grunted.

Unlike Kevin and his buddies, no one here responded to his toughness except for a tiny lift of eyebrows from Cindi and Serena.

Jude shrugged. "I kinda got beat up after school."

Melinda pushed off from the wall. She sashayed over to him like a lioness, slow and intent. "I like it," she said. "You're gonna have a…" She reached up and gently but firmly touched the cut. "…a nice little battle scar."

Jude's entire body was in tumult. Nothing would settle or stop.

The only way out was to talk. And talk cool. But he was prepared.

"You guys do pills?" he asked.

But Greg and Melinda immediately exchanged looks that laid out some kind of warning.

Greg waded in, "Never, man. Why?"

Melinda was suddenly wary, and physically drew away. "Never, ever." Her eyes fired caution at Greg and everyone's demeanor was suddenly remote and brooding. Then to Jude, she said, "The only people who would ask something like that are narcs or dealers."

Jude shrugged again. "I just thought…" He tugged out his baggy of pills. "If you wanted some."

"Never, ever," Melinda repeated. She was warning everyone off, as if Jude were offering poisoned candy. But her eyes locked on the baggy as it dangled in his hand.

"I'm not a narc," Jude said. "My dad is a doctor. He has big bottles of these. He won't even notice some are missing."

Greg squinted, "How big?"

"Ten thousand pills in each."

"Sheeeeit," Greg said. "And what are they?"

Jude felt the high of the marijuana taking him. It made him feel like he was holding the conversation from the end of a long rope that reached into space. He knew he needed to be serious, but Greg's response, the Sheeeeit, seemed funny, and it kept getting funnier as Jude mulled it over. He shook his head to remove the silly grin he felt spreading on his face and held up the bag. "Blue are Valium. White are amphetamines. And the yellow and red are seconal barbital."

Greg looked around the group and ended with a long look at Melinda. She met his gaze evenly, severely. Still looking at her, he asked, "How much?"

Jude shrugged. He hadn't considered selling them. He had brought them as a means of entry. A way to be cool. "I don't know. I've never…" Now Jude looked at Melinda. She returned a retreating stare that told Jude he was on his own. He looked at the others. They watched as someone might watch a knife fight, distanced and curious. He listened to the crisp sounds of the kids on the grounds behind him, and the rigid zip of car tires over pavement on the street.

He realized with a start that he was staring at a lizard on the wall under the fence. Time was getting away from him. He shook the bag, coaxing his attention back to the plastic. "Right now, they're free," he said finally.

"You willing to take one?" Greg asked.

"Ah," Jude looked at the bag. He had no idea what the pills would really do, but he decided the amphetamines would probably be okay. "I guess so. Sure."

"A Valium?"

Jude shrugged. "Okay." He opened the bag and tugged out one of the dense blue tablets. He stared at it a moment as though its impact were scribed on the surface. He'd seen his father's little pile of pills by his plate at dinner. There were always two little blues. One should be no problem.

Jude pushed the pill to the back of his tongue and swallowed. He wondered what it would do to the disjointed, funny, and slow world of the marijuana high.

"Look," Greg grabbed Jude's shoulder, gave him a slight shake, and then let go. Jude wavered there, forced to concentrate on standing up. "We can't exactly afford to trust you. And, I mean, you could already try to get us in trouble with the pot. But Melinda said you were cool. And pot isn't such a big deal. But, pills, Mr. Glenn doesn't like pills."

Jude looked around, suddenly consumed with worry. "Who is Mr. Glenn?" he asked.

"The Assistant Principal. He's the discipline dude. He breaks up the fights, calls the cops, checks on probation, truants, all that crap." Greg leaned in close, conspiratorial, "He's the campus *pig!*"

Jude felt a shiver slip through him as though someone had pulled a zipper. Just beyond the shiver came a wall of sleepy oblivion. Where he had been frightened and keyed up a moment before, now he felt mentally world-weary and physically quite tired.

"Free?" Greg asked.

Jude displayed the bag a moment, and then handed them to Greg. "But this never happened, right?"

"This never happened," Jude said, "because we never… spelled it."

"Awesome, dude," Greg spun half around. "Words!" he spat.

Jude felt a new presence hovering at the periphery of the group and let his eyes travel there. A stringy black kid stood there. He was familiar somehow, like maybe Jude had seen him around. Silent, brooding, he was standing just inside the school gate, as though he might disappear again.

"Lance!" Greg called out in greeting. "The universe, too, has its spells!"

Lance squinted, made no move.

"I'm telling ya, dude," Greg told him. "We are here, brother. We're doing the good work. We're making words right out of sound, and sound right out of..." Greg threw his hands up and splayed his fingers dramatically. "Right out of *air!*"

Lance raised his chin slightly and Greg nodded. Then Greg held up the bag of pills. "And we have provender!"

Lance took five silent steps toward Greg. He still wore big black boots, and his clothes were a sort of wrap in black and red and gray that cocooned his torso down to his knees. On his legs he wore tight gray jeans.

He leaned over Greg, his hair slipping down in straggles and shadowing Greg's face. Into his extended hand, Greg poured a colorful pile of pills saying, "Bless us Father for this, our daily high!"

Lance smiled. "Amen, brother," he said. His eyes slid across the group.

Jude looked down into Lance's pale brown palm and the pile of pills at its center while he felt a rending, almost eviscerating roar filling him. He blinked and sat bolt upright. He knew that sound.

Jude looked out past the fence to the street. The roar deepened and ripped at the afternoon. It was loud and kept coming closer. It was louder still and came closer still.

And then it was there, Paulo and his hawg, the roar calmed to a throaty, clattering burble. Paulo sat astride the machine and raked across the kids with piercing eyes. His blond henchman was ten seconds behind, the gravelly boom of his motorcycle filling in the already overflowing niches of sound. Jude tried to disappear into the wall but felt forcibly excluded from its overly dense molecules.

Greg and Melinda stood and glided to meet Paulo, their arms melding and their heads forming a singular kiss as they moved toward him. They tossed their hair and it rained down together, hers longer and thicker, but his nearly the same color, and intermingled like some new possibility of animal.

Melinda threw a leg over the back seat and wrapped her arms around Paulo's denim coat. Greg clambered on behind her. Paulo stared hard at Jude, his face unchanging, but his expression stark and nasty.

The bike barked out a wall-rattling blast without moving, and then hopped forward and started rolling. Greg waved, called out, "'Turn off your mind! Relax! And float downstream!'" Then they were gone, the little parade of racket, the sound of the bikes receding deeper and deeper into the city.

Theo and some of the others were straggling off toward Bronson. Lance was nowhere to be seen. Mike, Cindy and Serena remained, leaning against the fence. When Jude surveyed them, Serena's dark eyes had settled on him. Unmoving. But not unkind. Just… what? Waiting? Consuming? Ridiculing?

He felt trapped.

He carefully enacted a goofy smile across his face. Then he leapt to his feet and headed for his bike. The world around him wobbled and jerked like a carnival house of mirrors, but no matter where he looked, he couldn't find his reflection.

He was too high to go home.

He rode north and then, instead of east to home, at Sunset Boulevard he turned west. He clipped out along the cacophony, letting his brain and body bask in whatever he had ingested.

Billboards loomed over him. Buildings thrust and towered. Cars snapped past. Buses chased him, hissing and sighing with hydraulics. He shot past the Hollywood Palladium and the Cinerama Dome. Mythical places, really. He couldn't imagine entering either one. And then a mile or more of small businesses, pushy cars, and the occasional home.

Soon he was waiting at the light at Crescent Heights. It was a wide intersection, and Sunset curved here. Looking down Sunset to where it slipped from view, it felt like an entrance into another world.

A lot of this had to do with the sudden cluster of billboards and imposing buildings, but even more it was the people on the street. The light changed and Jude rode into Sunset Strip.

He was woozy and strange. The world around him was floating and he slid effortlessly through it. There was nothing he didn't see and feel. The whole broad fabric of experience spread out and came into him as though time and space and mass were all being perfectly stretched and organized and brought here to be carefully fed into his body.

The glittering glass and metal of the traffic, the rock music thrusting from cars and shops, and the sunlit skyscrapers all nattered insistently. They nearly shouted excitement and progress, entering Jude's body somehow bigger than they really were.

At a light, music slipped from a car spilling a poppy and weird soundtrack.

Wowie zowie, your love's a treat
Wowie zowie, you can't be beat
Wowie zowie, baby, you're so neat
I don't even care if you shave your legs

Inside the car, a man with a headband and a massive beard watched Jude. As they pulled away, he lifted his hand and formed a peace sign—two fingers raised in a V.

Jude rode. His eye missed nothing. People loomed from hollows and curbsides. There were dirty kids with their hands out. A man with a guitar, singing. A girl in a torn white dress and dark blank eyes danced next to him. There were young girls in little groups of twos and threes in miniskirts, made-up like dolls, with stacked hair and tall white boots.

Their eyes, all of them, reached across the rigid march of time and experience and saw and plucked and ... fathomed. This was a tribe and he was rolling through their territory, their enclave. When their gaze flickered over Jude, he could feel himself being woven into a hundred flowing rivers of experience. He was passing into them just as they were passing into him.

At the next light, the same car sat next to Jude. The music pulsed. "Hey, you know something people? I'm not black but there's a whole lots a times I wish I could say I'm not white."

He was looking at the Whisky-a-Go-Go where a turgid line of

hippies and other oddballs stood and sat outside, waiting for tickets to something. Their eyes, individual and in groups, flitted toward him and then slipped past.

A kid, no older than Jude, was moving down the line with his hand out. He wore a low black hat, a purple vest with no shirt, striped and dirty bell-bottoms, and bare feet. Several of the hippies smiled at him and pushed things into his palm. Coins, joints, candy bars.

The kid turned his eyes on Jude, and Jude felt the boy's gaze pursue him as he passed.

Slowly and suddenly, the desperation and cloying fear in the scene rose up and closed over the glitter and hype. The boy was his brother. Or Jude himself. Just on the other side of coincidences and circumstances. The kid was rumbling around inside Jude, tearing covers off everything in Jude's pristine life. His clean white room. His neat T-shirts and jeans. His ordered family. But more than that, Jude's simple and naive view of the world and the future, a place of normalcy and certainty, a place of intention and reason and...

It was all fraying.

Jude, for the first time in his life, felt like he was part of reality. His eyes gathered these people as theirs gathered him. He was a stranger, a hick kid from Indiana, but it was all really just chaos, and Jude was another random, colliding, particle in it all.

The light changed and Jude stood on his pedals. He lifted his face to the sun. He felt tears on his face.

seven

SOMETHING HAD HAPPENED, BUT JUDE WAS OUT of the loop. His mother was beaming if only intermittently, as if she weren't fully convinced. His father was home early. He was cagey, looking at once less upset—his posture was more relaxed—and more upset—the set of his jaw and a darting, unease in his eyes. He carried a large clear iced drink with him everywhere.

Jude watched them acutely. His mother was woven of simple stuff: everything in its proper place, please. His father, he realized, was far more simple than Jude had ever imagined: he was literally playing King of the Mountain against all comers. He said things like, "He's going to need to learn his place. That's all there is to it." And "I will not stand for this behavior. Not in my house."

Jude took that realization in with glee at first. He had finally unraveled an important part of his father's machinery. But, with a little time and distance, he slid back into doubt and then disbelief. His father, a pediatrician, a man who got straight A's in a straight line from kindergarten through two medical degrees, couldn't just be playing a muscle-bound game of King of the Mountain.

But then his father was back in Mark's room, dragging out the records and music books that their mother had carefully put back after Mark left. "This is over," he growled. Everything he said demanded his mother and maybe even Jude as the audience. "There will be no more childish behavior from a seventeen-year-old in my house." He went back in for the acoustic guitar.

Jude tried to find out what was going on.

"Hey, Mom," he caught her off the phone while his father was in his den. "You seem like you're in a good mood. Did you hear something about Mark?"

"Oh, I'm sure Mark is fine. He'll be home soon, don't you think?"

Jude stared at her. She was watering plants in the living room. She poured water from a pitcher into two more plants and then looked up, a studiously blank look on her face. "Jude? Don't you think?"

He said, "I wouldn't know, Mom." He went upstairs.

He didn't ask his father. If you asked someone playing King of the Mountain a question, that person had power over you. They knew that you didn't know something. They knew what you wanted to know. And if they knew the answer, they had power as long as they knew the answer and you didn't.

And Jude was realizing that this was how his father always treated him.

He heard his father snarking in the hall. Jude's mother was dragging Mark's books and records back down the hall to Mark's room. "It's what he likes to do." Her voice was plaintive, but her actions were decisive. "And he's gotten very good at it."

"Well," his father's face was nearly purple with anger, "you're on your own then, goddamn it. He's no son of mine. I'll tell you that." He stormed down to his den and slammed the door.

That evening, Jude was sitting on the iron cage outside his window when a taxi pulled up in the street below. He watched his brother Mark step out of the cab, a guitar case in his hand.

From this distance, Mark looked like a young Indiana boy come to Hollywood. He glanced up at the house, and then turned back to pay the driver. His smile was crooked, fearful, as though he were wreathed in expectations he already knew were hopeless and false. But this was where the taxi stopped, and this was where he'd paid to go, and this was home.

Jude watched him mount the steps, his gaze again lifting to pan across the windows and doors when he reached the lawn. He saw

Jude then and Jude raised a silent hand in greeting. Mark nodded, his jaw set, and focused on the steps again.

Jude pulled himself back inside the house as he heard the door-bell ring. He heard his mother say, "This will be him," and felt his father disappear into the den.

"Mark!"

"Hey Mom," his brother said, nonchalant and worldly.

Jude listened to a scuffling of hugs and the awkward bumping of the guitar case.

"I'm so glad to see you!" his mother said. "Are you glad to be home?"

"I guess," Mark said, his voice constricted with doubt and regret.

A long moment of silence passed. Jude visualized his mother, her hands neatly, tightly pressed against each other, and then separated, and then pressed together again. She always performed this slow, silent clapping when she was nervous or upset.

"Well," she finally said, "I think your father is on a call with the hospital. But I expect Jude is upstairs."

Mark said, "Okay."

"Are you hungry? Something to drink? Dinner will be ready in half an hour."

"Okay."

Jude heard him coming up the stairs. He slipped out into the hall to watch his brother's homecoming. And then she said, "Mark?"

He stopped, half-turning his head.

"Please don't do that again?" It was a question.

Mark was silent. Jude watched his jaw work.

"Promise?"

Mark looked to the top of the stairs, his exit route. "Sorry, Mom. I can't make any promises."

He stood a minute in the silent slipstream of his words. Then he started up the stairs again.

Jude watched him from behind, sitting in the hall outside his bedroom door. He found Mark weirdly and suddenly admirable and strange. He had walked out of the house. He'd broken the brittle illusion of unity and safety, of family. Now that he was back, Jude felt like it couldn't have been more shocking if a goldfish had slipped out of its aquarium and was now, with a shrug, slipping back in.

Mark turned at the top of the stairs and looked at Jude, "Hey, brother."

"Hey," Jude lifted a hand. He felt like a ten-year-old.

At dinner the conversation was about anything but Mark's adventure, and it was isolated to Jude and his mother. She talked about maybe joining the PTA at Jude's school. Then she asked Jude about Kevin and if Jude had any other friends. Then she wanted to know about Jude's classes and then his teachers. Then she asked how his bike was working, careful not to mention the accident.

Jude found himself eating quickly and answering slowly, adapting to his mother's tense line of questioning. His father ate slowly, the working of his jowls apparently a source of great study, almost pleasure. His father's eyes also traveled slowly, but Jude saw there was a pattern. His father would slip a bite into his mouth and incline his head so that he was looking slightly down on the table. Then his chin would point at Jude on his right, swing far left to his mother, and then return center to Mark, his eyes following with each motion. The look at Mark would hold a long moment while his jaws worked slowly to a swallow, and with each rotation around the table, his eyes slowly hardened to an icy glare. Then it would all start again.

Mark ate casually. He popped bites into his mouth and chewed, his eyes moving with ease to the three other people, but also around the room and through the doorway to the dining room. He looked like a foreign student, not understanding the conversation and curious about the strange habits of his hosts. Every few times his father glared at him, Jude saw, Mark would stare back with bland interest, holding his gaze until the angry old stranger looked down again.

With his mother asking questions, Jude chipping in answers longer than he would ever have allowed before, and his father and Mark locking eyes in a rigorous cadence, Jude felt pinioned deep in the inner workings of a tightly wound watch. His gear, the flywheel, felt like it was spinning hot and fast, but no matter the speed it wasn't driving the gears. Time refused to pass.

His father, in his sloth-like movements, stopped once, focused on Jude just as Jude was cleaning his plate.

"How are your grades?"

Jude's mouth was full. He chewed and formulated an answer.

But his father wasn't done. "Because we'll need at least one of our kids to make it through school. That way," his father chewed the food in his mouth with three slow workings of his jaw, "That way, you can take care of your brother." His eyes slid to Mark. "Bail him out of jail. Put him into rehab programs. Loan him money. Go find him drooling on himself in a flophouse somewhere. And give him an early burial." He chewed again, just two times, eager to deliver his punchline. "Maybe even shed a tear or two over his grave."

"Lyle!" his mother crowed. It was the enacting of her If-I-say-your-name-you-have-gone-too-far rule.

"Well, it's true," he said. "Maybe only statistically." Three slow chews. Four. "But that makes it even more likely."

Mark through all of this kept his eyes on their father and smiled blankly like everything was spoken in Russian.

Then Mark, his plate clean, picked it up and balanced it in one hand. Looking at their father, he said, "And who's gonna cry over your grave?" Then he stood and left the room.

Jude watched. His father swallowed, but his jaws kept working. His face darkened and his eyes narrowed. He held his knife and fork on either side of his plate as though he were trying to crush them.

There was a crack as he slammed the butts of the silverware on the tabletop. "Get back in here!" he yelled at Mark.

Mark came back to the doorway and reached out so he was holding both sides of the doorframe. He wore heavy-framed glasses, the silly haircut, and short-sleeved plaid shirt. Indiana clung to him. But his bearing was Los Angeles, California.

"You will not speak to me that way in my house!"

Mark smiled. "Well, Mom asked me to come home until I finish high school. That's…" he squinted, "eighteen, nineteen months. We don't really have to talk between now and then."

Jude thought his father's jaws might snap.

"Mark!" now Mark was placed on motherly alert.

"And then, it won't much matter 'cause they'll ship me off to Vietnam to go fight in your dirty war."

Their father had stated his beliefs at other dinners that

Communism had to be eradicated wherever and whenever it cropped up. It was a disease. And, as far as he was concerned, the Vietnam War was doing exactly this: eradicating the Communists.

"Then I'll fill that grave you're worried about, right on time." Mark released the doorframe and walked out.

Jude lifted his empty plate, ready to leave. His father snarled, "Stay at the table until the whole family is through."

Because the machinery of dinner had been so poorly tuned, his father had half his food still to carve and chew. But the gearing was apparently set. He didn't speed up. Jude sat looking at his plate, working his lips into and out of a frown, acting as though he were thinking deep thoughts.

Finally, his mother, seeing the machinery of her husband slowing to a near standstill, said, "Jude, you can go on upstairs and do your homework."

He hefted the plate and escaped. His father didn't stir, a forkful poised forgotten two inches above his plate.

Upstairs, Mark smiled with lazy ease. He said, "Jimmy got us tickets to the Doors Friday at Cal State."

"Mom and Dad won't let us go," Jude said.

"Yeah they will," Mark's certainty was final, complete.

"Okay," he said, not believing. "But that's crazy talking, and I gotta do my homework."

Mark said, "Wait." He lifted three or four LPs off the turntable and slid the bottom two into sleeves. "Listen to these. All the way through."

Jude spun and left his brother's room. The records were *The Doors*, and *The Doors' Strange Days*.

Jude felt like a moth against a light bulb. He saw the heat, he felt it, he battered against it. But it remained remote. Who was this boy, his brother? Where had they landed? It was as odd as the Emerald City. As weird as Wonderland.

JUDE put the LPs on his turntable and started it. As "Break on Through" crackled out, he decided to try to write something for the journal assignment. If it *was* an assignment. He laid out a yellow legal pad and two pens and sat down at his desk. The turntable spun, the dull red label with the distinctive 'E' for Elektra Records seeming to rush around the outer edge.

Jude wished he could capture that. Precisely that. The world was spinning, but he was out on the edge and it was going too fast.

He had believed, sitting down, that he was going to write about his brother and his parents, or maybe Lacey. But he realized he would never turn in something that was that personal and… what was it? It felt dangerous?

His mind spread over his recent days and geographies. Like passing at low altitude in a jet, vistas popped open and closed, but mostly the past was closed to him. It evaporated almost as quickly as it was poured out.

But in his mind's eye, in one of the opening vistas, he saw the black man. Jude closed his eyes and remembered. He had hardly thought about it at the time. He'd been riding his bike through the city almost randomly in the days when his brother was missing. It wasn't planned exactly, but he would ride and ride and ride, and then, something would attract him like a glade in a forest. Maybe it was a little park, a fountain, a steel table and chair chained outside a carwash. He would stop and sit for a while, not thinking so much as just watching, and perhaps, under the surface, processing.

He looked for a way to start it…

I swear, on a bike, Los Angeles is like one big sewer. You ride down tubes filled with turds and piss. The lights are valves. Green means flush. And it's nice to find a little beach along the side where you can just sit and watch. Barnsdall Park, or Ferndell, or the high wall that runs behind Tower Records on Sunset Boulevard.

Yesterday I rode down the Vermont Avenue sewer and came out on a big open corner at Santa Monica Boulevard. It was paved and ugly, and ten busses were waiting with the engines running so it stank.

But there was a guy.

From a distance, he just looked crazy. He was wearing dirty white sweatpants and a blue and white striped jersey. He had on ragged old tennis shoes, and he wore a blue

Dodger's hat. He was so black that when he was in front of the blacked-out store windows behind him, he looked like a hat and shirt dancing by themselves.

The weird thing was his baseball mitt, and then there was the fact that he was playing baseball. All alone. With no ball. And in a stadium.

"It's Sutton at the bag," he called out. "He's dropped the last five men, all strike-outs. Can he do it again?"

He warmed up his shoulder and toed the pitcher's mound. He was announcing. "Ken Harrelson in the lineup for Ramon Webster. Here's the pitch, low and inside." He pitched, then he turned to face the on-coming pitch. He swung deep and long, like Mickey Mantle, and then the bat was gone and he pumped his fist with perfect umpire authority. "Steee-rike One!"

It was an LA Dodgers game—there were pennants hung from a shopping cart nearby and there was the Dodgers hat. I'm pretty sure it was a game against the Kansas City Athletics. My cousin in Kansas raves about Ramon Webster.

Two pitches later, "Harrelson sends it down the third baseline! It stays in bounds!" The black man jogged three paces, dipped and scooped a ball. "He's rounding first! Lefebvre in left field with a throw to second!"

The black man unwound a slow and elegant shot, his body extended in a perfect lazy textbook throw from left field. Then he spun and looked and leapt straight up, glove raised high. "Safe!" He called out. "Ron Hunt with the catch, but Harrelson is in underneath. He's safe! He's dusting off! KC is on base, and Campaneris is at the plate!"

He bent down and picked up a resin bag from the mound and dusted his hands. It was so real I thought I saw it fall and raise a cloud of dust as it landed.

He wound up for the next pitch.

Jude shoved the pad away. It wasn't what she wanted. It wasn't what she asked for. But it was what Jude understood needed to be understood just now. That people performed on their own little private stages. And talking about a crazy stranger, instead of about his friends or his brother, or himself, it felt safe. He let "Moonlight Drive" on *Strange Days* recede, then he flipped the records over and started the side twos. He took his book and climbed out his window to the cage.

AT SCHOOL, Jude felt like he was pedaling a unicycle. He used to ride his neighbor David McKay's unicycle back in Indiana. He'd never gotten proficient at it; David didn't ever let him ride it for long. But the experience was still there in his muscles and brain. It had been like riding the tail end of John Hancock's pen as he signed the Declaration of Independence.

If possible, the experience at school was even worse. A John Hancock at least followed a path. It flowed. But Jude felt like he was riding the unicycle over broken pavement. Open crevasses flared out below him, curbs loomed, debris was scattered about. He was seriously off-kilter.

In social studies, Mr. Diaz asked if any of the students had ever done drugs. Jude, his experience so raw and new, and feeling for a moment like he was among friends and peers, almost lifted his hand. Instead, he scratched his nose and let his gaze sweep the room.

No one raised their hand.

"That is the right response," Mr. Diaz said. "Because, if you had raised your hand, I am bound by law to report you to the administration, and they are bound by law to report you to the police."

He walked to the window and peered out at the sun-drenched lawn, the building's shadow hugging close to the wall at this hour. "Any of you know about Haight-Ashbury?" He kept looking out and didn't turn to see if anyone had raised their hands.

"Heard of it?"

Jude flitted his hand a bit. He felt he had to acknowledge to Mr. Diaz that they had talked about Haight-Ashbury when Jude had asked about his brother.

"Haight-Ashbury," he said, finally turning around. "Have you seen a storm drain after a heavy rain?"

Kids shrugged, nodded, or just waited.

"Debris all piled up against the grating? Trash, branches, lost shoes?" He moved slowly, philosophically across the room. "Well, that's Haight-Ashbury."

Ten dramatic seconds were required before he made it across the room to his wall map of California. He faced the room. "Anyone know where it is?"

Mr. Diaz let his eyes travel over the room. He was going to wait.

Jude put up a finger and half a hand.

"Jude."

"It's in San Francisco."

"It's smack-dab in the middle of San Francisco." He reached out to the left of the state map to the inset that showed San Francisco. He tapped the center of the city. "It's a neighborhood, and what did I tell you about neighborhoods?"

The class was silent. There was an air of disappointment to Mr. Diaz, a fatalism. In the room, it felt like some sort of punishment was coming.

He raised his voice, pronouncing a lesson. "Neighborhoods are magnets that attract the dominant culture that's already there, or is filtering in. Neighborhoods tend to be homogenous!" He moved from the map, heading along the chalkboard toward the back of the room. "Some economic or cultural shift occurs, and a new kind of resident moves in. That resident thrives for some set of reasons. Their success attracts other, similar residents. The prior residents find it harder and harder to stay. Maybe it costs too much, or maybe the new residents are the wrong race or religion, or too poor or too scary, or for that matter too rich and too demanding. Pretty soon, the new residents drive out the old." He coughed. Shrugged. "The factors that help new people get into a neighborhood are usually trends. That means the reasons the neighborhood works for the newcomers keep improving. And those same trends can work hard against the current residents."

He crossed behind the desks at the rear of the room and came up along the windows from behind Jude.

He stopped next to Jude. In a quieter voice, not lecturing, he said, "Your brother ever show up, Tangier?"

"Yeah," Jude said.

"Thought he might. But if he was still missing…" Mr. Diaz

returned to his slow march. "Well, like I told you, you could look for him in the Haight." Jude had the distinct impression once again that Mr. Diaz thought him naive, rich and coddled. And that all added up to white.

Mr. Diaz stopped at his desk at the front of the room and sat on the corner of it. "The debris, right? The Haight is where disaffected kids are turning up. Mostly white kids like most of you. The Mexican kids, the blacks, most of them don't have to leave home to hit bottom. That's 'cause they're already there.

"So, this one little area in SF, that's where American youth is going. Mostly to overdose and die."

He peered over their heads and out the window.

"I'm telling you this, so that if you ever get the idea in your head that you should pack a few things in a rucksack and run away to Haight-Ashbury, that you should know that you are heading toward the drain. The great drain of American white kids."

His eyes snapped back to the class. "Don't get me wrong. I'm not saying there isn't a war on that needs to be protested. I'm not saying the battle for civil rights is finished." The bell rang but no one moved. "I'm saying just don't be a deadbeat."

Jude wobbled, at least mentally, to the door. Diaz called out at their backs. "Don't forget your homework. Chapter five in the text." Jude ducked involuntarily. The book sat unread on his desk at home.

Then he was in the hall, the wobbling worse, his head reaching ever farther above the unicycle. He got his lunch and topsy-turvyed out to Kevin and his friends. In some recess of his mind, he was sure that now he would calm down and things would stabilize.

They didn't. Last week these kids were his best and only friends on earth. Today, they were petty, frightened, and stupid.

"Your brother's an idiot," James said. "He's gotta get into college to avoid the draft."

"Yeah," Henry said.

"I don't know," Jude said, "Mark says the college deferment will be gone by the time he turns nineteen anyway."

"Fuck, it better not be," James scowled.

Kevin caught Jude's eye. "His brother, Vincent, is at UC Berkeley. He's twenty."

"He's applying for grad school," James said. "Just to stay out of the draft."

Ten minutes later, as they scrunched their bags and fired them at trash cans, James pronounced, "Your brother?" Jude met his gaze. James's lip was lifted in a sneer. "He's fucked, man."

At the end of the day, wobbling or not, Jude decided he would try to see Lacey again. He mounted his bike and pulsed uphill from school, passing the looming, sun-splashed wall of KTLA's soundstage on Bronson. He crossed Sunset, keeping his eyes open now, always alert for Hector and his friends.

But as he reached the corner at Harold Way and was just about to turn, his bike snapped to a hard fast stop and he spilled past the handlebars onto the pavement.

"Fuck!" he leapt to his feet and there they were, Hector and his two goons. They had emerged from between hedges on the darkened lawn of the first apartment building. A broken length of broomstick had been stabbed into the spokes of Jude's bike. One of Hector's friends—it was the same two boys—was flipping an unopened switchblade in his hand. The other held a bottle.

"You been avoiding me, honky," Hector said.

Jude took a step toward them, fully intending to just lay into Hector with all the crazy he felt coursing through him. And fuck the consequences.

"Hey, man!"

Jude followed the eyes of his antagonists. The tall blond hippy from the house across the street was once again playing Frisbee. And now he was standing five feet away between parked cars.

Without a word, Hector and his friends melted back into the shadows and disappeared past the corner of the building.

"Wow, man," the hippy said, "what was that all about?"

Jude shrugged. "Yeah, they're the ones that busted my bike up a couple weeks ago."

"Bad karma, dude. Bad karma."

"I guess."

The hippy's smile was wide and goofy. The hippy shrugged, "Well…" He moved his hands through the air as though weaving something there in front of himself. "Hey, man, my name is Chris

Marley. But you can call me Marley, man. That's what my friends all call me."

"Okay, Marley," Jude watched himself being alone and adult. "I'm Jude. Jude Tangier."

"Cool. Like the city."

"I guess so."

"I'll call you Tangier, okay?"

"Okay." He didn't quite understand.

"It's like," he lifted his hands toward the sky, as though draining his explanation right out of thin air, "man, it's like 'my people' and 'your people,' you know, and not just, you know, *instances.*"

"Okay." Jude tried to sound more convinced.

"I mean, do you dig it?"

"Yeah, maybe."

"Cool, Tangier. So, right" The man bounced a bit, nodding with his head and entire torso. "Well…"

"Hey, thanks, ah, Marley," Jude shrugged again. "You know, for getting rid of Hector and his buddies."

"It's all exactly cool, man. Exactly, like with complete precision. Because that is the work of peace in the universe. That," he stressed, *"That* is the work! I mean, right? Gotta cleanse the world, one moment at a time. And every moment is like, *now.*"

"Right."

"Yeah, all right, Tangier!" The hippy lifted a hand, high and flat toward Jude. Jude stared at the hand, and then past to the scraggly man behind it. "Give me five, dude!" The hand made a short movement toward Jude. Jude lifted his hand in a mirror image and the hippy grinned and then slapped his hand against Jude's.

"Cool, man."

"Cool," Jude said.

"You wanna get high?" the hippy asked.

"Ah, I'm sort of meeting someone, so thanks, but…"

"Yeah, man," the hippy smiled blissfully. "I totally get it, man. Time waits for no one, man. Time waits…" his eyes traveled across the sky over the street. The hippy turned and followed his own gaze.

"Time waits…" he said again.

Jude watched the hippy wander back across the street, then bent to inspect his spokes. One broken, two bent. He carefully twisted and yanked the broken one until it came out and bent the others a bit to make sure they cleared the forks. Then he climbed back on his bike and rode down the sidewalk.

Marley waved as he rode away. Jude lifted his hand and then dropped it back to the handlebars.

At the Crestview, he slipped up the stairs, sliding first along the watchful gaze of the women in the yard, and then of an Asian woman approaching along the balcony. But, he stopped with his knuckles three inches from Lacey's door. A male voice inside the apartment issued like a foul dark cloud from the open windows.

"I don't give a fuck," the voice crackled with anger. "You don't fucking *use*."

Silence followed.

"You fucking *hear* me?" The voice was nasal and carried a whine inside it.

"I hear you, cowboy." Lacey's voice was tired, soft, small.

Jude hovered, his knuckles still frozen in the air. Then he drew them away and let his arm drop to his side. There was an air of completeness to her voice. She knew the man. Though his voice bristled, she didn't sound scared.

The Asian woman slipped past him, her eyes raking his face as slowly and carefully as a Zen garden.

Jude looked out over the street. The dense thrum of the freeway, the jagged and constant honking and sirens from the boulevard, the bird-like jabbering and tittering of the women below—it all passed into him and through.

Suddenly the door opened and he was face to face with Paulo. The man's scowl pushed out in front of him, lit and electrified by startling blue eyes. It pushed past his thick black moustache and unkempt hair and out over his uniform of denims and emblems.

Jude stepped back.

Paulo squinted down at Jude. "The fuck you want, punk?"

"Just…" Jude looked past him into Lacey's apartment.

Paulo stepped out and reached behind himself and, stabbing Jude in the chest with a stiff finger, pulled the door shut.

"She's *busy*!"

"Okay," Jude took another step sideways and back.

"So take the *fuck* off." Paulo, his eyes locked on Jude, whistled piercingly.

The blond guy that followed Paulo around appeared from around the corner downstairs. He looked up and started moving across the lawn to cut Jude off.

Jude nodded at Paulo's idea as though it were a logical one. Then he turned and left, heading toward the front stairs.

The blond man was waiting at the foot of the steps. Jude grinned at him, like there was no big deal. Then he spun away, ducked under Paulo's swinging arms, and shot down the backstairs, taking three and four at a time.

Paulo leaned over the railing above and growled down, "Get the little fucker, will ya?" He slammed his fist on the railing, releasing a loud *bong* and making the whole balcony hum.

Blondie stared at Paulo for a moment. Then shifted his gaze to Jude as he leapt from the stairs and rounded the shrubs. He looked back at Paulo, and then his body startled as the command registered. He spun on the grass and hobbled in his big heavy boots to his motorcycle.

Jude heard the rip and roar of Blondie's engine as he unlocked his bike. Jude grabbed the handlebars and shoved the bike fast out ahead of him along the pavement, leaping on and slamming his PF Flyers into the spinning pedals.

As he hit the street, he steered right for Blondie. Blondie had already pulled away from the curb and had anticipated Jude would turn the other way. But Jude slipped past and Blondie was left working through a slow U-turn in a narrow street with a massive motorcycle. As Jude shot past him, he had a moment of satisfaction seeing Blondie's eyes cloud and a frustrated snarl pass over his teeth.

Jude hugged the corner hard and shot east on Harold Way. He pumped hard in pure, heartbeat staccato. The bike lunged with every pump. Hanging left, he rode against the oncoming traffic. There was none, but he figured Blondie would keep his Harley somewhat legal.

But Blondie had other ideas. He gunned the engine as soon as he hit Harold Way and blew past Jude. Fifty feet ahead, he angled the motorcycle sharply in front of Jude. They were a few feet from Van Ness where the offramp surfaced.

Jude jumped his bike onto the sidewalk. Blondie saw the move and leaned back along the street, expecting to cut Jude off at the Stop. But Jude cut hard left and slid down along the passenger side of the cars exiting the freeway.

He heard Blondie twist angrily at his throttle, the engine bleating like an enraged old bull.

Jude stood on his pedals, looking ahead to find a gap in the cars, and then he looked back. Blondie was coming, riding down the glass- and trash-sprinkled shoulder against traffic.

Jude took the gap in the cars, dismounted and jumped the guard-rail, and pedaled on up the on-ramp on the other side, relaxed now.

At the top of the onramp, Jude stopped and looked back. Blondie was trapped by the guardrail, scowling at Jude, flipping him off, and waiting for a break in the traffic that would let him turn around.

Jude's body positively rang with pleasure. He shook a fist at Blondie and yelled, "Dumb fuck!" He got his bike underway again and yelled again, "Dumb motherfucking fuck!" And gaining speed, he jumped off the curb at the other side of the freeway bridge and, fueled with fear and adrenaline, Jude blazed through traffic like a hawk tearing through a canyon.

At home, Jude lay on his bed and queued up the two Doors albums. He listened all the way through the two sides before dinner was called.

eight

THE HALLS WERE SPLIT WITH SHAFTS OF SUNLIGHT. But with the intermingled darkness and the floating motes of dust, it felt like he was underwater. Jude navigated as under a reef, pushing past dense schools of fish, the lone groupers, the blowfish, the scary Moray eels, until he could get to English.

Two feet from the door, ready to dodge right to avoid an oncoming kid, he looked up to see Melinda. She was smiling and on a collision course from the side. She rammed her shoulder into his, laughed, and said, "Where you been, stranger?"

"Oh, hey," he felt himself color. "I gotta, you know, I gotta get home after school sometimes."

"Hey, come sit over here," she grasped his hand and pulled him along with her, back into the crook of the L of desks. Jude sank into her lavender smell and wafted along. He felt weak and helpless, and he realized he didn't want to feel anything else.

"Hey," Melinda lifted her chin only slightly at the girl sitting where she directed Jude. The girl got up and moved one seat over. The seats weren't assigned but were worn into a regularity of habit. He plumped down in a seat with the word RACIST carefully carved in the desk.

Jude's new place in the room upset the order of things and the consequences dominoed out. He felt the shift, every single shift, in his body. It seemed like every other kid that walked in found their seat overrun and scanned the room to find the source. Their gaze eventually lit on Jude.

"So, this *Catcher* book. You read it." Melinda leaned forward and into him to talk. The angle made a curtain of her hair, a curtain that framed her face and created a space so intimate and so filled with her breath and faint perfume that Jude shuddered with pleasure.

"Yeah, I read it." His voice came down to meet hers, quiet, almost secretive.

"I don't get it," she said. "Like, is there anything to get? Except that he's a pisser and a wanker?"

Jude shrugged. "It's about Phoebe, I think," he said.

Melinda's eyes widened and jetted about, seeing nothing as she took this in and thought about it. Then she burst out, "Holy smokes! Jude the dude!" She grasped his hand with hers and just held it while she stared at his eyes. "You are like the smarts, Jude. The smarts. I totally see that! You just like spelled the whole book, dude!"

"Let's get started," Ms. Loral called out. "I see we've moved around a bit today. That's good to do sometimes, don't you think?" But her eyes too wandered suspiciously along the rows until they finally settled on Jude. She didn't like Jude sitting with Melinda.

"All right then," her voice was dry, "shall we discuss what's happened so far in *Catcher*?"

Melinda's left hand rested on Jude's forearm, casually possessive, and she raised her right.

Ms. Loral turned her shoulders to square up to Melinda. Her arms were crossed tightly. She raised one hand slightly and pointed, "Melinda?"

"Yeah, I was just talking to Jude, here, and I feel like, now I get the whole book."

"Oh?," Ms. Loral pivoted her shoulders back along the front of the class until she'd run down the rest of the class. Then she rotated back. "Can you share your epiphany with the rest of us?"

"Well, I just said I didn't get it, like the whole thing," Melinda flipped her hair back. "And Jude just said, 'It's about Phoebe.'"

Ms. Loral nodded, thoughtfully, the sides of her mouth stretched down a little.

"And it just kinda hit me that, you know, Holden thinks being a catcher in the rye is about running around keeping little kids from falling over a cliff."

"Yes…" Ms. Loral sounded doubtful.

"I mean, he's keeping Phoebe safe, or I mean, that's what he wants to do."

"Well," Ms. Loral flicked a hand dismissively. "It's definitely an idea worth considering."

Jude surprised himself and spoke. He felt he needed to finish the explanation in order to protect Melinda, and to protect his idea. "Well," he said, "It's sorta… He thinks he can save Phoebe, but instead, Phoebe saves him."

All eyes shifted to him and he shrugged, looked down.

Ms. Loral pulled her head back and pursed her lips. "How so, Jude?"

He explained. The book had sung strangely to him as he read it. He felt like the inept boy in the pages was harmonizing with him, even through the odd turns of phrase and the strange and fractured landscapes of the East Coast.

"Holden hates anything phony. He wants everything to be true and honest and, I don't know… immediate. But, no matter where he goes or what he does, everything anyone does is phony. But, it's worse than that because everything Holden does is phony too. And, by the end, he knows it.

"Phoebe is the only one that's true."

"Well…" Ms. Loral nodded, her mouth a hard line saying 'No.'

Jude could feel her about to say something like, 'Interesting idea.' He wanted to head her off, but his notion that Holden giving his sister his hat was the author's signal that their roles were changing seemed flimsy.

Ms. Loral nodded. "Interesting idea." She turned her shoulders. "Anyone else?"

"I thought he was an idiot," a kid named Mike said. "Like he should be in an institution. Like, who let him out? And like, why do we have to read about a crazy person?"

The class laughed with him.

"Another interesting idea," Ms. Loral said shaking her head. "I'm sure we'll have some interesting papers on this one."

Melinda winked at Jude and shook her head. Which he took to mean that she agreed with him and the rest of them, including Ms. Loral, could all take a leap. He decided he would go to the auditorium after school today.

Ms. Loral started handing out the book for the next class assignment. It was a pink-bound paperback with a black-and-white photo of a weirdly retro hippy couple.

"We're going to try an odd new book called *Trout Fishing in America*. It's by Richard Brautigan. Very quirky. I think you'll like it."

Melinda accepted the book from the girl in front of her by plucking it up from the corner. She dangled it like it was a dead rat. She rolled her eyes, saying, "Odd and quirky, by which she means 'Cool enough to trick kids into reading it.'"

It was a skinny book. Jude liked that.

AS SOON as Greg saw Jude coming, he rose from his cross-legged position on the pavement and danced from one foot to the other. "Oh, far out," his smile was infectious and Jude grinned back. "Here comes the Candy Man!"

Jude shrugged. Melinda, who had been leaning against the outer wall smoking a cigarette, pushed off and came toward him. She threw her hair back and her arms out wide as she did, clearly sweeping in to hug him.

Jude felt a jolt of fear that nearly paralyzed him. It shot like a steel ramrod right up his spine. His smile froze and his legs carried on like sticks. He thought about veering away, but his spine couldn't turn. He took the warm, soft impact of her like a wave passing over him.

"My hero," she called out, releasing him. "That book is nutso! And Jude unraveled it with, like, three words!"

She leaned in and kissed Jude on the cheek.

"I…" he spit out past dry lips. "I… I…"

Greg slapped him on the back, laughing. "Out with it, son! I, I, I, ah say, I ah say," taking on the voice of Foghorn Leghorn, "out with it, son!"

"I have some pills," he said.

"Told ya!" Greg danced again. "The Candy Man can!" He grasped Melinda's hands and they swung around each other like square dancers. "Those! Those shameless, nameless little friends were awesome, man!"

Jude passed out his entire pocketful of pills. Theo, Mike, and Serena were there also. When he handed five of each color to Melinda, she said lightly, "Love you, dude!"

Jude nodded hard and said, "Hey, love you. Too." A blush swept through him and his entire body jerked with embarrassment. Jude felt like everyone noticed.

He accepted the small blue glass pipe and lighter, his back carefully to the gate and sidewalk. If James or Kevin saw him... He coughed again. He couldn't seem to get it right. On the second round, he found a hole on the side of the pipe, and he plugged it with his finger. He lit the lighter and drew in a hit, deep and smoky. Better and better.

Then, feeling like it might be a cool thing to be doing, he said, "I'm supposed to go see the Doors Friday with my brother." He was going to ask, 'Are they any good in concert?' But Greg and Melinda and Theo all swooned with excitement the second they heard.

"Most awesome band, maybe ever!"

"My brother has seen them, man, at the Whiskey! Says they're the most monumental mind-blowing act ever!"

"Nothing like it."

"Massive envy, man!"

"Do you have their new record? I spun it like fifty times after it came out. 'People Are Strange,' man. 'Moonlight Drive.' And, fuck man, 'When the Music's Over!'"

"Yeah, man, the whole 'Love Me Two Times' thing is just the hit, just sugar on the pill, man."

"Did you see them on Ed Sullivan? Fuckin' groovy, man. They freaked!"

Theo lifted the pipe and lighter to smoke. He tipped the flame into the bowl and then pulled the lighter up and away from the pipe. The flame stretched across the space between, the suction holding it in the pipe, his hand pulling the source away like taffy. He pulled it three, four, inches out before narrowing the gap again.

The others began arriving—Steven, Cindy, Pete. The pills were gone, but Greg shared his stash with them and inspired Theo and the others to do the same.

Jude knew he probably would not have wanted to share. It seemed to Jude that Greg lived outside the tiny frame of humanity that had been granted him. He boomed, he rattled, he reached. He just... exuded.

Cars began pulling up to pick up the other kids. Greg and Melinda climbed into a Volkswagen van driven by Greg's older brother, Fritz, they called him, the one who had seen the Doors. Introductions had to be made. Theo got into a new, white Mercedes Benz.

With Greg and Melinda gone, Jude didn't really know the other kids and so he shuffled around a little on the sidewalk. Steven was there, lighting the nub of a joint. Cindy and Serena were leaning on each other, back-to-back, passing the blue pipe back and forth. Cindy and Mike were talking closely, like maybe they were a pair, and Jude hadn't noticed until now. Mike grabbed the joint every other pass.

Jude felt like he should say something. He peered off in the direction of his bike.

Then he looked back at Serena and Cindy. "Is it, like, cool to smoke pot on the sidewalk? I mean, why don't we get busted?"

Cindy smiled at him and rolled her eyes. But she had smoke bottled up inside and she wasn't about to speak.

It was Serena who answered. She held the pipe in her fingers and peered at Jude, her eyes just as flat and dark as ever. "No one fucking cares."

"There's like cops everywhere," Jude pointed out. There were routinely two police cars parked at the campus every afternoon, one out front, one at the rear entrance by the PE building.

"That's for the other kids," she said. She took a long deep hit.

Jude drew down his eyebrows in disbelief. "Who exactly?"

Cindy sneered at him. "They bust the black kids and the Mexicans. And they scare the rich white kids. But they could give a shit about the low-end white kids like us." Then she and Serena pushed off each other's backs and turned to face one another. Their hands went out, showing each other off as examples. "Except!" Cindy laughed.

Serena finished for her. "Yeah, except! What the fuck are we?" Cindy was black, and Serena was a cinnamon-skinned Mexican girl.

They clasped together in a hug, laughing.

"Well," Jude stepped forward, took the pipe and lighter from Cindy and drew down hard on it. Mike, crouched in front of Cindy, watched him, appraising. Jude held the smoke in and gave the joint to Serena. Their eyes locked and Jude suddenly felt like Serena was the strangest, most intense person he'd ever encountered.

Her dark eyes and dark hair set off a delicate face. Her eyeliner arced out at the sides of her eyes. Her lipstick, too, was dark. It all seemed impossible and even wrong, but, maybe it was the marijuana convincing him otherwise. She was, just then, the most incredible person he'd ever met.

She smiled as though she knew exactly what he was experiencing.

She held the pipe close to her, but turned it, offering him another hit. To get it, he had to step toward her. He took it, and just inches from her face, he took a hit, her eyes still hard on his.

A song slipped into his mind.

Before you slip into unconsciousness,
I'd like to have another kiss.

Her smell was over him. Her hair enclosed them. It shone like a perfect black ethereal curtain. It seemed to cut all sounds. He broke eye contact and stammered. "I gotta-got-gotta..." he shrugged, almost helpless. "I gotta go."

He clumsily stumped off down the sidewalk, almost bowling Mike over, to the sound of the girls tittering. He found his bike, mounted it, and rode north.

AT THE Crestview, Jude crossed the lawn and mounted the stairs as quickly and stealthily as he could. Once again Frenchie's pale friend was standing on the walkway in the shadows. Her eyes tracked Jude, but still, she made no motion and said nothing.

Lacey's door stood ajar and Jude stopped in front of it. He looked at the pale girl again, then knocked and waited. Then, feeling the eyes of the women on the lawn below on his back, he pushed in and pulled the door to behind him.

Music played. It was the new Procol Harum song, "Whiter Shade of Pale." The song was a bit like the Doors to him, laced with odd lyrical turns and luscious music. But where the Doors songs seemed to be filled with portents of strange storms just over the horizon, evil hidden in people's hearts, and death, "Whiter Shade of Pale" felt mysterious, fickle and even fun.

The kitchen was empty with several plates and bowls cantilevered on the sink. The bathroom door stood open and he glanced in. He knocked lightly on the bedroom door and, after a moment, pushed it open.

No Lacey.

He felt he had known this when he entered. Even from the walkway outside, the rooms had been missing her vital presence.

He wandered back to the kitchen and surveyed the mess. He felt badly for Lacey, that this crust of the past few days should remain. Then, with an almost physical start, he went to the sink and started the water. While he waited for it to get hot, he pulled silverware from the stacks of dishes and scraped old cereal, brown lettuce, spaghetti noodles, and hard clumps of rice into the trash. Then he plugged the sink and squeezed a thick stream of pink Lux dish soap under the running water and watched it suds up.

The radio played commercials and blared with the robust bark of the DJ. The next song they played was a Byrds song, "So You Wanna Be a Rock n' Roll Star."

The dishes done and stacked in a drainer on the other side of the sink, Jude began retrieving pots and pans from the stovetop and sinking them beneath the suds.

"What exactly are you doing?"

Jude, caught in a reverie, lurched and peered out toward the backlit door. Lacey was rimmed with bright light, her eyes and mouth smiling inside the halo.

"You don't have to do my dishes!" she cried out. Then she swung toward the couch and tossed down a large red plastic basket full of laundry.

Jude raised his hands in innocence and retreat, "Sorry!"

"But, hey," she laughed at him, "you don't have to… But don't let me stop you!"

Lacey came into the kitchen and kissed Jude on the cheek. Jude felt the odd swoony critter lurch and awake inside him. Her smell was earthy, warm, uncluttered. He clung to it like a soap bubble.

"It looked like, I don't know…" He shrugged and dunked the pan he held back into the steaming suds. "…like it needed some help."

"Yeah, there's a reason it looks like it needs some help," she snapped a shirt out of her basket and began folding it, watching Jude. "It's because it does."

Jude kept a weather eye on Lacey as she folded. He leaned into his work and felt a blooming, complete pleasure in the scenario he found himself in. He felt like an actor who was thawing out to become a human. A boy cracking through to become a man.

He stopped to tally his day. His last hour or so, really. Two kisses from two beautiful women. Two kisses from two beautiful women. Two kisses…

"Sorry about Paulo," she said.

"Paulo?" Jude pretended the name didn't ring every bell of memory so loudly that it cleared everything else from his head.

"You know." She leveled a gaze at him that said, simple and clear, 'Let's not pretend, okay?'

"Oh, yeah, that guy."

"Yeah," Lacey smiled weakly. "He can be an ass."

"Yeah." Jude finished the last pan and wiped down the countertop and then the stove before he drained the water. "His buddy, too."

"Yeah," she agreed. As he dried his hands, Lacey said, "Help me with the bed?"

"Oh, ah, sure." He blushed. Something about entering her bedroom set off his body in surprising ways. His muscles tightened and he could barely walk. He moved almost robotically.

But, in the room, windows open, the radio lilting the Beach Boys' "Sloop John B," and the quotidian act of making a bed all sharpened his physical pleasure, pushing his discomfort down into darkness. He absorbed her movements and lived inside the slippery smells around him. He concentrated on lofting the sheet between them until it bowed upward like a sail, and then bringing it down in unison with Lacey's movement so that it squared over the mattress and cinched under the corners.

He helped her in the bedroom until the bed was made, and then helped her fold a slew of other sheets, one after the other, until she had a stack of pastel sheets in blue, yellow and rose.

She talked the whole time. "I'm not a California girl. And for sure

I'm not a Los Angeles girl. I think I told you, I ended up in Atlanta. My parents moved there when I was like twelve. I never fit in there. And I don't fit in here, either."

She caught his eye. He was openly assessing her long blonde hair, the even tan over her long, bare limbs, and her lightly freckled cheeks. She was a poster girl for Southern California, and as far as Jude was concerned, Los Angeles.

She laughed. "I know, everyone says the same thing. I look like a Southern California beach girl. But it just isn't in me. I've never lived in a place where it snows, but I think I'd rather."

Jude watched her and listened. She was wearing a white cotton blouse tied across her midriff and short jean shorts, all worn and torn. Her feet were bare. He wondered what it would be like to someday touch her.

Someday.

Really.

Touch her.

It all seemed very foreign to him, and yet he could think of no other destination anywhere in his future. Even when he forced himself to think ahead, he would get a flickering of home and his family's faces, like some kind of dishwasher ad in *Life* magazine. But the faces were all somehow soured and they were impossible to hold there for long. Or he could see himself confronting a paper notched with typescript on a desk, maybe ready to turn in. But that evaporated too.

"You lived in the snow," she said. "What was that like?"

"It was a major pain," he said. Then he shrugged, "But also pretty cool, actually."

"Like how?" Lacey lit a cigarette, started it, and then propped it in an ashtray on her bedside table.

"I liked the skating and sledding. A good snowball fight. And…" he shrugged again.

"And what?"

"Just the snow. It's so amazing when it starts. And sometimes you get big storms and it drifts really high. You can dig fortresses and tunnels under the snowbanks.

"I don't know, it just changes everything. You wake up some morning and everything is completely different—it's eerily silent, cold, and white—and that's cool."

"Yeah, maybe that's why I want to go to the snow: I need a change. A whole complete change." She laughed. "Like a whitewash."

As they folded the last sheet, Jude asked, "So, like, do you…" He shrugged. "I mean…"

Lacey laughed, "C'mon, spit it out." She tugged on her end of the sheet, pulling Jude off balance for a moment.

"It's just…" He looked at her eyes. Piercing. Blue. "Like, are you gonna get married? Have kids?"

"Ha!" Lacey drove her hand into the halfway point between them, striking a fold into the sheet. "Not me."

"But, why not?"

Lacey looked around the room and raised her hands as though she were presenting evidence. But then she started, snatched up her cigarette and pulled hard on it. "Let's go in the other room," she said.

Jude maneuvered out ahead of her.

"So just ask yourself," she said. "Why would I?" She stabbed the cigarette into the ashtray on the kitchen table. "How many married people do you know that are happy?" She started into the kitchen but spun on her toes, dialing in her argument. "I mean, are your parents happy?"

"I don't know," he pushed the ashtray an inch away, pulled it back. "I guess not so much."

"Well, I don't know any. And who'd want to bring a kid up in this world anyway?"

He agreed with everything she said, but right there in the middle of his agreement, his entire vision of life and success was being threatened. Worse, his future with Lacey was also threatened.

Jude sat at the kitchen table while Lacey put away the rest of the laundry. If there was one thing he was certain about, it was that he didn't want Lacey to change. And definitely, he didn't want her to move. He felt, actually, that what he'd really like is to have her be his, and his alone. He picked up her cigarette and put it to his lips and drew in lightly, the ember crackling softly.

"You know," Lacey came back in the room and watched as he set the cigarette back down and blew out the smoke. "I'm not as bad as you think."

"I don't think you're bad."

"Bull!" she laughed. She crossed and snatched up her cigarette.

Pulled in a deep puff. Stood over him, her hips just a short two feet from his nose. She handed him the cigarette and blew out. Then she grasped his chin and met his eyes. "I have a memory, Jude. I know I've been a bit of a—no, I've been a full-on—mess when you've come by."

Jude tried to shrug, but it felt weird with his chin in her hand.

She let loose, grabbed the cigarette back and drew in.

"All I can say is…" she spoke through the smoke in her mouth and lungs. "Well, just wait. You'll see. It ain't easy." She handed the cigarette to Jude and whirled away. "But I shouldn't say that. Maybe for you, it will be."

"Maybe," Jude said. But in his mind's eye he was alone. Cut loose. Nothing was easy now. He suspected things were just going to get harder.

Lacey carried a folded stack of clothes to the bedroom and returned.

"My brother came home," he said.

"Oh! Hey!" She stopped in the middle of the room, hands out as though exclaiming on the size of the new topic. "That's a good thing, right?"

"Yeah, I think so."

"It is," she forcibly replaced his doubt with her certainty. "You gotta try again. I mean, leaving is a huge thing. It's as big as a snowstorm, right? It changes everything. So you go back and see what changed, and if you still don't like it, well, then you gotta go."

Jude nodded. But, he followed her metaphor down its path in his thoughts, and he saw the soggy, smashed look of the gardens and flowerbeds after the snow had mostly melted. He felt like this was closer to the truth. That Mark's return was more like that day when you realize Winter is over. Instead of crisp newness there's a dingy patch of ground that everyone had been pretending was abundant and green. Instead, it was trampled, frozen, gray and muddy.

Lacey began putting dishes away in the kitchen. "Thank you again for doing the dishes! That's pretty groovy. No one, I don't think, has ever washed my dishes for me."

"Really?"

"Really. You want anything to eat? I gotta eat some breakfast!"

"Um, no thanks. Isn't it kinda late for breakfast?"

"A bit. But, I got up at three," she said. "And I wanted to get the laundry in before the other girls."

"Oh." Jude couldn't follow, but he let it lie.

He thought about his news while she pulled out cereal and milk and a spoon. He was uncertain of it. At school, it was an effective bragging point. But would it be with Lacey? He didn't know.

He dragged carefully on the cigarette and finally said as he exhaled, "I'm going to see the Doors Friday. With my brother."

"You are *what?*" She spun and stared at him with her mouth open.

"Going to see the Doors."

"You are *not!*"

He grinned. "Yeah, I am."

"You're too…" She raised a hand to her head. "Jesus!" She spun away and lifted her spoon, shaking it at the wall as though she were using it to punch out an argument.

"I'm too what?"

She whipped back around. "You're too *young*, okay?" Then she threw her spoon across the kitchen. It bounced off the table and flashed past Jude's nose. "I know you don't want me saying that, but it's *true!*"

Jude picked up the cigarette. He felt immeasurably old. Sad and old and yet so terribly young and childish. He didn't dare look at Lacey. He could feel tears in his eyes. Lacey seemed like a tiny chip of a boat somewhere near the horizon, distant and receding. His fingers shook as he took a drag.

He looked away to where the spoon had landed, wiped his eyes, and said, "Yeah, well, I'm a little kid, and I'm going."

"Ah, fuck," Lacey snatched the cigarette from his fingers and drew in deeply. He looked up at her and felt the childishness even of his defensiveness. He moped sullenly like he might if his mother said he couldn't stay up to watch "The Twilight Zone." She pushed the smoke out in a dense cloud. "I'm no good at this," she said. "You're just gonna have to forgive me." She went back into the kitchen to retrieve her breakfast. "Or else forget me. That's what it always comes down to, anyway."

"I'm not gonna forget you," Jude mumbled.

158 · *If They Say I Never Loved You*

"What?" She set her bowl at the table.

"I said, I guess I'd better forgive you then."

She laughed. Tossed her hair back. "You're rich, you know that?"

"Why shouldn't I go to see the Doors?" he asked.

"Well," she crossed her legs. "Now that we're talking about it, I've changed my mind. You should go. But be careful, okay? The crazies and nutjobs come out of hiding when the Doors play."

When he left, he stood at the door a moment, looking back in. Lacey was organizing loose laundry into piles. "Thanks," he said.

"Thanks?" She cocked her head at him.

"I like talking to you."

"Good," she turned a flat, frank gaze on him. "I kinda like talking to you, too."

"Okay," he lifted a hand.

"I want to hear about it," she said. "The concert."

"Oh, yeah, for sure."

"See ya, Jude." Her smile lit her face, but she didn't leave the couch area like he thought she might. Just a little peck goodbye maybe? But no. He trundled down the stairs, feeling like his tennis shoes were heavy as mud-caked snow boots. He clambered on his green Sting-Ray and rode for home.

nine

THE CAR WADDLED SLOWLY ALONG THE FREEWAY.
The Doors' music pelted the interior from an eight-track player that
glowed from under the dash. It was the second of these other-worldly
devices that Jude had seen now, the first bulging from under the dash
of Russ's Gran Torino.

"The End" was playing. "The blue bus is calling us. Driver where
you taking us?" Jimmy's father was driving. Jimmy's step-mother,
Nina, was also in the front. The smell of her like a faint garden filled
the car. She kept up an excited patter with Jimmy's father, calling him
Ricky, but she kept turning to include the boys.

In the back were the four boys, Jimmy, Jimmy's cousin Ralph,
Mark and Jude. It was a brand-new black Lincoln Continental, with
rear doors that opened toward the front. It was a big car. Wide. Even
with four of them in the back, there was room. Mark and Jimmy sat
in the middle with the view out the front.

With Ralph—a guitarist, though Mark said he was horrible—they
carried on an avid conversation about who was the best guitarist in the
world. Jimi Hendrix was winning. Jeff Beck and Jimmy Page of the
Yardbirds were contenders. Eric Clapton of Cream, Pete Townsend
of the Who, made it into the mix. Mark wanted to include blues
players Peter Green and Mike Bloomfield, but Jimmy and Ralph had
never heard of them.

Jimmy's step-mother—she had said, 'Call me Nina,' when they'd picked Mark and Jude up—talked about the L.A. music scene. Where the Doors got started, the evolution of Crosby, Stills and Nash, the start of Buffalo Springfield, a singer named Joni Mitchell. She made it sound like she knew the musicians and had been hanging out in the studio when they made their records.

Jude squeezed against the door and, because it was what he could see, he considered the debris on the roadside. There were the occasional hubcaps, shredded tires, paper bags, a pair of jeans, a bent up Montana license plate.

They parked nearly an hour after the concert was supposed to start. But when they emerged from the car they couldn't hear anything.

"Between bands, maybe," Jimmy said.

"Are there other bands?" Jude asked.

"Ooooh yeah," Jimmy's father said enthusiastically, right behind Jude. He and Nina were dressed very hip. She was a slender, pale-skinned woman with long black hair and slightly Asian eyes. She wore a white hat, a white leather coat, a short white leather dress, and white boots above her knees. The dress had round holes in it filled with clear plastic, each a portal to a patch of Nina's pale white skin. She looked sexy and fun, but to Jude, the matching cold white leather also made her seem galaxies distant from his scruffy little realm.

The dad, a tall, round-bellied balding man, was wearing moccasins, striped bell-bottoms and a red-and-white shirt with fringe on it. His gray tufts of hair were longer than Jimmy's. He had a scraggly gray beard flecked with black and white. He looked old. He said, "The Nitty Gritty Dirt Band and The Sunshine Company are opening."

"Couldn't be two worse bands to open for the Doors," Jimmy said.

"Why?" Jude asked. They were making their way across the large parking lots. Being late, they were parked in a separate lot and police were directing them along fences at right angles to the gymnasium where the concert was being held.

"The Sunshine Company is like the Mamas and Papas," Jimmy

said. "Just fizzy pop music. And the Nitty Gritty dudes play the same thing, fizzy pop, but all hillbilly."

Jude could care less. He was just glad to be here. In fact, he was a bit stunned to be here.

⸻

THE EXPLOSION Jude had anticipated at home had never happened. Sure, Mark had said don't worry about it. But Jude had not really believed him. The days leading up to the concert had simply come and gone, and the only evidence Jude could see of stress caused by the impending date were his father's darting, suspicious, angry eyes at the dinner table.

Jude was well-attuned to the faint waves of tension in the house. Sometimes, he was caught by surprise—some sudden flare-up of fury on his father's part—but that was rare. His father was a powder keg and there were events like a poor report card or a call from the neighbor about a broken fence or dirty swimming pool and Jude could predict the timing and method of the explosion.

With the Doors concert, Jude had anticipated an explosion precisely the night before. It would come as dinner wound down, as Mark settled his knife and fork into his plate with finality. Then their father would say something quiet, like 'Don't be expecting to go anywhere anytime soon. Your grades aren't good enough.' Or maybe it would be, 'I think the next couple of nights we'll need to review your homework before you consider yourself finished.'

There would be some surprise stumbling block, some rule that randomly emerged, like a semi-truck bearing down out of a fog bank.

But the Doors concert never came up. Not at dinner. Not even the night of. Their father worked late that night, and wasn't home by the time they left.

Jude had to believe Mark's version of events: their father was not stopping them from going because he was basically on detention from their mother. On detention because he'd caused Mark to leave home and Mark was being given a sort of reparation for his suffering.

It had weirdly converted their father from a seething knot of anger with a feather-weight trigger to a dark storm that lurked on the horizon. Too far away to cause immediate damage, but big and powerful enough to race down on them unexpectedly.

It just hadn't happened.

It was surreal.

⌐⌐

THEY encountered police. And then police, and then more police. In the remote lot it was a cop here and there. At the outer edge of the main parking lot, it was pairs of uniformed police. Then, as they got closer, it was pairs of pairs. Outside the entrance, it was twenty or more cops wearing helmets with bulletproof face shields, their billy clubs out. Jude walked past one who stared hard at him and snapped his club into his open palm.

Weaving among the police were hawkers selling Doors T-shirts and scalpers selling tickets. Jude knew their tickets had cost $15. The show was sold-out and hawkers were offering tickets for $40 and $50. People were eagerly buying them up.

As they neared the gymnasium, they passed a troupe of Hare Krishna dancing, singing and jangling finger cymbals. They were young, healthy, sometimes beautiful people. Jude couldn't for the life of him understand why they did what they did.

Right in front of the ticket takers, at the four widely separated entries across the front of the building, there were musicians. A singer-guitarist, a saxophonist, a singer with a tambourine—singing "Mr. Tambourine Man," of course—and a group of three with a fiddle, a guitar and a banjo, all singing.

They were late. They offered up the tickets at the door and Jude made sure he received his torn half. They'd missed the Sunshine Company. The four boys stood near the rear of the hall for the Nitty Gritty Dirt band. All the pluckety mandolins and violins made Jude itchy. But it was the saccharine singing that made him want to leave the building until the band was done.

He shifted his attention to the crowd.

From where he stood, it looked like everyone was ignoring the Nitty Gritty Dirt Band. They clustered and hailed each other. It seemed like everyone knew everyone else. Girls shrieked and hugged, men grasped shoulders and pounded backs. High-fives were raised. They wore leather and denim. They weren't the flower children hippies. This crowd was bikers and druggies, a special brand of hippy. And anywhere Jude looked long enough into these groups, he saw cash and drugs changing hands. Little baggies, cigarette boxes, little squares of paper, and individual joints passed at hip level, while green wads of cash passed a few inches higher, near the belts.

There were tables near the rear of the hall selling shirts and stickers. Radio stations vied for attention with huge emblems of their call letters on the walls. He saw kids his age all over the place. Not a lot of them, but more than he'd expected. He felt better seeing them.

The hall was a pall of smoke, and the smoke smelled strongly of marijuana. When Jude asked about it, Jimmy produced a Marlboro cigarette box and shook it open. It was filled with marijuana cigarettes. "Let's join 'em," he said.

Jimmy's parents had stood with the boys for a short while, mainly it seemed, for the two of them to point out all the famous people they knew or saw in the crowd. "There's Neil Young," Jimmy's father pointed out. Nina said, "He's talking to Twiggy!" Jude looked across the floor at a man with muscular sideburns and fair slouch leaning down to an impossibly thin, short-haired blonde girl. It looked like a Saint Bernard about to eat a Chihuahua.

They found, or supposedly found, Steve Winwood, Allen Ginsberg, Sonny Bono, James Brown, Jack Nicholson, Mary Travers, Joni Mitchell, and Ricky Nelson. Jude recognized Sonny Bono and Ricky Nelson from television. But the others could have been complete fabrications.

Then Jimmy's parents had flaunted their backstage passes and wandered away. Now though, they were loose in the crowd. Jude could see them easily. Jimmy's dad was older than nearly anyone else there, and for sure no one else was wearing a crazy white outfit like Nina's.

The wait for the Doors seemed interminable. Even feeling a bit high, Jude was bored and worried. All he could do was tag along with Mark and his friends, and they were eagerly following scents Jude couldn't smell. They had to see if they could see better from the top of the bleachers. They couldn't. Then they had to see if they could get into the locker rooms because they decided that was where the Doors would be hanging out. They couldn't do that either. Then they needed to find a place to smoke more weed. At least that was easy.

Then, when the Nitty Gritty Dirt Band had been off-stage for almost an hour, canned music blaring over the sound system, it was time to get as close to the stage as possible. To Jude, it felt like he was chaperoning a party of over-excited ten-year-olds.

Everywhere they went the older boys were oblivious to the scowls of the older people they pushed past. Elbowing through the crowd to the front, Jimmy treated it as though he were making his way through a bunched-up herd of Holsteins. He angled through sideways, squeezing and pushing. He reached back and pulled Ralph or Mark through after him.

Jude felt sensitized to the anger they were leaving in their wake. The four of them were like bubbles rising toward the stage to what Jude visualized as a sealed top. Every new space they gained together was smaller and tighter than the last. He was afraid that when the Doors took the stage, or when they pissed off the wrong people, the four of them would be crushed or split apart, or just beaten up.

"Should we all have a place to meet up?" Jude shouted at Mark when they were compacted into a new space together.

Mark either didn't hear, or ignored him. Mark was on tiptoes trying to look over the heads in front of him. A roar rose from the stage area and quickly spread. A hoppity-skip trill on the organ danced out over them and repeated, and repeated, and repeated. It was familiar. Then the guitar ground down through the organ notes and Jude recognized "When the Music's Over."

People around them surged forward. At the same time, half of them were swaying back and forth. Jude felt like seaweed in a tidepool as waves rushed in.

Jim Morrison was visible in snatches between the bodies. He wore a long, black jacket, open; a loose white shirt, almost a blouse; and black leather pants. As the song exploded, and Morrison leaned into it, Jude had the feeling of watching something caged. Morrison prowled, he snarled, he snapped. But he also slipped away easily down avenues in the music, eyes closed. Then, as though seeing words near the surface, he would raise the mic and report them, discuss them, expose them, sing them.

Jimmy urgently pressed forward. His ambition to touch the stage was unspoken, at least to Jude, but it was all-consuming. Jimmy kept looking back at the three of them, his face set and determined, sweat-sheened, hair askew. Then he would turn back to the wall of people and duck and drive forward into the fissures in the crowd.

Mark followed. Ralph, an apologetic look back over his shoulder at Jude, went next. And then Jude, feeling he had no choice if he wanted a ride home, chased them into the closing seams.

They finally were clustered maybe fifteen or twenty feet from the stage. It was great for them, Jude thought. They could look up at the stage instead of forward through the taller heads and shoulders. They had a great view of Morrison who seemed unconcerned with the audience, his back to them. But they could also see Robby Krieger, eyes closed, riding his guitar like a steed into the music. Ray Manzarek was on the opposite side of the stage, but Jude could still see his narrow, professorial face, the flashing glint of his glasses. And behind them, the driver, the drummer, was John Densmore. Jude only glimpsed Densmore, his arms and hair and sticks, steady and wild, stitching the whole thing together in time.

Jude was sure he had no expectations. This was his first concert. But it turned out he did. He expected to recognize the songs. He also didn't expect the band to open with "When the Music's Over" with its refrain of *"Turn up the lights, turn up the lights!"* And then, deep inside the tune, the band was seeming to unravel. Morrison was all but gone in the wings of the stage. Densmore suddenly released the beat and the loose herd of instruments with it. Manzarek kept along on the beat for a few bars, but then he wandered into a tempoless solo that Krieger jabbed with anguished, abstract, and almost random guitar licks.

After the caterwauling carried on for far too long, Morrison, head down into the mic, his face hidden by his hair murmured.

Something wrong, something not quite right,
Something wrong, something not quite right,
Something wrong, something not quite right,
Touch me baby all through the night.

The drums woke up slowly and pursued him, and the music threaded around his voice.

Won't you be my whore, I want you, I need you
Give me a sign
Give me a look
Send me a book
Drop me a line
It's almost time
Give me a sign
Right now, right now
Now, now… now.

The music faltered again, slipping off into a thrumming of wind, a random knocking, something lost and faltering. Then Morrison shrieked and shouted.

Why were you born?
Tell me!
You must know!
Why, why were you born?

The start of the lines was an existential wail. They dropped through longing or grief and ended in condemnation. Morrison shrieked again, elemental, tribal, and the drums rose and—*crack!*—they were back into the raunchy run of the song.

The crowd hooted and shouted until it rose to a roar that overrode all but the drums and the bass. The bodies packed tighter. The song tightened and closed. And Jimmy's determination doubled. Another organ lilt followed by a stretchy guitar riff, and the band launched into "Soul Kitchen."

Jude couldn't really see what happened, but ahead of him, there was sharp jerk in the unbroken flesh of the crowd. The jerking roiled and spun for a moment, and then Jude saw Jimmy pass overhead on a score of raised hands. He was no more than a pale and crumpled package marked for delivery to the rear.

Then, the bodies ahead of Jude parted slightly and spit out Mark and then Ralph. Mark fell to the floor. He got up and brushed off. Then he shrugged and they all turned and started their retreat. They were mostly just ejected by the greater organism that danced in a thrall, but there were elbows thrown and sour glares. Jude could feel it in their dismissive eyes: 'Kids!'

Towering above them were slender, beautiful young women riding the shoulders of men. One wore nothing. Her legs were bare. Her chest was bare. Mark turned to look back at Jude in stunned disbelief. Jude ducked past her protruding knee, and looked up through the sensual architecture of her body. Her eyes fell to his and she grinned at his gawking face. Jude ducked away and pushed on.

They found Jimmy several minutes later. The band was hovering through "People Are Strange," and Jude, in full agreement, felt like he was looking at Exhibit A. Jimmy was sitting in the bleachers, about as far from the stage as someone could get. He was sullen and angry.

"Where-a-fuck you guys *been*?" he greeted them. His shirt was ripped and dirty, and his nose was bloodied.

Jude watched the band. People kept popping from the rear of the mass and staggering away. One stopped five paces out, leaned over and puked over the floor. One was a topless girl. As she made her way toward the bathrooms, men in twos and threes veered to her, grasping at her breasts, kissing her face, and then released her. She continued on her course as though the encounters were an inconvenience, an obstacle course on the deck of a pitching ship at sea.

The mass of bodies that filled more than half the gym was dark and urgent. Jude sensed them. They were obsessed, morbid, compelled. If not for the lit stage, and Morrison with the mic stand stabbed and grounded into the body of the place, the crowd could be some dark cult of lost souls.

The rest of the night became Jimmy's escape. As badly as he needed to get to the stage, now he had to get home. "Where's my dad?" he kept asking. But the show reeled and shimmered in seeming eternal darkness, and people around them became, if possible, more manic and demented.

When Jimmy saw Nina, her white costume flickering near the locker room doors, he launched an expedition to reach her. *"You know the day destroys the night…"* The audience surged and crowed to the recognized song. *"Break on through to the other side!"* The song urged them on, Jimmy just as furiously parting the seas as before.

But when they got to Nina, she was kissing a strange man, and his hand—clearly visible through one of the clear round portholes in her dress—was well up inside her skirt. Her eyes were closed, her jaw elevated. Jimmy stood five feet away and shouted at her. She didn't hear and he went to her and yanked on her arm. "Nina!"

She turned blank eyes on Jimmy and, after a moment in which she seemed confused, turned back to the man. He was a tall, lanky man in a black suit with a black shirt and a white tie. He was clean-cut, but his face was deeply tanned, almost ruddy, and a sharp white scar split his upper lip. His eyes were piercing over thick red lips, and it was Jimmy they sought to pierce.

Jude saw it coming. Jimmy reached out to grab Nina's arm again and the man's reddened, ringed hand slipped from Nina's clothes and cleanly swatted Jimmy in the head like he was one of Emilio's bees.

Jimmy flew off his feet and landed on the wood floor. By the time Mark and Ralph had pulled Jimmy back to his feet, Nina and her friend had slipped away.

In the car, all the way home, Jimmy sulked. He snatched angry glances at Nina and muttered "Whore," under his breath. Jimmy's father drove and talked about how amazing the show had been, never noticing Jimmy's swollen lip and darkening cheek. Nina sat in the front, her eyes glazed, head lolling, and smiling blissfully. She sang snatches of lyrics, "Love me two times, babe!"

When Mark and Jude were let off, they stood on the curb and watched the taillights of the Lincoln sink down the hill. "Fuck," Mark said, "that was bitchin, man! That was pure fuckin' groovy!"

Jude shrugged. The concert had been a strangely puny and difficult thing for him. A pain in the ass, really. But he saw it not through his eyes, but Lacey's, and then Melinda's and maybe Greg's. He couldn't wait to tell them about it.

He looked up at the house and saw the silhouette of his mother watching them from the living room window. They went up and closed the door behind them.

JUDE got to see Lacey for a moment on Sunday. He'd gone on Saturday but Frenchie had stopped him. She had been standing on the balcony in her blue silk robe talking to an older man in a suit.

As soon as Jude set a foot on the steps, Frenchie had called down, "She's busy."

Jude looked up. Frenchie was looking at him, her face serious. The man was grinning down at him.

"Oh, okay," Jude said.

"Saturdays are busy," Frenchie said. Her hand was clutching the man's lapel.

"Okay."

Still grinning at Jude as though he were on the inside of a joke, the man reached inside Frenchie's robe. Frenchie pushed his hand down and away, but he just reached in again and this time Frenchie didn't stop him. Jude could see the orb or her breast under the man's hand. Her eyes lay on Jude flat and dark.

Jude spun away and climbed back on his bike.

He returned on Sunday. He felt just as compelled as Jimmy had been at the concert, he realized. He circled the block twice, and seeing it as lazy as any school day, he parked his bike in the alley behind the trash cans and walked nonchalantly to the stairs. Only the walk was in sunlight. He ducked to the stairs in the shadows hoping to make it to her door without interruption.

The split second before he knocked, Penny opened her door at the far end of the balcony. Jude halted his hand, turned it into a short wave, and then knocked.

Penny came along the walkway. She was wearing a T-shirt and maybe nothing else. Her bare legs and the movement of her body under the shirt pounded in his eyes. Penny stopped beside him and he realized his mouth was open and his eyebrows arched. He tried to haul his face back into the realm of normal.

"Hi Jude," she wrinkled her nose in a way that Jude found intimate and exciting. "Folks around here like to sleep in when they can, you know."

"Oh," his voice was small. He looked out at the sunbaked street. It was after three in the afternoon.

"Maybe come back tomorrow," she said. But Jude knew he couldn't. Mondays was when the Paulo guy was there.

"Oh, okay, thanks," his voice shrinking even further.

Then the door opened.

Lacey stood blinking with tousled hair. "Jude." She smiled at Penny.

"Sorry sweetie," Penny said. "I was just sending him on his way. You go back to bed."

"No, that's all right." Lacey was wearing a man's button-down shirt with high cut-outs on the hem on either hip. "I'm awake. He can make me some coffee while I shower."

"All right, sweetie," Penny threw Jude a disapproving glance. "Whatever you say."

Jude stepped in past Lacey and worked his way toward the kitchen. "Thanks," he said to Lacey.

"Thanks?" she asked. She closed the door. She looked so warm and vulnerable standing in her living room in that shirt.

"Yeah, I kinda get kicked out sometimes when I come by."

"Yeah," she said. "I'm not surprised." She pulled her hair back off her forehead, out of her face. Then she pointed to the bathroom and went that way.

Jude started water for the coffee, set up the coffee brewer, and then started washing dishes. He heard the radio from the bathroom and then the water, drowning out the music. He dreamed of Lacey's wet and naked body while he scrubbed a pan with hardened spaghetti on the sides.

One short knock hit the front door and then it opened. The door swung in suddenly and Jude looked up into the face of Russ. The big black man filled the door. His eyes roamed the room, but quickly found Jude standing in the kitchen. Seeing Jude, Russ's yellow eyes seemed to glow with hatred and anger.

"We had us a contract-o-pact, little honky bitch," he said.

Jude held up the pan. "I'm just washing some dishes."

"I don't care if you're retrofying a new fucking kitchen," Russ moved two steps deeper into the living room. "You gone, boy. *Now.*"

"Well, I'm making some coffee. It's on the stove." Jude felt like he was ducking punches.

"*Fuck* the coffee," he jerked a thumb toward the door.

"Lacey's gonna…"

"No," he snarled, "Lacey *ain't* gonna!"

Russ moved toward Jude with surprising speed. He lifted Jude by his left forearm, swinging him past the kitchen table and flinging him into the living room. Jude landed on his feet, but cracked into the coffee table and he went down against a chair, and then, to the floor. The room shook with the impact.

Russ was over him, lifting him by the front of his shirt, sneering down, all teeth and leathery neck, like some old crocodile. He smelled overwhelmingly of body odor and cigarettes. Jude's tiptoes clipped the carpet as he sought some contact with the earth. But Russ scooted him out the door, turned the corner, and fired him toward the front stairs.

Jude stumbled and dragged his knuckles against the stucco wall. He fell to one knee. The skin was peeled from his knuckle. In its place was a ragged whitened field that was prickling with growing red dots of blood. The sting of it brought tears to his eyes.

He stumbled to his feet and angled for the stairs. The pale girl sat on a folding lawn chair by Frenchie's door. Jude met her eyes and felt tears start. He hardened his face and hurried past. But he was hauled up short by what he saw as he went by.

The girl sat, like all her poses and postures, like she was half-dead. She kind of slumped, ethereally. But as Jude moved by her, he saw that her right arm was in a cast and that her face had a bruise bigger and darker than Jude's had been.

The girl's eyes pulled up slowly to meet his.

"Ow," he muttered, unintentionally.

"*Move*, motherfuck!" Russ's bellow hit him like a bat. Jude started and shot down the stairs. When he turned the corner of the building, he saw his bike lying in the middle of the driveway. Russ must have come back from somewhere in his car, or maybe taken the trash out, and had seen the bike.

Jude climbed on and rode away.

The whole world was stacked against him seeing Lacey. He didn't understand it. There was some mysterious chasm between himself at fifteen and the world of adults. The chasm seemed vast but completely empty as though it didn't really exist. And yet…

He rode home and locked his bike in the garage. He mounted the stairs and went up to his room without eating and curled up on the planter cage outside his window. He didn't cry but he wanted to. There was a massive knot in his chest.

After an hour of sheer, ruinous existence, he got up and grabbed the Malcolm X book.

He couldn't see how this Malcolm X had become a leader of any sort. His life was filled with posturing and crime. He lived among prostitutes. He smoked pot, snorted cocaine, took heroin. He tricked people. He stole. As Malcolm X said himself, he hustled. He hustled drugs and gambling bets, card games, and whores. The whores, according to Malcolm X, were black women who did strange things for white men. And white women, even the married ones, he assured the readers, routinely went to Harlem to have sex with Negro men. When Malcolm X ended up in prison, Jude rolled his eyes at the shenanigans Malcolm X had just gone through, shut the book, and climbed back inside.

He sat on his bed and stared dolefully at the bare walls. Bob Dylan's "I Want You" came on the radio, and Jude listened, thinking about Lacey, until the lump formed in his chest again. He clicked it off and for the first time in months, sat in his room in complete silence. Birds were shrieking in the trees.

⌒

THE TALE of the concert had somehow soured by the time Jude could tell it on Monday. He told Kevin and James and the guys at lunch, and then he told Melinda and Greg and pals after school. But all that came out of him was the crappy side of the concert. The dense crowds, Morrison being high, Jimmy getting swatted around, people puking and stumbling, cops everywhere, and Nina getting felt up by a stranger.

James, hearing the litany, kept nodding as though he'd known all along. "Concerts, man," he said, passing judgment on the entire rock culture. Henry said, quietly, "Actually sounds kinda cool." Jude and James exchanged a look: Henry was just immature.

After school, Melinda was watching him talk about the concert as though she were seeing a deeper, truer, and uglier Jude. But he couldn't help himself. Jude just couldn't remember any good parts about the concert.

He felt like they were all watching him, clinically, fatally. Even

Serena. The fleeting moment of light he'd seen in her eyes the week before was extinguished.

Jude sat and watched the hippy kids all leave. He stayed at the school, leaning against the auditorium wall in the hot sun. He felt hollow and stilted. He had no place he wanted to go. Well, he wanted to go to Lacey's, but it was Monday, so between Paulo and Russ, he doubly couldn't. But there was nowhere else he wanted to be. Certainly not home.

He sat and felt the tug of routine. His life was ordered and the ordering alone dragged him from one moment, one encounter, one place to the next. He watched kids climb into cars and wondered what lay down their tunnels of time. Strangers on the street passed on their way from and to. All places he couldn't access, couldn't even imagine. Places they came from. Places they went. People they knew and loved and lived with.

On his bike, the path led simply home. Even when he detoured. Even when he stopped in some odd place, like Barnsdall Park with the odd Aztec-ish structure built there by Frank Lloyd Wright, or climbed the hills to the Griffith Observatory. Sooner or later, he still ended up back at home.

He found Mark playing guitar to a Hendrix record.

"So, what did Jimmy look like today?" he asked.

"Hah," Mark laughed. "He looked worse than you did after you got beat up. His whole face was black and blue." Mark didn't stop playing. He was playing an electric guitar he had somehow acquired after the whole guitar-runaway thing. The guitar was plugged in and turned most of the way down. Mark's guitar carved a clean groove right down into Hendrix's music.

"How come the whole guitar thing with Dad is just…"

Mark bounced his head through a couple bars and chipped out some high, warped notes. "Over?" he asked.

"Yeah, is it?"

"Because Dad's a pussy," he said. "And because if he won't let me play guitar, he knows I'll leave." He played three stunted chords right along with Hendrix, a high fast lick. "For good." Then he said, "And if I leave, Mom will never forgive him," lick, chord, lick, "for being the asshole that he is."

Jude retreated to his room. He had the morning's *Los Angeles Times*, fulfilling Mr. Diaz's directive. He skimmed an article about a civil rights trial that was to start in Mississippi the next day. But, paging through, the paper was one article after another about a disappointing world. It was all bombs, refugee camps, and war. There were people who died. A nun in Saigon had poured gasoline over herself and lit herself on fire. Jude thought it might be to protest the war, but it was, instead, a protest over government treatment of Buddhists.

Students had walked out of Ladybird Johnson's pro-war talk, while at another meeting, President Johnson, her husband, was saying things that Jude thought sounded anti-war. "We can take no pride that we have fought among ourselves like animals. And that is an insult to the animals who live together in more harmony than human beings seem to be able to do."

He did find one article he liked buried in the paper. An elementary school principal in Nocasio, California, Mrs. Garnet E. Brennan, had been suspended after admitting she smoked marijuana every day. Mrs. Brennan was 58, and she'd been smoking "one or two cigarettes in the evening to soothe herself" since 1949. She said marijuana was "not habit-forming" and she used it for "only beneficial results." She was surprised that the school district cared. She said, "The laws are unconstitutional since marijuana is a non-narcotic."

Jude smiled. He felt connected to this story at least. He tried to imagine Ms. Mantle getting high.

But within minutes, he saw Lacey in her men's shirt, her flashing smile, her long bare legs, and his heart had soured again.

He slept fitfully. In the minutes after the alarm sounded in the morning, he slid into a dream. He was a balloon floating up through a dusk-filled sky from a birthday party. When he looked down, Lacey was reaching for the string, and Melinda was pushing her aside, also reaching. Serena stood to one side, watching. There was a pleasure mixed into the loss he felt. Then they were gone and all he could see was the little boy who'd lost the balloon looking up, crying.

JUDE filled a baggy with more pills and rode to school Tuesday morning.

Walking into school, he was bowled into and toppled, the books and papers he was carrying fanning out over the linoleum. When he looked up to see whom he'd run into, Hector and one of his friends were there. Hector held an opened switchblade shining against his shirt. The other students kept moving, forming a dense, slow-moving wall around him on the floor. Hector leaned in. "Next time, mother-fucker, maybe I cut your guts instead a' your shirt."

The friend kicked Jude's hip, hard.

Hector and the friend faded back into the wall of kids.

Jude looked around. Kids cleared him like a traffic island, but they did not go around his papers and books. They walked right over and through them.

Jude rose slowly to his feet. His right hip ached and shot spikes of pain down his leg. He lifted and dropped the leg a couple of times to ease the inflamed joint. Then he bent to his books and papers, gathering them willy-nilly and stuffing them back into his pack.

He exited the scene quickly, but when he got around the corner, he stopped to brush himself off. His finger caught in his shirt. The shirt had a three-inch slice in it, just below the pocket.

In homeroom, he borrowed tape from Ms. Mantle. While she prattled on about some terrible event somewhere, a demonstration at a university back East, he used masking tape to close the sliced fabric from the inside of his shirt.

"It's the rock music," she claimed. "It's as if Ho Chi Minh or Leonid Brezhnev were writing it." Her eyes screwed upward behind her pale blue glasses, and her hands rose and clutched above her breast. "Communism. That's what's to blame! And it's everywhere!"

Several students were staring at her with hard or squinting eyes. They were discovering another enemy in their midst. Communism and rock music? What the fuck *was* this Communism thing?

In social studies, it was immediately apparent that something was up. Mr. Diaz was wearing a black armband and watched with hooded eyes as the students entered.

"Who saw *The Los Angeles Times* this morning?" he asked. "Anyone?"

Jude had glanced at it on the breakfast table, but nothing caught his attention. Two students raised their hands. But Mr. Diaz ignored them. He was too charged-up.

"One of the great—maybe the greatest—revolutionary leaders of the Latino freedom movement was shot and killed yesterday." Diaz stalked the front of the room. Jude thought he actually looked distraught. "Che Guevara… Ernesto 'Che' Guevara," he trailed off, and went to his favorite place to think and speak, the windows.

"Cuba," he said,—he pronounced it *KOO-bah*—"gained its independence from Spain in nineteen oh-two after the Spanish-American War. But, like so many Hispanic countries, Cuba was turned into the equivalent of a slave plantation.

"American companies went in and planted sugar cane. Over half the country's farmland was converted to cane. Wages were kept artificially and extremely low. And to keep it all in place, the United States installed puppet governments that kept the country in poverty, completely subjugated to the United States.

"You've probably all heard of Fidel Castro, the president of Cuba. He led the revolt that removed the puppet government of Fulgencio Batista. That's now. But before that, Castro tried more than once to take over the country in the name of the people, and failed miserably every time.

"After he met Che Guevara, a doctor and a surgeon who had traveled extensively in Latin America, and who had seen first-hand the ravages of nation-states enslaved by the economic giant to their north…" He scowled. "That's us."

He turned to face the class. "After that, Guevara literally wrote the book on guerilla warfare. Using his strategies, Castro's rebels—they were called the M-26-7—were able to invade Cuba and eventually take over the country.

"Guevara stayed for a while and then moved on to lead other rebellions. Yesterday…" Mr. Diaz's eyes traveled to the window, and far outside. "Che Guevara was killed while leading a small army in Bolivia."

The rest of the class, Diaz tapped one country after the next to the south of the United States and listed the export crops, the poverty levels, the puppet government, and the coups that had put them there. American-owned banana, sugarcane and rubber plantations stretched all the way down through Brazil.

Jude listened, but found Diaz's ideas slamming against the walls of reality. Jude learned United States history in Indiana. The country was founded on human rights. It was a perfect system of checks and balances—the executive, the legislative, and the judicial. The President and the Congress and Senate were elected representatives. The country was democratic and functioned within a capitalist system of competitive markets.

But, by the time he left Mr. Diaz's class, Jude was finding a set of ideas pooling into a low spot in his thinking. There was the Vietnam War and the draft. Jude knew nothing about either one really, but his brother said both were evil, and that the draft was designed to keep the wealthy kids out of the war and just send the poor kids.

Next to that idea was another that Mr. Diaz had planted, that racism and poverty were intentionally woven right into the American fabric.

Nearby, but not nestled down in there yet, was his thinking about drugs. He realized the article about Mrs. Brennan, the elementary school principal, and marijuana had surprised him in several ways. The coolness of the incident was skewed by her age—wasn't marijuana the drug of the young? And he wondered about the non-narcotic thing. If marijuana were legal, would it still be cool?

He thought about the sweet fuzzy highs he'd experienced on grass and thought, yes, it would still be cool.

He dropped his books at his locker and headed for lunch. He sat down with Kevin and Robby. Henry and James weren't there yet.

Robby punched Jude in the arm the second he sat down. "Man, I saw you hanging with Melinda and Greg last week, dude! What's going on? I mean, like, what is *that* about?"

"They're, you know," Jude shrugged. "They're actually pretty cool."

"Man, I like that Melinda chick."

"Yeah," Jude agreed.

But the conversation was stalling. They could all see James and Henry coming toward them, the two of them shaking their heads in flamboyantly staged motions of dismissive disgust. They stepped to the center of the area where the boys ate lunch and continued to stand.

James tossed his lunch to a bench and stood shaking his head,

"Jude, oh Jude, oh Jude!" He spread his hands: the world was his evidence. "We drove by yesterday on the way home."

He nodded at Henry and Henry said, nodding, "We drove *by*."

"They're *whores*, Jude." James bounced on the balls of his feet he was so pleased with his news. "They're prostitutes. Your little blonde girlfriend makes her money by *fucking strangers!*" He threw his hands up, shaking his head to rid it of the craziness, and the two of them sat.

"We drove past yesterday, and my Mom, even my *mom* knew," James continued. "We're driving past that apartment building and she's like 'Oh my god, there's a brothel not even a half mile from your school!' My fucking *mother* knew."

James was deeply pleased with himself. But Jude felt like his bones were crumbling inside his chest. The sordid sexual exploits of prostitutes in the Malcolm X book slithered through his mind like an old flickering movie. The soundtrack was broken in his mind. It kept repeating a woman's laugh and something like his father's Dixieland Jazz recordings.

He stared hard at James, his eyes surprisingly dry, and spit out, "I knew that." He stood up and grabbed his lunch bag. "You think I didn't fucking *know* that?"

He fired himself down the path and almost stumbled as he turned the corner. Tears came, and the moments, the people, the words… everything that had ever happened to Jude at the Crestview shot through him at the speed of light, and at the same time, moldered in his mind like slowly developing Polaroid stills. The women, the robes, the late breakfasts, Russ's warnings, Frenchie and the businessman. Duh!

But over and over as he lunged ahead, like Hector's blade slicing his shirt, he came back to making Lacey's bed and the stack of pastel sheets on the back of the couch. He couldn't get the feel of the soft cotton, the cool pastel colors, the number—the sheer number of them—out of his mind. Off his fingers.

And the smell…

Jude ditched English. Jude ditched band. Jude ditched PE. He burrowed back along the wall by the fence where Greg and Melinda would arrive later. He sat in the hot, hot sun, and imagined the light and heat searing-over the wound he felt. He pulled at it with his anger. Stitched it with his determination. Hammered it with the loneliness he felt, cast like a die on the pavement of this strange city.

Then, without warning, other memories flowed: Lacey's neck rising from her robe, her knees drawn up on her couch, the smell of her as he entered her apartment, her kisses on his cheek, and over each memory, the soft bells of her happy laughter.

Every time he thought the wound was closed and he was finally and truly nothing but a hardened soulless figment, she would rise slowly up again, and like her breasts breaking the surface of the water, take everything else away.

He wasn't aware that three classes and two and a half hours had passed. But suddenly, there was Theo, circling him, staring down, his hands out to his sides. More evidence. But this time Jude was the evidence.

"Hey, man," Theo moved without a lift or sway or swagger. His shoulders, buried under long dark hair, slid along level and square. "Are you, like, even moderately okay, dude?"

Jude was hunched over his knees, arms crossed and head down. He shrugged. "Never been better."

"Right…" he sounded doubtful. "You want, ah, like…"

Jude could tell Theo was considering real-world possibilities, like the nurse, a counselor, Jude's mother. Jude pulled away and lifted a hand slightly, as if to ward Theo off.

"Okay, okay," Theo lifted his hands in a sign of surrender. "How about some pot? Or," he spread his hands again, "I have a Nestlé Crunch."

"Yeah," Jude squinted up at Theo. "Let's get stoned."

Theo was always turned out. Today he wore a pair of deep purple bell-bottoms that looked crisp and store-bought. On his feet were black leather boots that looked like something the Beatles would wear back in the day. His shirt was black, collarless, and buttoned like a priest's, and over it he wore an old-fashioned yellow-and-black striped vest. From the vest pocket, he produced a joint and a lighter.

Cindy arrived, and Mike, and then Serena. But Theo and Jude were already deep, or high, or, "Man," Theo grasped Jude's shoulder and giggled, "I think we've left the fucking building, man."

To Jude, there was a pact now forged between himself and Theo, a pact that was hard to concentrate on and keep here in these fleeting instants, but that was physical and real. It had to do with lifting off in some way. Getting higher than high. And it had to happen now. And not just now, but down inside the *now* of the now.

As soon as he thought the idea, Jude knew he was already there. Before now, Jude had never really smoked much. A couple of hits. And then light tugs to brighten the ember if the joints kept coming. But now... he was going to *smoke*.

He saw and talked to Greg and Melinda and the rest. But he could, at any moment, draw his gaze onto Theo and the two of them locked in, swapped the joint, and smoked. And they elevated...

It felt like they were on a merry-go-round that clattered louder and spun faster with each passing minute. It felt like they were descending insanely deep in an ocean and the crush of water squeezed sound and light and brain cells. It felt like...

"Here's the dough, man."

Jude popped to the surface—a surface—and received a small roll of bills from Greg. He was at ninety... about ninety-three degrees from Jude, Jude decided. Melinda was ratcheted into the conversation at one-twenty-four. Or minus fifty-six. Or... He felt like he was being swallowed by a geometry problem.

He found it quite hard to get the baggy of pills out of his pocket. It seemed slippery and distant, and he kept forgetting what it was he wanted to accomplish.

But Greg seemed happy. He was now holding the bag. That seemed right. So Jude shifted his focus to making sure the bills made it into his pocket.

Then something was there like a cross between a semi-truck and thundercloud. Jude stepped away from the intrusion, still trying to push the money deeper into his pocket. He was certain that, whatever else was going on, that pushing this wad deep down would somehow save him. But he couldn't. His hand wouldn't work right. He was high above the earth, pinned, and just below him was a raven-faced man as angry as a swarm of bees.

Jude suddenly fell and felt like he'd been dumped into a stack of disconnected bones and organs. He couldn't move.

He mentally traversed his legs, in their various places; his arms, his torso, and isolated a definite problem. There was a hairy arm hard against his chest, holding him down. Unaccountably, he began to laugh.

But the arm ran right up into the sweaty armpit of a man. It was Paulo's henchman, Blondie, and suddenly Jude was icy clear and awake. Blondie slapped him again.

"Not gonna get away this time, fuckface." He loomed. The entire sky was his unshaven face, waxy flesh, and boiled eyeballs.

"I don't know where the fuck you're getting your shit," his voice was a surprisingly high-pitched rasp. He dangled the bag of pills. "And I don't know how the *fuck* you found the chicks at the Crestview." He reached forward and grasped Jude's shirtfront and pulled until Jude was off the ground. "But I have permission…" He stopped himself, grinned and chuckled. "No, I got instructions to rearange your face if I ever fucking *see* you again."

He thrust Jude back down against the hot pavement and stared down at him.

"This ends now you little fuck!" The man sizzled at him.

Then, Jude heard a jangling noise in his head. But it rang with the exact timbre of pavement. A wave of something dark moved out from the back of his head that he understood was pain, but it didn't register as pain. It was just a growing warmth filled with white-hot needles.

The blond man had dropped him and Jude's head had bounced off the pavement. He lay on his back looking up into Theo's placid face.

Theo helped him up and got him moving. But Jude was confused by his questions. "Are you okay, man?" "Where's your bike?"

Theo was acting as if the old reality were still in place.

Jude humored him. "I feel. I really do." He clambered up slowly, looking for the blond man. He was gone. Jude registered the sound of his bike, shifting through gears and drawing quickly away. Jude walked stiffly toward the gate, Theo staying alongside, one hand on his shoulder, the other against his chest as if Jude were ancient and could barely walk.

Bright pills were scattered over the dusty black asphalt. They sang with urgency, but Jude had trouble focusing, seeing them.

Jude let himself be led to the front of the school, and then, summoning great focus and balance, he made his way across the front lawn with Theo at his elbow. Mr. Glenn, the assistant principal, was on the lawn, talking with a couple parents. There were teachers out and about. Jude lifted his chin and tried to appear completely sober.

They came to the bike racks where four or five other students were unlocking and preparing to ride. Jude stopped, waiting for some of them to clear out. The steel racks looked to him like a massive pincushion, and as dangerous.

But when one kid left, two more would push in, ambling along between rows.

"Which one is yours, man?"

"Theo," Jude said.

"Yeah, man, I'm here. Which bike?"

Jude stood blinking and trying to focus. "It's gone," he said finally.

"You sure?"

Jude pointed. A chain with a blue plastic slipcover was hanging from the third rack in. One of the links had been cut and bent.

Theo went over and plucked the chain off the rack and, as he straightened up, he slowed and then bent back over. He brought the chain back and held it up. "You're sure this is yours?"

Jude reached out and worked through the combination, 32-15-26. It felt like he was spinning the lock face underwater, slowing before each number and creeping up on it, as though it might move if it felt the spin of the dial approaching. Then, surprisingly, the lock snapped open. "Cool, man, I can do the combo."

Theo nodded, waiting. He was closer to Earth than Jude. Practically standing on it, Jude thought.

"Fuck," Jude said, seeing the event take place in his mind. "Fucking Hector."

"My Mom can give you a ride home," Theo steered Jude away from the rack.

"Who the fuck is Paulo," Jude asked.

Theo ignored the question and directed Jude across the grass. "Where do you live?"

Jude reported the address a number at a time, and tagged the street on after like hitching a wagon to a horse.

Theo got Jude to the curb. The new white Mercedes sat in the street out past the parked cars. A woman sat at the wheel with a steep wave of silver- and blonde-streaked hair and sunglasses with lenses the size of drink coasters. She was leaning over peering out at Jude.

"Is he okay?"

"Yeah, he's okay. Someone stole his bike." Theo opened the back door and gave Jude a nudge. Jude didn't move. He was staring at the white, white woman in the white, white car. She was like a cartoon or a mirage. "Can we drop him? He's just up on Normandie."

"Sure, why not?" She blasted Jude with a white smile.

Theo walked Jude to the back door of the car. He said, "Paulo is Greg's step-dad." But it was such an unexpected statement that it entered Jude and made no sense. A scene of Paulo sitting at a dinner table with Greg, the older brother that Jude had heard about, a little sister Jude added from nowhere, a wife/mother, and all lit like a happy family in a Norman Rockwell scene. Paulo was holding a carving knife over a roasted chicken.

Insane.

Theo closed the door after Jude and got in the front. Jude looked at the seat next to him. Serena was sitting there. She looked worried to have Jude in the seat next to her.

He started a shrug but gave up on it halfway through.

Her eyebrows lifted in doubt, but she said, "Bike got stole, huh?"

There was something soft in her voice that brought Jude close to tears. He looked out the window at the cascade of students over the school's front lawn and bit his lip.

They pulled from the curb and Jude wiped a hand hard over his face to pull away the cobwebs of fear and defeat and sadness. He let his eyes wander in the car. It smelled like something royal. The seats were a creamy white-and-brown leather. Chrome and wood studded the doors and seat backs. But the smell…

He followed the smell. Soon it made him feel like he was flying, a fly-tiny speck in the vast space of the cockpit, seeing the amazing detail, the craft, the luxury.

"Awesome car," he said in his best fly voice.

He turned to Serena, "Are you Theo's sister? Or, or, like, his girlfriend?"

Theo, his mother, and Serena all laughed.

"No," she smiled at him. "And no."

"Okay," Jude settled back in the seat, feeling deeply proud that all the big questions had at least been raised. And answered. That was important.

He tried to look outside but it was too bright. He closed his eyes. Exactly how high was he?

He felt the seat flex down and wrap to touch his back shoulder-to-shoulder and butt-to-neck. It was cool and sweet. The smell oozed up and around him again.

Then he realized there was something else loose, hanging, treacherous somehow. He stared over at Serena, puzzling. His memory had something, but his tongue couldn't get the shape of it.

She met his gaze, easily. "What?" she said.

It was there. "So, what are you doing in Theo's mom's car then?"

She laughed again. "I live down the street from Theo."

"Oh. Of course you do." He settled back once more but was up almost at once. He twisted back to Serena and feeling more serious than perhaps ever, he asked, "Are we moving?"

Serena reached out, put her hand behind his neck, and pulled Jude's head down into her lap. "Lie down," she said. "Rest."

Jude closed his eyes again and quietly and perfectly entered some sort of heaven made of the smell of her and the feel. His face was lying on her thigh. Her fingers worked slowly, maybe even absently, in his hair. But it was like being massaged by the planet itself.

When he was exactly six galaxies deep, as light and airless as a wish, Serena gently tugged his hair. "This your house?"

Jude squinted out through the glass at the house up the hill. "Yeah."

"Okay, you make it up the stairs okay?"

"Can't I just stay with you?" Jude asked.

Serena pursed her lips as though she were considering it. But she pulled his hair again, "No."

Jude sat up, gathered his backpack, and clumsily clambered out. Outside the perfectly conditioned air of the car, the day settled over him like a blanket fresh from the dryer.

Jude crossed the street and waved at the car from the stairs. It glided off silently.

Serena's gaze remained ahead. She didn't turn. She didn't look back at him.

ten

SATURDAY MORNING FINALLY CAME. JUDE HAD ditched school on Wednesday and Thursday and claimed illness on Friday. He was wallowing in a misery that was deeper than his guilt and fear about missing school.

It was weird, in fact. He felt like the guilt and fear had less to do with the school and his classes than it did his new friends and even his teachers.

He lay on his back after he woke and thought about the one ray of hope there had been. But it was a false hope, he knew. The dream that was Serena was like the basketball hoops at the county fairs back in Indiana. From head-on, they looked real enough, but step to the side and you could see they were flattened ovals that barely fit a ball. He could shoot all night and never hit a shot.

Before he'd even crawled out to pee in the morning, Jude looked up from his bed to find Mark standing over him.

"So what the fuck is going on with you?" he asked.

Jude shrugged and squinted at him. He felt like a fish at the bottom of an aquarium. Mark rarely came in his room, and more rarely had any interest in his life. But... not a fish. A person. A person under water.

"Mom says you got your bike stolen."

"That's, like, normal in L.A.," Jude said.

"Normal until it's you," he said.

"Maybe."

"You selling the pills?"

Jude shrugged again.

"It's creepy," Mark said. "I knew everything about you in Indiana. 'Cause everything you did, every teacher you had, everywhere you went... I'd already been there. I knew all your friends' older brothers and sisters." He walked past Jude's bed and sat in the desk chair.

"Now," he shook his head, "I don't know fuck-all about you."

Jude sat up. Yawned. A month ago, even five days ago, he would have nearly swooned to get his brother in his room, much less for him to have some interest in Jude's existence.

"Like I know anything about you," Jude said.

"Yeah, well, you've never known anything about me."

Jude shrugged. That was sort of true.

"So what the fuck is it like at LeConte?"

"If I knew," Jude rolled his eyes around his room, "I'd tell you."

"You know something."

"I know I don't know shit," Jude flounced back down. Then it started like air pushed from a balloon. "I don't know. It's like I hated the hippies when we got here. But now they're sort of my friends. This one girl, Melinda—she has a boyfriend, Greg—but she's nice to me. She said she liked my assignment in English.

"And Greg is cool. He buys the pills mostly, but he's pretty crazy just generally and I hang out with them. And there's this girl, Serena I like that's there.

"But mostly, there's this woman, the one that bandaged me up on the way home after I got beat up. Her name's Lacey. And she's older, but I think she needs help. There's this fucker who bugs her, and it turns out to be Greg's—the hippy Greg—it's his step-father. Guy named Paulo, and he's a fucker—a Hell's Angel—who is almost always there and mean and, I don't know."

"Whoa," Mark nodded appreciatively at the outburst. "What happened to the Kevin kid that you hung around with?"

"Yeah, I still hang out with them at lunch, but..."

"But what?"

"They're calling Lacey a… a… I don't know. They're saying she's a prostitute."

"Whoa, dude, is she?"

"Maybe," Jude admitted. "I guess so." He shot it out nonchalantly. But at once, his face scrunched and tears welled. "Fuck," he said.

Mark was practically bouncing on the desk chair. "No, man, that's so cool! My little brother, hanging out with prostitutes!"

"Yeah, maybe." Jude rolled away and stared at the bathroom door. "I gotta get ready for school, man." He didn't, there was time, but he knew the mention of school would clear Mark out.

"Cool, dude. You're gonna have to take me by there. I gotta see this!"

When Mark left the room, Jude pulled his knees up tight to his chest and held them there. The pressure seemed to stem the quavering that fluttered just below his breastbone. He glowered at his walls.

In the last few days, ever since the Doors concert, he'd been lifting concert posters from telephone poles and bulletin boards. The Doors at Cal State was there. A ragged one for the Monkees at the Hollywood Bowl from last summer that he'd discovered on a telephone pole under several archeological eras of more recent posters. An upcoming concert by the Who. A Jimi Hendrix poster. With each poster, with each removal and transporting, with each careful tacking to the walls, Jude felt he was remaking himself, slowly but surely, into someone Melinda and Greg would find cool, and that maybe even Lacey would admire. That maybe one day, he would like, too.

A raw folk song came on the radio.

The stories of the street are mine, the Spanish voices laugh
The Cadillacs go creeping now through the night and the
*   poison gas*
And I lean from my windowsill in this old hotel I chose
Yes, one hand on my suicide, one hand on the rose.

To Jude, it felt like that, suicide and a rose. As if there might be some choice he could make, and the options were that far apart. Right now, the rose was far in the distance, out of sight behind hurricane fences and frosted glass.

TIME kept on stumbling. Feeling like he had no place and no direction, Jude felt ostracized, excommunicated, truly outside. He felt he was a moth again, battering again against the glass of windows, lantern shades, light bulbs. The glass was age, friends, knowledge. He couldn't find a way through. And he wasn't sure anymore what light he wanted to reach.

Jude felt a visceral spiral in his chest and gut. It was a roller coaster, the centrifugal force of descent as powerful as the weight and velocity of a thousand pounds of steel running down a coiled carnival ride. But it wasn't thrilling. It was sickening. It was an acceleration into fear and fate, into the mud of being. Into the sewage of living.

He lay in the emptiness of his room after dinner. The night and the weekend stretched out ahead into a horizonless plain. His brother was out at Jimmy's. His parents were watching television and punishing the vodka bottle.

Jude felt nothing but left out and unwanted.

He took a notepad out onto the window cage. The night was warm and nearly windless. The city smelled hot and dry. The lights below flickered in the heat, like the stars above. He set the nib of the pen on the paper and waited.

> Everything is either in or out. And the lines between them. See someone you've never seen before, and you know right then, in, or out. Crazy lady on the corner, talking to the yellowing teeth she's holding in her hand—out. Black kids on the bus watching me like they're waiting for the kill—out. Pretty girl, my age maybe, a pony tail—in. I wish.
>
> You don't have any clue who you are until you see yourself from their eyes. That's not so hard to read. The pretty girl would see me—did see me—and lowered her eyes. Not batting her eyelashes but pretending I didn't exist. The black guys. An old man and his kids. The crazy lady. They would all see me and look right on through.

Jude uncoiled from his bent-over writing pose and leaned back against the cage. "So fucking what?" he asked the evening air. "So fucking what?"

There was a sliver of a thought. More of a fantasy, really. He saw the pretty girl look down in his mind's eye and saw the thing that was himself get up and sit down beside her. "Hey, how'ya doin? I'm Jude."

It seemed so simple. To just enter the world. To just... As if... As if he were part of it.

At that moment, Jude could see all the way down his life. It was the same dismal shuffle as it was to climb on an RTD bus and head for the back. His shoulders were turned at an angle to avoid bumping into anyone. His eyes scanning for a safe place to sit, to be. But there was never a safe space. Never a welcoming.

He was a true outsider.

He lifted the paper and tore it away from the spiral steel cord that held the notebook together. Then he let it drop. It shot downward, slicing most of the way down before it caught the air and suddenly swooped, wild and fast, out over the ivy. In a couple of confused rustlings, the paper tumbled along the top of the ivy leaves for a moment, and then rattled loudly and flopped, already wet, on the ivy.

He climbed back inside and stood there a long time. He was as close to the only 'in' he had in the world—his bedroom—and he still felt outside. Not just unwanted, but unseen, unknown. Non-existent.

There was no way in. Nowhere to even try or start. He was...

The word that rose up in him was *nothing*. Nothing. Nothing. Nothing. And everyone seemed just fine with that. Even his parents.

He crossed to his bed and opened the drawer by his bedside. On the sheet by his pillow, so he could cover up if anyone came to his door, he spread his collection of pills. He sorted them by color and made a loosely organized American flag in red-and-yellow, white and blue.

He mulled the colors, the sizes, the expressive potency of the pills. He had pulled them out with some notion that he might just take them, all of them, at once. He could finish the charade of son, brother, student. He had no friends. That was just a simple truth. For the people he cared about, he was peripheral at best. For the people he wanted to avoid or exorcise from his life, he was expendable himself.

He boiled it down over and over. It was a simple accounting that remained the same regardless of how many times he reworked it. He was a dweeb from Indiana. His hair was short and cut funny. His clothes were practically fresh out of a corn field. So there was that. Then there were the social barriers. He didn't know these people, and they didn't know him. They said and did strange things. And though he was doing his best to say and do those things too, he didn't. And the people he felt were looking out for him a bit, Kevin and Ms. Loral, seemed completely hopeless. They weren't going to help him.

He could just go to sleep. He could see his relaxed form on the bed, fully and finally finished.

But an electric fear bubbled in him.

He could hear the weeping. Only his mother would probably cry. If anyone. He thought about the shock and surprise at school. "He was such a well-adjusted young man. He had everything to live for."

Serena's eyes would fill with tears. But would they really?

He knew his father downed three or four Valiums every night. So he collected a small handful of the Valium, most of the blue part of his flag, and scooped the rest back into the drawer. He looked into his palm. Ten of the little blue pills rolled about.

Then Jude stripped, went in the bathroom and turned on the radio, and started a hot bath. He poured a glass of water from the sink. He downed the pills and then he stood looking down into the tub. He decided he didn't want to be naked, so he retreated to his bedroom and pulled on his swim trunks.

Then he slipped back into the bathroom and slid down into the tub.

"I'm a Believer" by the Monkees closed out and the DJ announced a song sung by Erma Franklin. A bumpy, dark song came on. *"Take another little piece of my heart now baby!"*

Jude sank into the song and felt his body accepting the hot water of the bath. He remembered hearing "Kind of a Drag," "Incense and Peppermints," and "Somebody to Love." He remembered crying. The tears flowed from his center, whatever that was, and streamed down his face, feeding the bathwater. And then they oozed back into his body, making the cycle endless, timeless.

He didn't remember Mark draining the tub and pouring cold water over him to wake him up and get him out.

Mark told him later that he'd come home and heard Jude sputtering in the water. Not sputtering, actually. But that would do. Mark had called out. He'd knocked. He'd finally just come in, and Jude was half under the water, eyes rolled back white as marshmallows.

Jude only remembered waking up in his bed in the raw light of day and rushing to the bathroom to puke into the toilet. Afterward his legs and arms felt like warm Red Vine licorice sticks that had been left on a sunny sidewalk, and his stomach would not settle.

He spent the entire day under waves of nausea, his tongue rising in his throat like a turd that would not flush, his head filled with a battering, angry, army of swollen pain.

WITH NO BIKE to ride, he took the bus in Monday morning, walking the last blocks to school. It felt like he was approaching his fate. The best thing he could find to do with himself, and he realized he'd been practicing it all weekend, was to cease caring.

But one thing he could do…

After homeroom, he went out to the bike racks and scoured them for a sign of his bike. It was like hunting for one noodle in a tangle of cooked noodles. There were a couple hundred bikes and the shapes they took and the colors made it all an indistinguishable mass.

He started at one corner and walked down along the row. Like a farmer sowing a field, he turned around at the end of the row. Three rows in, toward the back of the racks, he saw a bike that looked like his, but it was black. It had the same Schwinn seat on it, the same bent tire with the missing spoke. He pushed his way to the bike and stood over it. It was his.

Jude looked around him. No one about. He bent and touched the frame. The paint was sticky.

He lifted the lock and looked at it. It was a decent-sized steel chain locked together with a standard Master combo lock.

Jude scanned the area again and then knelt down. He set his backpack down and pulled out the short-handled sledge he'd taken from his father's tool bench that morning.

Then, propping the lock just so against the edge of the bike rack itself, Jude lifted the sledge and fired a blow at the side of the lock. The impact rang out through the metal rack and the lock carromed away, smacking into the spokes of his bike.

He pulled the lock back over and saw that he'd managed to dent it.

The bell rang announcing the start of second period. Jude ignored it and set up the lock again. He lifted himself slightly to peer over the bikes at the school. There were two kids coming toward the racks. This time, he let the sledge fall hard like it was his last and only chance.

The lock shot back into the spokes, but this time in two pieces. The hardened steel shaft skittered along the pavement.

He loaded the sledge back into his pack and then stood and pulled the bike out from the rack. He walked it out to the front of the racks, and locked his bike up with a new, more impregnable, Master lock and a big new cable.

Jude stood, sighed, and headed for math class.

The rest of his day lumbered at him like the dark tunnel he knew it to be.

Mr. Diaz was absent and the sub, a dried-out husk of a woman in her forties maybe, and wearing a severe blue dress suit and crisp white, long-sleeved blouse, told them to read twenty pages in the book. Frank, the black kid, stood up, pulled his things together, and left. The teacher, Miss Fletcher, asked Bonnie Argyle in the front row, "Who was that young man?"

"Um, who? I didn't see him. I was reading."

"Who was the Negro boy who just left this room?" she demanded of the whole room at once.

A kid in the first row by the door, Jude knew him only as Red, said, "Joe Kendricks."

"Joe Kendricks," she repeated and turned to her class role. "I don't see a Joe Kendricks on this list," she said.

"Yeah, he's a new kid," Red said.

The teacher scribbled the name on her ledger and pinched her lips at the closed doorway where Frank had left.

Jude sat there wanting badly to get up and leave also, but he couldn't muster the courage, and after fifteen minutes of inner turmoil, he gave up on himself. Now, it would be too embarrassing and stupid to get up and leave, and the other kids would just say 'Jude Tangier' when the biddy asked his name.

At lunchtime, James had it in for him, calling him a whore-lover, and so Jude left the group again—maybe for the last time, he told himself—and ate his lunch alone.

In English, Melinda seemed to ignore him. He couldn't be sure. He sat in his normal spot in the left bank of desks. She sat to the rear on the right. Ms. Loral was talking about what a great book *Charlotte's Web* was. Maybe so, Jude thought, but it was a kid's book. He'd read it in third grade.

In band, distracted, he didn't hear Mr. Denny barking at him. Denny was always barking. But rarely at Jude. Jude did what he could to keep up, just enough to avoid getting a baton or music book thrown at him.

But this time, Jude jerked backward in his seat and nearly toppled into the trombones as his trumpet sang in his hands and a loud ping rang out. Mr. Denny's baton went sailing.

"Mr. Tan*gier*!"

Jude blinked and stared wide-eyed at Mr. Denny.

"We're playing 'Hungarian Dance,' not 'Semper Fidelis!'" Denny stood as tall as he could muster up on his raised conductor's stand and stared at Jude.

Jude unconsciously turned his head slightly one side, unwittingly signaling that he had no idea what Denny was talking about. The words 'Hungarian Dance' and 'Semper Fidelis' sounded strange to him, though he'd heard them both fifty or more times by now.

But Denny saw the movement and clamped his lips tight. Then he slapped his own music stand aside and barreled through the other kids in their chairs so fast that all Jude could do was watch him in stunned silence.

Jude saw the meaty paw of the man lifted, open and high, and then the back of Denny's hand slammed into the side of Jude's head, knocking him over. His trumpet flew and rattled, while Jude flailed down into the spit stains where the trombone players emptied their horns on the concrete floor behind his chair.

Denny shot past him and scrabbling loudly, recovered his baton.

He thundered back past Jude, and snarled, "You, Mr. Tangier, you need to toe the line!" Then he mounted his stand and said in a quiet but quivering voice, "Where were we now?"

Jude stayed where he was for a long minute. Then, as the music began again, he stood, grasped his trumpet, and edged down the row past the other trumpets. He took his trumpet to the back of the room, set it in its case, and clipped it shut.

Then, hauling the awkward case, he walked out of the band room without looking at Mr. Denny.

⌐

"SO, you wanna *walk* home?"

Melinda and Greg had left already, climbing into Paulo's truck. But Theo was there, sleepy-eyed and pale, a quiet smile that never wavered.

Jude reared back, his face registering surprise. "Walk?"

"Yeah, you know," Serena scissored her fingers in the air. "Walk."

"Um," Jude laid out the long city blocks, end-to-end, in his head. To her house and then back to his… It was going to be three miles or more.

Jude looked at Theo. "With Theo?"

"Of course with Theo. You want him to walk home alone?"

"Ah…"

"Besides," her smile, close and warm, broke over him like a wave, "we need a chaperone, don't you think?"

Well, wow. The entire time he would be with Serena, a beautiful and intriguing girl, and supposedly Theo was just a third wheel. "Okay, well, sure," he said.

Serena scrunched her face at him. "There's no hurry, right? I mean, we've got all afternoon."

"Right!"

Jude diverted them through the halls of the school and crammed his backpack into his locker next to his trumpet. His trumpet could fucking rot. His homework could fucking wait. And his bike… He thought of it out there, covered in tacky black paint. Well, it could just fucking stay here.

"Crazy, right?" she said, as they popped out of the crowd of kids on the front lawn and started up Bronson.

"Crazy?"

"I mean, kids. I mean, us. I mean, school. I mean, people. Like," she spun once and her dark hair formed a lustrous dark cloud around her. "Like human people."

"Yeah, well, when you put it like that."

Serena laughed. She tugged at Theo's sleeve. Theo was sailing along behind them like a helium balloon. He was cheerful and mute.

She nudged up against Jude's shoulder and said, "Well, at least you're funny."

Jude felt himself blush. What did that mean? 'At least?' "Are you... I mean, is someone, like, making you do this?"

"Do what?"

"Um, walk home with me?"

"Jeez, Mr. Jude," she pushed his shoulder, "don't take everything so serious!"

At Sunset, they crossed over and Serena led them into The Phosphorescent Psychedelic. It was a head shop. Jude had looked through the front windows of the shop ever since he'd started at LeConte. He hadn't realized it, but he thought of it like he might a cigar store, or Frederick's of Hollywood: off-limits.

But here he was, parting a bead curtain and ducking in. The Rolling Stones' "Out of Time" was filling the shop. Jude smiled at the thought of Ms. Mantle stepping in here, and finding the music of Ho Chi Minh "everywhere."

Serena nodded at the guy behind the counter, and said "Hey, Charlie."

"Hey, Serena," he said, "what's up?" He gave the paper he was reading a snap and turned the page. It was the *Los Angeles Free Press*.

"Not much. This is Jude."

"Hey," Jude said.

"Hey," Charlie said. Then he said, "Hey Theophilus," and snapped the paper again.

The shop was much cooler than the blazing heat outside. The space extended in near-dark deep into the building. Glass cases lined both sides. These were lit from within and provided the main light source in the room. They were cluttered with pipes of all descriptions, little metal roach clips, leather and beaded necklaces and ankle bracelets, decals, incense, and one whole case dedicated to rolling papers.

Posted on the top of every glass case was a hand-inked sign stating either FOR TOBACCO USE ONLY or NOT FOR USE WITH ILLEGAL SUBSTANCES."

Shelves on the walls held larger pipes and candles, gauzy fabrics, hats, woven bags. And everywhere the walls were exposed, posters filled the spaces. Black light bulbs glowed from the ceiling and set the colors in the posters alive, the reds and greens and yellows urgent against the black backgrounds.

In a display case near the back were three big glass devices like he'd seen in Penny's apartment. They were like a vase that had been bred with a massive spider. A sign beneath read HOOKAHS.

A poster display unit hung from the wall in the back, a big metal contraption that paged like a massive book. Across from that was a cabinet full of LPs. The sign above it read PSYCHEDELIC MUSIC.

Theo crossed the room to the LPs and began fingering through them.

"Come on," Serena led Jude toward the back where they passed through another beaded curtain. A sign on the wall beside the curtain said NO ONE UNDER 18 ALLOWED.

Serena ignored the sign.

This room had a single glass case. Behind that case sat another young man. He had long straggly hair and a beard tied into knots with beads all framing a narrow, serious, and off-color, almost yellow, face. He glanced up from his book, "Heeey, Saa Reee Na!"

This space was completely papered with posters, pinned to the walls at all angles. At either side were booths with dark curtains.

"Hey," Serena responded. She went straight to the case and leaned on it. "You're still here."

The young man smiled up at her, "Yeah, hippies are dead. Long live the hippy."

"Unbelievable, right?" she said. Jude watched her ease with the man. It showed in her fluid posture against the case, the flip of her hair out of her eyes, her unhurried conversation.

"Well…" The man rolled his head back and searched the ceiling, also completely papered with posters, "it's different there."

"Oh hey, Bongo," she turned to Jude, "this is Jude." And to Jude, "The first head shop ever, the Psychedelic Shop, in the Haight—you know where that is?"

Jude nodded. "Yeah, the Haight, I do."

"Well, they had this head shop there, and they shut down and gave away all their shit. But it was part of this big celebration thing they called the Death of the Hippy. It like happened, like I don't know, last month."

"Yeah, well," Bongo said. He set his book face-down on the glass. Jude scanned the title, *Yoga: Immortality and Freedom* by some strange name. Bongo's hands and fingers were long and graceful with each knuckle and joint pronounced so that they looked almost alien.

"So you're not going to march on City Hall and burn an effigy?" she asked him.

"No man," Bongo was concentrating on something in a drawer that Jude couldn't see. "See, that, the Haight thing, that was runaways and drugs, man. That was like, you had the purists, you know, the real hippies, you know, and all this freeing of the mind, and this whole, you know, deconstruction of the… like the…" Bongo set a tiny trans-lucent envelope on the counter and shoved it at Serena.

"Like the whole fucking culture, you know?" Bongo was back on track. "And it just fucking magnetized, and pretty soon you had half the fucking runaways in the country coming in, so it's this kid element," his eyes shot up to Serena. "I mean, no offense, but you're no runaway."

"I like to work from within the system," she smiled at him, the envelope held crisply between two fingers.

"So yeah, and then the vultures descended, man. I wouldn't have believed it if I hadn't been there myself. The whole Haight, man, is just fucking drugs and squalor, man, drugs and fucking squalor."

Serena tipped something from the envelope onto her tongue and then rolled it back into her mouth. She held out another one on her finger to Jude. It was a tiny little pyramidal thing. It looked like green plastic.

Jude opened his mouth and she stuck it on his tongue. Bongo watching them, was nodding, his long, articulated fingers tugging at his beard, one beaded strand at a time, as though he were counting them.

"So yeah, man, they held the wake like a couple weeks ago. But here in L.A.…." His voice rang with disappointment. "Hippies are scattered. They have no place, you know, and so they have no voice. And no—fucking hell, my brain—no vision, right?"

"Right," Serena said. "Well, I'm glad you're here Bongo."

He smiled beatifically. "Hey, you know what?"

"What?"

"Me too. You know? Me too."

"All right," Serena faced Jude. "Grab a booth and I'll be right there."

"Um," Jude stared at her. He was at sea. He had no idea what to do in the booths.

She saw his fear and patted him on the chest. "Don't worry. You'll figure it out."

Jude walked off toward the booths and turned to look back. Serena and the Bongo guy were opening a door into a back room.

He ducked his head and stepped into the nearest booth. Inside, the booth was papered with posters like the walls of the room outside. A black light pulled the colors out. Two big bean bag chairs in dark colors lay on the floor filling most of the space. In the back corner a stereo console glowed with four sets of headphones hung on two wooden pegs poking from the side of the console. A collection of twenty or so LPs were stacked below it.

He went to the records and flipped through quickly.

The first record he recognized was a Byrds record, *Fifth Dimension*. He shrugged and grabbed a pair of headphones. They were ratty, the vinyl at the ears cracked and dirty. But that was what was there, and so he pulled them on. He queued up the record and slumped down in a bean bag.

Jude's mind was wandering up the sunlit sidewalks that took them closer to home. He was with Serena. It was what he had expected. Serena was beautiful. Interesting. She smelled so good, like sun-warmed flowers and cinnamon. And she seemed to know exactly who Jude was. She knew how to talk to him. How to make him do things, and talk, and even laugh.

He suddenly realized he was deep inside a poster. It was the sole black-and-white poster in the space. It was an aqueduct that flowed down along a brick causeway and among ornate pillars. At its end was a waterfall that plunged back impossibly to the beginning of the stream.

Then the music hopped and "Mr. Spaceman" was on and Jude was smiling. He closed his eyes and soared out into space, feeling completely untethered from the booth, the head shop, even Los Angeles.

Where was Serena?

Then she was there. She was stacking another record onto the turntable.

She flopped down beside him in the same chair. The heat of her hip and leg against his blasted a fire in him. He lay there and stared at her. She lay with her head thrown back and her eyes closed. Her soft lips were parted and she seemed to be drinking the music in through every pore.

"Eight Miles High" came on and the guitar solo slithered through him, aimlessly. He was determined to have a thought, and it was this: He was high. He was higher than high. Maybe eight-and-a-half miles.

The music was entering and weaving through the posters above him. It emerged in shapes and new colors. He could move right inside the music and travel with it. He sailed down highways on a motorcycle, feeling himself deep-chested, masculine, a force. He swam along the endless river, endlessly pouring back into himself. He slipped inside a Beatles poster and found himself curled on a couch against... he looked up behind him. He swam in Serena's warm eyes. He smelled what he imagined was Norwegian wood.

A song played that was driving and repetitive. It sounded to Jude like they were singing right to him: *"Don't ride the music, baby, don't ride the music."* It felt like they knew what he had been doing, and it had been forbidden. Or maybe... there was just a better way.

But then the record player clacked and clattered and a new disc spun. Crunchy chords bulged and he knew it was "Purple Haze." He felt his brain reweaving itself, casting off all sorts of strange ideas and ways of thinking, and seeing new ones and new realities. It was as if the skin of the world had been peeled back and he could now see... what? The obvious?

It seemed like five days later that Serena took him by the hand and pulled him upward.

"Bye!" she called out to Bongo.

"Hey, come back anytime, baby," he said.

She grinned at him.

Jude tried to say something but couldn't tell what came out of his mouth.

Serena pulled him through the outer shop, clutching at Theo as she passed him. Jude stopped and dragged against her pull. "Hey, wait," he said.

"Whaaaat?" she was exasperated. "I'm dying here! Let's get some aaaaiiiir!"

"Just a sec," Jude held his ground. "What," he pointed, "are," then threw open his hand, "those?"

"Oh," she relented. If she could educate the yokel... "Those are hookahs."

"I can *read*," he explained to her.

"You smoke pot in them, hashish, you know. They're like party bongs." Theo smiled up at them blissfully.

Then she was done with the lesson, and he was yanked bodily out into what felt like a solar flare. Cars flicked past alight with bright chromatic reflections. Drivers bared their teeth and scrunched their noses at Jude like ferrets, their venomous gazes caught in the warp of time and slowed to a crawl just so he could observe, see their greedy, swollen path. People were such... such...

"Animals!" he said aloud.

"I know, right?" Serena steered Jude east down Sunset. Theo was bumbling along with them, hardly aware. He *looked* stoned. Jude wondered what the three of them must have looked like out here on Sunset Boulevard at three in the afternoon.

Serena...

He watched her move down the sidewalk ahead of him. She was a point of light, a creature of mystery and beauty, a myth, a vision. She was so sexy and fun and certain. Jude found himself laughing and jogging to catch up to her.

They stopped on the bridge over the freeway and watched the great course of concrete plumbing at work draining, draining, draining. People fired by convictions only they themselves could perceive, but which now Jude could see, not in content, but in something more powerful: the human rubric.

The word hung inside him, rubric. He understood it, and it had a shape, like Escher's self-feeding waterfall, but he couldn't remember where the word had come from.

"I made it up," he said aloud, both as a conviction and an awareness.

"Made up what?" Serena pulled him east again.

"Rubric."

"Awesome. I always wondered who made up that word."

"We…" Jude was slicing deeper into his insights as though his attention were a blade designed for exactly this. "We. Invent. Every. Single. Word."

Theo nodded at his shoulder, his eyes passing into and through everything.

"No. Really?" Serena was ahead, pulling at him like a child leading him to a candy store.

"Every word we speak," Jude said, "is made right on the fucking *spot*."

"Right on. So how come I know what you mean?"

Jude saw it as clearly as the layer of smog over the city. "You have to see it," he told her. "Words are a thin little layer over us. Over everything we do. We think they make us not animals. Every single thing we say is that, man."

"Is what?"

"So groovy," Theo said.

"I am not an animal," Jude answered.

"I am not an animal!" Serena screamed to the sky, her whole body giving in to the call. Jude was suddenly restored to himself, whatever that was, wherever it had been, and he felt the flush of embarrassment. But Serena rounded him off in front of a large plate glass window and his attention slipped out again.

This was her candy store.

Jude turned to look. Before him was a deep red car. A sleek, low Alfa Romeo two-seater. It shone from the inside out and had a wide-eyed, eager innocence about it. It took some time for his eyes to reach out from the chrome medallion, the low dense black grill, and the sweeping curves of the fenders to include the whole car. Then it was inside him, whole and complete.

"Oh my god," he reeled back, "I'm stuffed!"

Serena laughed and pulled him away. But then she was holding him close and peering at him. "So, what the fuck is going on with your face?"

The shiner was gone. Jude had no idea what she was talking about. He turned back to the glass and stared at himself. He looked strangely stringy and hollow. He couldn't see his face in any detail.

Serena touched his right ear and he felt the burn. The memory of Mr. Denny's blow to his head returned. "Oh, that," he said. "Mr. Denny hit me."

"Holy shit," she grinned, "the band teacher? For a pale-ass weasel of a kid from Indiana, you get in front of some weird shit."

"Pale-ass weasel of a kid," he said.

Theo echoed the sentiment, "Pale-ass weasel!" He wove his fingers through the air in front of his face. "But that's *me*," he proclaimed. "I'm the palest of the pale-assed weasels around!"

Serena locked her eyes on Jude's. "You know what I mean!" She clutched his arm tight against her and guided them on down the sidewalk. He could feel her breast. He could feel himself flowing out through his arm and into her breast. He could feel her lying naked against him.

He was expecting to walk her to her door, but instead they walked him to his. His brain was still slicing and looping and flying and crawling. He could see that both Theo's and Serena's eyes were dilated dark pits. He stopped on the sidewalk below the house.

"I can't go in like this," he said.

"Hey," she said, grasping his shoulders. "It's literally no big."

"Serena, I can't pull this off," he said. "I'm soooo high!"

"Yes you can," her voice was bright, cheerful.

"Stay with me?" he asked.

"I gotta get home."

"What did we take, anyway? Was that like, LSD?"

"I knew you were smart. Almost exactly like it." Behind her, Theo opened his arms and turned his eyes toward the sky. Manna was falling into his arms. Jude could see it. Packets of liquid blue sky wrapped in golden auras. Theo was letting it fall over him, his face turned up into it, blissful. But to Jude, it felt like a pounding rain.

"Okay, so what do I do?"

Serena smiled at him. She raised her hand and placed it on his chest. Then she leaned in and kissed him on the cheek. "I guarantee," she said, "you'll figure it out."

Jude watched her walk up the street, tugging Theo now. She was aware, he could tell, that he was watching her.

At the corner, she turned and waved. He waved back.

He stood on the sidewalk for a long moment. Outside the rain of manna, or light, or alien snot bubbles, or whatever it was, there was something else. Something floated in his mind like black stepping stones. They, too, were slippery with a golden aura. But they led somewhere.

He stared at the things that were not really there, not understanding. He knew he was at the end of them, and that he could not touch even one of the stones.

A car swept past, the swish of air and the grind of engine snapped through his haze.

He was where the stones led. He was the destination.

Then he suddenly sighted down the length of them and saw: Serena had asked him to walk home with them. She'd said Theo was their chaperone. She'd introduced him to her friends at the head shop. She'd given him LSD. She'd kissed him.

It was as straight a line as could be. Black dot after black dot. It was like pouring electric coffee in his veins. He felt, in that moment, as solid and real as he had ever felt in his life. He had a girlfriend.

JUDE needn't have worried.

His mother was leaving as he came in. She was wearing a dress which she hardly ever did unless she was going to a dinner, and hauling her expedition purse, the large white one that could hold a book, a couple magazines and her knitting.

"Aren't you late?" she asked as she swept past him.

"I walked home," he said.

"Why didn't you take the bus?"

"I didn't feel like it," he said. But then his mind spiked with fear. Did that sound too casual? Too vague? He blurted out, "I just wanted to walk."

"Well," she was standing on the front porch now, the hot sunlight casting a glowing and flowing halo over her that Jude could watch but not enter.

"I don't know when I'll be back," she was saying. "I put dinner in the refrigerator with instructions for heating it up." She raised her eyebrows, "Are you capable of doing that? Heating up the dinner?"

"Probably," he said. "Where are you going?"

Jude could feel the distance between them. It sat there like a desk or counter-top that neither of them quite approached or touched. It was always there, always had been, but never a separate, labelled thing like this. Like the black man in the pawn shop, everything was a negotiation, and one with the chance of losing out, of disappointment.

He found himself circling back through his memories again, memories that lay like brightly lit shop windows where stiffly acted vignettes were played out, all down a dark street, one-by-one into a past that slipped, after twenty or so windows, around a corner.

He knew what he was looking for, and he peered into the memories as he passed them. He wanted to find the last time his mother had hugged him. As he slid past the windows, he kept seeing moments when he could have anticipated that she might have hugged him—when she learned Hector had beat him up, his first day at LeConte—but in which, without even a glance into the window of time, he knew she didn't.

He was quickly out of Los Angeles and looking into windows of moments in Indiana.

But, he was pulled out of his reverie by his mother snatching at his shoulder. "Jude? Are you okay?" She was leaning in, peering closely at his eyes now.

He was sure his pupils were vacuous and black like Theo's and Serena's had been.

He looked away. "I'm fine," he said. "Just thinking, you know, homework and trumpet and, you know, figuring out when I should do the dinner thing."

Her hand fell away. "You can do your homework while the food is in the oven. But put the timer on. And stay where you can hear it."

"Right," he said. "Is Mark here?"

"Mark is at Jimmy's house."

"Okay. Where are you going?"

"My friend Barbara was stung by a bee and she's allergic. She's at the hospital."

"Oh." Jude looked down through the living room. It seemed wide and empty. It felt as big as an airplane hangar.

"Bee sting?"

"Yes, a bee sing. They can be very bad for some people. Allergic reaction. Like Barbara."

"Oh. Okay."

She looked down at her watch. "In about an hour." She looked back up at Jude. "That's when the dinner should go in the oven."

She clattered down the steps to the garage and Jude closed the front door.

Even though he could feel the complete absence of other beings in the house, he hollered, "Mark!" He waited and felt the physical, luxurious, practically velvet, silence. It enveloped him in its certainty.

Jude grinned up at the ceiling and howled. "Aaawhooooo!"

He wasn't hungry. In fact, his stomach felt like he'd swallowed a baseball mitt that he couldn't digest. But his brain was singing, his eyes and ears were vessels for a flood of reality that he'd never tuned into before, and his soul—if that was what it was—his core, his meat, his being, was flaccid and drunk with the experience.

He went upstairs, replenished his pill cache and searched for any other stocks of pills he might have missed. He found several small bottles, and he opened each and read the names, and determined to keep an eye on them. If some were unused, he could pilfer a bit.

Then he went to his bedroom, stacked Jimi Hendrix and the Byrds on his record player, and lay back on the bed.

Ah! But are you experienced?
Have you ever been experienced?
Not necessarily stoned, but beautiful?

Well, yes I have, Jude thought.

He ate dinner late, but it didn't matter. Mark came home at six, but their mother and father didn't get home until after ten. Their cheeks glowed and their happiness was palpable.

"You were at Barbara's that whole time?" Jude asked his mother when she came in his room to check on him. His father leaned in at the door, looked over his room, scowling at the posters on his walls. Then he left.

"Oh, well, she was at the hospital," his mother said.

"So you were at the hospital this whole time?"

"They released her and we all went out to dinner. That's all."

"Okay."

Jude lay back in his bed and saw his parents like two animals that had pulled their legs from a trap for a night. They were celebrating their escape from their children.

⌒

THE NEXT morning, Jude left the house early. Kevin was supposed to meet him on his bike, but Jude just ran down the hill to catch the bus. He felt like Kevin and his pals were fading. They were being shits to him, and besides, they weren't really needed, especially now that Serena was his girlfriend.

He jogged down Bronson from the bus stop and made it to school nearly twenty minutes early.

He went past the bike racks and saw that Hector, or whoever, had found his bike again and had some displeasure to express. The bike had been flipped upside down, the spokes of both wheels kicked in, and the seat stolen. But the new lock had held.

Jude was surprised by his reaction. He simply saw it as causing him to walk home from now on—but with Serena. So there!

He sat on the large concrete pedestal to one side of the stairs and looked out over the lawn. Slowly, kids and cars began arriving.

Then it was ten minutes before the bell and the cars and kids came in a dense wave. He saw the creamy white Mercedes arrive with Theo in the front seat. Jude was acutely attuned to the back door. As Theo stepped out, he saw the rear door crack open and then swing wide.

It was Serena. Jude was in motion before her head had cleared the door.

She was laughing with Theo as the car pulled away and Jude approached.

"Hey, Foxy Lady," he said. She was wearing a long, lightweight, pale blue sweater, fixed to her hips with a dark suede leather belt, and she wore matching fringed leather boots over white jeans. She shook out her dark mass of hair as she stood. Unbelievably beautiful, Jude thought.

He stepped up to her, ignoring Theo, and leaned in and kissed her on the lips.

Serena drew back as if he'd stung her. "Whoa!"

Jude stepped back a single pace. He searched her face. She wasn't frowning. Just surprised. Maybe it was okay.

But then he looked at Theo. Theo's eyebrows were arched high and he was scanning the kids nearby. Everything slowed.

Then it began. Jude felt twenty, or maybe forty, eyes pinpoint him and watch. Jude could not see, but he felt, the awareness of the incident flow out and away, forever escaping his grasp, slipping over the lawn and through every mind and eye. The drama would continue to unfold, but all the information was already there. Jude, the awkward kid in awkward clothes had just kissed the steamy Serena and she had pulled back. She had rejected him. He was pink as roses.

Jude wanted the unfolding to never take place. He could try to be funny, but he could only envision his imaginary quips falling flat. Instead, he bit his lip, flashed Serena a look of pure hatred, then dragged that same scouring look across Theo, and turned and left, slicing straight through the clusters of kids.

"Hey," Serena said in his wake. But it was a weak effort. The sound quickly died behind him.

It didn't matter anyway. He was already committed. He traversed the lawn toward the big wooden front doors of the school, pushing harder and faster as he went, as the kids on the lawn seemed intent on staying away from him. But he finally mounted the stairs into the school and ducked quickly down the hall, away from the kids and their horrible witnessing.

She had betrayed him. She had led him to believe, and then she betrayed him in public, in front of everyone.

He was heading for his locker. By the time he got there, he knew he wouldn't be going to homeroom. He was going to skip that class—fuck the absence he would get—and he might just ditch the whole goddamned day.

He was going to put his books in his locker but his locker wasn't an option. Someone had kicked in the door of the locker. Not enough to get into the locker, or at least it didn't look like it, but enough to bend the hinges into unopenable, frozen, metal knuckles.

Now there were two sources of twisted metal in his life—his locker and his bike. Okay, three. There was whatever was happening in his chest. His life, which had seemed to be blessed just ten minutes ago, was imploding all over again. He saw the legion of faces and heard the voices of all the people here set out against him. There was Hector's scowl, Paulo's murderous mien, Russ, James, Mr. Denny, his father, Melinda, and now Serena. And even Theo. How could he have expected anything different? His throat began to close and tears started.

Jude steered through the halls and out the back of the building. As he pushed through the doors, he lifted the shoulder of his shirt to wipe his eyes. When was this misery going to end? As he passed the auditorium and the dusty little rectangle where the hippies sat after school, he slowed only long enough to slip his social studies and English books into the gap between the wall and the fence.

He kept his notebook. It felt like it might be his only friend just now.

Then he set his jaw and barreled out past the gate. It all felt so small and dirty in the morning shadows. Like the whole fucking school. Small and dirty.

Jude turned left and headed away from Bronson, toward Van Ness. On Van Ness he turned south, away from the school and away from home.

Five minutes later, he was standing on Santa Monica Boulevard watching a large gray-and-black hearse swing under a stone arch that read HOLLYWOOD CEMETERY. Three black limos followed, each turned cumbrously from the boulevard, in over the gutter. Several passenger cars followed the limos.

Jude had spent time in the cemetery back in Indiana, but he'd climbed the wall at the back to get in and hid whenever someone came around. He didn't think a kid was welcome in a cemetery. But he decided to just see what happened, and he walked in the front gate.

A man in green overalls was driving a small tractor across the lane in front of him as he passed the gates. Another man in a suit and tie stood outside the stonework office building to his left. The staff seemed unconcerned at his presence. Jude walked purposefully, angled away from the office to the right, and no one said anything to him.

Jude wandered the grounds. He could see that the larger struc-tures, the mausoleums, were at the rear and to the east. He wanted to get over there, but maybe later. Just now he saw the hearse and entourage of cars ahead of him and he set out to circle the grave-side party at a fair distance.

A corrugated aluminum awning set on long, high steel legs stood on little black tires over the gathered mourners. They were in folding chairs, each chair hidden by a green slipcover. There were maybe thirty people. Women wore hats. The men wore dark suits. A couple who stood at the rear of the group, just outside the shade, leaned on each other and looked on. They wore modern clothes. The man wore a pale yellow suit with matching bell-bottoms. His hair was a blond cascade that fell past his shoulders. The woman wore a white, lacey dress, quite short, with cowboy boots.

Jude could see a man in a black suit and some kind of long vest at a podium. Past him and in between the raised stone markers on the browned lawn, as Jude moved slowly along, he caught sight of the coffin poised over the grave on a shiny chromed pedestal.

It would be a relief to be dead. To just flick off this crackling static of attention he felt from others. To end, once and for all, his parents needling, their expectations. To send Serena and Melinda and Lacey, and Kevin too, a fuck-you they would never forget.

Feeling flickers of LSD still alive in his brain, he could see people in a new way. They looked like costumed rats or monkeys. They studiously picked clothes for an occasion as if it would separate them from animals.

Then Jude saw it again in a flash, the entire history of humankind: it was all of it, clothes and manners, ceremonies and speeches, a fierce effort to not look like animals. The world spun out from where he stood in a latticework of human endeavor. Roads went to everywhere. Jets and boats crossed the water. Buildings cluttered every landscape. And all of it, to Jude, seemed a desperate, clawing, fierce attempt to not be animals.

Meanwhile, here was a crowd of critters with sharp white teeth and nervous hands. Strident chirps and barks, darting eyes. Walking on two legs, dressing up, and chattering away with words. It was not going to save them. The grave in front of them pulled silently at their fates.

He gazed over the cemetery walls at the Wilshire District a mile off to the east. Those skyscrapers were nothing but upside down rabbit holes. The people scurrying every which way were no more than

210 · If They Say I Never Loved You

rats or mice, just breeding away, and hiding their meaninglessness behind their walls and cars and clothing.

To seal it all in, there was either the Bible or there was science.

It was all there at the graveside. It was simple and stark as the steel and aluminum. Meaninglessness compressed and organized while a man spewed words over it and the mousey little people made damned sure they believed.

"Holy shit," Jude said aloud.

He angled on around them, watching them as they rotated within his field of view. A trumpeter stepped from under a tree well to the rear and played "Taps." Jude knew from his own trumpet studies that the tune was sometimes called "Butterfield's Lullaby," or "Day is Done" after the first line of the lyric.

Music too. Just another way that humanity mounted evidence that they weren't animals.

Seeking shade, he nestled in under a large fir tree next to two large white raised tombs. They were maybe sarcophagi. Was that the word?

He let the smell of grass and stone bake into him. He watched tiny vignettes as they played out in his little visual avenues. There was a groundman smoking a cigarette, studiously out of view from both the funeral party and the office. There was an older couple who performed a slow ritual over the cleaning and flowering of a grave.

A beautiful woman with long, dark hair strode past on the roadway. Serena popped into his head. The bitch. He lifted his notebook and slapped it down on his thighs.

I could rip her heart out
I could pull her teeth
One by one with pliers
Lay em out in the street
Make a little necklace like its pukka beads

She said she loved me
She kissed my mouth
Now I gotta get all those demons she let in
I gotta get em all out

Take me back to Indiana
Where the corn grows in rows
Take me back to Indiana
Where love ain't just for show

He lay on his back and watched the sky grow taut and pale as the morning's smog stretched over the city.

He listened to the grind of the tractors, the blare of lawnmowers, and the distant river-rush of traffic with the endless threads of sirens.

The next thing he knew he was waking up.

He felt refreshed and stupid. Why had he let some girl mess with his head like that? She was just another mouse in her little mouse outfit, enacting her little plays about liking him when they were alone and then rejecting him when the other mice were about. He would go back to school like nothing happened because… Nothing had! Nothing!

Besides, he told himself, he had Lacey, and Lacey was above all this crap. Lacey would totally get his whole thing about the mice and the people and the Bible and science.

The whole fucking planet, the entire human race, was just a fool's errand on the way to nowhere.

He didn't know what time it was, but the light and the relentless disk of the sun made it look like it was maybe ten A.M. or so. He stood and looked down at the tops of the two sarcophagi. His hand rested on the tomb of Constance DeMille. He looked at the second tomb. It was the namesake of the street behind their house, Cecil B. DeMille. He'd heard the name. He knew deMille did something in the movies. But he'd died in 1959. Almost ten years ago.

Jude cut straight through the graves and walked out to Santa Monica Boulevard. A time and temperature display above the mall outside the cemetery read 91 degrees and 10:21 A.M. If he hurried, he would make social studies. What would Diaz want them to take seriously today?

JUDE slid into his seat just as the buzzing bell to announce the start of fourth period died. Diaz was in a state. He stalked the front of the room, snapping his wooden pointer in his palm.

"Is it wrong that Joan Baez led a protest outside the draft offices in Oakland yesterday?" His jaw jutted forward, his hair was more of a tangled mess than usual. "Or…"

But as he reached the windows, he stopped. "But wait," he held the pointer out at the far end of its arc. "Do you even know who Joan Baez is?"

No one spoke.

"No one?"

Jude had heard of her, but didn't know who she was. The Argyle girl started to raise her hand, but then pulled it down before Mr. Diaz saw her.

"All right, so let's get that straight." Diaz retreated to his desk and took his perch at the front corner.

"Baez is maybe the top female recording artist in the world today. She's a folk singer the likes of Pete Seeger, and more recently, Bob Dylan." Diaz spun his finger in the air like he was moving a newsreel forward. "Most people know her now as Dylan's girlfriend. And most of her music lately is Dylan's stuff.

"But most recently, she's been a lightning rod for these anti-war protests. Singing and recording protest songs and lately, getting right down in it, she's showing up at the protest marches and doing shows for free."

Diaz surveyed the room. Jude looked over the kids as well. Their faces were closed, bored, or even asleep.

"Yesterday, Baez showed up with some three hundred protesters at the military induction center—the offices where they induct or take in new army draftees—in Oakland, California. Almost half of them, a hundred and forty people, were arrested."

Diaz sat with raised eyebrows and his pointer still poised, but motionless. He was still wearing the black armband. The one for Guevara.

"You people have to start *reading* the *newspaper*!" He leapt up and started snapping his pointer again. "So I'll ask again, was Baez in the right? She and the other protesters blocked the doors of the building, and told the draftees to stay home and throw away their draft cards."

Owlishly, Diaz continued to strut, but his audience remained silent.

"Mister Hillman, do you have an opinion?"

"Sure, I guess so," the kid grinned. "I think the Rams could go all the way this year, sir."

"There's hope even in the darkest places," Diaz smiled weakly.

Hillman frowned, confused.

"If, by your silence," Diaz continued pacing, "you condone Baez's behavior, then you're also saying the United States Army which is conducting the draft, and the Oakland Police who made the arrests, are in the wrong."

Jude didn't know where Diaz was going with this, but with his windows on the world suddenly scraped clear by his bout with LSD and the graveyard, he raised his hand.

"Mr. Tangier," Diaz leveled his pointer at Jude.

"Well," now that he had the floor, his ideas seemed a little frayed. But he pushed on. "The army and the police are right by law. But Baez is also right by law because she has freedom of speech."

Diaz had spun away from Jude while he was talking, ready to correct him, but he stopped as he reached the doorway. He spun back. "That," he snapped the pointer in his palm. "That is pretty much the crux, right there.

"So, Tangier," he moved back the center of the room. "Who wins?"

Jude puzzled on this. His first thought was 'No one.' But he thought about the millions of mouse-like people all reading the news accounts all over the country. Maybe even over the world.

"The protesters win."

"Because they have morals on their side?" Diaz's smile was tilted, sly.

"No. I mean, maybe in the long run. But yesterday they won because they got in the news."

"Well, well, well," Diaz nodded at him. "Someone's been paying attention in class."

After class, Frank, the sullen black boy, went out the door shoulder-to-shoulder with Jude. He looked at Jude with his flat dark eyes and said, "This is a white man's war against the brown infidels. It's not about morals. It's about money, motherfucker."

Jude shrugged and said, "Probably."

"Definitely."

JUDE ate again with Kevin and James and Robby and Henry for lunch. Or he tried.

James was on the attack the second he saw Jude. "It's the whores' boy!" he crooned. Then he retold the entire story of Jude and the whores for the sheer pleasure it gave him.

Then he took a new tack. "Then you're too chicken to hang out with us because we don't like hooors?" He went on to describe Jude's actions, ducking and leaving under fire from James the day before.

Then, still not getting Jude to bite, he said, "But now you're back because your hippy chick wasn't really your hippy chick and she totally dissed you in front of the whole school this morning."

Jude ate his lunch and listened to James pick at him.

"You got nothing to say for yourself, dweeb?"

Jude scrunched up his empty lunch sack. Then he lifted his eyes to James. Sentences flared in his mind, filled with venom and heat, but then died.

He wanted to defend himself. He wanted to skewer this smug ass who stood on the sidelines and sneered. He wanted to scrape the entire mess off of himself and this planet like a smelly wad of dog-shit off a shoe. But every utterance that rose to his lips was empty on arrival.

He finally said, "Not to you." Then he looked away across the schoolyard. He was expecting nothing except to sit there while the conversation among the boys slowly picked up again about a girl in their Temple classes.

But seated at a table by himself, out in the middle of the schoolyard, was stringy Black Lance. He sat alone, a flattened bag in front of him, his hands working over the surface of it. He wore his big black boots, and with his long hair and small-boned structure, looked ethereal, like a wraith held down by boots.

Without a word, Jude stood and left. He heard the conversation behind him die and then spark back into life and get back on course.

Jude walked out on the yard and sat across from Lance. He felt nervous, and worried that Lance might just get up and leave. But so far, Lance hadn't even raised his eyes to acknowledge Jude. Jude asked, "Whatcha doing?"

Lance now looked at Jude. His gaze was studied boredom, or maybe patience, his head held at a slight angle.

Then he slowly lifted the bag and revealed what was under it. Clean, deep cuts in the table top showed. Jude squinted. It was a word: COWARD. The only letter left to finish was the *d*.

"Where you get your stash, son?"

Jude stared at the word, trying to grasp why the effort, and exactly how Lance was doing what he was doing. His statement had kind of crept out and Jude was only aware he'd said something after it was out and had sat there between them for several seconds.

"My dad," Jude said. "He's a doctor."

Lance nodded, laid the bag down, and began working at the table again. Jude watched his hands as he worked. His left hand held the bag, much like you would hold a paper you were drawing on. His right hand held a short, blocky black-handled knife and with this, through a surgical hole cut in the bag, he slowly and carefully dug deep furrows in the wood. Every wood chip he released, he swept into the bag.

"Hector still bothering you?" It didn't look like the kid was carving up the table. But it looked strange, what he was doing. It looked like maybe he was dicing his lunch up into tiny bits.

Jude shrugged. "Stole my bike last week. But I stole it back. Put a better lock on it."

Lance nodded again. Carved. Bagged chips. And every few seconds his eyes would rise and scan the schoolyard.

"But then," Jude squinted out across the yard with what he imagined was a good imitation of Steve McQueen, "he couldn't steal the bike 'cause I put a new lock on it. So he busted it all up and left it locked up."

"Sheeeet man," Lance grinned. It was the first time Jude had seen his teeth. They were an even white surprise coming from his, so far, dour moods.

"Yeah, and then," Jude shook his head, "and then, he goes in and kicks my locker door in so I can't use it."

"Fuckin' A, you got yourself one true enemy, man."

"Tell me about it."

"Well," Lance swept a few wood chips into his bag and lifted it away from the table. COWARD stood out pale and bright in the wood. "Maybe there's something we can do about Hector."

216 · *If They Say I Never Loved You*

"Yeah?"

"Maybe, yeah."

His jaw worked while he considered his carving. "And I also seen you was having a word or two with that blond dude . Friend of Paulo's."

Jude loosed a deep sigh. "Yeah, so? Not much that can be done about that bastard."

"I'm just," Lance pulled off a perfect beyond-the-horizon squint across the pavements. Jude's McQueen was trumped. The whole place felt suddenly like a prison yard, their lives suddenly mean and gritty, their mutual circumstances desperate. "It's just that maybe I can offer something of a solution."

Jude shrugged.

"So tell me, brother, you got stash today?"

"Maybe," Jude was cagey, more acting out the Steve McQueen moment he was imagining than being in the real situation. He never left the house without a baggy of pills in his pockets now. He looked around the playground to make sure no one would hear him. "But, yeah, I've got stash."

"So," now Lance peered cautiously around the yard, "you understand the risk you are under *right now*, yes?" Lance stabbed the tabletop with his finger to hammer down those last two words.

"I guess so."

"Motherfucker," Lance was suddenly right up in Jude's face, practically snarling. "You just told *me*. Greg knows. Melinda knows. That means *every one* of their fucking *friends* knows." His face was a blank, like the wall of truth. "And you are *carrying*, dude."

Lance sat back again, his eyes traveling out past Jude again, and said quietly, "Any one of those people, including me, brother, could be a fucking narc."

Jude shrugged. "Yeah, I guess so." But Jude trusted his sense of people, and their honesty.

"Are you crazy?" Lance shook his head. "Do you know what happens if the wrong people find out?"

Jude had no idea, but he tried to form his facial muscles into a still mask. "Yeah sure, I mean…"

"You *don't* know, honky." Lance laid his hand flat over the carved word, COWARD. "What happens is, you're outta here," Lance jerked his thumb over his shoulder.

"That might not be so bad," Jude laughed.

"No, honky," Lance leaned in again, emphasizing his words. "I mean you're outta public school. You're maybe in continuation school with all the hardasses—and they would eat you for fucking breakfast—but more likely, you're in juvie with the *hard* hard-asses.

"And you gotta police record, and you aren't worrying about friends or girls or drugs, man. You are quite fucking literally covering your *ass*! You get me? You are worried about getting the fuck out *alive*!"

The bell rang, and Jude felt the tension of being late for English rise up in him. But it quickly capitulated to the feeling of his heart being roughly scraped raw with Lance's dire words. Neither of the boys moved.

"Look," Lance flicked Jude's knee with a knuckle, "Here's the deal. First off, I can sell what you supply. I can get Hector and Paulo off your back. Hector because I know where that motherfucker lives, if you know what I mean. Paulo because you'll be clean if you're not carrying, and not selling. 'Cause man, you know this is his turf, right?"

"His turf?"

"Pot, mescaline, LSD, uppers, downers. The chillins here," he put on a down-homey Negro intonation, "they be buying from Paulo. Or, to be more accurate, from Paulo's blond boy, Rudy."

"But then, how do you sell the stash I have?" Jude asked.

"I already work with Paulo. I sell his shit."

Jude sat silently for a minute, considering. A hundred questions arose. But the school grounds were emptying quickly. The noise and the students were siphoning off into the buildings.

"Paulo never needs to know. I just sell a bit more. The demand is there, dude."

"I don't know," Jude said. He liked being a drug dealer. It made him cool. He could tell people, and it made an impression. And there was the money. He had a roll of bills at home taped to the back of a drawer. At just $2 a pill, and with nothing for him to spend his money on, it had quickly topped $500.

"You'll make more money than you do right now. I guarantee you that."

"Yeah, but…"

Lance jutted his chin quickly past Jude and Jude turned. Mr. Glenn was lumbering across the yard toward them.

They stood together and Lance held a palm out flat and low. Jude swiped it with his own palm and started to turn.

"Hey," he said.

Lance turned to look at him.

"The words."

"The words?"

"I see 'em around. 'Honky,' 'White Trash.' And ah, 'Coward.'"

Lance measured the distance Mr. Glenn still had to clear with his lumbering hobble. Then his eyes met Jude's. "They're mirrors, man. Show the real you."

Jude felt circles making circles in his brain.

"Dude," Lance said, "I'll come by this weekend."

Jude stopped his retreat. "What? What for?"

"I gotta see the stash, man. I can't be taking chances." Then Lance ducked and was moving away. Jude spun and hustled for his English class before Mr. Glenn could get to him. Instead, the big man barked out helplessly after them, "Get to class, boys!"

Jude heard Lance say, loudly enough, "I ain't no boy, mother-fucker."

"What was that?" Glenn called out. "What was that you said?"

Lance sent a look at Jude and then slipped inside.

eleven

JUDE'S NEW BIKE WAS DARK BLUE. A SIMPLE FIVE-speed. Used.

His father had taken him down to McCutchen's Cycles on Vermont and had bullied his way into another negotiation.

The assumption, Jude was surprised to learn in the store, was that he would buy a new bike. But Jude didn't see the point. Maybe he would have wanted a new bike—a red one with bold knuckles of chrome—a month ago. Maybe even a week ago. Now he wanted something that would disappear among the other bikes on the racks at school, and would offer a thief nothing worth stealing.

His father had actually remained standing in the aisle of new bikes, reading the brochures while Jude retreated to the corner near the repair shop where the used bikes hung from hooks in the ceiling.

The dark blue bike was listed at $45. It was a Schwinn Collegiate with 26-inch wheels and a 19-inch frame. It had simple flare handlebars, and a flat, triangular seat. It had steel fenders also painted dark blue, a feature he would have avoided, or vowed to remove in an earlier life. The bike looked new except for a few scratches on the bottom of the frame. The brakes, tires and cables all looked good.

"This one?" His father's voice close behind him startled him. He reached past Jude and shook the bike like it was a carcass and he wanted to make sure it was dead.

"It looks like a good bike," Jude said.

"A new bike like this is probably sixty-five dollars," he said. "This is used."

Jude looked across the room at the lone saleswoman and felt sorry for her. She saw Jude's glance and started over.

"Looking at the used bikes today?" she said. Her nametag read BEVERLY. She was maybe twenty-five, her hair piled into a beehive. She wore pedal pushers and a white blouse with McCutchen's Cycles of Hollywood embroidered on the breast.

"Well," Jude's father shook his head, "we were looking, but the prices for the used bikes…"

The woman's smile faded a bit, but she waded in. "Mr. McCutchen prices the used bikes based on industry guidance."

Jude's father smirked. "But we're not an industry. We just need a bike for my son to ride to school."

She smiled without warmth.

Jude drifted away, touching the new bikes, looking down through the glass cases at the shiny new derailleurs and gear hubs. He saw his father shaking his head, a look of disgust across his face. A few more words were exchanged and he threw his hands up and turned away.

"Jude!" he called out, and they left.

In the car, his father said, "Well, we'll go to Sears and get you a bike there. That woman was just rude."

But Sears' bikes were new and expensive. So were the bikes at Bicycle Village and A-Jack's. They went to Vermont Lawnmower where there were a few used bikes, but nothing that suited.

Jude's mother got the whole story when they got home. It was the criminals, the greedy shopkeepers, the clueless salesgirl that sent them home empty handed. His mother's response was, "But he needs a bike to get to school."

Later that day, his mother drove him back to McCutchen's and she paid the $45 for the used blue Schwinn. Other than fuming through dinner, his father didn't say anything else about the bike.

WHEN Lance arrived Sunday, Jude had forgotten he was coming over. The whole bike thing had swollen over his attention and Lance and his visit had wicked away.

Now Lance was at the door looking very black and dusty, like someone out of Mark Twain, and Jude's mother was standing aside like he might be carrying vermin.

"Your friend Lance is here," she said to Jude as he stood at the top of the stairs.

"Hey, man," Lance said.

"Hey," Jude said. "Come on in."

"Why don't you come on down, Jude, and I'll get you boys some Kool-Aid or a pop?" Every other word or so she said was a little harder than usual. But Jude could read her. She was telling, not asking. Having a black kid in the house was scaring her.

He decided not to hear her though. His father was out on a run and if Lance were going to see the pills, now was pretty much the only and ideal time.

"Thanks, Mom, but we have some homework to do." He half-turned on the stairs and Lance took the signal. He crossed the hall and climbed the stairs. When he reached Jude, he slapped him on the shoulder like an old friend. "Things cool, dude?"

"Things are cool," he said, and they ascended the stairs together.

When they reached the midpoint in the upstairs hall, Jude could feel his mother listening acutely below them. So he went past his parents' bedroom door and said, "I finished reading the book, but I don't really get the ending."

Lance dovetailed perfectly. "Yeah, no kidding, dude."

In Jude's room, Lance stopped and held out his hands. "Fuck me, man! You are in the fucking lap, dude."

Jude shrugged. "Maybe. I guess."

"I'm telling you, dude. You are on the front of the fucking wave."

Jude could sort of see the room from Lance's eyes. It was a big room. It held two twin beds, a dresser, a desk, and a chair, and still had lots of floor space to spare. The windows looked out over Los Angeles or up to the Griffith Observatory. The closet behind him was a big open square of hardwood flooring and clothes and shelves with books and records.

It was, Jude had to agree, a little nuts.

Lance was slowly cycling along the walls, looking at the scores of concert posters and record sleeves and magazine photos.

"Look," Jude said, "I'm guessing my mom has gone back to the kitchen. We gotta do this quick before she comes up or my dad gets home."

"Then let's do this quick." Lance broke away from the walls and went to the bedroom door. Jude tugged it open and listened. Then he led the way.

The two boys slipped out and along the hall. Jude cut in at his parents' bedroom door, then took a sharp right into the master bath. Lance was on his heels.

Jude stopped in front of the mirrored cabinet and met Lance's eye. If there was to be some drama in the moment, this was it, and Jude felt he had to provide it. He held for three seconds, five, and then yanked open both doors at once. There, like three little kettle-drums, sat the bottles of pills.

"Holy shit," Lance was impressed. "Man, dude, I mean, I was like thinking," and he held out his hands to depict a much smaller size of container. "That's like fucking *industrial*, man."

"Bitchin', huh?"

"Truly," Lance reached in and spun the top of the amphetamines. He plucked out two and popped them into his mouth like they were Life Savers.

He held out two additional pills to Jude and Jude held up one palm to the pills. "Naw. Besides, we gotta get out of here."

Lance reached out and touched Jude's sleeve. He said, almost reverently, "They're always here like this? He never moves them?"

"Never," Jude took the lid to the big pill jar from Lance and closed the cabinet. He yanked Lance's sleeve to get him out of there.

When they got to the hall, Jude turned them toward the back yard. He felt he could maybe avoid having Lance and his father cross paths if they were in the yard.

"Okay, motherfucker," Lance slapped Jude on the shoulder again. "You is all true, man. You is all full and whole true." He cycled around the back yard with as much awe as he had shown in Jude's bedroom. "I have seen it with my own eyes, brother."

"Well," Jude was swatting at bees. "I told you, man."

"I know you told me, man. But you gotta know, brother, most

people I deal with are flat out motherfucking liars, man. They've got the soul of a snake, the heart of a fucking toad."

Jude stared at the boy as he stood at the edge of the lawn. At this end, the yard crested at a wall that dropped twenty feet down into the neighbors' garden. Past the wall and the low hurricane fence that ran along the top, was all of L.A., from downtown, through the Wilshire District, and all the way to Santa Monica and the hazy lump of Palos Verdes in the distance.

"Un-fucking-believable, man. Just completely off the fucking rails, dude."

Ten minutes later, Lance had climbed over the back fence and had disappeared into the gardens of the house down the hill. "See you tomorrow," he'd said back through the fence.

AT SCHOOL on Monday, Jude removed the lock from the trashed black bike that had been his, and at the far corner away from the black bike, slid the new lock through both wheels and the frame of his new used bike.

In the hall after social studies, Jude shook his locker door until it popped open. The maintenance guy had reshaped his locker door, but the fit was imperfect. You could slide a sandwich in through the slot at the top. But the door opened and closed, if reluctantly, and the lock sort of worked.

He watched Serena cross the hall on her way to class. The sight of her made him feel wilted inside. She was wearing a beige miniskirt and a white blouse. She looked delectable. But she was walking with Cindy and they either didn't see Jude, or more likely, just ignored him.

Grouchy and hurt, he stopped off in the boys bathroom in the downstairs hall on his way to homeroom. He tugged the plastic bag from his pocket. The night before, he'd carefully counted out 50 blue pills, 50 white pills, and 50 of the red-and-yellow caps and rubber-banded the bag shut. Now he slid the bag in behind the first toilet in the row, the space behind the tank just sufficient.

When Lance had told him where to leave the stash, Jude was surprised.

"Why in the downstairs bathroom? It's, like, always crowded.

Mr. Glenn is in there checking up on things every day, a couple times."

"Yeah," Lance nodded. "Exactly."

Jude got it. Right under their noses. The least danger by choosing the most.

Through the day, Jude kept feeling like he was literally looking for himself. He sat with Kevin and James and the others at lunch again. But now he had no girlfriend, no Lacey, his brother was back home, and he wasn't even a drug dealer anymore.

Melinda smiled, but thinly, when their eyes met in English.

As English was close to ending, a girl walked into Ms. Mantle's class and handed her a note. Ms. Mantle unfolded it and read it, and then stepped over to Jude and refolded the note and slid it onto his desk. Another thin smile.

He lifted the note and opened it. "Jude Tangier is to see Mr. Glenn during Fifth Period." The handwriting was hurried, and the two Ns in Glenn had come together to masquerade as an M.

Jude knew what it was about. He hadn't gone back to band for almost a week now. No one had said anything to him about it. He had simply been going out behind the auditorium and slipping in under the shade of the bougainvillea that climbed the outer fence. Out there, he read a book or just lay and watched the parched sky drain its heat down onto the black pavement.

He shrugged and let his gaze sweep the room. Kids were looking at him, including Melinda. When he met her gaze, her eyelids lifted. She was curious and she was expecting, he could tell, that he would tell her what was up when they left the room. But he didn't like Melinda just now.

Jude looked up at the clock. Two minutes to the bell. They had their homework assignment. A kid was trying to explain why he couldn't do it.

Jude, after a full day of not being able to find himself, found that other parts of him were also missing, like a certain amount of fearfulness. He understood his options, and normally would have just waited for the bell and then tried to avoid Melinda in the crush. Instead, he lifted his books and stood. With a slight nod to Ms. Mantle, and lifting the note aloft as evidence, he left the room.

He had stopped at the downstairs bathroom three times since he'd left the baggy of pills. It had still been there every time. Now he stopped and closed the pale green stall door. He sat and reached down and back in what was now a well-calibrated movement that avoided touching the toilet itself.

The baggy was gone.

Jude felt relieved, but then the feeling stalled. He wondered: what if he went into Mr. Glenn's office and the baggy was sitting on the desk? What if Lance was there, busted? Or worse, narcing on Jude?

"Fuck," he said aloud.

The outer door was shoved open and now the rush of boys into the bathroom between classes had started. Jude stood, flushed the toilet, and left.

Jude slipped into the administration offices and sat in one of the sleek, old-fashioned, dark wooden chairs without announcing himself. The words WHITE TRASH were carved in the seat of the chair next to his. The words had been sanded and stained to try to hide them, but they still stood out starkly. He opened the *Autobiography of Malcolm X* because that was what had been sitting in his locker, and more or less pretended to read.

Students were threading in with notes from teachers, or asking for something for a class. One kid, a boy Jude didn't recognize, came in holding his stomach and claimed he was sick. He sat near Jude for a while, his eyes traveling sheepishly over Jude and then around the high-ceilinged room.

The bell rang and activity died down. The secretary, Mrs. Flowers, came out and let the sick kid through the swinging gate. She took him to the Nurse's Office. Jude was alone in the little entry area.

A substitute teacher arrived and began handing over materials for the teacher. Mrs. Flowers stood tall and cool behind the counter explaining that a sub might still be needed tomorrow.

"Okay, well, just call me," the sub said.

Jude heard a door open somewhere behind the counter. "I don't know where he is." It was the gruff, anger-laced voice of Mr. Glenn.

The sub smiled—thinly—and left.

Then Glenn was at the counter leaning in toward Mrs. Flowers, "Where is this Tangier kid? Did you send the note to his class?"

"Oh yes, Mr. Glenn, we did. And Ms. Mantle sent a note back saying he did receive it."

"Miss," he said.

"Miss, sir?"

"She's not married. She's Miss Mantle. This 'Ms.' stuff is no different than calling a 'custodian' a 'maintenance engineer.' It's all lipstick on pigs, you ask me."

Then Mr. Glenn's eyes slid past the counter to the chairs. "Who is this young man?"

"Oh," the woman just noticed Jude. "Well, I don't know."

Jude carefully read the sentence on the page, pretending not to hear.

"Son?" Mr. Glenn said.

Jude blinked, but didn't look up.

"You!" he called out. "Young man!"

Jude lifted his head and peered across at Mr. Glenn.

"Who are you, and what are you doing here?"

"I'm here to see a Mr. Glem."

"Glem? *Glem*?" Mr. Glenn was leaning far over the high counter now, as if taking Jude's shoes into account would complete the explanation he was looking for.

"Are you Tangier?"

"Yes, sir."

"It's Glenn… G L E N N, Glenn. Let me see that note."

Jude closed his book and stood up. He found the note in his pants pocket and placed it on the counter.

Glenn snatched it up, read it, and then, with a single lifted eyebrow, looked at the secretary. He tossed the note on the counter and said, "Well, come on. Let's get this over with."

Jude followed the man to his office. He moved in a sideways lurch, the left leg stiffer and maybe longer than the right. He wore a gray jacket, but when you looked at the fabric closely, it was actually a white jacket with a dense black weave over it. It made Jude think of a used car salesman.

"Sit, sit," Glenn said when they were in his office. The big man balanced a moment, hands on either arm of the chair holding himself above the seat. Then he lowered himself in and sighed.

Jude stood just inside the door. The room was dominated by Mr. Glenn's desk. Sunlight passed through the Venetian blinds and fell in tiny slivers that cut across Mr. Glenn and the floor. On either wall behind the desk and beside the window were bookshelves. There were exactly six books in the cases. The rest were stuffed with plastic binders of various sizes, each with a carefully typed label. The labels somehow communicated the moldering boredom possible for an adult life. There was a *Los Angeles School District Administration Training, July 1962,* a *District Council on Juvenile Delinquency—1964 Findings,* and *Standards and Policies in Los Angeles District Junior High Schools.*

Glenn rolled his hand impatiently over the space above his desk, "Sit, sit!" The big man grimaced out a smile of sorts.

Two chairs sat in front of the desk and Jude sat in the one closest to the door. He scanned the desk which was messy, but showed no evidence of a baggy full of pills.

"Mr. Tangier, can you tell me why you haven't been attending your band class during this period?"

Jude shrugged.

"I don't read shrugs, Mr. Tangier. I'll need something a little more specific."

"Mr. Denny told me to get out and stay out."

"Please, a teacher at this school would never say such a thing."

Jude immediately knew where he stood. He was used to this from his father. Jude was the child in the adult world. His word was less than nothing here. He shrugged.

"You're going to tell me that Mr. Denny told you to leave his class and never come back?"

Jude shrugged again.

"If I call Mr. Denny in, maybe with your parents here, for a conference, do you think he'll agree with what you're telling me?"

Jude shrugged, then said, "Sure. Unless he lies."

Mr. Glenn's face darkened and his eyes flashed. "We will not talk about teachers that way at this school."

Jude shrugged again.

228 · *If They Say I Never Loved You*

"You have," he looked up at his wall clock, "thirty minutes left of this period. You will return to band and begin attending class *today*. Do you hear me?"

Jude combined a shrug with a minimal nod.

"Any more trouble and we will have that conference, young man. Do you hear me?"

Jude made no movement.

"All right, get out of here. Mr. Denny is expecting you."

Jude hefted his books and left through the door they'd entered. Outside in the hall, he opened his locker, propped his books against the trumpet case, and slammed the locker. Then he walked out the rear doors of the building, past the band building, and sat down under the bougainvillea. Today was not the day to go back to band.

AT THE BELL, Jude went to wood shop, then PE, and then he was back. He was hoping for a smoke before he climbed on his bike and headed for home. He was holding out hope that Russ would be gone and he might see Lacey today. The marijuana would help. It would calm him down.

He was also hoping to see Lance, with maybe some signal or word that all had gone as planned. And, ideally, he would be able to ask about Hector.

Theo and Serena were already there. Theo was seated against the fence in the shade. Serena was leaning on Theo's shoulder, talking close and quiet to him. Her laughter bubbled up like champagne, brightening the dusty space around them, but hardening in Jude into something brittle and painful.

Theo lifted his chin, said "Hey Jude, the dude, the pale-ass weasel." Serena barely shifted her eyes, glancing at Jude and then returning to her whispers and laughter.

"Hey," Jude said and sat in the hot sun across from them.

He lifted his face and pretended he was being absorbed by the sun. He closed his eyes. He ascended up through a sunbeam in an attempt at mental purity. But Serena and her coy, distant smile were there, a floating sweet aura around her. She slowed his ascent. Cluttered his mind.

Beyond Serena, though, a true smile, the real center of things, was Lacey. Just the pureness of Lacey behind a maze and concentric ring walls.

"Hey man," Jude was jostled back into reality. Greg had slid up against Jude's left hip as he sat. "I hear, man."

Then Melinda shoved in on his right and Jude felt like a magnet with opposite poles from theirs, like he should pop out from there, and get far away.

But they both pulled in tight against him and Greg went on. "You, my friend, are now a Capitalist!"

That sounded bad. "Well," Jude started.

"But, hey man, nothing wrong with Capitalism. Especially with drugs. You gotta protect yourself. Right?"

"Yeah, I guess so." A shadow fell over them. Jude looked up into Lance's pale eyes.

"I told them, man, so they would, you know, know." Lance looked away and spoke to the enclosed horizon of the fence line. "You're not carrying anymore, man."

Melinda grasped his arm. "So," she pulled herself tight against him, "what was the note?" She leaned across him to talk to Greg, "He got a note from the office in English today."

"Cool, man," Greg nodded sagely. "Lay it on us, dude, what was it all about?"

"Band."

"What the fuck?" Greg asked.

"You've never gone back," Jude said to Greg. "To band. What do you do during fifth period now?"

"You were in my band class?" Greg opened his eyes wide in surprise. "So you were there for my..." He lifted his hands as though he were holding drumsticks. But his eyes had slid past him to Melinda.

"Yeah, I was there," Jude said. Then for Melinda's sake, he said, "Mr. Denny flipped out. A full two-minute drum solo on 'Twinkle, Twinkle Little Star.' I think everyone flipped out a little bit."

"Yeah, it was a truly true bitchin' moment," Greg claimed. "But now I've got Study Hall for fifth period, and if I don't show on time and stay until the bell, I get detention." He grinned. "The artist as criminal, man!"

Melinda tugged at Jude's arm, laced her fingers in among his. "So what happened to you in band?"

Serena spoke up from across the pavement. "Denny cocked him one." Jude could sense she was involved in the conversation because he was sandwiched between Melinda and Greg and Lance, and then she'd seen Melinda take his hand.

"Cocked you one?" Greg punched Jude's shoulder. "That's just groovy, dude. He and I never came to *blows*!"

Jude looked up at Lance. He stood in line with the sun, but his shadow stopped just short of Jude. The brilliant halo of light hid Lance's face. But he was listening.

"Yeah, I was playing the wrong piece or something," Jude said. "Kinda daydreaming." He met Serena's eyes. She didn't look away. "And he fired his baton at me. Then when he came to get it off the floor, he back-handed me. Knocked me out of my chair."

"Fucktastic!" Greg said.

"So the note was like…" Melinda wanted the punchline.

"I had to see Mr. Glenn today, and he said I have to go back to class."

"Did you go?"

Jude shrugged, "No."

"Way, extremely cool," Greg pronounced.

A joint came their way from Theo and Melinda pulled on it, the ember bright and crisp. Jude took it and smoked, and then handed it to Greg.

The red Ford truck rumbled into the street and Greg and Melinda gathered their books. They both took another pull at the joint and then handed it off to Theo and ambled out through the gate. Paulo peered out at them from behind the wheel of the truck.

"Is he ever happy?" Jude asked Lance.

Lance smiled to himself but said nothing.

"Like I don't even get him, man," Jude pushed on. "What's he doing at the Crestview?"

Lance's eyebrows arched high on his forehead. Then he looked around the yard, circling down to the area where they were. He looked hard at Theo and Serena, then he sat next to Jude. He said quietly, "So, what the fuck you know about the Crestview?"

Jude shrugged. "I have a friend there."

Lance laughed. "You?" He was shaking his head. His smile remained wide. "You gotta friend at the Crestview?"

"Yeah, why not?"

Lance leaned closer, impressing on Jude to be quiet. In a near whisper he asked, "'Cause you're a punk ass kid is why?"

Jude shrugged. He didn't much like Lance just now. He hardened his voice, hoping to sound businesslike. "What happened with Hector?"

Lance kept smiling and shaking his head, all the while staring at Jude.

Jude asked again, "So what about Hector?"

"You are full of surprises, White Boy." He peered across at Theo and Serena. The two of them were peering back, clearly wondering what Lance and Jude could be talking about.

"Mr. Elizado is taken care of," he said finally. "Hector and I have reached an agreement."

Jude nodded judiciously, as though there were things about this statement to consider.

"And the baggy?"

"Handled," Lance picked at his teeth with a thumbnail, staring at Jude. "Anything else you need to ask me about, boss?"

Jude pushed off and exited through the gate. He looked back at Lance and found Lance's eyes on him hard and wary. Jude looked away.

⌐⌐

ON WEDNESDAY, Jude rode to the Crestview to see Lacey. With his big lock, Jude locked his bike at the apartment up Canyon Drive from the Crestview. The apartment had a covered garage and Jude rolled his bike in between two rows of small, locked storage units for the tenants. He locked his bike in the open space between the units and crossed the alley.

The Crestview was busy. Jude could see that as he rode past, and again as he approached from the rear. The sun was blazing hot in mid-October and doors were open, bright clothing hung dejected in the windless air, rhythmic bass thudded out on four or five competing beats, and most of the women were out on the lawn or on the balconies.

Using Malcolm X's description of how men moved about around

whores, Jude acted like a john himself. It was simply a matter of acting like he had an appointment, someplace to be. He just needed to avoid seeing Russ or Penny.

He skirted past the pretty black woman at the bottom of the stairs and ascended the steps two at a time. The first women he encountered, leaning back on deck chairs with feet up on the railing, were Frenchie and her pale friend.

"Hey Frenchie," Jude said, keeping his voice matter-of-fact.

"Hey, if it isn't the street fighter. Jimmy? Right?" Frenchie asked.

"Jude," he said. "Close though."

"Yeah," she said, unimpressed with herself.

The pale girl curled back up into herself, her feet pulled up onto her chair. But Frenchie left her feet up on the rail, blocking his way.

He looked over the pale girl. Her face was much better, still bruised, but less swollen and dark. She wore the same cast, but dirty now. There were penned names in red and black and blue on the plaster.

Jude waited for Frenchie to drop her feet and let him past, but Frenchie tugged at her cigarette and slowly exhaled, the thick white smoke hiding her eyes. She said, "You coming through or what?"

Jude frowned at her, not sure what she meant. He edged closer and she finally lowered her legs and sat up. When Jude met her eyes, they were as always flat and still. But now that he was right up over her, he saw she had a half-moon of a bruise on her right cheek. She had caked it with makeup, but it shone through, dark and bluish. His eyes wandered down her. There were three bands of bruise on her left arm. She sneered at him, knowing what he was seeing. She said, "Don't you be fantasizing about me back in your little bedroom." She twirled a lock of her hair around a finger. Then she said husky and whispery, "'Cause you can't even handle the pretend version."

Jude felt his face and neck flush and he shot past her. Frenchie laughed at his hurrying back. At Lacey's door, like a little kid that needs to pee, he knocked once and entered.

Lacey was sitting at her breakfast table with Penny and another woman. Anchoring them there, centered, was a wide ashtray with three spiraling trails of smoke. They were all looking expectantly at the door. Lacey smiled when she saw who it was. But Jude saw Penny's face cloud over, and then clear, but forcibly. The other woman, the redhead who'd been up in Jude's face out at the curb that day, just smiled at him, but coldly.

"Sorry," Jude said. "I shouldn't just…" He gestured at the door. "But I saw Paulo do it. You know? And if I stand out there knocking…" He shrugged. "Russ, you know?"

Jude flushed again. He felt like a twelve-year-old.

"Hey, everybody does it except the people that don't even bother." Lacey leveled a look at Penny.

"Hell," Penny pushed a shallow smile out, "we all do that around here." Her fingers waggled in the air.

Jude nodded and felt himself trapped in the small space just inside the door. He was held back by Penny's scowl that lurked just behind her smile.

"So, yeah," Penny said, "we're kinda in the middle of something." Lacey and Penny were dressed in shorts and T-shirts. The redhead wore a kind of loose beach dress. They were all barefooted. Lacey's hair was pulled pack into a braid. The braid started on either side of her head, over her ears, and Jude found this new and exciting.

"Yeah, true," Lacey spread her hands and laid them flat over a ledger that was opened in front of her. "We should probably, you know, finish this."

"Oh, yeah," Jude started out of his frozen state. "I mean, I just came by to apologize."

"Apologize?" Lacey sounded incredulous. "For what?"

"Oh, you know, last time I was here."

Lacey's nose scrunched and ducked her head as she remembered. "Yeah… you disappeared."

"Yeah, well," Jude started.

Lacey waved a hand over the table, "No big, Russ told me."

"Told you what?" Jude wanted to know.

"That he kicked you out, and you are never, ever, ever to come back here—*evah*—until after you turn twenty-one." She lifted her eyebrows and smiled, expressing her inability to change Russ or the situation.

"Yeah, well," Jude started.

"Yeah well what?" Penny asked, an edge to her voice.

"There's no law he can't be here, though. Right?" The redhead was coming to Jude's defense.

"Actually," Penny said, ready to dig into something.

Lacey laid a hand on Penny's arm to stop her. "It is illegal for you to be here after like six or seven at night. But as long as it's just a residence…" Lacey shrugged. "I don't know, but I don't think it matters."

"Cool," Jude said.

But Penny was shaking her head. "Not if the manager," she tossed her head toward the front of the building, "and that's Russ—says you can't be here."

"Well, Jude's here now," Lacey said. "Leave him be."

"Yeah," said the redhead.

"We have things to do here today," Penny reminded her.

"We can do them," she said. "Grab a Coke or something," she said to Jude, "and grab a couch. We're almost done."

A smile spread wide across his face. He didn't dare look at Penny because he was sure he would be gloating. Then, when he tried to move, he lurched. He'd become so locked in, every muscle tensed, he hadn't even noticed.

He crossed stiffly behind them and entered the kitchen. It was, as he now knew was the usual, a mess. He opened the fridge, pulled a Coke out, and pulled the tab. Then he set the can on the counter and turned on the hot water.

"Jude! Don't do my dishes!"

"You know I don't mind," he said.

Penny laughed aloud. "Hell, if I'd known he was doing your dishes when he came over, I'd be having him over, too."

"I'm in twenty-two," the redhead said. "You know… when you're done here."

"I can't get him to stop," Lacey said, shaking her head.

Jude shrugged and began herding the silverware from across the counters toward the sink. He shoved the stopper in place and squeezed dish soap in under the faucet.

He sipped his Coke, sorted and stacked dirty dishes, scraping garbage into the trash occasionally, and waited for the sink to fill with steaming hot water.

When he turned off the water, he could hear the women talking. But it made no sense. Penny was saying, "If he keeps taking the nut, he's no different than the Walker brothers."

He put his head down, let their voices become a hum in the background, and scrubbed dishes. He listened, but only a few statements made any sense to him. Then he finally began to piece something together when Penny said, "You're not going to have enough to get out until, shit, like nineteen seventy-five."

Lacey's eyes were hard. "He promised me six months."

"Yeah, well," Penny waited until Lacey lifted her eyes to look at her. "You knew when you started that the deal was shady."

"At best," the redhead said.

"Yeah," Lacey capitulated. "I know."

"So what are you going to do?"

"I don't know. If I ask him for my money, he's going to go off the fucking handle, start thinking I'm going to jump, make my life hell, and after all of it, he won't give me the money anyway."

Penny nodded and laid a hand over Lacey's wrist. She looked back over her shoulder at Jude. Jude met her eyes briefly, but then turned back to the dishes.

"It's not like we're street walkers, or stuck on Third Ave," the redhead said. "Or catching crumbs on Highland."

Penny nodded. "Wendy's right."

Wendy saw Jude watching them with interest. She lifted her chin at him to include him in the conversation. "There's a whole…" she lifted her arms up as though lifting the veil from reality, "a whole ecology of whores out there."

Penny rolled her eyes, Lacey smiled down into her cola.

But Wendy rolled on. "You got a thousand runaways a month coming into L.A. Maybe more. Hell, probably more. Definitely more! Girls, boys, it doesn't matter, kid." Jude's mind played out an amalgamation of his many rides down Hollywood Boulevard. There were the clusters of kids his age and older with backpacks and sleeping bags. There were the loners at street corners, their hands out for change, the pairs of them with one singing and the other battering away at a guitar. They were as routine, he realized, as the garbage, and for some reason, even less visible to him.

"They show up, and to eat or find a safe place to sleep for a night or two, they end up fucking strangers." Wendy plucked tobacco from her tongue. "But no one in their right mind wants to do anything with these kids, you know. 'Cause they're illegal, they're dirty, they're sneaky. You fuck one and her friends show up the next day and rob you blind. Or they work with the cops and get you busted on a two-sixty-one or a two-eighty-eight."

"Statutory rape," Penny said.

"Or lewd acts," Lacey finished.

"Right. Sorry. That's cop lingo. But, you know, if you're poor or desperate, then that's your market."

Jude had stopped washing the dishes and now leaned his hips against the counter, listening.

"The whole thing is so fucking dangerous that the natural thing is to find yourself a pimp. I mean, if you're going to keep at it.

"Of course, the smart ones find themselves a pimp right off. And pimps, if they're smart, they're out checking out the new blood and recruiting the best of them.

"But a pimp, that's when you're in the business. 'Cause now you have protection, someone to watch your back. And for the john, you got someone to ensure the girls are in check. They're not going to rip you off or follow you home."

Wendy sat back in her chair, pleased to be the lecturer with an attentive audience. She took a deep drag on her cigarette and waited five luxurious beats before she blew out the smoke.

She leaned forward and tapped the ash off the end of her smoke, then sat back and held the cigarette near her head, almost aristocratically.

"And pimps, usually they have a place, or access to a place. Flea-bag motel, a flophouse, or some such. And in that ecology, just chicks with pimps, that's a big chunk of the business right there.

"That's us too, you know." Her eyes and cigarette hand made a quick rolling motion to take in the building where they sat. "I mean, the Walker brothers own this building. They pay Russ to run the place. And this is where they send their better clients. I mean, you know, they've got like a hundred girls on the street at any time. And when they got a girl starts getting a repeat list, they bring her into a place like this."

"Repeat list?" Jude said.

"Guys that request them, come back over and over, you know?"

"Oh."

"The Walker brothers have got like three places like this. Hollywood, Sunset Strip and one down in Venice Beach. Seventy-five, eighty girls. Maybe more."

Penny's brow was furrowed. She plucked up her cigarette and pulled quick and hard.

"Wha's up witch chu?" Wendy drawled out.

Penny scowled and spoke before she'd let loose of the smoke. "They've got more like two hundred on the streets, and you forgot the place they've got downtown for the high-end escorts. It's like three hundred girls they're running. Most of them pull a couple hundred a night. We're pulling twice that on average. And that's every day of the year. I've done the math. It's thirty million bucks a year."

She sat back and blew the remainder of the smoke from her lungs. "That's like a hundred grand a year per girl."

Wendy's eyes fired. "Yeah, but we're not getting fucked over by the bosses. They're not pushing us out as soon as the next hot young thing shows up. We're not getting tossed into their private party vans. We're not getting beat up because johns will pay extra to beat up some helpless chick. We're worth something to them because we got *class*."

She flicked her cigarette in the direction of the ashtray, the ash fluttering to the table and floor. "We've got it fucking good, bitches. And some of us make it to the big time."

Penny laughed. "No one in this room is gonna make the big time." She plucked up her wineglass and drained it. "Well," she flipped her hand, "'Cept maybe Lacey. You could do it if you wanted to."

Jude, wanting this to go on, and afraid any noise from him might break the spell, couldn't help himself. "What's the big time?"

"Oooooh, what's the big time, he asks!" Wendy raised her hands and shook them high over her head like a southern preacher. "We're talking escorts! The bitches that make the big bucks. Grand a night with one guy. Sometimes more. They live in fancy flats in high-falutin' neighborhoods and have a car and a driver and a fucking house staff to cook and clean and dress them. It's fucking *amayyyy*zing!"

"It's not always like that," Penny said.

"Besides," Lacey turned to look at Jude wistfully, "It's really lonely work, and probably, in a lot of ways, they don't make more money really."

"They make a ton more money," Wendy protested.

Penny lowered her head and swiveled to face Wendy in order to deliver the news to her. "We're all employees," she said. "Our incomes might be different, but you can bet that after expenses, not one of the girls ever leaves with a nest egg. I bet even the smart ones, when they get out or get pushed out, barely have enough to pay first and last month's rent in fucking Reseda."

Penny slumped back. Then Wendy. Lacey leaned back more leisurely. She lifted her cigarette and smoked. Jude thought her movements exquisite.

Penny said, "And that's what we're talking about here, Wendy. We're figuring out an escape plan for our girl, Lacey." She leaned forward and poured another finger of wine into her glass. "'Cause if we can do it for her, maybe we can do it for us."

"But look," Penny said, turning to look at Lacey, "you gotta move slow on this. Right?"

Lacey nodded. She took another drag and lowered her head. Jude watched her profile behind the veil of her blonde hair.

Penny drank off the wine again. "All right, we'll talk again soon?"

Lacey nodded again.

"Right now," Penny patted Lacey's hand, "I suggest you lose the liability."

Lacey's eyes rose to Jude. She frowned through her hair, with a 'What's-the-big-deal?' air to her.

"I'm serious," she said.

"I get it," Lacey said. "Everybody's serious."

Penny patted Lacey's hand once more, then she rose and with a scowling shake of her head directed at Jude, she headed for the door. "You coming?" she asked Wendy.

"Yeah, yeah, I'm coming."

Wendy stood and wavered in place for a moment. Then she shook her head to clear it, and she pushed out the door behind Penny.

Jude turned back to the sink and washed the last couple of spoons while the dishwater drained. He rinsed them and slotted them into the drying rack. Then he grabbed a moderately dry towel from the hook by the sink and began wiping down the counters.

"Jude, thank you, but you don't have to do that." Lacey had come to stand by the refrigerator, watching him work.

Jude stopped and stood straight. He looked at her. She was more human to him than he'd ever seen her. More human, in fact, than he'd ever seen anyone. That was it, wasn't it? That people put up a front. Always defending themselves, or with someone like Greg, pushing themselves out at other people. But for most of us, he thought, scared and worried, trying to hide and talk and act all at once.

This humanity was a strange thing. It made Lacey almost completely and impossibly unsexy, and yet he felt himself filled from the very center of his chest with a nearly suffocating bloom of love like he'd never felt.

"What's wrong?" Jude asked quietly.

"Nothing, really. Nothing."

"You told me about the Paulo thing," Jude said. "Is he the one that took your money?"

Lacey registered surprise that Jude knew, that she'd told him, but she said, "Yeah. Yeah, he's the one."

"I'm sorry," Jude said. "He's a scary dude."

Lacey nodded and smiled at him.

"What?"

"I don't know," she said. "Most men, you tell them some guy is stealing from you or hurting you somehow and they swear they're going to take care of it." She stepped into kitchen a pace and popped open the refrigerator. She bent down, her long, creamy thighs there in front of Jude, strong and pale and soft.

"Does anyone take care of Frenchie?" he asked.

"What?" Lacey half-stood in surprise. "Frenchie?"

"I mean…" Jude pointed to his cheekbone.

"Oh that," Lacey laughed and ducked back into the refrigerator. "Believe me, Frenchie can take care of herself. You want a beer?"

"Ah, sure," he said. He turned and wiped down the last section of countertop and hung the towel. When he turned, Lacey was leaving the kitchen with two bottled beers.

She folded herself down on the couch and set the beers on the coffee table.

"What's Reseda?"

"Reseda?"

"Yeah, the Wendy chick. She said that's where, I don't know, cheap housing is, I guess."

"Oh, right. Reseda is just a shit town out in the Valley. Ten square miles of shit apartments."

Jude surveyed the living room, seeing that there was room next to her, but that he should probably sit in the chair across from her. Of course, he didn't want to sit across from her. He realized as he stood there that at this moment, his satisfaction and pleasure in the world could be measured in inches from Lacey. It could be a unit of measure: IFL. The fewer of these there were, the better off he was. The more of these there were, the darker his day would be.

He hesitated at the corner of the table, almost freezing in place again. Then he awkwardly lurched and lumped onto the couch. He settled in and looked at the beer, then at Lacey. He was seven IFL.

"San Fernando Valley," she tossed back her hair. "That's where Reseda is."

He picked up the beer, a Pabst Blue Ribbon, and sipped. He'd tasted beer before, but rarely, and now it tasted like sour piss. But Lacey tilted her beer and pulled several gulps down quickly.

Jude tried to mimic her, but just got one swig in before he choked and coughed.

"Sorry," he said.

Lacey didn't seem to even notice.

"So," Jude said, "I have some money."

Lacey's eyes flickered, as though she were returning from somewhere far off, then she looked up at Jude, smiling. "That's sweet, Jude, but I can't break your piggy bank."

"It's not my piggy bank," Jude said. He was hurt that she would once again treat him like a child. He was sure they were past that.

"I don't mean..." she started.

"It's drug money. The pills I sell," he said. "I can get you five hundred dollars tomorrow. And more pretty soon."

"Five hundred?" He could tell she was surprised.

"Yeah," Jude swigged at the beer again, willing himself to not taste the stuff until it had gone down. "How much does the Paulo asshole owe you?"

"It's not..." she started but stopped. She centered her gaze on Jude's face. "He owes me more than a grand."

"Okay, well, I'll get you five hundred tomorrow, and another five hundred in like…" Jude had no idea how much money he could expect from Lance, but Lance had said it would be better than what he was making on his own. He'd been selling for over a month, so… "I don't know for sure, but maybe in a week or two."

"You would do that for me?" she asked.

"Of course," he said.

Lacey smiled and shook her head, then she leaned across, pulled at Jude's shoulder. As he leaned down toward her, following the pull of her hand, she met his lips with hers and she kissed him.

The kiss wasn't the dry, quick thing he'd felt before. It was a warm, deep, resonating echoing shower of light and heat through his inner realm. When she pulled away, it felt like his soul was being detached, cell-by-cell.

Lacey cast a melancholy smile at him and said, "I sure hope you're not doing this because you're falling for me."

Jude frowned. "Why is that?"

"If we're friends," Lacey held his hands. "If we're friends, then we'll always be friends." She nodded her head at him waiting for him to agree.

"Sure, I guess."

"But if you're in love, then, at some point, you're going to get your heart broken. And you won't forgive me for that. Not for a long time."

Jude pondered this, but found no way into the idea. What he was feeling was, he was almost sure, love. It was certainly not friendship. But it didn't feel like he had a choice.

"In the meantime," she smiled again. "While you were busy hating me—fully justified, by the way—I would miss my good friend, Jude."

"I doubt I could ever hate you," he said.

"Yeah, it surprises just about everyone."

Jude's face clouded. He was about to ask what she meant, but she spoke first.

"No one can imagine hating someone they're in love with. Then," she leaned in and kissed Jude once more, this time on the corner of his mouth, "they can't believe they ever loved the person they hate."

Lacey finished her beer and snapped it with finality on the table.

242 · If They Say I Never Loved You

She unfolded her legs out from under her and then stood. "So that's why I hope we're friends, Jude. But we are, right?"

She reached down and helped Jude to his feet.

"So, should I…"

"If you do, I'll pay you back. I swear."

"I don't care if you pay me back."

"Yeah, right," she laughed.

Then Lacey hugged him and Jude felt his erection press against her. Jude gulped air and goggled his eyes until they were almost painful.

She released him keeping a hand on each of his shoulders. "I should never let you in here. But, you're a sweetheart. And a friend. And you will get over me." Her face opened into a grin. "You'll see."

IT WAS as if the world were a tumbler on a safe and it had rotated the last, final click. Suddenly the latch had popped and the safe was opening with a silent sigh.

Jude woke up feeling ecstatic. He untaped the roll of bills he had behind his drawer and shoved it into his pocket. He scooped another perfect 50/50/50 of pills into a baggy. As he dressed, he found himself nearly dancing in his bedroom. Then, he hopped on his bike to an inner soundtrack of pleasure and play, even as Kevin rode hard to keep up and kept throwing 'What-the-fuck-is-wrong-with-you?' looks at Jude when he did catch up.

Outside the bike racks, Jude and Kevin encountered Hector and one of his henchmen. Jude heard Kevin behind him utter "Shit!" But Jude had Lance's word. He rode straight to the racks and dismounted, not five feet from Hector.

Jude expected maybe angry, molten silence, but instead, Hector met Jude's gaze and, very slightly, lifted his chin in very cool, very understated, recognition.

Jude also lifted his chin, and began to wonder what Lance had said, and who this Lance character was.

Hector ambled off while Jude and Kevin locked their bikes.

"What the fuck was that about?" Kevin asked.

"I don't know for sure," Jude said, "but I think Lance talked to him."

"Lance?" Kevin was agog. "Lance Wilhite?"

Jude shrugged. "I don't know his last name."

"The kid you were talking to a couple days ago at lunch?"

"Yeah, him."

"Yeah, that's Lance Wilhite." Kevin made it sound like he was a criminal, FBI posters in the Post Office and all.

"What's wrong with Lance?"

"Man, he's like seventeen or something. He flunked out of King like twice, and he spent some time in juvie, and now he's here." Kevin shook his head. "But fuck, man, he's old enough to be in high school."

"Well, he said he would help me with Hector, and it looks like he did."

Kevin cocked his head at Jude, working the angles. Then he pulled back and began nodding. "Right, your dad's pills," Kevin pronounced. "You're giving him your dad's pills."

"Even if I was," Jude said, determined to be more cagey than he was accustomed to, "I wouldn't. I wouldn't tell someone like that that I have pills."

Kevin smiled and let his eyebrows climb in disbelief. "Right. He's practically the *only* person you *can* tell something like that."

In his locker, Jude found a sealed white envelope, the kind that would hold a small Thank You note or invitation. He wanted to open it, but felt too many eyes around him. Even if they weren't watching him now, they were potential eyes. Just try tearing open a private note in a crowded hallway...

Instead, he ducked into the downstairs toilets and entered the first stall. He hooked the baggy behind the toilet and sat down to tear open the note. But he was running late, so he skimmed the note—it was an invite—but his eye jumped to the signature. In a rounded, looping hand, Serena's signature hung just above the bottom of the paper. The *a* at the end of her name had been converted to a tiny heart.

Jude stuffed the note in between pages of a book and stood up. He flushed and left, feeling like his entire body must be glowing. A heart!

In homeroom, when Ms. Mantle assigned them time to work

on any homework they might need to do, he finally felt he had the privacy to read the note. While Ms. Mantle prattled on about "the horrendous state of student skills these days," because no one was coming to her optional study skills class at lunchtime, Jude opened his book and laid the note open inside it.

"Hiya Jude!" was penned at the top. A printed invitation followed. It was a Halloween party at Serena's house on Saturday. It started at 6:00 and went "until it's over." Costume prizes. Then at the bottom, Serena had written, "Hope you can make it! Luv ya, Serena." And the *a* was still there: a little heart.

At lunch, Lance bumped into him in the crowded hall and spun on him. He grasped Jude by the shoulders and got into his face. He spit out in a fierce voice, "You gotta watch where you walking, honky bitch!"

Jude pulled back, but was pinioned by Lance's clawlike grasp. He dropped his books and with a start realized he'd been on the verge of wetting his pants. His face burned and reddened.

"And," Lance leaned in closer and snarled in an almost silent, hoarse whisper, "check your pockets."

Then Lance shoved Jude a pace back, spun and left.

Jude stood a long moment, just feeling shock. But kids were walking right over his books and papers. He bent and began pulling everything together. He looked for the card from Serena, but didn't see it. Feet and legs kept plowing right through. No one stopped to help.

He finally saw the card and he lept between kids, grabbed it, and slipped it into *Trout Fishing*.

As he stood, he pulled a tightly-rolled wad of paper from his pocket. It was money. At least a hundred dollars. Maybe more. He stuffed it back in his pocket and headed for math.

~

IT TOOK Jude until Saturday morning to get the accumulated bills to Lacey. On Thursday, as Jude had done his usual reconnaissance, swooping around the corner fast on his bike, Russ had been out watering the front lawn.

"Hey! I see you, you little honkey mo-fuckka!" He slashed the water in an arc after Jude. "Get the fuck outta here!"

Jude ducked down, the water nowhere near him, and added speed.

On Friday, before he'd set foot on the bottom of the stairs, Frenchie had stepped to the rail above and said, "She's busy."

Jude's face had burned with shame and jealousy. He wanted to go up and pound on the door and yell, "I have the money! I have it, and now you can quit!"

Instead he had retreated up the street, locked his bike, and then made his way back down behind the apartment buildings across the street. He sidled out along the drive where he could watch the front of the Crestview.

He was standing in a narrow drive with bushes along one side. He slid in behind the bushes and leaned against the stucco wall.

Not two minutes later, Lacey's door opened and a man stepped out. He wasn't what Jude expected. The figure was a man wearing a white dress shirt, sleeves rolled to below the elbow, and black slacks. His shoes were black canvas. He wore a gold watch and a small gold chain around his neck. Sunglasses hid his eyes. Jude guessed him to be thirty or forty years old.

The man looked up and down the street, as though he thought someone might be following him. Then he spread the fingers of both hands out in front of himself like he was about to fly, and then balled them into fists. He rolled his head on his neck once, twice, and then several more times, almost luxuriously. Then he headed for the front stairs.

Frenchie was still on the walkway, cigarette smoke trailing away above her.

Jude watched for another ten minutes, but Lacey never came out. Then a chubby bald man ambled up the backstairs and, with a nervous nod at Frenchie, went to Lacey's door.

Jude felt his face crumple and tears start. He burst from the bush and hurried back behind the building. He was sure Frenchie had seen him.

He went home with a shiv of hatred under his heart. He would just keep the money. His mother was always telling him to save for college. Perfect! He would sock it away and when the time came, he would just pay for his own fucking college.

He sat on his bed and carefully laid flat and recounted the money. Still seven hundred and eighty dollars. He folded it over once and it formed a nice fat sheaf of worn bills. He lifted his mattress and stuffed it under.

There was no escaping it, though. Always, from under the darkness of the sea inside him, there was the light that was Lacey. He would focus himself on her taking one sweaty fat man after another into her bedroom, as he battered his mind with hatred and disgust, and then, off to one side, as if off-stage, he would hear her laughter or feel her kiss on his lips, her hand on his face, and the entire sea of darkness would drain away in an instant. He was…

He didn't know what he was.

He could tell he wanted to be right. He wanted his mother's moral compass, even if it pointed somewhere strange. He wanted his father's certainty and fury. He wanted his brother's detachment and incisive focus on something inanimate.

But what he had instead was the experience of being flushed through dark pipes through unexpected feelings, through insane curves, down harrowing drops, and into bizarre destinations.

He had no real friends. He thought he'd been acquiring friends but he had exactly one telephone number and that was Kevin's. Or, well, he had Serena's now because it was on the invitation. But he would never call her. He wished he knew Theo's phone number, but he'd never thought that Theo was really a friend. Now, he felt like Theo was possibly his only friend. Problem was, they'd never really 'made friends.'

Music fell away from him. It all sounded tinny and futile. Juvenile. He couldn't read. He tried writing, but the only sentence he finished was the first one: 'Fuck!' He would smoke pot, or take some Valium, or even LSD, but he knew none of it could touch the ragged 'high' he was living.

He entered Friday night like a vagabond entering a foreign city. And he just lived through it. It was all he could do.

He told his mother he had a lot of homework and went upstairs and closed his door. He crawled out his window to the cage and laid on the steel slats watching city lights crackle on in blocks, and house and apartment lights pop on one-by-one. He tracked the flaring lights of police cars and ambulances. He tried to guess where the triangular pinpoints of light in the sky, the jets, were going.

At some point, he finally fell asleep.

When he woke, he was in his bed and the ceiling was boxed off in great rectangles of reflected light from the city. His window was still wide open and the radio on. He must have come inside by himself because his mother would have closed the window and turned off the radio.

He laid back and was engulfed by black emptiness.

JUDE woke with a start.

He reached under his mattress and felt for the big flat sheaf of bills. As soon as his fingers touched it, he was already rolling from bed. He left the bills there and got himself dressed. The radio was playing "The Beat Goes On" by Sonny and Cher.

The day outside was misty under early reddish light. His window was still open and a chill lay in the room. He looked out before pulling it closed. The pastel stuccoed houses outside looked bright and cheerful like saltwater taffys. Past the houses, a downtown skyscraper was slashed with a deep orange flame of reflected sunlight. The streets and buildings in the distance fell under a blue shroud.

He knew it was early, way early, but he grabbed the money and stuffed it into his pocket. Then, in silence, he let himself out of his room, down the stairs, and out the kitchen side door.

He tilted his bike toward town and he let it gather speed. The streets were nearly empty and rather than the seedy gutters he usually saw between dusty buildings, they seemed avenues of possibility.

At Canyon Drive, he locked his bike behind the apartment building across the street from the Crestview. He hitched his pants up on his hips and headed across. The place was quiet. No one was out or at a window. There was no music.

Jude mounted the back stairs and, rolling along the outside of his soles, he slipped down the walkway in silence. At Lacey's door, he didn't bother to knock, he just tried the knob.

It was locked.

He hadn't realized it, but his entire plan—he hadn't even realized he had a plan until this moment—had hinged on the door being unlocked.

Jude's blood turned to cold sludge. If he knocked, he would probably alert other people that he was there. He didn't want that. If he waited, he knew he could wait all day for a chance to talk to her and it might never come. And even if it did, he could still be seen in the half-minute it would take him to cut from cover and run to her door.

He looked out at the street. His eyes welled with tears. He realized that he hadn't expected any obstacles. He'd felt so right about what he was doing, and right not from his tiny little human stance but right from the Big Right, whatever that was, that he was certain, from the moment he woke… he hadn't considered anything between himself and Lacey.

Feeling exposed, he looked across toward where his bike was locked. But retreat seemed impossible. The whole thing might unravel. The whole thing, even in his own mind, might unravel.

Jude turned back to the door, this time as its own problem. He tried the knob again. It was still locked. Then he stepped back and looked at the door in its milieu. There was a little black metal stand with a plant. Its tendrils were touching the white painted surface of the walkway. Next to this was a cross-hatched black rubber door mat.

Jude lifted the mat. No key. He lifted the plastic container that held the plant. He fingered the dark soil. No key. He ran his fingers over the top of the doorframe, his eyes constantly darting left and right. No key.

He stood back one more time. He felt like he could just give the door a swift kick just below the door knob and it would pop open. But he would probably also wake other people up, and might scare Lacey.

Ready to give up and retreat, he shifted his attention to the window. The window was partly open and the screen was bent. He lifted the screen tight against the top of the frame until the bottom edge was clear and he popped the screen out.

Jude pushed aside the curtains and angled the screen into the apartment. He leaned in and set the screen quietly against the inside wall. Then he reached over and unlocked the door.

He was in.

He closed and locked the door, and then closed the window, trying to lift the reluctant aluminum frame to keep it quiet. It sort of worked. The window finally latched with a click.

Jude slipped into the darkened living room. There was a sour smell lingering in the shadows. The kitchen table, he saw, was cluttered with newspapers and clothing. A couple of potted plants looking yellow at the far edge. The sink was piled with dishes again. He focused. He crossed the room taking in only dimly the cast of the furniture and the sharp eyes and images that watched from the photographs.

Her bedroom door was open and he stopped just outside to look in.

He could see Lacey from the shoulders down. She was spread-eagled, lying on her stomach, under the sheet. A fan murmured on low in the window. Jude wanted to see her head, her hair. He edged in further.

This room smelled cool and sweet. It was as if the air were laced with nighttime and forests and a distant rainstorm.

He entered her room.

For a long moment he drank her in. What would it be like, he wondered, to come into that bedroom every morning to bring her coffee and maybe the paper? To see her roll over and smile at him? At *him*!

Maybe… no definitely… she would pat the bed beside her and Jude—he saw himself in just a pair of boxer shorts—odd because he wore briefs—would slide in next to her.

For just a moment, Jude knew what it would be like to inhabit the exact center of the universe. He felt infused with worth and love. Whether she knew it or not, Jude and Lacey belonged together.

Lacey's face was toward him, but hidden by her hair. Jude knelt down near her bed. He raised a finger, and without touching her skin, started at the temple and pulled her hair back from her face. It was like unveiling a saint. His breath caught and his eyes welled just a little.

"Lacey?" he whispered, his voice suddenly quavering.

Nothing.

"Hey Lacey," he mastered his voice.

But she didn't stir.

Jude reached up and laid his hand over hers. Quietly, he said, "Lacey, I'm here," and he squeezed her hand.

She opened one eye, unfocused, mouth open over a small spot of moisture on the pillow. The eye closed again.

Jude squeezed her hand again, "Hey, Lace."

Both eyes popped open and she jerked her hand away. Her whole body jerked back away from him.

"Hey, sorry," Jude fell back himself. "It's just me!"

"Fuuuuck!" Lacey squinted up out of the covers. She took in Jude and then scanned the room as though reading the patterns and density of the light.

"Jude? What the fuck are you doing here?" She mumbled the words as she rolled away from him and settled with her back to him. "And what fucking time is it? It's *way* too fucking early."

"Sorry," Jude watched her shoulder rise and fall with her breathing. "I tried to come by the last two days, and I kept getting kicked out."

Her breathing was slowing, deepening.

"I brought the money," he said, pulling the sheaf of bills from his pocket. It smelled like old dried lettuce.

Lacey drew in a deep breath and rolled back to look at Jude. "I'm sorry, Jude. I don't get up at whatever the fuck this hour is, ever." But she settled onto her back, her eyes open, reading the pale blue light on the ceiling.

"What is it, like eight in the morning?" She raised her hands overhead and stretched.

"Maybe a little earlier." Jude could see the pale green glow of the bedside clock. It was 7:15 A.M.

"All right, all right," Lacey laid her arms over her face and eyes. "You're here to do me a favor. A huge, massive favor. I can wake up for that." She lay there without moving though, and Jude feared she would fall back asleep.

"And you're right," she continued. "It's hard to get in here sometimes. For someone like you, anyway."

"No shit, man," Jude tried to deepen his voice to sound cool and physically older while the topic of his youth was under discussion.

"But I'm here now," he said, changing the subject. "And I do have it. Seven hundred and eighty bucks."

"Whoa!" Lacey dropped her arms from her face and then propped herself up on her elbows. She shook her hair back and looked at Jude for the first time. "That's a lot of dough, Jude." She was wearing a baseball-style T-shirt with dark blue arms that stopped mid-forearm. It made her look so young and fresh, and breathtakingly beautiful.

Warily, almost shamefully, Jude let his gaze slide down the bed and out to the floor and chair and bedside tables. The bedroom, compared to the living room, was relatively neat. Clothes were hung in the open closet and shoes were lined along the closet floor.

The neatness felt like an anomaly. There was also a small array of pink and blue and yellow and green bottles on the bedside table on the far side of her bed. And then there was, in the closet, a hamper full of sheets.

He felt the stab of jealousy and looked back at Lacey's face.

She had been watching him.

She laid back and reached out and grasped his hand. "I can't even begin to fathom…" she started. "But, look, if you loan me that much money, maybe this ends. Like soon. Right?"

Jude nodded and felt his face crumpling again. He bit his lip and stared past her. But tears stood in his eyes and he took in a quick stabilizing pulse of air.

Lacey scooted back and tugged on Jude's hand. "Hey," she tugged again, "Come here."

Jude felt as limp as smoke. He rose and flowed along the flue onto the bed.

He sat.

She patted the bed, just like he'd imagined.

He lay down, curling up tight. But he felt awkward and stiff and out of place. He was a foot or two from Lacey, facing away from her. He was wearing jeans and T-shirt, his flannel shirt, and his high-top PF Flyers.

Lacey pushed on his back. "Hey, this is my *bed*. Take off your shoes."

Jude kicked his shoes off, then toed his socks off one after the other. He still felt wooden and strange, but then Lacey spooned up against his back, and the sweet, soft flush of her breath on his neck, and the warmth of her body, and the curled innocence of their bodies struck a hammer blow in his chest. Tears flowed silently down his cheeks and his breath caught and surged. Lacey pulled him closer, tighter, and he melted into her.

She talked softly behind him while he buried his nose in her sheets and reveled in the smell. And cried quietly. She talked about going home maybe, just for a day or two. But that she could get a fresh start. "I can teach school, I think," she said. "Did you know that?"

He shook his head, No.

"Yeah well, but not here. I can't teach school around here."

"Why," Jude croaked out.

"It's expensive to live here. More than a teacher can make. And…"

"And?"

"These people…"

Jude knew what she was talking about. Or believed he did. She'd called them the Walkers. They owned the building. They owned the women who worked there.

Jude pushed back against her. He nestled in closer.

And then he smelled coffee.

Sunlight was sharp and stinging in his nostrils and he felt like he was held down by a dense wet spiderweb. His eyes were crusted and his lips were chapped. He rolled over into a strange shell of a place he couldn't identify. Then he heard music, and it wasn't the music, but the volume, the exact precise volume of it, and the pinpoint location of its source, that he recognized. That little black Panasonic radio, its hopeful little antenna thrust up from its table in the living room, became the center of meaning and his entire geography and history leapt from it in an instant.

"Fuck," he groaned.

"Hey, bright eyes," Lacey swept into the room and threw a pillow onto the bed past his face.

"What happened?" Jude asked. "Did I fall asleep?"

"Yep, you did."

"What time is it?"

"Almost noon. You hungry?"

Jude sat up and swung his legs off the bed. He realized with a start that he wore just his T-shirt and his underwear. His flannel, pants, shoes and socks were folded and set on the chair by the closet.

"Yeah, I guess so."

"Come on," Lacey stood for maybe just one second there at the door, but Jude drank her in and stored the moment like a gold medal from his grandfather. She was wearing two tank-tops and short cut-off jean shorts. Her feet were spread apart and she had lifted her arms out to the side. She was an expression of happiness and light and possibility.

Then she was gone.

Jude stood up and pulled on his pants. He buttoned the fly and headed for the front room.

"I'm making you a grilled cheese. That sound good?"

"That sounds really good."

He plunked himself at the table which had been mostly cleared, and just as he dropped his head into his hands, Lacey slid a steaming cup of coffee under his nose. "Wake it on up, buttercup."

Jude sipped at the dark liquid and felt the first shockwaves of the caffeine roll through him. He reached into his pocket and tugged out the cash. He placed it on the table and then shoved it away from himself and toward Lacey in the kitchen.

When she emerged from the kitchen with a bright yellow plate, she slowed and then stopped. She set the plate next to the money as though one some kind of an exchange for the other. "Jude." She sat and slid the plate toward him.

"Jude," she said again. "Are you sure? I mean, I'll pay you back, but really, you don't have any proof of that. You don't know me, Jude. Not at all."

Jude bit into the sandwich and chewed. He felt a thousand things at once. His body was hollow and limned with webs of drowsiness. His blood was crackling with coffee. His eyes were swollen and heavy-lidded. His lips dry. And this talk of trust and knowing, it fired off entire galaxies of thought and reaction.

Jude plucked up a few potato chips from the plate and crunched them to paste. Then he took another bite.

"I'm serious, Jude," Lacey reached across and touched his elbow. "You should use this money for college." With her other hand, she pushed the cash a few inches back in his direction.

He said nothing. The weariness he felt was the weariness of his certainty. He was tired of the world pushing him to do and be and think things he had no wish to. It was like advertisements, just so much irrelevant noise.

He finished his sandwich, polished off the chips, and then sat back with the coffee cup in his hand. Lacey sat there watching him, her look confused, her head sometimes tilting like a cat confronted by a strange noise.

Jude looked past her at the kitchen.

She read his look. "No!" she stood. "You are *not* going to do my dishes again."

Jude looked away. He felt sixty, eighty. Impossibly wise. There were bald, open truths now, and nothing else. He was fifteen. That was just what it was. And he was in love with a woman maybe ten years older. And she was a whore. And she would probably be leaving. Probably soon. Using his money to do it. He had a dizzying vortex inside. He suddenly felt like he might never see her again.

But that too was just another of the truths. Nothing to be done about it. No amount of moaning or crying or fretting would change it.

"I gotta go," he said. "I didn't leave a note or anything."

"Jude?" Lacey sounded scared. "What's up? You're kinda acting crazy here."

"No," he said and swung his eyes to meet hers. He could see her, maybe for the first time, as the impossible, stumbling, troubled and troublesome storm that she was. Her eyes were lined with surprise and exhaustion. Her mouth was tightened by fear. Even the cast of her shoulders and neck—she was on the defense. It was like she never knew where the next blow, the next problem, the next shock would come from.

"I'm not crazy," he said. "I'm just a kid." He stood up and without clearing his plate, he went into the bedroom and sat on the chair. He pulled on his socks and shoes and then stood and tucked his flannel into the side of his jeans where it wouldn't catch in his bike chain.

When he came out, Lacey was standing there waiting for him.

She had the wad of money in her hand. She waited until Jude met her gaze.

She said, "One thing you are not, Jude, and that's a kid."

Jude shrugged. He looked at the door. It was the first time he had ever wanted to leave Lacey's apartment.

"I've been around," she said. "You know that about me." She took a step that effectively blocked him from the door. "And I'll tell you this, I can count my real friends on *one* fucking finger." She held up her hand with the index finger raised.

Jude met her eyes again.

"You know who that friend is?" she asked.

Jude shrugged again.

"That friend is Jude Tangier."

He knew she was being dramatic. He was not her one true friend. But he cried because she was crying. But it was literally tears falling from a hollow. He felt gutted, solemn, weary. He almost spoke. He thought that Penny, Frenchie, and maybe others, must be friends. But as soon as he began to think it, he thought of his own 'friends.' No one from Indiana had written him. Kevin was fitful as a butterfly. Greg and Melinda were conditional at best. So was Serena.

Lacey flipped the money onto the table and came to Jude. She took his shoulders and pulled him to her. She hugged him and they cried together. He could feel her chest heaving in a tempo off from his own. Her arms were tight around him, and his found their way around her. He hugged her like a tree in a tornado.

He let himself sink into the warmth of it, the rawness. He pressed his face into her hair and shoulder. He drank in her smells. His hands and body read hers with something deeper than need or memory. His tears welled up from somewhere deeper than had ever *been* there before. And for a while, the depth kept getting impossibly deeper.

She finally loosened her grip on him and leaned her head back. Her face was a mess of tears and she laughed when she saw his face. "We're quite the pair," she said and wiped his face from top to bottom with her bare hand. He reached up and did the same to her.

Jude jutted his chin at the money. "I'll have some more next week," he said.

"Jude, really."

"Really."

He wove home through the early afternoon traffic like a porpoise in the waves. He was mindless. He was completely untethered. He was a molecule inside the existence of existence. His bike leapt and swerved and jumped and hopped. He slipped between the great walls of buses and the galloping cars. He shot over curbs. He shot up alleys and down delivery ramps. He rode.

As the pavements jarred and jumped beneath him, a crazy-quilt of concrete, asphalt, paint and glass, he pressed his mind ahead. He wanted to project this incredible experience out into the future. He wanted to tell Mark, Kevin, James, Greg and Melinda, Seren...

"Holy shit!" Jude whispered to the street. Serena's party was tonight.

FOR THE PARTY, Mark let Jude borrow a suede jacket he'd worn for a play in Indiana. He'd been an Indian in the play, and the jacket had fringe running up the bottom of both sleeves and it crossed the back of the jacket at the shoulder blades.

From the bottom and back of his shirt drawer he pulled out a T-shirt he'd bought a month earlier but hadn't dared wear yet. It was the first piece of clothing he'd ever bought for himself. It was a long-sleeved T with the bottom half consisting of vertical red-and-white stripes and the top half a single white star on a blue background.

For pants, he pulled out his most outrageous pair of flares. His mother refused to buy him true bell-bottoms and he couldn't imagine trying to buy himself a pair of pants. But these were striped, also vertically, in tans and browns.

His shoes would have to be his PF Flyers.

But Mark topped it all off to perfection. When he saw Jude dressed up two hours before he would ever have to leave, he laughed. "You look like a lost kid from Indiana."

"Fuck," Jude's blood slowed and darkened in him. "I'm like..."

"Hey man," Mark said, "me too. Just a minute."

When he came back he stepped in behind Jude and slid a rolled bandanna over his forehead. It was poorly folded and loose, but it hid the weirdly angled bangs Jude had carried with him as his badge of innocence from Indiana.

"Cool," Jude said.

"Yeah, man, that nails it."

"So groovy," Jude's head bounced in what he imagined was a hippy-like hip agreement. He could feel, and just about envision, what it would be like to have hair down around his shoulders.

"All right, dude, you're ready for the big party." Mark walked around him, assessing. The music from his turntable cut at the end of the Beatles' "I Want To Tell You" and he and Mark could hear the searing blaze of Hendrix from Mark's room.

Then, as Mark was leaving to go back to his room and probably continue practicing guitar, Jude had a flash of recognition. He was dressed like Paulo. The shirt—he hadn't ever realized this before, not even when he was buying it—was almost identical to the first one he'd seen Paulo wearing on his motorcycle. And the suede jacket was another thing he'd seen Paulo wearing.

Jude could feel guilt and shame slide across his face. Greg and Melinda, and probably everyone else there, would just say, "Oh hey, cool Paulo costume." And then they would run off and tell Paulo that the creepy kid from Indiana had come to a party dressed just like him.

Mark was slowed by the events crossing Jude's face. "What's up, man?"

The doorbell rang.

It wasn't often the doorbell rang, but when it did, it did more to impart the size and grandeur of this house than anything else. It was a single *bong* tone, but a deep peeling bong, one that didn't sound electronic. It sounded like old brass and filled the halls and rooms with its suddenness and presence.

Jude and Mark looked at each other and waited. "Got To Get You Into My Life" was chirping merrily on the record player.

A few moments later, they heard their mother pulling open the door and her typical cheerful greeting curve sharply downward. A deep, gravelly voice started in and Mark and Jude edged to the bedroom door. A man was asking for "Doctor Tan-gee-air."

"Tan-jheer," their mother pronounced the name for him. "Just a moment."

Their father was out in the backyard. He was laying out in his swim trunks sunning. He nurtured his tan every chance he got. Even,

Jude knew, sunning in the nude when he thought no one else was home.

Their mother got halfway up the stairs before she stopped. "Oh my, I'm sorry." She glanced over her shoulder at Jude's bedroom door and pegged them standing there. "Boys, go get your father."

Then she spun and trotted back down. "Please, I'm forgetting my manners! Come in! Have a seat in the living room! Can I get you something to drink?"

Jude rushed through the connecting bathroom behind Mark and shot a look out his bedroom door. From there, they could see down into the entry hall. Two men in gray suits stood there, hats in their hands.

"Cops," Mark whispered.

Jude felt the word pass through him like a bolt of lightning. "No fucking way."

"Way," Mark said. He sneered, "Maybe they caught the old man being an asshole to someone else, and they're taking him for twenty-five-to-life."

Jude felt like a wooden model of a bird was being unfolded inside his chest. There was no room for the thing inside him. It felt like it was going to unfold no matter what and break anything in its way. He felt like his entire childhood of innocence and stupidity was about to come home to roost.

He ducked around the corner into the sunroom and went to the back door. He tugged it open and looked out. His father lay on a chaise on the patio where the neighbors couldn't see him. Next to him was his huge, pale-blue plastic iced tea glass, empty but for a small hill of ice cubes on the bottom.

Jude called him, "Dad, some guys are here to see you."

But he didn't stir.

"Dad!"

No movement.

Jude finally crossed the lawn and nudged the chair with his foot. His father's eyes fluttered open. "Wha?" He almost barked the word. He sat halfway up and then slumped back. His eyes rolled and then popped wide open before closing again. "Wha?" Quieter this time.

"Some guys are here to see you."

"Some, wha?" He slowly licked his lips and laid his hand over his eyes.

"I was sleeping," he said.

"Yeah, Mark thinks they're cops. And they're waiting in the living room."

"What?" The last T on the word was crisp and his father sat up straight and sharp. "What? Cops?" Then his face clouded and he turned an angry scowl at Jude. "Why didn't you tell me?"

Jude shrugged and backed away.

Their father leapt to his feet and spun on Jude. "What on earth are you wearing?" Then he was in the house in three leaps and the screen door banged shut.

Jude slipped back in the house and rushed down the hall to his room. His father was behind the closed bedroom door getting dressed. Jude closed his bedroom door and ripped off the headband. Then he quickly stripped out of the hippy clothes.

He got dressed in a pair of plain flared blue jeans and a striped T-shirt. Then he grabbed the baggie of pills out of the pocket of his Sunday blazer in the closet and the small baggie of pot in the other pocket. In the bathroom, he dumped the substances into the toilet, bags and all, and flushed.

The bag of marijuana circled the drain like a big jellyfish, a bubble of air caught inside. It didn't go down. And worse, as the flushing subsided, it rolled to one side and the air escaped, pushing a small floating pad of crushed leaves out over the surface.

"Fuck," he flushed again.

Mark looked in. "They can hear you flushing the toilet," he said. "They probably know what you're doing."

Jude hadn't thought about that.

Jude pulled two squares of toilet paper and carefully reached down into the bowl. With the squares he carefully wiped out the last few little leaves that clutched the sides. The wet wad of paper he took to the window over his sink and threw it deep into his neighbor's trees.

When he turned back, Mark was shaking his head. "Let's just hope no one is watching from the street."

"Fuck," Jude felt beset.

He ducked back into his room and quickly picked up the scattered costume, shoving it into his clothes hamper.

He stood a moment, staring at himself in the mirror as if just encountering his estranged twin for the first time. The boy staring back was foreign, desperate, lost. He wasn't the scheming, dealing, daring master of the underworld he'd imagined.

In the hall, he heard his father clear his throat, preparing for the audience.

Jude rushed down to Mark's room. From there, the door cracked open a finger's width, they could hear better.

"Doctor Tangier," Jude could feel the man stand up, extend a hand. "I'm Detective Kiplinger, and this is Detective Rose. Can we speak privately?"

"Of course," his father's voice barked with authority. "We can talk in my den."

"Nothing I can get you gentlemen?" Their mother teetered at the entry to the living room, her voice shaky, her hands weaving quick designs in the air.

"No thank you, ma'am."

But the other man, his voice raspy, said, "If a coffee isn't a problem…"

"Oh, it's no problem at all."

Jude took a lower slot in the doorway, and Mark leaned in above him, so they could watch the small procession of men's shoes and slacks go down the hall to the den.

As soon as the three men passed, Jude looked back up at Mark and they silently agreed. They slipped out of Mark's room and shot out the back door. It was a hot day. There was a good possibility the den doors were standing open to the patio on the side of the house.

Mark led the way. They turned the corner from the back yard and could see the doors, all four of them, glass-paned, tall white doors, thrown open. He sidled silently down the stone stairs. Halfway down he stopped and Jude pulled up just behind him.

They sat that way a minute, tuning their ears to the sounds. But the men's voices were deep and hard to hear.

Mark slid down two steps and Jude followed.

They heard their mother knock and deliver coffee. "Anything else I can get you? No coffee for you? You're sure? Lyle?"

"No, no thank you."

Jude could imagine the scene. His father would be sitting in his chair and the two detectives would be sitting on the couch, a foot lower. They would sit forward, their knees high and their elbows propped there. It was his one of father's defenses against being short.

"What can I do for you gentlemen today?" he asked.

"Sir," the Kiplinger man said, "I'll cut to the chase here. Your son has been selling drugs at school, and we have evidence that the drugs may be coming from your personal supply."

Mark turned an eye on Jude. It wasn't accusatory, but a kind of 'Oh, fuck' look.

"My son?" he sounded incredulous but only for a second. "Damn it, I should have known. He's been…" When he spoke again, he'd gotten up and he was right at the door. "He started playing guitar and listening to all those drug songs. And he ran away from home recently. I'm sure he stayed in a drug den for at least some of that time. But I just had no idea he was stealing drugs here at the house."

Jude and Mark exchanged wide-eyed looks.

"There is also good evidence that he has been consorting with, ah, well, several prostitutes, sir."

"Prostitutes?" Jude could practically hear the anger crackling from his father. "Prostitutes? Where? Who?"

Mark looked back at Jude again. This time it was an 'Oh, fuck, they've got you nailed' look.

"Well, sir, it appears there is a woman that has befriended your son."

"Oh my god. Is he…?"

"We don't have that kind of information, sir." Then he asked, "How old is your son, sir?"

"He just turned seventeen. But I just had no idea…"

"Seventeen?"

"Yes," their father turned away from the doors and sat back down heavily. "We just moved here from Indiana a few months ago, and I simply underestimated the impact and influence the big city drug culture would have, I guess."

There was a moment of silence.

"You say he's been selling the drugs?" He sounded cagey now. "How do you know it's him? What is this evidence you have?"

"You said your son is seventeen?" Detective Kiplinger came back to his question.

"Yes, he turned seventeen in, ah, June I think."

Detective Rose asked in his raspy voice, laced with doubt, "A doctor's kid, seventeen, and he attends LeConte Junior High?"

"LeConte?" They heard the creak of his chair. He was up again. "That's my youngest, Jude."

"And how old is he, sir?"

"He's fifteen."

"Well, he's the one who's been selling the drugs."

"I find that…" but he let it trail away.

"You understand that, because he's a minor…"

"Sssst!"

Mark and Jude nearly leapt. Their mother was standing in the yard above them frowning down on them. She gestured wildly for them to come back up the stairs.

They unfolded from their seated positions and slipped up the steps.

She grasped Jude's arm and pulled him away from the stairs. Mark followed in their slipstream. "What on *earth* are you boys doing?"

Jude shrugged.

Mark said, "Listening."

Their mother's face was set and hard, but as soon as Mark spoke, a wedge of doubt appeared.

"So, if you were listening, what were they talking about?"

Now Mark shrugged. It was Jude's fate and he was going to leave it up to Jude.

Jude said, "They're here because I was selling Dad's drugs at school."

"You were *what*?" She released his arm and pushed him away, shocked. She took a step back from him, her face astonished, disbelieving. "My *son* was *selling… drugs*?"

Jude shrugged again.

She reached out and grabbed his arm again and half-led and

half-dragged him into the house. Mark shut the door behind them and she corralled them both into Mark's bedroom.

She pushed Jude so that he sat on the bed, her form looming over him.

But before she said anything, they could hear the door downstairs opening. Their father was saying, "My license is down at my office, but I can show you where I keep my prescriptions."

The three men trumped up the stairs in single file. When their father reached the top of the stairs, he pushed Mark's bedroom door open two feet and leaned in. It was as if he knew Jude would be there.

"You," he speared Jude with a withering glare and spoke just above a whisper, "You, young man, are in a world of trouble."

Behind him, the Kiplinger man stood looking past their father into the room. His stare was directed to Jude, and it was bland, implacable, merciless.

Jude felt his innards melting and turning to ice all at once. His stomach was physically cramping from fear.

Without breaking his gaze from Jude, he said, "Let's see this supply, sir."

A few minutes later, their father emerged and moved down the hall, his eyes scouring Mark's open door for signs of Jude. Jude couldn't move from the bed, so he kept his eyes on the floor. Still, he was hyper-aware of his father's glare.

The two detectives came after him with the three bottles of pills.

"Ma'am," Kiplinger leaned into the room, "we're taking Doctor Tangier by his office to retrieve his medical license and then down to the station."

She raised a hand to her throat and opened her mouth. Her eyes were pained. It took a moment before she spoke. "I don't understand." Her eyes shot past the man to the other detective. "Is he under arrest?"

"Not formally, ma'am. Not at this time," the detective was a blocky man, with a dark ring of oily hair around a bald pate. He held his hat in his hand, almost apologetically, spinning it round and round. Jude concentrated on the dense dark shadow of whiskers on the man's face. Each one, if you bothered to look, was a tiny black dot. It was like an infestation of tiny insects, he thought.

"But you should know, ma'am, that your husband *is* the culpable and liable party in this circumstance, and depending on other parties involved, he may be arraigned and could face criminal and possibly civil charges."

"I don't understand," she took a step toward the detective, as though she might grasp his sleeve to keep him from leaving and taking her husband.

"It's simply this, ma'am. If one of the families of the young people who purchased and consumed these drugs wishes to file charges, it would be your husband who is liable since he is both the responsible parent and the source of the aforesaid drugs."

"Oh my god!" Now she pushed right past the detective. "Lyle?"

"It's going to be fine, Ann. You'll see."

The three men retreated down the stairs and Mark followed his mother out onto the landing. Jude couldn't move. He was peering into a bottomless pool of guilt.

"Sir," he could hear the men just fine. "I'm sorry, but by law we must handcuff you in order to escort you to the car."

His mother gasped. Her voice filled the entryway and shot upstairs, "He is *not* a criminal!"

"Well, ma'am," Kiplinger said, "that's entirely possible. But there are rules, and we follow them, because that's what we expect everyone else to do."

"But he shouldn't be led out of this house in handcuffs like a common criminal!" she barked at him. "These people are our neighbors!"

"I'm sorry, ma'am. The rules are the rules."

"Oh my god." Jude imagined her biting a knuckle, her forehead pulled into sharp, converging lines.

Mark turned to look at Jude. Mark's face was a malevolent grin. He was thrilled to see their father handcuffed and led away.

Jude felt the pool rising inside him. He dropped his chin and closed his eyes.

Then he heard the raspy voice of Detective Rose. "Hey, where's the kid? He's coming, too."

JUDE glanced at his father as he reached the bottom of the stairs. The three men were waiting for him. The detectives flanked his father, each holding him loosely high on his arm. His father's hawk-like gaze was on Jude. All Jude could read from it was… he was going to go with happiness, but it was more than that. His father was gleeful. Gloating. He practically sneered at Jude.

The men backed up a step to make way for Jude.

Jude glanced at his mother. She looked like a complete stranger. Her face was ghostly and drawn as though she'd seen an accident. She was watching the proceedings as though helplessly watching blood drain from him and maybe from his father.

She lifted a hand to her throat and her mouth tightened.

Jude stepped past the men to the front porch. Then, head bowed slightly, he led the men down the 37 steps to the street. At the street, he looked both ways and then crossed over. The detective's car was obvious. There was a late-model, black Ford Galaxie at the curb.

He went to the car and waited. He slipped a fleeting glance over the houses above and around them. The windows flashed and glared like angry eyes. Every single one felt like it contained someone he knew. The neighbors, his brother and mother, but also, oddly, his friends from school, his teachers, his friends from Indiana, his grandparents, his cousins.

As soon as Detective Rose opened the rear door of the car, Jude slid in and across. Rose helped his father duck in after him. His father had run earlier and then had gone out in the yard to sunbathe. He hadn't showered. A warm, cloying odor wrapped Jude's nostrils as his father settled in as best he could with the handcuffs.

"I'm sorry," Detective Rose said. "I can't take them off in the car. We won't be long. We're out of the Hollywood Division."

"Don't worry about me," he thrust his chest upward and out. "I'll be fine." Then he lifted his chin to signal he was above all of this. And ignored Jude to signal that Jude wasn't. Jude was in fact the cause of it all.

Jude leaned his head against the window and let the blocks roll by. It was a strange time in Los Angeles, early afternoon on a Saturday. Traffic was heavy, regardless, and the sidewalks thrummed with a misplaced humanity. There was a huge black woman wearing a vast dirty purple robe. She waddled along, grinning without teeth, and waving a cardboard sign at them. It read, GIVE ME SOME FUCKING MONEY… PLEASE. Another man, also black, tall and thin and dark as ebony, was wrapped in a white sheet and he wore a white turban on his head. Hippies were sitting on the curb smoking what appeared to be pot.

It was a circus out there.

The detectives talked between themselves as they drove. But the windows were down and Jude couldn't hear them. It felt like he and his father weren't even there. Or were luggage.

Jude kept toying with that one thought in his mind: that he was the cause. He had never even questioned the idea. He just was. Any time there was trouble anyways. He hunted back through the events—walking back from the cops arriving, to Lance, to Serena, to Mr. Glenn, to selling drugs, and to Mark running away... all the way back to Hector and even beyond, to the fact that they had moved here in the first place—and he could not quite get the cause to stick to any one thing or person, or even moment...

When they got to the Children's Hospital, Detective Rose and Jude's father went in. Jude sat in the car with Detective Kiplinger who seemed perfectly happy to chew a toothpick and squint out at the foot traffic entering the rear doors. The two came back out with a set of simple picture frames.

Then they drove back the way they'd come.

Detective Kiplinger pulled in next to an old, imposing building with an American flag waving out front. The structure was brick with a red-tile roof. It just two stories, but it looked as tall as a three or four story building. The windows on the first floor were up high and they were long and tall. So were those on the second floor.

Kiplinger opened Jude's door and Jude slumped out. He heard Rose getting his father out on the other side. They entered the building at the side door, passing two uniformed officers heading out. Gruff greetings were passed among the police, and Kiplinger held Jude's arm as they entered.

They ascended stone stairs and entered a high-ceilinged, short and narrow hallway. Cherry-dark wood paneling was cut with pale green frosted glass. Doors had green glass panes with gold-leaf lettering and numbers. DISPATCH—1010. STAFF SERGEANT, LIEUTENANT BRIGG—1017. And PATROL—1025.

A counter opened on the left and a craggy-faced man in police blues and a black-visored police hat was seated behind it. He was talking dispassionately to a man leaning behind and next to him. "She's

got two kids now. Six and maybe four. I don't know if the whole college thing was worth it."

The other man responded, "Depends. Who'd she marry?"

"A plumber," the man said.

The two men watched Detective Rose fill in a form and shove it
across to the seated man. The seated man lifted his chin but didn't
move to touch the paper.

Then Kiplinger touched their arms and Jude followed Detective
Rose through the door marked PATROL. They entered a large open
room with lots of desks and activity. The ceilings were as high as the
hallway, at least twenty feet above them. The vaulted shape of them
amplified the sounds.

The place felt like a cross between an ancient church and an old
public bathroom. Along the far side were wood-and-glass enclosures
built out into the room. The detectives led them straight across toward
these, shooting decisively through the maze of desks and people.

They directed Jude and his father to sit on a dark, scarred, wood-
en bench that reminded Jude of a church pew.

"We'll get you accommodated in a minute or two," Detective
Rose said. Then he spun away and navigated to a desk near the back
of the building and close to the side with the enclosures.

Jude glanced at his father. His father was waiting for him. He
met Jude's gaze and half-grinned like he did just as he was about to
play a trick on someone. "Well," he said, "you've done it now. You're
probably going to spend a few years in juvenile hall."

Jude wanted to sneer back at him and snarl, 'I don't give two
fucks.' But instead he just pouted. Inside he was fuming. He knew
he should be worried about juvenile hall, and maybe about Lance,
or Greg and Melinda. Maybe even Serena.

But he wasn't worried about them or even himself. Maybe it was
because whatever was about to happen to him was beyond his imagi-
nation. Or maybe he was just consumed with hatred for his father.
This man had spent the better part of the last five years—and maybe
before that—taunting and shaming and belittling Jude and Mark at
every opportunity.

On the road trip out to California, his father had told Jude, "You
have good eyesight. Why don't you keep an eye out for Chimera gas
stations? They have the best gas." Of course, Jude never saw one

because there were no such stations. When they got to Los Angeles, he gave Jude grief for not finding any. Then he laughed openly as he told Jude the truth.

Then, not so long after they'd moved to Los Angeles, his parents had had a cocktail party to meet the neighbors. Jude, talking to the Fords from across the street, not knowing his father was nearby and eavesdropping, had been trying to explain what they were doing there in Los Angeles. "My dad is a baby's heart doctor," he'd said. "Apparently they don't have one of those here at Children's."

"Oh," Mr. and Mrs. Ford were thrilled with the information. "It sounds like he'll be doing a great service."

Then his father was there, suddenly looming at Jude's right shoulder. "Ap-par-ent-ly," he stressed each syllable as though the word were made up, "but not acc-ur-ate." He strung out that word too. "I'll be joining two other physicians in the Pediatric Cardiology department. But it sounds like our little Jude is going to be giving political speeches pretty soon with all these big words!"

Jude had blushed horribly and ducked out of the room like a six-year-old.

There were his endless rules, too. The short hair, no bell-bottoms, no rock music, the chores, the low allowance that their mother doled out semi-secretly, and always 'Home by dark!'

But worst of all was what Mark referred to as the scrambled eggs. He explained it to Jude. "Mom is always telling us to be quiet when Dad's home and that he works hard and had a hard day and all that crap. Emilio's dad is the same way and his mother calls it 'walking on eggshells.' Being quiet to keep him from getting pissed. But with our dad, the eggshells are already broken. He's always pissed. He's just looking for an excuse. We're walking in scrambled eggs."

That was pretty much it, Jude decided, The fucker. His father was just a black cloud that hung over Jude's life day-in and day-out.

Detective Kiplinger came and got his father and walked him to one of the enclosures. He opened the door, his father stopping and glaring at Jude with venom in his eyes, then he let his father in and Kiplinger leaned in and said something. Then he stepped out and closed the door.

Jude sat staring glumly at the floor thinking that a show of remorse might help. This morning, he'd felt like he was twenty years old, smart and free and starting to have fun. Now, like a marble in a pot that had stopped spinning, he was back at the bottom. He was a fifteen-year-old kid as wet behind the ears as you could be, still smelling like Russ's turnip truck from Indiana.

The plain old wall clock that hung on the wall to Jude's left read 2:12. He leaned back, swinging his feet so that his heels scuffed on the linoleum, and watched the activity in the room. It was like watching an ant hill. There was purpose and pattern but it was all a mystery to Jude. He thought for a while about where the anthole was, that place where, if you poked a stick, it would cause every single ant, or in this case, cop, to go a little crazy.

Detective Rose took a coffee in to Jude's father, but the two detectives ignored Jude. They sat at their desks and talked into their phones and occasionally leaned over their desks to talk to each other.

At 2:34, a woman in uniform approached. "Let's get you fingerprinted." She was a youngish woman, maybe Mexican, thick in her body and slow moving. Her uniform bulged and popped as she walked.

Jude followed her to the counter. They passed behind it and entered an office where a setup for fingerprints and photographs was arranged.

The woman got every single one of Jude's fingerprints including his thumbs, her hands grasping his and carefully rolling each fingertip first on the ink, and then on a white card with squares marked for each print. Her breath was disturbingly sweet, like a warm chocolate bar, and came in hard gusts through her mouth.

Then she led him back to the pew.

At 2:56, a different young woman who worked at a desk near Jude's pew crossed over and spoke to Detective Rose and he nodded. She left the room through a side door and came back five minutes later with a bottle of Coke.

"You wanna Coke while you're waiting?" she asked him.

"Sure," he was thirsty and the notion of the sugary flavor sparked his taste buds and body.

She handed him the bottle. "They like to make folks wait," she said. She wore the standard dark blue police uniform, but with extra seams and darts to accommodate her femaleness. Her hair was a flop of blonde as though it had been formed in some intentional way earlier but had been knocked aside somehow during the day—Jude imagined her wrestling and handcuffing a criminal. Her face was pretty, but her eyes were green, flat and bland, like she was practicing not caring.

"Wait, like how long?" Jude asked.

"They'll talk to you before dinnertime," she shrugged. "I mean, probably."

"Oh," that seemed like eternity just now, but then, what lay just beyond the end of that eternity wasn't somewhere he wanted to arrive. So, well, what the hell.

"What are you here for?" she asked. "If you don't mind me asking."

"I was selling my dad's pills," he said.

"Your dad's pills? Where does he get the pills?"

"He's a doctor."

"Oh, yeah, that makes sense." She nodded and almost smiled at him. "So," she made a tiny apostrophe in the air over his left eye. "Where'd you get that? She was referring to his scar.

"Some kids beat me up after school," he said. "I'm kinda new here. We moved from Indiana like, I don't know, three months ago?"

"Oh, wow," she said. "So maybe a little culture shock?"

Jude shrugged. "Sure, I guess." That was it. Culture shock. But it was more than that now, of course.

"You're lucky. It's kinda sexy," she gestured to the Coke. "Is that going to be enough? Have you eaten?"

Jude hadn't eaten lunch, but he wasn't in the least hungry. "No, I'm good, thanks."

"Well, I'm Officer Linda Umler. If you need something."

At 3:15, Rose and Kiplinger opened the door of the enclosure and went in.

At 3:32, Jude saw Lance enter the room from the same door they had come in earlier. Lance was alone. Jude's spirits lifted. If there was anyone who could maybe get Jude out of this, it was Lance.

Jude had assumed that as soon as someone was picked up by the cops that everyone who knew that person dove for cover. But maybe

Lance was as good as his word. He'd said, hadn't he, "I can take care of you, even if there's trouble."

Lance had the same past-the-horizon gaze, commando-like garb, and nonchalant shuffle. He lifted his chin at some of the police officers, but the officers didn't respond. They just stared at the kid as he passed them. Jude took it as a show of courage, real or not, as Lance crossed the cluttered room.

Halfway across the room, Lance caught sight of Jude and Jude saw a dark cloud pass through his eyes. But then it was gone. He raised a hand in greeting and set a new course to head for Jude.

"Duuuuude!" he said. "How incredibly inconvenient, man. Right?" He lifted a hand and Jude met it with a slap.

Lance sat down next to him. "What happened, man? I just heard like literally ten minutes ago." His voice wasn't quite a speaking voice and not quite a whisper.

Jude dropped his voice below Lance's. "How can you be here? Isn't this like the lion's den?"

"Ha," Lance nodded at him. "That is exactly what it is, man, the fucking lion's den. But the laws of this jungle, man... You gotta be able to pass right under the lion's nose without getting caught."

"So..." Jude's gaze swept the room.

"They think I'm an informant, man. I give them bullshit tips." He slid a conspiratorial look across the room. "In exchange, they usually leave me alone."

Jude kept peering fiercely around the room. The cops were mostly ignoring these two kids on the bench. There were other men on benches along the walls, but they were handcuffed to steel rings bolted to the wall or floor. Something was amiss. Jude wanted to understand, but he felt like he was looking down through dirty water.

"Look, man, I get it. Up is down, and down is up half the time. It is royally fucked up. But, here's the thing, little man." He dropped his voice to near silence. "We're doing illegal shit. You and I know it shouldn't fucking *be* illegal. But it is. And to get by, dude, everybody's got to have a play." His voice was gentle. As easy as the truth.

Jude squinted. He tried to look savvy, discerning, suspicious.

"Take your friends, man. Greg, he never buys or sells. He hides behind Paulo. He uses, and supplies, but always small amounts. He's been hauled in like five times, but never with enough to bust him.

"And Melinda, she's riding his coattails."

"What about Theo?" Jude asked. "And Serena?" He watched a pair of cops unshackle a man in dingy jeans and no shirt and lead him to a room.

"Theo is the real deal, man. He's Greg's main customer. His parents have the bucks and so things go down behind the walls and gates up at their house."

"And Serena, she's your classic blow queen."

"Blow queen?"

"She gives blow jobs or sex for drugs. Keeps the transactions fairly small and non-monetary, you know. That's a quarter of the girls in junior high, dude. Half of the high school."

Jude's stomach lurched. Serena?

Her smile at him as she had disappeared with Bongo... it returned to his mind like a memory of a bad meal.

"And you know what happened to Rudolph, man, right?"

"Rudolph?" The name was familiar but it brought no one to mind.

"That tall blond guy? Rudy. Rudolpho. Rudolph. Follows Paulo around?"

"Oh, yeah." How could he have forgotten Rudy? "What happened to him?"

"Paulo found out he was skimming."

"Skimming?"

Lance clicked out a 'tsk-tsk' to show his impatience with Jude's naivete. "Drugs. Money. Chicks. Whatever, man."

"Oh."

"Not just fucking 'Oh,' man. Paulo got rid of him, man."

"Got rid of him how?" Jude was whispering and realized their conversation was getting more and more hushed, more and more secretive. This, while they were sitting in full view in a police station.

"Look, man," Lance straightened up and let his gaze slide out over the room. It settled on the desks where Rose and Kiplinger sat. Jude took it as a sign that Lance was done talking.

"Wait a minute," Jude said. "How do you know this stuff?"

Lance leaned down and let his hand rise slightly until he was scratching the back of his neck. A smile played on his lips. "Hey man, the dude was encroaching, man. Encroaching."

"So you…" Jude had a sudden flash of reality. The room he was in, the light that pressed in, the wooden chairs and benches, the milling dust motes, and most of all, Lance. It was all suddenly absolutely mundane. As tired and existent as an old rug. And somewhere, just past that old rug, was an inert man with dense blond hair and a thick moustache.

Lance was asking him something. Poked his knee. "So, man, what the fuck happened?"

"Happened?"

"To you? Is that your old man in there?" He gestured with his chin at the row of holding rooms.

Jude shrugged. Nodded. Lowered his head. "Couple of cops came to the front door and busted him and hauled me in with him."

"When did this happen, man?"

"I don't know, like one o'clock?"

"Oh, man, that's good. I mean, they like to bust people at bad times, you know? Like between three and six in the morning. Fucks you all up cause your whole body is like half-asleep."

Jude could only see the march of shame down their front stairs in broad daylight. He winced with the memory of the blank eyes of window glass.

Lance scanned the room. "So, who brought you in, man?"

Jude jutted a chin toward the empty desks at the back of the room, "Guys named Kiplinger and Rose."

"Cool man," Lance stood. "I'll do what I can do, man. Hang loose."

"What happened to the Rudolph guy?" Jude asked.

Lance drew a quick finger across his throat. "Gone."

Lance crossed the room to the desks where he leaned in and spoke to another man in a suit sitting at a nearby desk. Lance nodded as the man spoke and pointed to the enclosures. The man nodded back at Lance.

Jude watched as Lance walked to the enclosure and knocked. The door opened for several long seconds while they spoke, and then Lance was admitted and the door closed.

Jude would have given his eyeteeth, whatever the fuck those were, to hear what was being said in there.

At 3:47, Lance and Detective Rose emerged. They walked to Rose's desk where they spoke over a paper on the desk, their fingers pointing to words as if verifying their meanings.

Lance plucked a pen from a chipped white coffee cup on the blotter and signed the paper. He stood and shook Rose's hand. Rose headed back to the enclosure and Lance made a pistol with his fingers and fired a round at Jude, winking. Then he was gone.

Two minutes later, a man in a much nicer suit than the detectives came in from the door nearest Jude. His suit shone with green-and-gray hues and he carried a wine-red briefcase that perfectly matched his belt and shoes. He wore thick black horn-rims and looked like a skinny Clark Kent.

He made no stops and took no detours. He went straight to the enclosure and knocked. He opened the door and went in without waiting. Two minutes later, he was out the door with Jude's father in tow. Kiplinger came out and then Rose. They watched as the man led Jude's father in Jude's direction.

"Hi, Jude?" The man let loose of his father and shook Jude's hand. "I'm Martin Freisen. I'm an attorney for the American Medical Association. I'm here to take care of things on the legal end."

"Okay," Jude said. His father was standing there looking smug, his eyes remote and cold on Jude.

"First things first," he pointed to the door he'd come in. "Let's get you both out of here."

Jude stood and set his Coke bottle on the arm of the bench and, with a quick prod from Mr. Freisen, led the way through the door. The three of them passed through a much more professional or public-facing realm. The hallway was wide and clean. A free-standing drinking fountain hummed. A glass case contained trophies and photos of police officers in graduation-type gatherings and alone.

A big wooden counter ringed one side of a large lobby and another hall shot off to their right flanked with an American and a California flag.

Mr. Freisen spoke only to Jude's father, but Jude listened as though his life depended on it, because of course, it did.

"So, the AMA fields this kind of thing more often than you'd think. The cops know: trying to book a physician is like catching water in a sieve, but they hope *you* don't know that. They're hoping to put the scare in you, get you to implicate yourself in crimes that don't even exist, and maybe get you into a jail cell before our office finds out."

He led them across the sun-blistered parking lot to his spanking new two-tone, four-door Cadillac DeVille. The body was a dark blue, the top a white fiberglass thing that looked like it could be removed. Jude slid into the back seat and felt the tight, solidity of the slam of the door resonate in his bones.

As Freisen pulled to the exit of the lot, Jude's father said, "We need to make a brief stop. It's right on the way."

"Sure," Freisen said, "which way?"

Pretty soon, his father had them driving down Bronson and Jude was wondering who on earth would be at school on a Saturday afternoon. But Jude felt the car turn off Bronson and he lifted his head to look out. They were turning onto Harold Way. Jude's heart sank.

His father was leaning forward, looking at addresses. When they reached the Crestview, he pointed, "This one, right here. The one with these floozies outside."

Jude could feel the rush of his father's anger, even from the back-seat. It was his father's reactions to being there. It was the way he spit the word 'floozies.' It was his impatience with the motion of the car, the door popping open before Freisen had even located a place to park. When Freisen slowed, he just pushed the door further open so that Freisen had to stop or clip the door against a parked car ahead.

"We'll be right down," Jude's father got out and opened the back door for Jude. "Let's go." His jaw was set.

He grabbed Jude's shoulder as soon as Jude stood and marched him across the street toward the women sitting in their chaises and lawn chairs. The women had gone silent and were watching the drama develop of the man leaping out of a big Cadillac and grabbing his kid. Jude stumbled in the street and his father literally lifted him back to his feet and impelled him forward.

"Hey, it's Jude," Jude heard a sing-song voice call. He panned across the women's faces. Wendy fluttered her fingers at him with one hand while lofting a wine glass in her other hand.

As they reached the curb, Jude's father snarled at Wendy, "What you've done to my son... And what you do anyway... It's *disgusting*." Wendy's eyelids fluttered once, twice and then went still, her eyes cold and piercing at Jude's father.

His father snarled, "He's just a *kid!*" Then he thrust Jude toward the building, barking after him at Wendy, *"Disgusting!"*

At the stairs, he shoved Jude upward without slowing. Jude stumbled again, his hands dropping to the steps to regain his balance. This was utter hell. He didn't want to be here and he thought about the possibility of just hitting the top step and taking off down the walkway and down the backstairs at a run.

But when he hit the top, he glanced at Penny's screen door and saw her eyes peering and wide past the screen. Down the way, there were four women, all leaning on the railing. They'd been seated, but had gotten up to watch the drama below. Two of them turned and slipped inside at the sight of Jude and his father. A third tripped lightly down the stairs.

Only Frenchie remained on the walkway. She sat back down in her chair and watched Jude and his father with calm eyes, as though measuring the minute difference between reality and her prophesy that Jude would come to no good. She was leaning back in her chair, her long pale legs bare to the hip. But Jude could only see her dark, almost-searing eyes.

Jude looked for the pale girl but she was nowhere to be seen.

At Lacey's door, his father pulled him to a stop and banged three hard knocks on the door. Music thrummed from inside. It was a Donovan song, "Season of the Witch."

Jude wanted to concentrate on some core feeling in this horrible moment, but he couldn't find a single feeling he could pluck out and name. It was like a mudslide. There was just a dark turgid mass. There were fleeting glimpses of fear and shame, fury and hurt, defeat and powerlessness.

He looked down the way at Frenchie who watched Jude and his father with a smirk not unlike his own father's. Out on the lawn, the women were staring up at the spectacle. His father raised his hand to pound again when they heard a voice inside, "Coming!"

Then the door opened and there was Lacey.

Her face flickered with a tiny light when she saw Jude, but quickly resolved into a question mark. She was wearing blue jean shorts and a jersey T-shirt.

"Are you Elizabeth Kingman?" Jude's father was accusatory, his voice loud and gruff. "Or in whore terms, *Lacey*?"

She looked at Jude, and then, knowing full well what was happening, she looked at Jude's father. "What is this?"

It was as if someone had poked his father with a stick. He exploded. He stepped toward Lacey, shouting. "You have been consorting with a fifteen-year-old boy!" He was a foot inside her apartment and she tried to block him with the door. "He's is my son! He's a *kid* for Christ's sake!" He shoved Jude forward like a rag doll, an exhibit of a being with no inner motivations or judgments. His fingers dug deep into Jude's shoulder.

"Look, mister," Lacey said, bracing herself behind the door.

Then Jude felt his father sucked away from his side, his grip on Jude's shoulder suddenly gone.

"What the unholy bleeding motherfuck do we got us here?" Russ was on the walkway, Penny two paces behind him, and he was dangling Jude's father from one arm like a little boy. "Is this another piece of shit off the turnip truck?"

Russ was dressed in his uniform of ragged robe, stained sweats, and a tank-top T-shirt. The slippers on his feet were old tan corduroys, stained and torn. His eyes were yellowish orbs stricken with harsh, red blood vessels. His lips were purple.

The color had drained from Jude's father's face and Jude saw him look terrified, perhaps for the first time ever.

Penny shook her head at Jude and looked past him at Lacey. "You okay?" she asked.

Penny...

Jude stared at her in disbelief. She was wearing shorts, a blouse tied off at her midriff, and her big blue sunglasses. Her hair cascaded in a flounce of loose curls, her face was rouged, and her lips bright red. Her skin was so tanned she might have been half-lizard. She

was all legs and bosom and lips. She was like a neon sign that read
WHORE, on or off.

A slicing of fear touched the back of his throat. He turned to
Lacey.

Her eyes were hard on Jude's father, and flashing past to Penny.

But midnight had suddenly come and gone and Cinderella's
coach and gown, and her glass slippers, were suddenly, in Jude's eyes,
scapes of bare flesh, a tight T-shirt to show off her breasts, short tight
shorts, and worst of all, her brightly painted toenails, the polish crisp
and flaming red.

"Maybe I just extricate this piece of trash over the railing?" Russ
was in Jude's face.

"Let me go, you goddamned animal," his father had recovered
and was batting at Russ. "Do you know who I am? I'm a doctor. I am
a physician. I can have you shut down. All of you!"

Russ shook him. "Hey! Motherfucker! Pacify yo ass!"

His father barked, "That is my *lawyer* in the street!"

Russ smiled. "Right here, mister? And right now? We are talking about the law of gravity. Maybe your Mr. Lawyer can shine up a
lawsuit on *that*."

Silence fell in around them all, slowly, timidly. His father and
Russ stared at each other. Jude could see the ridiculousness of his
father, his toes an inch off the ground, Russ holding him there with
no apparent effort.

Jude's father's face curled into hatred. "That *whore*," he pointed
at Lacey, "has been forcing drugs and sex on my *son*!"

Russ glanced at Penny, then Lacey. Then he turned to Jude.

"She has been having sex with him after school for the last month!
She will go to jail for this!" Jude's father was bellowing now, his face
red and enraged. He slung fists at Russ, but half-heartedly like he
didn't actually want to touch the man.

"Miss Lacey?" Russ asked quietly.

"Russ," she stepped all the way out on the walkway. "I know you
didn't want him around, but he's a friend. We never..." She shook
her head. Then she shook it again, clearing something away. She took
another step closer to the fray. Her voice got harder. "I never did,
and never would have. Jude's a friend." She looked at Jude. "Jude's
a *friend*."

Lacey spun and rushed back to her door. She stopped on the threshold and spit out, "Jude's *my* friend, mister. If you don't know who your kid is, you prick, that's *your* problem." There was a momentary lull as everyone just kind of stared at each other.

Then Lacey, reloaded with new venom, said in a hollow voice, "I'm glad I'm not one of your patients." Then she slammed her door. Windows all up and down the building rattled.

When Jude looked back at Russ, Penny was gone and his father was standing on the walkway, cowering back from Russ's big fat finger. "You heard the lady, you little man-twerp. You get the fuck out. And don't you *evah* come back."

Jude's father retreated from Russ, but he spit and howled like a cat. "I'm calling the police. In fact, we'll just go there *now*! You will be in jail or out on the street by the end of the day. You mark my words!"

As he shuffled past Jude, he grabbed Jude's shirt and dragged him along. Jude felt like a mouse the cat had caught and was wearing to a mere nubbin of life before finally killing it. But, Jude knew, the death—the escape really—wouldn't come for many years. Not until he was eighteen and off to college. Or until he'd had enough and he just ran away.

His father shoved him ahead at the stairs and Jude stumbled down. His father ranted all the way down the stairs and across the lawn. "He's a *minor*. Do you know what that *means*? That means every last one of you will *go to jail!*"

Across the street, Mr. Freisen stood holding the back door of his Coupe DeVille. His eyebrows were raised, but otherwise he was silent and placid. Jude was propelled from the curb by his father, and fired headlong at the car. "Get in and shut up!" he snarled.

Jude slumped into the back of the car as the door slammed shut. He looked up at the Crestview. Russ was leaning on the railing upstairs, a single thick middle finger raised at their exit. Jude tried to find some evidence of Lacey in her window, but there was just the silvery reflection of nothing at all.

Mr. Freisen counseled Jude's father to call the police when he got home rather than, as his father put it, "marching in there and demanding justice."

But even at home, his father demanded an audience for his drama. He demanded that Jude sit in the den on the couch while his father shouted into the phone. But his father shifted quickly from "the disgusting scum of whores and drug-dealers in this city," some of whom he had now positively identified for the police, to "the lazy incompetence of the LAPD."

"Who do you think writes your goddamned paychecks?" he shouted into the phone and slammed the receiver down.

He rounded on Jude then, angrier than any time yet today. "You are *grounded*! You are not to go anywhere near that den of whores and drug-dealers. If I find out that you have, you will lose that damned bike of yours, and all your records, and all that crap comes off your walls."

Jude watched his father sputter and fume and said nothing.

"Go to your room! And stay there!"

Even as he climbed the stairs, he could hear his father launch into his litany to Jude's mother. His voice was high-pitched and screechy.

Jude went in his room and closed the door. He scanned the walls. The images of rock and revolt were dense now. They had multiplied rapidly. Jude had started adding record sleeves and posters or photos that came in the records, as well as concert posters and cut-outs from magazines. They were climbing up out of easy reach now, and were starting to overlap.

His parents hated the images. Worried over them. Sniped at him about them. But now, what had been a gesture of defiance suddenly seemed juvenile and fanciful.

Starting right by the door, he started removing the posters from the walls. He plucked them one after the next and began stacking them on his desk.

Mark pushed in from the bathroom. "Whoa, dude, what the fuck!" He was upbeat, bouncing on his toes as he walked.

"Yeah," Jude agreed. "What the fuck?"

"So?"

Jude shrugged.

"The fucking *cops* hauled you *and* Dad away, dude." Mark slumped down on the bed.

"Yeah," Jude paid close attention to the tacks and tape, making sure the images were kept as pristine as possible, but nevertheless tearing and crumpling some corners.

"So what happened, man?"

"We sat at the police station for half-of-fucking-ever. Then some lawyer showed up and sprang us. Then Dad dragged us all to the Crestview and he accused Lacey of giving me drugs and having sex with me."

"Holy shit! He met your prostitute?"

"She's not my prostitute. She's my friend." Jude laid a Byrds flyer onto the growing stack of images. "She even said so."

Jude recounted the manhandling by Russ, the ride home, and the phone call.

"The fucker," Mark sliced out in a harsh whisper. "He deserves to get taken down, man." Mark rolled off the bed and went to the window to look out. "So they're not going to arrest him? Dad, I mean?"

"I don't know," Jude said. "Probably not."

Mark turned back and leaned against the sill. "So what the fuck are you doing?"

"Taking down the posters and shit."

"Why? Is Dad making you do that?"

"No. He threatened to." Jude tugged down the Beatles *Revolver* poster he'd gotten from Platterpuss Records.

"So why take them down, man?" Mark slumped down on the bed. "You should leave them up to piss him off."

Jude shrugged. He didn't know what to say. He looked down the wall at the hundreds of images to be pulled. "I guess I don't want to feel like this is my room anymore. You know?" Jude looked across at Mark. He was nodding in agreement. "I mean, I feel like I gotta be ready to leave, you know, any minute."

"Yeah, I dig it, man." Mark's sideburns were coming in. Jude was envious. They drew down his cheeks into a sharp flare that ran toward his chin, a full public confirmation of his independence. "I totally dig it. 'Castles made of sand slip into the sea eventually.'"

"Yeah. But it's hard to tell if this is a castle or a prison."

Mark reached out the window and grasped the bars of the window cage. "It's definitely a prison."

～

DINNER was another chance for his father to claim higher ground in the drama he'd set in motion. "I imagine the police are raiding that den of whores right now."

But Jude's mother shushed him. "Lyle, we don't need to talk about this at dinner." So their dad shut up and was held to wordlessly grinning and gloating, occasionally shaking his head in happy wonder at his imaginings, all through the meal.

At the end of the meal, as his father stood to go, leaving his plate behind for Jude to clear since Jude was on dishes, he looked at his watch and said, "End of the floozies."

Jude did the dishes and retreated up to his now bare-walled bedroom. He felt as blank and hollow as the walls. He could hardly see five minutes ahead. He knew he wanted to avoid his father. He knew he was trapped in this house, grounded. He knew he wanted to leave, and he wanted everyone to know it.

He didn't want to read.

He didn't like the tinny cheer of the radio.

He didn't want to write in the journal.

He put on the last record Mark had loaned him. It was John Coltrane's *Ascension*. Jude had tried to listen to it twice already with no luck. The fractured, beatless, disorganized flush of sounds was grating. He could hardly stand a minute of it.

Now, he set the record on the turntable and clicked it on.

The crazed flows of saxophone, piano, bass and drums felt like his blood and nerves. The stuttering beat felt like his heart. The mystery of it, like a veil of meaninglessness and chaos, was a depiction, a telling, an enactment of his life.

Jude felt himself sinking into the music and the music rising back up out of him. It was... he looked for the word out on the very edges of his words. It was... metabolic. It was as if Coltrane had entered Jude's soul and simply played what he found there.

Serena rose up out of the mash of sound. Jude watched her move in his mind. She was dancing to the music, a kind of physical flow over the top of the cacophony. He could smell the spicy fragrance of her, sense the dark depths of her eyes, and feel the luxurious swale of her flesh.

She was unaware of him. Of anything.

Slowly, the dim edges of the space lifted, light touching them. It was a ring of men. Men in business suits. Men in hippy frocks. Men in work clothes. They watched Serena dance with as much hunger as the disgust that Jude felt.

Tears slid down the side of his face. The idea of her bent and broke in him like bones. He'd hoped. He'd wanted.

Jude's mother shook his shoulder and he started. He'd fallen asleep. It was full dark outside.

"What is this awful racket?" she asked.

The record was playing over and over again. Jude didn't know how long he'd been asleep.

"John Coltrane. It's one of Mark's."

"I can tell. I hope you don't like it."

"I do like it," he told her. "Now."

She rolled her eyes. "You boys don't need to rebel against *everything*."

Jude crossed to the record player and carefully lifted the needle and shut off the player. He sat in his desk chair and faced his mother. She sat on the end of his bed. She was wearing navy clam-diggers and a white and navy blouse. Her face was dark and serious.

"Jude, I think you owe us an explanation."

"About what?" he asked.

"About all of it. The drugs. The… the… the prostitutes." Her eyes were traveling the walls, observing them minutely. There were tack holes, yellowed slivers of tape, a few paper corners still there high up.

"There's nothing to explain," Jude spoke wearily. He set his elbow on the arm of the desk chair and covered his eyes with his hand.

"There most certainly *is*. You almost got your father *arrested*. He could have gone to *jail*."

Jude shrugged. "That doctors' lawyer said he could get Dad out of anything."

That seemed to launch an avalanche of thoughts in his mother. Her eyes flickered and slipped off to a middle distance.

"Regardless," she came back. She leaned in and spoke in an urgent whisper, "Jude, I cannot help you unless I have some idea of what happened."

"It was nothing," Jude said. But it registered in him: she wanted to help. He looked out the window a long while. He finally said, "It's just, that day I got beat up on my bike, Lacey and Penny cleaned me up and put bandages on me, and ah, Frenchie, she sewed my pants back together."

"Oh my God," his mother spread her hands wide over her knees, leaning slightly forward. "Jude, I had no idea you'd been hurt that badly."

"It wasn't so bad."

They stared balefully at each other for a few moments. Then Jude said, "So I went back to thank them. And Lacey and I got to be friends."

"And this Lacey? This is the Elizabeth person?"

Jude shrugged. "I don't know. She's Lacey."

"Is she the one who told you to get drugs and sell them?"

"*No!*" Jude snarled at her. She'd learned that from his father, always jumping to the most negative conclusion possible. "I learned about the drugs from Dad. He dragged me in the den after Mark ran away and showed me the amphetamines, the barbiturates, and the Valium, and told me how kids used them. I just grabbed some to be cool with the kids at school."

"You mean, like Kevin?" His mother held high hopes for Kevin to be a good influence, a clean kid.

"No," Jude picked up the record jacket for *Ascension* and began to study it. "Other kids."

"What other kids?"

"Just some kids."

"Like this Lance kid?"

Jude remembered Lance had come to the house, so she was blaming him for Jude's downfall now. "Yeah, sorta."

"But your father said that he's the one that got you into all this trouble."

"Lance?"

"Yes," his mother ran fingers up into her hair and pulled outward, fluffing her hair into a larger profile. "He's what they call a 'narc' or something. He's an undercover police officer."

"He's like, a *kid*," Jude stressed.

"Well, I guess he's small for his age."

Suddenly, Jude couldn't get the dots to connect. Lance had sold Jude's supply and given him the money. He was selling the drugs to people like Greg and Melinda. He'd given Jude the full amount they agreed on. He'd taken care of Hector for Jude.

But two things stood out in his mind now. One was when Lance was standing in his parents' bathroom staring at the bottles of pills and he'd said, "They're always here? He never moves them?"

The second one was when the detectives were at the door and Rose had said, "We know where you keep the pills."

Jude felt betrayed and hurt and he wanted his mother out of his room. He changed the subject to one that would get her to leave. "So," Jude looked up, "how did Dad get off? Did he bribe the cops?"

"What on earth? Jude, what exactly do you mean?"

"I just thought that, even if I have to go to juvie, then at least Dad would go to jail for a while."

"Why on earth should your father go to jail?"

"Why shouldn't he?"

"Jude," his mother stood, her eyes flashing with anger. "He's a medical doctor. He has a license to have those pills in this house. He is protected by law."

"Doctor heal thyself," Jude uttered quietly.

"What did you say?"

"Nothing."

twelve

JUDE SWOOPED DOWN OUT OF THE HILLS ON Monday morning, just glad to escape the gloom of the house. Either his mother or his father, or both, had been home all weekend, and every time Jude left the house—to go to the backyard to sit in the sun or to the garage to clean his bike—they asked him where he was going and when he was coming back in.

His mother did take him out for errands on Sunday. Not much was open, but she dragged him through Sears and Macy's. She was mostly quiet and unresponsive, but he was no better. He figured that to passersby they probably looked like there had been a death in the family.

She had poked at racks and cycled through whole sections as though she were lost. Then she found clamdiggers and blouses that looked like her clothes at home, and she cheered up and bought several items. After that, they sat in the shoe department where she talked about espadrilles with the salesman and tried on twenty pairs or more. She bought a beige pair and left with her head up, her shoulders back a bit. She was restored.

When they got home, his father had a shit-eating grin on his face. It was a look he wore when he had done something malicious to someone, and he always thought being malicious was funny.

It was like when their neighbor back in Indiana had been a car geek who liked to brag about how well he could tune a car to get good gas mileage. Jude's father had siphoned gas into the man's Volkswagen bug over a period of weeks until the guy was practically dancing in his driveway over his mileage.

Then, his father had started taking gas out.

It had surprised Jude how reactive the man was. One day bloated and bragging, the next, silent, tinkering, upset. His father played the man for weeks like that, reveling every night at the dinner table. Then, when he finally told the man, the man pretended to laugh it off. But he never spoke to Jude's father again—just glowered at him over the hedge and went inside whenever he saw him. There was not even a goodbye when they had moved out.

Jude got to see his father's malicious grin quite often when he was younger. His father used to tickle Jude mercilessly. Jude laughed and cried and hated every moment. Then, one day, while Jude was watching television, his father approaching with that grin spreading like a stain, Jude determined he would not be ticklish anymore. He must have been ten or eleven.

His father's fingers dug in under his arms and Jude felt the electrical impulses of resistance shoot through him. His whole body wanted to pull away and defend himself. But instead he willed himself to raise his arms out and to feel the fingers. Just feel them.

Surprisingly, they felt stubby, hard, and stupid.

Jude felt his father searching for the place that would ignite Jude's resistance, but Jude just closed his eyes and waited. Finally, Jude heard his mother say, "Lyle, leave him alone. He's not in the mood."

The fingers stopped. But when Jude opened his eyes, he looked straight up into his father's fury. His cheeks were flushed. His mouth was twisted into a snarl. He looked like he was about to hit Jude, but instead he pushed off Jude to stand and stormed out of the room.

Jude turned back to the television and found his brother staring at him, mouth open. "Whoa," he'd said, "what happened to you?"

Jude had shrugged. "I guess I'm not ticklish anymore."

So now, seeing the grin, Jude knew his father would only have the shit-eating grin if he had done something that would hurt Jude in some way. It couldn't have been the posters on his walls; they were all gone. Besides, Jude's father never came into his room. He thought through his other possessions.

There were three things he could think of. It could be his record collection, the clothes he'd bought with his own money, or his new bike. He stared at his father and shrugged. He could have them. All of them.

He had gone to his room and confirmed that it had not been his records or his clothing. Later, he went down to the garage and opened it. His bike was still there.

He was walking up the stairs when he realized what it might have been: his father had moved or secured all the drugs.

He was curious to find out what he'd done—Jude was sure he could find his father's stash—but he was pretty sure there would be some kind of a booby trap. His father would want evidence that he'd pissed Jude off. So, when his father and mother announced with a bit of dramatic fanfare Sunday night that they were going for a walk and would be gone for 'over an hour,' Jude just lay back on his bed and continued reading.

An hour or so later, his father had been sullen at dinner. Jude had not tripped his trap.

So, come Monday morning, Jude had had enough of his family life to last him a lifetime. He rode fast across the fragmented pavements, jumping curbs, slicing in behind buses only to slingshot past as they pulled to the curb.

He locked his bike out front at LeConte and grabbed his backpack. He stood and started to turn. But there was someone there. Jude started, fear flushing through him like ice water. A foot away, Lance's face loomed.

"Mo Tha Fuck A," Lance hissed, leaning close. "You are supposed to be in juvie. What the fuck you doing here?"

Jude shrank back. "I, ah…"

"You, ah…" Lance mimicked him, "you, ah…, you got off 'cause you a white boy."

Jude shook his head. "No, I got off because my dad's a doctor. He's allowed to have the pills."

"Yeah, and you shoulda gone to juvie for stealing them and selling them." Lance was different than Jude had seen him before. He was wearing the same loose-fitting, near-shapeless clothes and big boots, but he was intense and shaky. His hands kept scratching at his forearms. His eyes darted. He licked his lips. And blinked. A lot.

Jude stepped back, resting one hand on his handlebars. "The cops said you're…" Jude stopped. He wasn't sure he could say this here.

Lance finished for him. "The cops will say anything." He dropped his voice low, "They want you to think I'm a narc so you won't bother finding out what's really happening, how they really knew you were selling."

"How did they know?" Jude asked, looking past Lance at the kids filing into the school.

Lance stepped in closer and leaned in. "Maybe it's one of your little hippy friends. You ever think of that?"

Jude stared at him blankly. He couldn't quite imagine any of the kids being narcs. But he realized that it was because he assumed these kids had known each other for years, like he had known kids in Indiana.

Then he thought of Kevin and his friends. Kevin might. He'd ratted Jude out to his mother. And James… Jude felt shaken.

"Well, I gotta get to class," Jude said.

Lance leaned in again and whispered urgently. "You. Say. Nothing." He straightened and gazed at the front door. "Not to anyone." He drew a finger across his throat. Then he spun away and clumped off in his boots.

Jude slipped into homeroom as the bell was ringing. But Ms. Mantle did not even let him sit down. "Jude Tangier? Mr. Tangier?"

Jude slowed and then stopped. She was holding up a sheet of paper. Her expression was icy. "You're wanted down at Mr. Glenn's office."

⌐⌐

MR. GLENN kept him waiting. He was out talking to Mrs. Flowers, the office secretary, when Jude arrived. And he saw Jude come in. But he just frowned and retreated to his office. He didn't call Jude in until second period was well underway.

The secretary, one finger pushing her pink-rimmed glasses high on her nose, opened the gate and said, "Jude Tangier." Then she led Jude to the open office door and stepped aside. Jude entered.

Mr. Glenn was deeply invested in one of his binders. It lay open on the side desk and he bent over it with a yellow Hi-Liter pen.

Jude sat and waited.

Finally, Glenn dropped a bookmark into the pages and flopped the notebook shut. Then he glanced quickly at Jude and rolled back in his chair, the wood squeaking and the bearings ratcheting out a series of metallic clicks.

He raised his chin and nodded his head in self-agreement and then leaned back still further. "Mr. Tangier," he steepled his fingers and didn't smile.

Jude kept his chin lowered and watched the man from under his brows.

"Mr. Tangier, for a young man who narrowly missed going to juvenile hall, I would think you might be a bit more communicative."

Jude shrugged very slightly. He waited.

"Do you know why you're in here?" Glenn asked.

Jude shook his head, 'No.' He could make a good guess. They were going to punish him one way or another. Or maybe, just maybe, he realized with a flicker of interest, they were going to ask him to rat on his friends.

"Well, let's get right to it, then, shall we?" He lurched forward and thunked his elbows on his desk. Everything about this man, Jude decided, needed heavy furniture just to keep him from banging his way right through everything.

He held up a page in front of himself. "You know what this is?"

Jude shook his head.

"This is your fate, son." He shook the paper so it rattled. "This is probably the first in a long line of such documents for you." His head bobbed in self-agreement again. "This, son..." he rattled the page again, "is your suspension."

He held it at arm's length away from his face. "Five days. That's a long one, son. Most are a day or two. But you got caught selling dangerous drugs. Last kid we caught doing that was expelled. That's right, *expelled*. He's up at San Quentin, now, I suspect. Ronald Sellars. He was a hard case."

Jude waited. He didn't know what a suspension was exactly.

"So..." Mr. Glenn slid another page out onto his desk. "This is for you." He pushed the page toward Jude and Jude leaned forward to look at it.

"Take it," Glenn said.

Jude pulled it off the desk and set it in his lap.

"You have until the end of second period to go to each of your classes and get your week's assignments and the teacher's signature. Every single class. Including band and wood shop and P. E."

Jude looked down at the paper. It seemed an innocent enough thing, paper. Especially just the one flimsy sheet. He could just tear it up and ride home.

He shook his head. He didn't have the courage to do that.

"Like now," Mr. Glenn urged, impatient.

Jude startled and stared up at Mr. Glenn. Then he looked up at the wall clock, stood up and walked toward the door.

"You understand what you're to do?" Mr. Glenn asked, his voice gruff.

Jude shrugged and left.

He followed the shortest route he could think of among his classes. Band was closest, so he went there first. It was the jazz band class period. They were playing the Mamas and Papas "Monday, Monday."

Jude entered the class and went straight to Mr. Denny's raised platform. Denny was looking exasperated with the students' limpid, stumbling rendition. But Denny always looked exasperated.

He saw Jude and rolled his eyes mightily, a horse seeing a snake. Jude thrust the paper at him and said nothing. Denny snatched it from him and slapped it down over the music on his stand. Still slashing along with the music with his baton, he read the brief note at the top. Jude had read the document on his way over. It said,

"Jude Tangier is suspended for five (5) days starting today, Monday, October 30, 1967. He will be allowed to return to campus, and classes, on Monday, November 6, 1967. Each of Jude's teachers is to give Jude any work or assignments for the next five (5) days. He will be required to turn the assignments in on Monday, November 6, 1967, unless otherwise noted by the teacher. Each teacher must also sign this form to ensure each teacher has seen this form."

There was a list of his classes in order, a blank for 'Work to be completed during suspension,' the teacher's name and a line below that for their signature. At the bottom of the form was signed Martin Glenn, Assistant Principal.

Denny, still thrusting his baton up and down, felt his vest pockets until a pen surfaced and he pulled it out and scribbled on the form.

He thrust the page at Jude, and Jude, even though he could tell the horrible tune was winding down, raised his voice and asked, "No assignments?"

Denny finally turned to Jude, took a swipe at him with the baton and snarled, "I don't care *what* you do." He scowled fiercely.

With the baton removed from the job of propping it up, and the dark energy pouring out of the short plug of the teacher, the music faltered and stopped. In the quiet, Denny kept on. "You're a miscreant. You're getting a head start on your life: suspension now, expulsion later, and jail before you finish high school."

He slashed at Jude again with his baton and snapped, "Mark my words!"

Jude shrugged. He looked at the faces that were staring at him. Then he left.

Wood shop and P.E. were easy. Both men read the note, signed the paper, and said something at least kind.

Ms. Loral stopped her class. She was standing at the chalkboard, a sentence pinned down and its parts labelled like a dissected frog. She was wearing a peasant dress, sandals, and a white blouse, looking more like a hippy than even Melinda.

"Review the next five examples in the book and be ready to talk about them," she told the class. "I'll just be a minute."

Then she pointed to the chair beside her desk and Jude sat down. He set the paper, now with three signatures scrawled on it, on the desktop. She pulled it over in front of herself and read it. Her eyes rose to Jude's. "I'd heard about all of this... this morning... in the teacher's lounge... but... well, I figured they must be talking about the wrong kid." Her hand lifted and ventured in his direction, but stopped.

Jude said nothing. He glanced over his shoulder at the class, trying to remind her that she had a classroom full of kids.

"Drugs?" she hissed. "What were you *thinking*?"

Jude shrugged. He hated questions like this. It made obvious, perfect sense to sell drugs and to take them. Selling drugs gave him money and it gave him an in with the in-crowd. Taking drugs gave him whole new perspectives, ideas, worlds. Only some stuffy old person trying to force kids into their overused, worn-out morality would ask such a question.

"I'm sorry," she pulled her hand back. "That's a ridiculous question. I imagine from your point of view that there are a hundred good reasons." She laughed. "Hell, just getting in good with someone like Melinda Eastwood. That's probably worth it right there."

Jude found himself nodding in agreement.

"Okay, look," she twisted the paper to an angle and signed it. She pushed it to Jude. "Here's your assignment, you write all of this up. It can be an essay, a set of journal entries, or, hell, if you want, write it as a story. You know, make it fictional."

"All of this?" Jude asked.

"Yes, the whole thing. Right up through getting caught."

Jude scowled. "Mr. Glenn wants the assignments in writing," he said. "I think so he can check them before I turn them in."

"Oh," Ms. Loral nodded slowly. "I see."

She pulled the paper back to herself and read it again. "There aren't any other assignments on the paper…"

"Yeah, that's band, and wood shop, and P.E. They didn't have homework for me."

"Okay, well." She stabbed her pencil tip on her desk calendar repeatedly. Jude could hear the clock ticking, and the metallic snap it made when it pushed forward at the minute mark. "Tell you what, let's make it a fiction piece. But it doesn't have to be about what happened. Any subject you want. Okay?"

"Okay," he said.

"And keep up with your reading and other writing assignments. You have those, right?"

"Yeah, right."

She jotted out the assignment on the paper and pushed it back to him.

Down the hall at homeroom, Ms. Mantle scrunched her lips into what Jude thought looked like a pig's ass and signed. Then she snapped at Jude, "I knew. I've known. All along. No good. No good."

It was Mr. Diaz who surprised him. He was in front of the class Jude should have been attending, his pointer poked against Vietnam and he was talking about "the mythology of winning this war." He glanced at Jude, and then turned back to the class. "No one, and I mean no one," he peered hard at the young people in the room, "is going to win this war."

Then he turned to Jude and held out his hand, still speaking to the class. "Give us a minute, will you? Get some of your reading done, or work on your essays."

Jude handed across the paper and Mr. Diaz took it lightly, swiveled around his desk and sat.

He pored over the paper and then looked up at Jude. "Look," he squinted hard, as though there was a mist between them, "you and I have talked about some of this. In class, and not. Your brother, your friends. I get it."

He swept his hand over the top of the paper, the gesture somehow encompassing the students in the room, the entire history of the class, the page, the administration, and even the world outside the windows. "Look, it is a bullshit, rigged game. It's like a maze where every path is flowery and sunny, but every time you almost get there, you find yourself back at the money machine, the police state, the powers that be.

"I'm inside that machine. You, too. And everyone you know. But here's the thing, the machine is working. Maybe it grinds us up, people like you and me, but it's working. Do you know what that means?"

Jude shrugged.

"It means that nothing that's going on is unexpected. The way money is designed, poverty is required. Without poverty you can't have the people on top, you can't have the endless Sisyphean hill that we all climb. And with poverty comes crime.

"But crime is expected too. Crime, my friend, is so essential to the system, so pervasive it should be legal." He smiled. "We pretend it's about *what* you do but legal is *who*. Nothing more."

Mr. Diaz leaned back in his chair. He was a small man, and still young, but his face was lined and hardened. His jaw was set, his eyes sharp, his movements were simple and few.

"So here's what I'm telling you. You have got to make a choice, and you've got to make it now, whether you're going to play—you know, be part of the system—or if you're going to play for the other side.

"Cause a life of crime is perfectly valid. But there's poverty crime and there's wealth crime. Poverty crimes, those are the ones that will beat your ass. You will run and you will hide. And they will likely find you. You'll go to jail. Then it's rinse and repeat.

"Wealth crimes, these are the lawyers and the politicians and the military-industrial complex mavens—they call them water buffalos because water buffaloes in the wild surround the watering hole and block other animals from drinking. These asses write the laws to take care of themselves. They never get caught 'cause they own the catchers, and 'cause they have money, and money can buy anything, including innocence."

Diaz steepled his fingers and smiled darkly at Jude. "So, I'm telling you, my friend, stay in school. If you're gonna be a criminal, it's best to be one in the system."

Jude rounded his eyes in surprise at the speech, but he said nothing.

Mr. Diaz grinned at him. "A bit much on a Monday morning, huh?" He leaned forward and inked his signature.

"Homework…" Diaz looked up at Jude. "Here's what I want you to do." He tapped the tip of his pen on the page creating a tiny flurry of blue dots. "I want you to read the newspaper every day. Basically front-to-back. Not the classifieds, but everything else—even the ads."

He popped forward and leaned toward Jude, "Just soak it in."

Jude nodded two times, then asked, "Do you want me to write something about it? Or…?"

"Just read the paper." He jotted the homework assignment on the paper and pushed it at Jude.

Jude nodded and stood up, but a question was jammed up in him, knotting his forehead. "I guess, ah…" He looked out over the class, then up at the clock. He was going to be late getting the paper back to Mr. Glenn.

"What is it, Tangier?"

"I, ah… I mean, I'm not sure what you're telling me. Like, what's the right thing to do?" Jude stressed the word 'right.'

Diaz laughed aloud, "Oh, that *is* the question." He turned to face the class. "Did any of you hear that? Jude just asked the million-dollar question."

The class stared back blankly.

"Jude just asked, 'What's the *right* thing to do?'" Diaz stood and set a hand on Jude's shoulder. "Here's the thing, class. Anyone can tell you—and your televisions will pound it into you—that there is a right thing to do, a moral high ground if you will.

"But the people who occupy the moral high ground—and I myself am one of them—are literally the people who keep all the criminals in business. We buy their products. We vote for them. We send our children to fight their trumped up wars. We give them thirty, forty, fifty percent of the money we earn in taxes.

"Maybe we pat ourselves on the back and go to church on Sundays, but I'll tell you this, the right thing to do is to find your self-respect, and…" his gaze rose to the maps on the wall, Los Angeles and the world "and figure out how to survive with that—your self-respect—intact."

The students listened with widened eyes and when he was done, they looked around the room at each other.

Then Diaz laughed again. "Hey, you're all gonna be fine. Not to worry." He gave Jude a light shove. "Hey, Tangier, don't you have someplace to be?"

"Yeah," Jude did have somewhere to be.

JUDE returned to the administration office, filled with impatience. This suspension was a boon. He could hand off this piece of bureaucratic crap to Mr. Glenn and then he could go see Lacey.

Jude pushed his paper across the office counter and waited until Mrs. Flowers saw him. Then he lifted his hand, leaving the paper there, and turned to leave.

"Young man!" Mrs. Flowers pinned him down with her pursed lips and a glacial stare. "Sit. And wait."

Jude sat. He tried, when he thought about it, to not fold or roll the edges of the paper. But the clock ticked dismally and the dirge of Mrs. Flowers's activities bored him. It was a conspiracy to murder his day.

The bell rang. Students and noise flushed down the halls. A few kids came in with papers to hand across the desk. A teacher stopped in, leaned close to Mrs. Flowers and shared some secret gossip. When she left, her eye found Jude and she glazed him over with distaste. Then she spun on her heel like Jude had personally insulted her and shot out of the office.

Finally, a buzz rose from Mrs. Flowers's desk. She spoke low into her phone, her hand over her mouth. Then she straightened and said to Jude in a very pleasantly unpleasant voice, "Mr. Glenn will see you now."

Jude stood and looked down at the paper. Two corners of the paper were recovering from being tightly rolled in his sweaty hands. The page had been folded several times and though it was unfolded now, it looked like Jude had pulled it from the trash.

He shrugged and pushed through the gate in the counter and headed for Mr. Glenn's office.

He knocked and waited.

"Yes," the voice was impatient, gruff.

Jude pushed in and stopped. It was disorienting. The blinds were up, indirect light filled the office, and a small vase of white and yellow flowers sat on his desk. Behind the flowers, Mr. Glenn was smiling, and not just smiling, but rising up to greet him as he entered.

It got worse. In the visitor's chairs, in the one furthest from the door, sat his mother.

"Please, young man," Mr. Glenn hovered over his desk like a manatee in business clothes, "have a seat."

Jude sat, the paper unconsciously rolling in from a new corner.

"As I was saying, Mrs. Tangier," Glenn sat, his chair bleating out with stress, "this is standard and required. Given Jude's mostly good grades, I did try to argue for leniency, but our principal, Mr. Thomas, said even his hands are tied. In all seriousness, selling drugs on campus is simply too grave a transgression. The district has its policies and they are inflexible in this regard.

"I will say this, Mrs. Tangier." He leaned forward, steepled fingers tapping together in front of a bland face. "Most children who participate in such activities go straight to juvenile detention, you know. And we rarely see them come back. To be frank, these students typically go on to the reform program over at King."

King was the mostly Hispanic junior high east of Vermont, known for its gangs and graffiti.

Glenn leaned back and crossed his fingers over his belly. He looked very satisfied with himself.

He popped forward. "In any case, young man, let me see your suspension form."

Jude unrolled the corner and flattened the paper over his thigh. Then he handed it across. His mother eyed the paper like it was the manifestation of all of Jude's faults. Mr. Glenn took it like it had once held fish entrails.

"Well…" he shook his head. "Very lenient. This is just not much homework for a week." He looked up at Jude and then his mother. "Let me just say, I'll contact each of the teachers and make sure they understood the expectation here."

Outside, Jude unlocked his bike and loaded it into the trunk of his mother's car. She waited with an air of hurried embarrassment while he loaded it. For his part, he was hotly aware that eight classrooms fronted on the street and that he was in full view of all of them. He guessed they both just wanted out of there.

As they drove north away from campus, his mother said nothing. Jude hunkered down for a silent ride home. But then, waiting for the light at Sunset, she said, "Where is this place?" She flicked her hand to gesture ahead of them. "The Crestview place?"

"It's nowhere, mom." Jude kept his gaze out the side window. "Besides, I'm not allowed to go anywhere near there."

"Nonsense," she said. "We can drive by."

Jude did not want to drive by the Crestview with his mother. She didn't need to see the women on the lawn, or the lingerie hanging on the railing. And they didn't need to see Jude being driven past with his mother, like Indiana tourists peering at the seamy side of Los Angeles.

She turned on the radio and with a deft spin of the tuner, landed on KHJ. "Soul Man" jumped out at them.

"Who's this?" she asked.

Jude shrugged. The song's name was practically the whole lyric, but he didn't know who sang it.

The music had the effect of lightening the mood, and as they crossed Sunset, Jude relented and said, "You have to take the first right up here."

"Oh," his mother acted surprised. "Okay."

The turn signal clattered and they were on Harold Way. The hippy house was quiet in its way. Just one woman sat on the front stairs, smoking a cigarette and flipping through an LA Weekly. But the place was clearly a hippy's crash pad. The windows were hung with embroidered cloth or Peace flags. An American flag hung upside down on the porch. Two Volkswagen vans and a battered old sedan sat in the dirt lawn.

Jude's mother saw the place and said, "Oh my, that's not it is it?"

"No, that's the hippy house."

"Oh, the Hippy House. I should have known."

They drove down the block and Jude, his curiosity piqued, decided to have her turn onto Canyon.

It was just after II A.M., and luckily, Jude thought, the women were not out sunning themselves yet. He pointed, keeping his hand below the dash, "That's it on the corner. You can turn left there."

They drove past slowly. Jude's eyes tracked the building for as much data as he could capture. Russ's door was closed. In fact, of the whole place, only Penny's door was open, and she stood with another woman on the landing. Penny wore PJs with short shorts. The other woman wore sweats and a sleeveless T-shirt. They were smoking and two coffee cups were perched on the rail.

Lacey's windows were closed and curtained. Same with Frenchie's.

The rest of the place looked fairly normal. Only one downstairs apartment had a towel and bathing suit hung over the back of a chair.

"Well," his mother refocused on the road ahead. "I guess I should be grateful."

"Why's that?" Jude asked.

"Well, they patched you up after those horrible boys attacked you."

"Yeah, they did."

At home, Jude tested the waters immediately. His mother opened the trunk and Jude removed his bike.

"So, can I go for a bike ride?"

"Of course not!" She slammed the trunk. "You are suspended from school!"

Jude trudged up the stairs to the house. As she unlocked the front door, she said, "No bike riding today. And maybe not tomorrow. I have to think about it."

His mother was actually angry with him. Usually she was only tentatively angry since his father's anger was enough to for everyone in the house.

When the front door closed behind them, Jude remembered Mark's assessment: He was shuffling down the halls of a prison.

JUDE was up early on Tuesday. He woke at 5:30 and slipped down to make a pot of coffee. While the coffee brewed, he sat in the dining room. It was directly under his room, and was the least-used room in the house, except for maybe the creepy, earthen-walled basement. He sat against the far wall where he would be able to look out over the city while also being able to hear the percolating coffee and any approach of his mother or father.

As the coffee maker finished, the device sputtered and hissed urgently. Jude waited a beat and then went in and got himself a large cup of coffee.

He was about to tip-toe back up the stairs when he realized he would be getting hungry and he did not want to have to come back down while his father was still in the house, or have to deal with his mother too early.

Jude, already in stealth mode, switched into high gear. He shot to the refrigerator following a path that he was mapping out in its entirety in his head. The path was clear all the way to his desk in his room. Now all he had to do was execute, shaving as many physical inches and seconds off as possible, to maximize his chance of missing his father.

As he tugged out the opened glass bottle of milk, he was reminded of the kid in the quirky book, *Trout Fishing in America*, that Ms. Loral had assigned. The kid in that book was poor, and he had an elaborate daily ritual to acquire and prepare a heavily watered-down batch of Kool-Aid. And at the moment, Jude felt akin: you specialized where you had to.

He pulled a tall clear drinking glass from the cupboard, and a butter knife from the silverware drawer and set them on the counter. Then he slipped into the pantry and grabbed two packets of

Carnation Instant Breakfast, the chocolate flavor. He tore these open as he ducked back into the kitchen and dumped them into the glass. He poured milk just past halfway to give him room and used the butter knife to stir. The knife gave him a nice flat surface to beat against the clumps of powder, and it reached deeper in the glass than a spoon.

Once the powder was mostly mixed-in except for a few, deliciously bulbous clumps of the exact right size to pop and flood his mouth with flavor floating on top, he topped off the milk and gave it a last stir. Then he licked the knife off and set it in the sink and turned to grab the empty packets.

His father was standing at the coffee maker, pouring coffee into a cup. He wore a pale yellow short-sleeved dress shirt, brown slacks and a dark blue bow-tie that looked mismatched with the rest of his clothes.

"Oh," Jude said. "Morning."

His father finished pouring, set the coffee urn back and turned and leaned against the counter, looking at Jude. He sipped from his cup. He squinted out the windows—the view was the dark, white wall of the Wallettes' house—and looked down into his coffee.

Jude felt the failure of his plan domino out through his muscles first, and then—*click, click, click*—begin to topple the ideas and urgency in his mind.

Not knowing what else to do, Jude picked up the empty Instant Breakfast packets, folded them over, and threw them away.

He glanced at his father to gauge what might happen next. He was smiling down into his coffee. It was a quiet, smug smile.

His father finally spoke after savoring several sips of hot coffee. "Not bad."

"Not…" Jude cocked his head like a puppy. "I don't…"

"The coffee. A good strong pot." He lifted his eyes to look at Jude. "How many scoops did you put in?"

"Five, I think. Maybe six."

"I think your mother only uses four."

"Oh."

Jude hovered near his own steaming cup and tall glass of chocolatey milk but not touching them, as though being detained. He had to hook his fingers into the back of his pajama waistband to keep his hands from darting around aimlessly.

"Well," his father set his cup down and stepped across to the refrigerator. He opened it and pulled out the square foil packet that contained his lunch. Then he picked the cup back up and drained it with one long gulp.

Without saying another word, he set his cup in the sink and left. Jude could hear him gathering keys and change in the den, and then, a minute later, the front door slammed shut.

Jude stood for a long moment, his fingers still hooked, but with no nervous pulsing in his hands or fingers. His father never let anything go. And a coffee and a chocolate milk were two things he would not have overlooked. He would have laid into Jude, 'Don't take those out of the kitchen. You're likely to spill. And who's going to clean up after you when you spill?'

Maybe, he thought, his father was happy to let Jude be dealt with by police and the school rules. Maybe his father was just in a good mood—probably because Jude was in trouble. But whatever it was, it was strange.

Jude took his beverages up the stairs and closed his bedroom door.

He listened as Mark left for school and his mother, within minutes, got onto the phone. He was thinking he would wait to do his homework until maybe the last day of his suspension, but he had nothing else to do and he ended up finishing most of it.

His mother looked in on him mid-morning. "All right," she said, "I'm going out to the bowling league. I don't think you should leave the house while I'm gone."

Jude looked her in the eyes and shrugged.

"Don't shrug at me, young man."

He kept his eyes on hers and did nothing.

She crossed her arms, but they didn't sit quite right. Her right hand grasped her left elbow, but her left hand reached up to her shoulder. It looked awkward and uncomfortable. She said, "I'll be back around one or two. There's left-over lasagna in the fridge."

"'Kay," Jude said.

When he heard the front door close downstairs, he crossed to the window and watched his mother descend the 37 stairs to the street. Her face was raised to the morning sun. She wore tan slacks and a pale blue blouse with a pattern of yellow flowers. Her step was light—she kept her bowling ball in the car. She was glad to be out on her own.

Jude felt like he understood her better.

Jude stayed at the window while she pulled the car out and pulled to the curb. Then she got out and closed the garage door and locked it. Jude waited until the navy-blue Dodge Corona had driven down the street and out of sight.

JUDE planned to wait half an hour before leaving the house, but he changed his clothes and was ready in just a couple minutes. Five minutes later, he'd already experienced one eternity. Two eternities was longer than he could wait.

Jude shot out the front door, slamming it behind him, and took the stairs in leaps. He had a momentary catch in his chest when he saw his father's car still in the garage, but quickly realized that his father had walked to work. It hardly mattered anyway. What could they do to him? What was left?

He rolled his bike out and locked the garage. Then he pointed the bike downhill and felt the conviction of gravity. He clattered over the rough and broken pavements, slipped around the buses, and sliced through the corners. He was a hawk piercing down through the winds and crags and trees of a deep canyon.

From Hollywood Boulevard, he took the shortcut. He turned onto the 101 south on-ramp with traffic, one driver flailing his arms and honking his horn to warn Jude. But Jude ignored him and rolled down to the halfway mark, hauled his bike over the guardrail, and then remounted and pedaled up the off-ramp.

At the top, he cut right and immediately saw the Crestview, a block west.

He cut sharply right again and pulled into the first parking lot behind the apartment building across the street. He rode up through three interconnected rear parking areas before pulling out to the street. Now he was well up Canyon from the Crestview.

His hawk-like persona swooped across the street to stay well out of the line of sight of the Crestview and leaned hard right to pull into the alley behind the building.

He rode to the next apartment and dismounted at full speed, riding deep into the under-building parking spots with just one foot on the pedals. He braked and hopped free, locked the bike to a stand-pipe against the wall, and stepped away from the bike.

He stood still in the shadowy hollow of the parking area. It felt like a great deal was at stake this time. Lacey was his last and only connection. No one else understood him, or wanted to. No one else even listened.

It was just after 10 A.M. It was before most of the women were awake. Maybe he would be in and out before even Russ woke up. His one big worry, he decided, was what he would do if Lacey's door was locked. He was afraid to knock, or at least not loudly. And what if Lacey was asleep and didn't hear him? Maybe the window would be open again and he could break in through the screen.

He took a deep breath and walked purposefully out toward Canyon.

As he rounded the dumpster by the garage where Russ kept his Gran Torino, someone stepped from the shadows.

Jude started and stepped back.

Hector stood in front of him, and coming out behind him were his two henchboys. They wore their uniforms of dark blue-and-black plaid shirts and blue jeans. On their feet were black boots.

Hector smiled, "He said you'd be here."

Jude looked past them to the building. He released a frustrated sigh.

"What's wrong, honky, we keeping you from something?"

Jude did not speak.

"We got something to show you, boy."

"Maybe I don't wanna see it," Jude said.

"Oh," Hector laughed, his face lifted in pleasure. It was disconcerting. Jude had never seen Hector laugh. "You're gonna wanna see this."

He lifted his chin to one of his boys and the boy walked toward Jude. The boy had no visible weapon, but Jude still felt threatened and he fell back.

"What's wrong, honky? Think we're gonna beat your ass again?" Hector laughed again.

The kid came close to Jude and then turned down the alley toward where Jude had locked his bike. Hector and the other kid came toward him. Jude didn't move.

The second kid had a broomstick and in a flash, smacked it against Jude's shoulder. "Move, dude."

Jude barely felt the blow. It seemed to blend in with a rising state of stunned bewilderment. Something was happening here that was bigger than a beating from a kid with a stick.

The first kid walked past the first dumpster and walked to a fenced enclosure just past the hedge. He tugged open the gate and revealed another dumpster.

Jude felt sure they were about to beat him up and throw him in. He backed off another step, preparing to run.

The kid with the broomstick lifted the metal lid of the dumpster. He pushed it up until it felt back with a loud bang against the fence. Then he peered in, and using the stick, rearranged something down inside.

"Take a look, cowpoke. We ain't gonna knife you," Hector laughed. "Not yet."

Jude stood his ground. He looked up and down Canyon, and then back down along the alley. He had good escape routes. But really he just wanted these monkeys out of his life so he could get on with it.

"You better not try anything," Jude snarled.

Then he strode to the corner of the dumpster furthest from them and looked in.

The first thing, the only thing, he saw was Lance Wilhite's face. His mouth was open slightly showing the edges of his straight white teeth.

Even a glimpse was enough to know, the boy in the dumpster was dead. His eyes were wide open, unseeing, and rimed with a whitish crust. His lips were pale, almost blue, and cracked. But mostly, he was still. Stiller than still.

Jude's stomach lurched. His hand rose and touched the filthy edge of the dumpster. He drew himself closer and stared. He felt his fingers shaking and his skin felt cool in the hot sun.

He looked up. Hector and his friends were lined up along the opposite edge, all grinning, watching Jude expectantly.

Jude looked back down. Lance's face and knees and boots were poking from a layer of crumpled newspapers, oily grocery bags, old clothing and scattered egg shells, orange peels, and lettuce cuttings. A desiccated cluster of dead roses lay down near his feet.

But, could it be fake?

Jude pulled indifference over himself like an old overcoat. He shrugged. "So?"

The kid with the stick waved it in the air once, drawing everyone's attention. Then he reached in and began plucking away the newspapers that were covering Lance. Flies rose and a yellow-and-green striped shirt was revealed. The shirt had three dark stains on it.

Jude met the gaze of the kid with the stick. The air felt still and dense as though it were slowly turning solid. Jude's fingers were still shaking and his tongue felt thick.

The kid raised the stick and snapped it down hard on Lance's forehead. The blow sounded dully in the metal container and raised a quick purple welt. But Lance did nothing.

Jude let go of the edge of the dumpster, took a single step away and bent over hard. He threw up into the narrow slice of dirt and jade plants between the apartment buildings.

"Hah!" Hector was exultant. He was at Jude's shoulder, leering down.

Jude stayed down, his hands clutching his knees. The vomit had left an unimpressive spray of wet over the jade plants, but nothing else was visible. The smell was troublesome, but it competed with the sickly-sweet smell of garbage and the Los Angeles perfume of old motor oil, bus exhaust and dust.

His retching subsided. His stomach was empty. The heat of the day was seeping into his back. But now it felt like his mind was blaring and wobbling inside his skull. What was happening? Why would Lance be here? Next door to the Crestview? With Hector and his gang there?

He pushed off from his knees and confronted Hector, his questions making him feel fearless.

"What the fuck, Hector?" anger bloomed inside the words, and

Jude stepped into Hector, forcing the boy to step backward. "Did you and your loonies kill this guy? What? Because he's a narc?"

Jude was still advancing, his voice rising. Hector, surprised, was retreating. The henchboys watched with open mouths, awaiting commands.

"What the fuck, Hector? Do I gotta call the cops?" Jude felt his hands and arms moving, his jaw was thrust forward. His brain was telling him these boys were dangerous, but there was a slice of new information that seemed real: He was mad enough to at least scare them. All three of them. And if they weren't convinced... The consequences seemed perfectly reasonable.

Hector's hands were up, flat palms to Jude like Stop signs. "Hey, Whitey, let's calm down." He gestured to his pals. "We just got word he was here, man. That's all, dude."

"Who said I would be here?"

Hector backed up against the side of a parked car and stopped. "Look man, I didn't know this little dude was your buddy."

"He's not my fucking buddy." Jude swung around. His eyesight was clouded with thick red orbs and his whole body, though he was untouched except for the bruised shoulder, felt bruised and sore.

His gaze travelled across the scene. It was a sad, quotidian splay of near lifeless back alley concrete, telephone poles, steel and chrome cars, and the squared canyon walls of stucco and plaster broken by the shine of empty windows.

He felt severed from it all, as though he'd been thrown on some alien planet. His mind jerked and bounced over it, not touching down. "Who?" he asked again. But he knew. It had to be Paulo.

But the corner of the garage at the Crestview was visible and the idea of Lacey drew him like a magnet.

"Look, honkey," Hector started.

Jude was already in motion. Worry sprouted, blade-by-blade, like a shimmering lawn inside him, and was soon blanketing everything. This was happening a hundred feet away from Lacey's apartment. What had happened to her? Did she know? Did the whole building know?

He raised a middle finger in his wake and surged away.

"Honkey!" Hector called after him.

Jude cut sharply around the corner of the building and took the steps two at a time. At the landing, he spun and peered down the walkway. There were two women coming up the front stairs, but he didn't recognize them. He glided to Lacey's door, knocked once, and then turned the knob and stepped in.

His body felt lit. She was going to be glad to see him. And he was glad to finally see her.

He opened his mouth to call out, but his voice was dead.

His senses were drinking in the scene, looking for the familiar, the beautiful, the aromatic, the loveliness of Lacey. But this room was… this room was completely different and strange.

He was in the wrong room.

But…

His heart lumped and pounded. Maybe the couch was the same, and maybe the kitchen table and chairs, but all the rest…

Jude stood in the open door, staring at the room. It was transformed into something so normal it was bizarre and strange. The furniture was the same, but moved. The place was immaculately clean. A bright red-and-yellow throw rug spread over the brown-and-beige shag carpeting. There were potted plants. A standing lamp of gilt gold. And in place of the dark and intimate photographs there were two movie posters over the couch, one from *The Sound of Music* and one from *Fiddler on the Roof.*

He lifted a hand and grasped the door frame. He realized he was trying mightily to force one notion in over another. He was ramming in the idea that Lacey had decided to redecorate, but the notion under it was sitting there unmoving, unblinking: that Lacey was gone.

And the music…

It was the Mamas and the Papas, "California Dreaming." And Jude somehow knew that he would hate that song the rest of his life.

But then Lacey came out of the bedroom, whistling. She was looking down, unfolding a towel.

"Hey, Lace…"

But his voice died again. When she lifted her eyes to look at Jude, she was not Lacey. She was blonde and almost the same height, but she was not Lacey. Her skin was reddish, her chin narrow and her cheeks wide. Her teeth were small, rounded a bit, like baby teeth.

"Oh! Wow!" The woman stopped. "I'm sorry, but, ah…"

"Where's Lacey?" Jude asked, his desperation rising.

"Oh, yeah, Lacey," she nodded, very seriously. "She moved out. Yesterday."

"Where," Jude felt his fingers knot into fists of impotence and frustration. "Do you know where…"

"I don't," she shook her head.

"Who are you?" his voice leaked accusation, and he regretted it.

"I'm Juniper," she said. "Juni for short."

"Hey," he said. Then he abruptly let himself out.

He headed straight for Penny's door. He wanted to be expedient, get in before Russ saw him, so he knocked once and grabbed the knob again. But this time the knob didn't budge.

He knocked again.

It felt like an eternity, but he finally heard her coming across the living room.

"Hey?" A pale face, blinking looked out. But it wasn't Penny.

"Is Penny here?" Jude asked.

"No," the woman blinked again, rapidly, and then slowly shook her head. "She moved. Are you like…" The woman pulled the door open a foot or so revealing her nightgown and bare legs. "Like her little brother or something?"

"No," Jude said, backing up, "No. I'm a friend."

"Well, I'll tell her if she comes by, and all."

"Ah, yeah. That would be great." But he knew he would never see this woman again, and probably not Penny either. "Yeah, well, I gotta go."

He spun to leave and almost bowled over Frenchie.

"I thought that was our little pervert mascot," she smiled crookedly at him.

"Frenchie!" Jude was thrilled. He'd completely forgotten Frenchie! He reached across the gap between them and touched her arm. Her eyes followed his hand and her brows rose in surprise. Jude pulled back his hand but blustered on. "Where did Lacey and Penny go?"

Frenchie laughed, one hollow bark. "Penny's down at the Yorkshire." She drew on her cigarette with exquisite purpose. Then she locked eyes with Jude and exhaled. The smoke forming a lazy, catlike cloud that sauntered out past the railing. "You know," she continued, "'cause the Walker brothers are pissed at her."

"Pissed, why?"

"Cause she helped Lacey leave."

"Why did Lacey leave?" He heard his voice rising and felt his desperation rising with it.

"Yeah," now Frenchie was nodding her head and curling her lip at Jude. "Because of you."

"Me?"

"You gave her a wad of cash, and she bailed." Frenchie laughed. "That messes up the whole system. You can't be giving a whore wads of money, boy, or they get these ideas." She tapped her head with her cigarette hand.

Jude shook his head. "But where'd she go?"

But a strange, serious man was suddenly standing on the lawn below looking up at them. He was thin, wearing a threadbare, tucked-in T-shirt and dark pants. His feet were bare. He had a shock of black hair and black eyes. His skin was almost translucent it was so pale.

Jude looked back to Frenchie.

"Don't worry about him. That's Clarence. He's the new Russ."

"The new Russ?"

"Yeah, Russ is gone."

"So..."

"I don't know," she finished for him. "And as for Lacey, hell if I know. She never did cotton to me. But..." Frenchie was wearing a robe over a bikini, and she pulled the robe open a few inches, revealing the pale swelling of her breasts, her rising thigh, "you can come do my dishes and leave me a wad of cash any time you want."

Jude was crumpling inside. There was a weakness in his chest that seemed to sluff away like a sand berm under the waves. In an instant, his eyes were welling.

"Oh shit," Frenchie cuffed him on the shoulder. "I'm joshing, Boy Wonder."

"Yeah," Jude said.

He felt stalled in time, as though the day's heat had coagulated and was holding him, and everything around him, locked tight like a bug in amber. The scrawny man on the lawn peered up at them. Frenchie watched Jude. Jude felt like if he could just find a thought in his head, find it and finish it, then he would be freed.

But his mind lay there blank and panting. Exhausted.

"Where's that girl?" Jude asked. It was a non-question, like the girl was a non-participant in things, a non-whore, maybe.

"What girl?"

"The skinny pale girl that was hanging around you all the time," he gestured with his chin to the chairs on the balcony on front of Frenchie's apartment.

"Oh, Denise," Frenchie laughed and frowned at once. "Yeah, she's gone, too."

"Denise," he said. Her name was wrong. It should have been Merry or Wendy or Roxy.

"Yeah. Gone." Frenchie pushed her chin out at the world beyond the walkway to indicate where 'Gone' was exactly.

He shrugged. The pale Denise girl had nothing to do with anything. She didn't matter. Just another thread in the vast tapestry of Los Angeles misery.

"Okay," he stared down at his hands. They were shaking. He shoved them deep into his pockets and then balled them into fists, hard against his thighs. "What happened to her?"

"Who knows."

"I mean," Jude shrugged and held it, his shoulders high around his ears. Why was he asking about this fucking Denise? "She was your friend."

"She was crashing in my living room." She stared hard at Jude now. She flicked her cigarette butt off the balcony, and while her eyes stayed coolly on Jude, both Jude and Clarence watched the arc of the falling butt until it dropped among the ferns and disappeared. Then Frenchie pulled a pack of cigarettes from her robe pocket. In studied, measured motions she slipped out a packet of matches, tamped down the tobacco, and scratched a match into flame.

Jude let his eyes linger on the pack, and Frenchie shrugged and offered him the flattened oblong shape. He reached across and pulled a cigarette from the pack.

"Hey kid," the man below spoke finally, his hand shielding his eyes.

But Jude ignored him, and bent to Frenchie's fingers where the match was burning down.

"I felt sorry for her," Frenchie said. "Happens."

Jude dragged hard at the cigarette and squinted through his own smoke.

"But spend half an hour with anybody and you find out soon enough they're in a mess for good reason."

"Yeah," Jude nodded, but couldn't imagine ever having enough of Lacey. He looked down at the man on the lawn. Then out toward the alleyway where he'd just seen Lance Wilhite lying dead in a dumpster. His eyes climbed to the rooftop across the street and then to the haze-locked skyscrapers downtown.

The distances were great, but Jude knew Lacey had had even greater distances in mind when she left.

When he focused again on the scene before him, standing on the lawn, halfway between the two stairways, was Paulo. He was wearing his biker gear, oily boots and jeans, torn denim vest, a white T-shirt with some kind of emblem on it, and a red bandanna. His eyes were on Jude and in his hand was a dull-bladed Bowie knife. He looked dour.

Paulo was ignoring the new guy. But the new guy started over toward Paulo, maybe ready to take control.

Jude had no faith that the stickman could exert any influence at all on Paulo. He looked up and down the walkway. A few doors were open now and women were standing in them, watching the scene unfold. From Lacey's old door, Buffalo Springfield's "For What It's Worth" was playing.

Stop, hey, what's that sound?
Everybody look what's going down.

He moved toward the front, and Paulo began to step that way. Jude did not want to deal with Paulo.

Jude looked at Frenchie. Her eyes searched his, but there was nothing she could do, and her expression was flat. He saw no way out. Paulo had him trapped.

Jude reached down in his pocket and tugged out the roll of bills. "Here," he said, and pressed the cash into Frenchie's hand.

"What?" Frenchie stepped back a pace like it might be a trick.

But she opened her hand wide to let the bills unroll in her palm. There were over two hundred dollars there. "What the fuck? Are you crazy?"

"Maybe," he said.

Letting go of the money had freed his thinking. He had his way out. He ducked past her and shot down the walkway. The shadow of Paulo was rushing along the lawn after him.

At Lacey's old door, the new mousey one was there, and without looking down at his pursuer, he raised an arm to slice himself into the room past her.

"Hey!" she squeaked.

But Jude barreled past and tumbled through the living room at a dead run. Imagined or real, he could hear the thunder of Paulo's boots on the stairs.

Jude ran into the bedroom and leapt across to the window. With both hands he thrust the screen out, bending the frame with a crack, and let it fall. Then he was out. The tree was there and he let himself down onto the limb, hanging by his hands. Above him, he heard Paulo's voice at the front door, and he dropped.

The second his sneakers hit the sidewalk below, he was running. As he cleared the back corner of the building, he heard Paulo. "Get your ass back here, you shit!"

The thundering started again, the whole building behind Jude filled with Paulo's rage, it's walkways and stairs exorcising him like a demon.

Jude ran to his bike. He flew past the dumpsters, both closed and mute now, and arrived in a slide across the dirty pavement. No sign of Hector or his hoods.

He spun the lock face forcing his brain to slow down enough to generate the three digits in correct sequence, and forcing his fingers to only do what they needed to do, and nothing more. It was 28. Two spins left to 9. He wiped his fingers on his jeans. One spin to 32.

The lock popped and Jude yanked the chain through the spokes in a clatter. He slung the lock over his shoulder, barely taking the time to snap the hasp closed over the last link of the chain.

He could hear the raspy clunk of Paulo's boots hitting the driveway. In his mind's eye, he could see Paulo lumbering like a bear. But a slow bear. Even the sound of the man's running feet was clumsy. He wasn't sure, but he thought he heard Paulo yell, "Where the fuck is Lacey?"

But Jude was on his bike accelerating down the alley and Paulo's shouting fell quickly away.

JUDE set a course for home, but fear crawled up his back and he took random turns and rode down alleys without traffic to make sure Paulo wasn't following him. His mind slopped about like an overfilled bucket. Lacey loomed, but if he let her in she brought panic and tears. Just past Lacey was the dumpster half-filled with trash and Lance's face peering sightlessly upward.

Jude pulled his mind in, drew down his focus, and rode harder. At the moment, there was the pavement, the traffic, and avoiding Paulo at all costs on the way home. As he crossed Hollywood Boulevard, his next absolute goal fired in his brain. He had to be cleaned up and hard at work at his desk when his mother came home.

He crossed Hollywood, crossed Western, and skirted along side streets below Franklin. He figured if Paulo was looking, he'd drive the main boulevards. When he got close to home, he crossed Franklin at Alexandria instead of Normandie and set in for the hard stand-on-your-pedals climb up that street, choosing to drop down from above the house instead of taking the direct route from below.

At home, no sign of Paulo, he opened the garage and peered into the dark. His mother was still out. He put his bike inside, locked up and hurried upstairs.

In his bedroom, he found himself in the mirror. Even though he'd had no real scuffle, his shirt was streaked with sweat and dirt and his jeans were torn at the knee and bloodied. He didn't remember how that had happened. The image of himself fired again. He had to be quiet and clean, sitting at his desk, doing homework. This was what his mother needed to see when she came home.

He quickly stripped off his clothes and stirred them into his dirty clothes hamper. Then he gathered up fresh clothes and started the shower. He hosed off, got dressed, and then dried the tub a bit.

His mother opened his bedroom door twenty minutes later. He was leaning over his *California and Society* text, taking notes.

"Jude?"

"Yeah?" he looked up.

"Did you go out on your bike?"

"No, of course not."

"You didn't try to see your friend at that awful… well… apartment building?"

"No, Mom. Besides, I think she moved."

"Why do you think that?"

"All the commotion Dad made over there, and the cops and everything."

"Hmmm," her eyes kept traveling the room, inspecting walls full of tack holes and old tape. "And you're sure you didn't go out?"

"Yeah, Mom, sort of sure."

But she wasn't convinced. Jude could see it. Some dark stone turned over inside of her. There was a slow hardening around her eyes. And when she spoke, her voice had changed. It lost its edge of concern. It became brittle and filled with conviction. "Well, maybe we've had just about enough of all this, too." She lifted her gaze out the window as she spoke and then got to the point. "I think you just need to calm down some, Jude. Be a part of this family again."

Jude watched her but said nothing. He knew, leave his mom to her own devices and she would, sooner or later, come back to thinking and speaking just like their father. It was what was called a closed loop.

She snapped her eyes on Jude. "Did you hear me?"

"Yeah, Mom. It's just, I gotta finish this chapter, and then I'm done with all my homework for the week. I guess I'm just trying to concentrate."

"I don't for a minute think that's what's happening here. When I tell you to stay home, you *stay home.*"

Jude shrugged and sat sullenly over his homework.

His mother released a deep sigh. "Oh. All right." She softened the line of her shoulders and smoothed the front of her blouse. "Have you eaten?"

"Maybe later."

Jude sat in the slipstream of her visit and felt the rime of panic and anger closing in again. But, with his mother in the house, he didn't feel like he had the freedom to think. Thinking for Jude was not some mere mental wandering. It was the thrust and feint of reality with real consequences in real time. He was afraid that if he had one particular kind of thought—like where Lacey might be right now—that he might be out the door and moving in her direction before he could do any of that wimpy kind of thinking—all strategy and insight and inaction.

The doorbell rang, popping Jude from his reverie. His mother yelled up to him. "Jude, Kevin is here!"

"Okay!"

Jude sat still and listened to the light banter downstairs. There were no words he could hear, just the cheerful discomfort of two people who barely knew each other and were a generation apart. It was like forks and knives at a nice dinner.

Then the soft pulse of Kevin's steps on the stairs. And then, a moment later, his bedroom door pushed in tentatively.

"Jude? You in here?"

"Where else, dude?" he rose from his chair. "You're pretty brave, coming into the quarantine zone."

Kevin smiled and nodded. "Yeah, well, I was warned."

"I can imagine. James probably had a thing or two to say. And your mom probably thinks I'm a hardened criminal."

"Yeah," Kevin was wearing his virtual uniform of slightly faded straight-leg jeans and a striped cotton dress shirt.

Kevin waited for more, but Jude remained silent.

Kevin sat down on the second bed. "So, what happened? How did you get suspended? I mean, we all thought you were free-and-clear."

Jude slumped down on his bed, facing Kevin.

"I guess it's automatic," Jude said. "That's kinda what Glenn said. Do the crime you gotta do the time."

"Yeah, but…" Kevin's brow gathered over the missing puzzle pieces.

"I know, I was never arrested."

Kevin was animated, "Yeah, exactly. Like, how can the school, you know, say you were doing something illegal if you were never even busted?"

"The school can do whatever they want is how."

Kevin nodded and peered around the room. His eyes fell on the shelves, the desk with its turntable, the big dark dresser, and then, like Jude's mother, stumbled onto the walls.

Then his gaze snapped back to Jude and he said, "So you gotta tell me, man, what went down?"

Jude scrunched and then pinched his nose as the events clicked through his mind. His brain was quickly sorting and ordering, laying down pieces of the story in their proper sequence and with the proper headlines—some headlines big and all bold, and others less so.

But the big headlines, the banner across page one...

LACEY MISSING!

LANCE MURDERED!

This was now the whole story, but he couldn't tell Kevin about it. Partly it was crazy dangerous to tell Kevin that Lance was dead in a dumpster off Canyon Avenue—Jude suddenly wondered if he should call the police and let them know.

But more important, and he had to remember this and be very careful, Kevin had gone home and blabbed to his mother once before. He was likely to do it again.

"Boys?" Jude's mother knocked and pushed in. She was wearing an apron and carrying a tray. "I brought up some cookies." She set the tray down. There were two glasses of milk and a plate of chocolate-chip cookies.

"Cool!" Kevin said.

Jude watched the unfurling of the moment. Mother in apron with tray of milk and cookies for teenage boys. If it were a film, he could feel the future scenes unroll with vapid placidity to a slow, smug death somewhere in front of a television with intertwined cigarette smoke and matching vodka glasses. He felt tired disgust. He was not a child. He could not be calmed down and brought back into the fold so easily.

When his mother left, Jude watched Kevin pick up a cookie and his glass of milk eagerly. Jude ignored the plate and watched his friend eat.

"So?" Kevin asked after surfacing from a gulp of milk.

"So," Jude began his telling. He created a hobbled version of events under the headline Kevin expected.

Junior high boy wronged by suspension!

By the time he'd gotten through Mr. Denny's response, he had reached up and grabbed a cookie.

Now he was thirsty. He reached for the milk.

THE MOMENT the front door slammed shut after his father in the morning, Jude was on his way downstairs. He'd made a mere squeak about being allowed to ride his bike today at dinner last night and his father had shut him down.

"You're not going to be out gallivanting after what you've done, young man."

Mark tried to jump in. "He got suspended. He's already being punished."

But Jude let it drop. He knew pressing his case would probably result in a specific and categorical ban on his bike or on even leaving the house.

He was keyed in, instead, to his mother. He knew she didn't much like having Jude home all day. Jude had had no real idea what she did with her days, but staying home even for two days was enlightening. She spent hours on the phone every morning, and then went out to shop or bowl or play bridge. She returned home a few minutes before he and Mark would arrive home and generally got back on the phone again.

So Jude entered the kitchen just as her hand was reaching for the telephone.

"So," he said, stalling her hand in midair. "Do you think I should stay inside all day?"

"No, of course not." She let her hand fall reluctantly. "But you heard your father last night."

"Yeah, well, it's not exactly gallivanting. I mean, I'm a kid in a city. All I can do is ride around."

"I don't know, Jude."

Jude pulled milk from the fridge and two packets of Instant Breakfast from the cupboard. He kept his face averted. His main concern was that she not see the blue hollows under his eyes. He had not slept. His mind was like a SuperBall fired by a gun into a metal trash can. His body, dragged along for the ride, felt like a rag doll.

"You'd rather I walked?" he asked. "Like maybe down to Hollywood Boulevard? Or up to Griffith Park?" Griffith Park, or at least the Ferndell entrance, was a known hangout of hippies, gays and bums.

His mother lifted the phone from the cradle while her eyes clouded in thought. "But," she'd leapt ahead to Jude on a bike, "you're not thinking about going to that horrible apartment building are you?"

"Mom," Jude drew the word out, stressing her obvious lack of thought. "Those women are whores. They don't get up until like three in the afternoon. And like I said last night, Mom, Lacey's long gone."

"Oh!" He'd shocked her. "Well…"

Jude stirred the clumps in the mixture in his glass.

"That's not all you're going to eat is it?"

"It's plenty, Mom. It's two whole breakfasts." He held up the two empty packets.

"When will you be home?"

"By three, easy."

"All right," she gestured with the receiver. "But only if you're home by three."

Jude drank off the chocolatey mush and set the glass in the sink. His mother was already dialing.

He rode down Normandie and turned left. He hardly ever went left from home. School, Hollywood Boulevard, Sunset Strip, the beach… everything was to the right. But the Yorkshire was downtown and downtown was left.

In the night, after Kevin had left, and really after dinner, and even later because Jude felt like Mark or his mother or father would intrude, Jude had sat up and thought through the events of the last few days and what he needed to do.

He burned through anger and frustration at Lance, Russ, Hector and Paulo. He assumed it was Paulo who had somehow initiated the course of yesterday's events. He must have killed Lance, or had him killed. Because Lance was outed as a narc. And then Paulo had told Hector to watch out for Jude and to scare him.

But Jude could not see why Paulo was so keyed in on him.

As he rode, tunneling through into the dense brown haze that stained the city, he wondered at his own sense of calm. He'd seen a dead man—not much more than a dead boy, really—and his stomach had turned. Then he'd gotten over it. Lance was a stupid ass to even be in Los Angeles, especially after he knew word was out about what he was doing.

He knew that if he could find Lacey, even to talk to her for five minutes, that this whole thing would come back down to earth. That his mind and body would not be fractured and screaming. That he could sleep again. Go back to school. Be a kid in his own house again, at least for a while.

At least he thought so.

He jounced past Echo Park Lake, three tall fountains standing above the sparkling green water. Old men and a few old women were sitting on the benches. Always alone. A couple out in a pedal boat. Swans and ducks.

He decided he should come out this way more often.

Then he passed under the 101. The density of the cars all around him, and even on the bridges above his head, was oppressive. But the way from here was downhill, and his bike sailed easily, rattling and hopping over the cracks and stones. The city skyline loomed straight ahead, great blades of buildings, taller to him than any man-made object he'd ever seen.

He angled left under the concrete pilings of another overhead freeway onto Second Street and encountered hills he had not expected. He assumed downtown sat on a flat. But a dusty, blank hill blocked him from the skyscrapers.

At Figueroa, he waited for a light. He was on the verge of the city, but the sidewalks were empty. The buildings here were stolid, dirty, and low. Cars and trucks packed the open concrete. The mass was salted with yellow and dark-green taxis. When lights changed, the cars leapt like shotgun blasts, all seeking some new, slightly better place in the mass before the next light went red.

Ahead, he could see a long curved tunnel with wall-to-wall traffic that passed through the hill. It looked forbidding to his bicycle. He crossed the intersection, and instead of entering the tunnel, he pulled left with the traffic and climbed a side street.

At the top, he hit First and turned right. The Yorkshire was on Broadway, and Broadway was a few blocks into the city. He rode to the top of the hill and stopped at another light. Across the street was the Ahmanson Theatre. The name was odd and yet familiar. He remembered that his parents had gone here for some event.

Now it was downhill again. He rocketed down, blasting through a yellow light, and at Broadway, light green, he leaned hard through the corner and fired himself down the street.

Now there were people. And the buildings ahead flowered detail like icing on a cake. He could see lumbering trucks down in the canyon of the street. Masses of people crossing at lights. Colorful theater signs rising above.

Jude passed a glass-fronted Goodwill store on the right. The street was densely packed with stores of every type. Bookstores, drug stores, furniture, clothing, jewelers, cafes. But more and more, the street was lined with jewelry stores. It seemed like every other store was a jeweler's.

People were dressed like downtowners should be, in suits and skirts, hats and briefcases. There were a few hippies in the crowd, mostly still islands with a guitar and a hat out for change, up against one building or another. Many others were dressed as though this street were barely outside their bedroom. They steered shopping carts among the crowds, they wore layers of overcoats, they yelled at each other and at strangers.

A long opening in the building ahead thrived with people. They were standing in lines onto the sidewalk and as he clattered by, he looked in to see an open-air market, but in a space hollowed out beneath a five-plus story brick building. Grand Central Market. There were neon signs in the dark interior, and the smell of cooking food and fresh coffee wafted across his path.

The Broadway, a block-long, multi-story department store went by on his left. It was a store his mother talked about on the phone. "The Broadway just doesn't carry shoes in my size anymore. They told me I'd have to special order them. Well, I just went to Mays. They had them." She told it like it was almost Biblical. The Broadway could be filling with toads as she spoke.

He rode down between the Million Dollar, the Arcade, the Cameo, the Tower, all big theaters with bulging marquees. He was tempted by the Woolworth's. His grandfather always took him to eat at the Woolworth's counter in Kansas City. But he pedaled on past.

In the next block he saw The May Company store his mother probably went to for her shoes.

When he got to the Yorkshire Hotel, the energy of Broadway was fraying. There were fewer people, and more of them were bums or near-bums. But they seemed tired compared to the bums up the street.

Jude found a place around the back in the alley to lock his bike. It made him nervous to leave it here, but his chain slipped through both wheels and behind a steel standpipe that ran up the back of a building. It should be okay.

Now he set about casing the place. If this was a whorehouse, he knew, then most people would not be up yet. There would probably be a Russ. But, unlike the Crestview where the doors faced the street, in this building, all the doors were inside in hallways.

He needed a way to find Penny, and then talk to her.

He tried the three unmarked doors on the back of the building that opened on the alley. Two were pretty obviously to restaurants. The pavement was dark and slick with grease, ragged mops stood behind a dumpster, and the smell was of rotting lettuce.

All the doors were locked.

He looked up the sheer wall above him. A rickety fire escape painted rust-red and flaking with dark patches of real rust, zagged down to the first floor and stopped there. A straight ladder was hitched to the railing and could be dropped to the pavement in the event of a fire. But there was no way Jude could reach it from where he stood on the pavement below.

Out front, Jude walked past the front of the hotel and peered in through the single glass door, but it opened on a barren hallway that stretched, light-by-light, into the darkness.

Jude crossed Broadway and leaned on a narrow section of brick wall that stood between a shoe store and a placement agency. Embedded in the bottom of the Yorkshire was Pig N' Whistle, a bar and grill that was already open at this hour for the hardcore drinkers. On either side were stores, shoes to the left and a jeweler to the right. The brick building that rose above all this was four floors of squarish windows topped with one floor of pairs of tall, arched windows with fancy filigree around them. Another steel fire escape, this one painted a fading pale green, split the face of the building.

The windows were all blank except one on the fifth floor where a woman was sitting on the sill in a nightgown, coffee in one hand and a cigarette in the other. She was staring out toward the horizon.

Jude knew he'd have to get in blind somehow. He would be likely to encounter some obstacle or resistance. But once in, he was certain that he could just wander the halls until someone left their rooms and he could ask about Penny.

He created a story for himself and crossed back across the street.

At the outside door, Jude looked up and down the street. A man, ten feet away, sitting on an upturned plastic bucket in front of the Pig N' Whistle was watching him, but turned away when Jude looked back at him. He had great black gouts of facial hair and wore a ragged blue parka vest and a soiled, bright red, woolen ski hat.

Jude made uncomfortable eye contact, then forcibly broke his gaze away, and pulled the glass door open.

In the reflection of the door, Jude saw the man start to get up off his bucket. Jude turned his head to look at the man, but he was heading away.

Jude watched him toddle away and he felt a small wash of relief. But the man turned in at the door of the Pig N' Whistle, and Jude imagined Paulo sitting there.

"Fuck," Jude said aloud.

He hurried into the hallway and entered a cloying, musty smell. The carpet under his feet was stained and worn, its greens and blues only visible at its edges. The hallway was long and tall with light sconces low down. It made the walls feel like they rose into a dark nothingness.

A single pay phone hung on the wall. It's hard chrome surfaces and stiff coiled-steel cord looked like something from a sci-fi movie. Stairs rose halfway back. A single word, LOBBY, was painted on the wall, a helpful arrow pointing upward. Jude climbed the stairs cautiously, but every second or third tread creaked or whined, some very loudly.

At the upper landing, Jude peered through the railing. The lobby was a dark hollow in the center of the building. A grimy, oversized chandelier hung over a space no larger than his room. A desk at the far end looked over the room and stairs. He saw no one behind it, but maybe they were seated or around a corner.

In the lobby itself were two once-red wing-backed chairs, now a rusty pink, and a large round low metal table with a glass top. The table top was strewn with car and sports magazines. In the far wall was an elevator.

A hall exited the lobby to the front and Jude could see a door down the hall. Another hallway went off the back of the lobby.

From where Jude stood, he could either enter the lobby or double back and climb the next flight of stairs. He took the next flight.

Emerging on the third floor, Jude found himself in a foyer midpoint in a long hallway that ran from the glass door out to the fire escape at the front to a small glass window covered with iron bars at the back. There were four doors on either side of the hall toward the front, and another four on either side stretching to the back. The elevators stood closed and sleepy on the far side of the foyer.

There was no action. No doors were open, and no sounds were coming through. He climbed to the fourth floor where a box of saltines lay on its side on the table. As Jude cleared the banister, two mice hurtled from the open end of the box and skittered across the rug to a shadow-bound corner and disappeared.

Still no action. No human action, anyway.

He climbed to the fifth floor and headed for the front of the building. He knew that the woman in the front room on the left was awake. He'd seen her.

Jude knocked on the last door, 501.

He could hear faint music inside, and possibly the clink of cooking utensils, maybe even a sizzle on the stove. But no one came to the door. Jude looked out the fire escape window for a moment and then returned to the door.

Now, as he raised his fist to knock, he heard the door, all the way down on the first floor slam and its glass shiver. It was just above faint, but dust seemed to jump from the walls.

He knocked once more, louder this time. It was a last-ditch effort before he would have to figure out someplace to hide. But it was also loud in the empty hallways. His rapping sounded, in his ears, like a pop-gun going off.

This time, the door rattled, rattled again, and then slid open three inches against a door chain. Inside Jude could see warm daylight, colorful furnishings, and a slice of a woman's face, guarded and squinting.

"Hi, my name's Jude," he almost whispered. "I'm looking for Penny, she's new here."

The woman shifted her head from a doubtful angle on the right to a doubtful angle on the left.

"But…" Jude looked to the stairs. The squawk and thud of steps and stairs was closer. He imagined Paulo, or whoever, bounding up a flight, looking up and down the hallway, and then bounding up the next flight. All too quick. "There might be some guy after me. Would it be all right…" His eyes, he could tell, were feeling desperate, and they fell to the chain lock.

"I don't know you," she said, her voice flat.

"I'm Penny's little brother," he said.

"So who's after you?" She pulled back from the door, still squinting and doubtful.

"The guy that made her have to come here."

"What guy is that?"

"His name is Paulo."

Jude could now tell that whoever was coming up the stairs was one floor below him and was starting up.

"There's someone coming," Jude said.

"Hey, like I said…"

Jude's eyes darted around the hallway. He was about to spin and race for the elevator, or the back hall, or… But his fear swept over him and he looked back one more time and said in the smallest voice, "Please?"

The woman shook her head and popped open the chain lock. "All right. For a few minutes." She opened the door but did not step back to make way. She met his eyes. She was short, maybe five-two, slender as a reed, with pale, pale skin and long dark, dark hair. Her eyes were a clouded gray-blue. She was wearing a light blue robe and, as far as Jude could tell, nothing else.

"No funny stuff," she said.

"No," Jude said. "No funny stuff. I swear."

She let him in and said to his back, "It might not look like it, but

I can take care of myself." She closed the door and quietly slid the chain lock back in place, and then, leaning on the door to ease their passage, she spun two deadbolts to the locked position.

Jude moved to the middle of her sunlit living room and turned to face her.

She smiled coldly at him, "You're not actually this Penny's kid brother, are you?"

"Well, no," he said. "But I really need to see her. She knows where a friend of mine went, and I need to find her."

The woman smiled to herself. She picked up her coffee cup and cradled it in both hands. "Well, I don't think it's an old saying or anything, but there should probably be one: 'Don't make friends with hookers.'"

She sipped her coffee and then jerked her head back up, tossing her glossy black hair in a graceful, nonchalant spray. "You did know, right?"

"Know?"

"That this place… Ah, your Penny friend, and ah, you know," her eyebrows arched, her head cocked, waiting for his reply.

Jude looked around the room. It was a roomy, warm space. The living room, a dining area, and the kitchen filled the front of the apartment. The kitchen was simply the far corner of the room with counters and a stove, a refrigerator and a sink. A door beside the refrigerator led, he assumed, to the bedroom and bath. The decor was ratty and dusty.

The two front windows sucked in great slabs of sunlight and looked out over the city center with its cluster of skyscrapers. The view gave the room a regal elegance that dissipated as soon as Jude let his gaze drift back inside.

"Yeah," he said, "I know."

The music that loped along quietly came from a turntable in the living room. It was unfamiliar to him, a high, lilting woman's voice, quite beautiful.

Footsteps in the hall stopped at the woman's door. Jude and the woman stared at each other. Then whoever it was knocked.

Icy chills ran through Jude and he considered running to the window to try to jump across to the fire escape. But the woman jutted her chin toward the door by the refrigerator, and Jude quickly ducked through the passage.

Jude listened while she opened the door and pulled it to where the chain stopped it.

"Hey," a gruff, terribly familiar, voice growled out, "you seen a kid in the building this morning? We gotta find him and get him outta here. Against the rules, you know." He was trying to sound boringly official, but he wasn't fooling anyone.

Paulo was still gunning for Jude, but why? Jude was suspended, and his drug-selling days were over. He assumed that would be clear to everyone involved by now.

"Yeah, well, no, I haven't. No kids. I woulda noticed that."

Jude looked around. He was standing in a short hallway the length of a bathroom door on one side and a narrow closet without a door on the other side. Beyond was a cool, blue bedroom with muted light. There was a window, but it had been bricked in and painted over when the building next door had gone up at some point in the long past. She had hung a small print of the Eiffel Tower in the center of the bricks.

"You sure?" Paulo did not trust her.

"Yeah," she said, her voice lazy, assured. "I'm sure."

"Against the law, too."

"Right," she said. She sounded sarcastic, and Jude worried that she would set Paulo off and he would try to barge in and search her place.

"If you see the kid," Paulo said.

"Yeah? If I see him?"

"If you see him…" Jude could hear Paulo struggling to gain some authoritative footing with her. "Just yell down the hall. We'll be around."

"Right," her voice was sarcastic. "Or should I call Bobby Walker? He's probably the one to call, right?" Bobby Walker must be one of the Walker brothers, Jude thought. Jude loved this woman just then.

"Look, bitch," Paulo snarled. "Just yell down if you know what's good for you."

"Yeah," she crackled. "If I knew what was good for me, I wouldn't be here. And certainly not talking to the likes of you."

"Just. Fucking. Do. It."

Jude heard his boots thundering away. Then he heard the door close, the jangle of the chain, the ratcheting of the deadbolts.

Jude emerged.

"So," the woman passed quickly across the room to the stove, "he was nice."

Jude laughed.

"So he's the bastard that's after you?"

"Yeah."

"What did you do to piss *him* off?"

"It's kind of a long story."

"I'll bet." She lifted a small silver pot from the front burner and refilled her cup. She turned to face him again, and leaned on the counter. "I only really know the girls either on this floor or who have been around for a while.

"I don't know any Pennys," she said. "But, I know a new girl came in day before yesterday on the fourth floor, and another on the second floor, a couple days back. That's the floor with the lobby."

"Yeah? Do you know which rooms?"

"Yeah, same as always. The new girls always get the room behind the elevator 'cause it's loud. I mean, the bedroom is at least on the opposite side of the apartments, but motherfu..." She stopped herself from swearing. She smiled, nicely this time. "Sorry. I started on the third floor in that apartment. All night long, your whole apartment is going clunk, gasp, bonk, shudder, bang." She laughed. "And it ain't the clientele, if you know what I mean."

"Yeah," he said, "I think so."

"Anyway," she smiled at him, "that's where your Penny is, most likely."

Jude nervously stepped toward the door, ready to go. "Thank you."

"No problem. A little unusual. Kid comes knocking. Ten in the morning. But no problem. Really."

She pushed off the counter and walked Jude to the door. "Those guys looking for you... do they mean to do you harm?" She gestured at the knot and bruise.

"Yeah, sorta."

"Well," she worked the bolts quietly. "What's your name, kid?"

"Jude."

"I'm Carrie." She poked a hand out and Jude took it. She made no grip at all, just held her hand out like it was an empty glove. He felt like he was supposed to kiss it, but he just held it a moment, shifted back and forth on his feet, and then released it.

"Careful on the second floor," she said. "Robby is the guy at the desk. Not going to be up yet, but he's got a room right behind the desk so he may hear you."

"Okay, thanks."

Jude crept to the stairs, sure that Paulo or one of his goons would be lurking, listening. He swung around the railing and looked up and down the narrow stairwell between the banisters.

He could hear Paulo's voice. It was distant and muffled. Maybe on the pay phone in the downstairs hall, Jude thought. He decided he needed to get down to the fourth floor quickly and knock on that first door past the elevator.

Jude pushed himself across to the wall side of the stairs and hugged it. He hoped the squeaks would be less at the edges. Still, every squeak or creak sounded to his ears like he was stepping on kittens and drums.

He heard the phone downstairs in the first-floor hall get hung up with a loud plastic clack and a ringing sound. So he took the last few stairs in two hops and pulled hard around the raised newel at the bottom. He landed softly and leapt on his toes the few paces to the first door behind the elevator.

He rapped quick and light, seeing in his mind's eye Penny wide awake and sitting in her living room.

Luckily, it was true! He heard the door hardware almost at once, and the door pulled open an inch. Then the eye inside widened and the door opened another inch. Then another.

"Jude!" It was Penny.

"Penny!" such relief flooded through Jude that he thought he might turn to water.

"Jesus, what are you doing here?" she pulled the chain lock and stepped back.

"Hi Penny," Jude walked in and, tears welling suddenly in his eyes, he grasped Penny like she was his mother. Or like she was who he wished his mother was, someone he could hug and cry with and talk to. Someone who understood. Who just fucking understood.

Penny reached past him and swung the door shut. Then she hung almost passively in Jude's grasp, her hands lightly patting his shoulders.

"Sorry," Jude pulled back and wiped his nose on his sleeve. "It's just…"

"It's all right, Jude. It's all right."

Penny was wearing a brilliant red-yellow-and-orange silk robe over blue PJs that were shorts. She looked tired to Jude. There were rings under her eyes and her hands kept flitting, her fingernails stabbing off to the left and right.

"What are you doing here?" she asked again, spinning away and heading for the kitchen.

Jude opened his mouth to speak, but Penny sliced in, "As if I need to ask."

"Yeah," Jude said. He stepped back to the door and slid the chain lock back in place.

"Paulo's here," he said.

"Yeah, I could hear him in the hall."

The robe was the one bright spot in the room. A single light glowed over the kitchen sink, and the rest of the room was a deep blue core that fell rapidly off into shadows. Jude followed it into the kitchen area.

"You can't go chasing her, Jude."

"I know!" The words burst out as if he'd been waiting for this. The force of it inside surprised him. He sucked in air to calm himself. "I know," he said again. "Of course, I know that."

Penny spun back and looked at him. "I don't even have an address for her, Jude." She turned to the stove, putting on water. "I mean, Jude," she flicked on the burner. "It's too dangerous for me, or you, or anyone really, to know where she is."

Jude slumped to a chair. "I gave the rest of my money to Frenchie yesterday," he said. Tears welled again and he wiped his eyes with dirty fingers. "I should have given it to you."

"Jude…" Penny's voice came soft and comforting.

"I just… I mean… Fuck." Jude's throat closed and a sob popped out of him. He tried to speak, to say 'I'm sorry,' but it wouldn't form in his mouth.

"Jude," Penny said. She cocked her head to one side, but stayed by the stove.

He turned in the chair and wept into the side of it. He tried to wipe his face, but the tears kept coming.

"What happened, Jude?"

Jude stood suddenly, his body unable to stay seated. He held the heels of his hands over his eyes and half-staggered to the couch in the dark.

"Penny!" he cried out.

"What, Jude? What is it?" She shut off the pot on the stove—it was just starting to boil—and moved it. Then she followed Jude into the living room and sat on a chair facing Jude.

"I don't know," he started. "Yesterday it seemed like, I don't know, like it fit somehow. Like, maybe like, it was logical or made sense. But right now it seems…" he had to let it go as tears backed up again and flowed.

Penny tugged a cigarette from a pack on the table between them. She lit it and handed it to Jude. "Here."

He took it and took a soft slow drag. She lit one for herself.

"I got there at like ten yesterday."

"Ten?" Penny waved her cigarette. "Wasn't it a school day?"

"I got suspended from school. And I thought early I might miss Russ and maybe Paulo."

"Suspended?" Penny sounded a little incredulous, like… Jude? A nice little kid like Jude?

"Yeah," Jude said, "just for a week."

"For why?"

"Selling drugs." He gripped his own knees, hard, trying to make a physical pain that would obliterate his mental pain. "That's how I got the money."

"Right," she said. "Lacey told me that."

They sat a moment, Jude gripping his knees still, and Penny taking a puff, releasing the smoke.

"Yeah, they'll bust you for that," she said. "So what happened?"

"Hector, the kid that beat me up the first time I met you, he and his buddies were waiting for me. At the Crestview." He shook his head to clear it of the image of the dead boy. "And they dragged me over there."

"Dragged you…? Why?"

"To show me. They had this kid. Lance. He was the narc from the junior high. He was…" Jude went silent under another surprise wave of bleak sadness.

"He was what? What about the Lance kid?" she asked.

"He was dead," Jude said.

Penny let out a deep sigh. "Jesus." She drew on her cigarette. "You're sure?"

Jude nodded solemnly. "Then, I found out Lacey was gone. And you. And Russ." Jude was finally feeling a clearing in his senses. "I mean, fuck Russ, but I kinda got used to him."

"Yeah, I know what you mean."

"And then Paulo showed up and I had to run."

Penny stood, patted Jude on the shoulder, and then crossed into the kitchen. She poured two cups of coffee, waiting for them to brew down through the paper filter.

While she waited, she cocked one knee forward, her foot propped on her other foot, and smoked, staring mostly straight ahead at the wall.

She lifted the two cups when she was done and headed back. "How much money did you give Frenchie?"

"Like two hundred and fifty I think."

She nodded. "That's a decent chunk, but probably not enough for her to get out on."

"Yeah, it was just spur of the moment. She told me all the news and I thought I'd never see you or Lacey again."

"Well, Jude, I'm glad you found me. I'll admit it's weird, but I am glad to see you." She set the cups down and sat next to Jude on the couch. "You're like a strange link between us all."

"Yeah? That would be cool."

He looked at Penny's eyes for a moment and then the feeling of his physical reality deflating like a tire, he slumped over against her. He pressed his shoulder up under her arm and lay his head on her arm. She acted like an old pillow, just taking the shape of Jude into her side and lap.

Jude was awash again. Tears kept coming, but they felt like lightning, striking down. He missed Lacey one second, but a moment later he would simmer down into the warmth and gratitude he felt curled against Penny. The pit he felt in himself was grief and it was pleasure.

He wanted to tell Penny he loved her. Because right now, he did. And really, she was the one who had come out in the street and convinced him to come in all the way back when Hector beat him up. He wanted her to touch his head, to caress his face. To look him in the eyes and say his name with that sweet sympathy she had used when he was hurt.

"Penny, I…" Jude started.

But she reached across and placed the flat of her hand on his chest. He felt the instruction to be quiet more than he understood it.

In that instant, he saw the great gulf that lay behind the pleasure he had been feeling. Pressed against a beautiful woman, he could not ever be part of her. She was even more remote than his adulthood. She was…

Jude gulped back a sob.

She was his mother, his father, his brother, his friends. She was Serena, Melinda. She was everyone who lived their lives outside of him, and who he would never, ever be with or of. He was separate, alone as a balloon let loose in the sky.

The woman he truly loved was Lacey. But he was alone and he always would be.

He felt freshly born, the icy disdain of the planet laid bare. His knees hurt where they curled tightly against Penny's thigh. His chest fought against the expanding anguish he felt and physical crush of crying. It was as if he were literally tying himself in knots for… for what? To have a stranger, a woman he would probably never see again, hold him.

He straightened a little, rolling his shoulders. Penny lifted her arms away from him and he squirmed. Slowly, he unfurled his body until he was just sitting there on the couch next to Penny. Their hips touched, but Jude hardly noticed.

Tears kept coming, but they just seemed… normal.

He wiped his eyes and looked around the room. Maybe the light had changed, but it felt more like his eyes had been replaced. He saw the lingerie draped over chair backs in the kitchen, dishes on the counter, shoes kicked off under the coffee table where they sat. A disarray of boxes and clothes and odd objects—a clock, a metal horse statuette, a stack of romance paperbacks.

Penny was watching him closely. He turned his head to look at her and was struck by the crow's feet at the outside edges of her lips and eyes. Her skin was pocked a little at her chin. A blackhead lay just under the surface on her nose.

But what startled him was what he saw in her eyes.

He saw raw fear. Not run-for-cover terror, or who-the-fuck-are-you defensiveness. No, she was staring out from that exact place he'd found in himself. She was alone. She was a star in the expanding universe, forever hurtling farther away from all the other stars.

For a moment, he felt sorry for her.

But then he realized that he really didn't feel sorry for himself. Not about this. Even thinking about Lacey, there was a spike of ice in his chest. He'd never felt love. That wasn't what it had been. He'd felt fear. He'd felt lonely.

Everyone was alone. Everyone.

Penny touched his hand. "Jude?"

When he looked back at her, she seemed to have seen his entire transition. She somehow knew where he'd been and what he'd seen. She knew that he was suddenly and irrevocably as cold as a killer.

"Jude," she grasped his hand in both of hers. "I'm, I don't know…" She looked past him to the door sunk in the wall past the refrigerator. "Do you want to…"

Jude shivered. Past that door was humanity's keening for connection and belonging. It was as futile as crying itself.

He leaned forward, elbows on his knees, and slowly shook his head. "I gotta get home," he said.

"Yeah," he could hear Penny pulling back, a sheen of hurt around her words. "Yeah, of course."

Jude stood, his joints, his posture, everything… different. His movements were simpler, scraped clean. But of what? He stood looking around the room. He had wanted to impress Penny. To be liked. Loved, even. And all that was gone.

Jude released a sigh. The world felt impossibly big and troubled. And pain and suffering moved through it like a river. Los Angeles—maybe all the big cities—were the reservoirs where the rivers emptied.

Jude looked back down at Penny. "If you write to Lacey..." he said.

"I told you. I've got no address for the girl."

"Yeah, I know, but if..." he stared at her until he saw it. She let her gaze ratchet down from a soft defiance to a look of acceptance, or maybe even permission.

"Please tell her thank you for me," he looked into her eyes again. He was surprised. She looked like a little kid, her eyes searching his face, her hands moving slightly as though they might reach out to grab his hand. Now it was her trying to find some connection between them.

But, with this new set of eyes, Jude wanted to think about Lacey. He stood in front of Penny and stared into the dark corner of the living room.

He saw Lacey as she was.

She had been in the same place as Penny, right where loneliness and fear tried to find a way to belong. Letting strange men into her bed and playing lover, mother, Earth.

The cool thing about Lacey was, she was getting out.

"Well," Jude said. "I hope Lacey makes it to wherever she needed to go."

Penny pursed her lips, nodded.

"I thought I loved her," he met her gaze again. "Maybe I did. Maybe I still do."

Penny shrugged, "Hey, Lacey's a pretty impressive girl. Lots a..." Penny stumbled over her words, pulling them back. "I mean, you know, lots a people love that girl."

"Yeah," Jude was grateful that she hadn't said 'guys.' But then again, he'd heard it, and seen it, the flow of men through Lacey's bed and life.

Maybe that was any pretty woman. Certainly, any pretty woman who was as sweet and easy as Lacey.

Pretty.

His brain formed the word: Wow. He'd seen his driving need to impress just minutes ago. But at this moment, he saw his entire time in Los Angeles as an effort to impress pretty women. He'd tried to impress others—Kevin, James, Greg—but they were peripheral.

He swept the room with his eyes once again. It kept changing structurally, in reality, each time his mind changed. It was valid, this work that Penny did. Real, vital, essential. It was an Emergency Room for the human psyche.

"Penny?"

Penny pushed herself up off the couch to face him. "Yeah?"

"You've been…" Jude shrugged. Tears of true gratitude sprung to his eyes. "Just, thank you."

He turned awkwardly and lifted his arms. Penny stepped into them and he held her as he'd never held anyone in his life. It was two souls, two beings, two people who knew. He felt her against him, his body thrilling at the warmth of her, the softness and shape of her. Deeper, though, he felt something else.

It was a long moment before Jude loosened his grip. When he did, it was Penny's tears on his shirt.

"I'm proud to know you, Jude," she said.

Jude smiled, with a flickering hint of a grin. "I'm lucky to know you."

"That's right, you little shit!" Penny punched his shoulder. "That's right! I practically pulled you out of the gutter. Rescued you! The beat-up, little lost pup. Brought you in and licked your wounds."

"Yeah, that too."

Penny laughed.

Then a silence settled over them. Jude felt the room change as though a cloud was passing over the sun. He let it sit over them for a moment, and then he took a deep breath, pushed out a sigh, and found the cold, steely center of aloneness again.

He leaned in and Penny leaned in also. They kissed, lips closed, but tight against each other. Penny's hand reached up and touched his forearm. The kiss ran through him in shocks and bursts. He shivered.

They parted. The softening release of her lips was more exciting than even the kiss.

Penny, her body up against Jude's now, lifted her hand and touched his brow. "That's quite a scar, sir. Sexy."

Jude laughed.

They pecked each other on the lips again, and Jude turned. "Thanks, Penny."

"Hey," she said. "Any time." But her lower lips was turned out and her eyes welled.

"Bye," he barely whispered it. He threw the deadbolts, dropped the chain, and with a last look at Penny, he let himself out.

As he was closing the door, he heard Penny's voice, soft and hollow, "Bye, Jude."

THE SECOND Penny's door clicked closed behind him, Jude knew he was in trouble. He felt Paulo looming, watching.

Weirdly, now he just wanted to get home. He wanted to get home and start all over. Start going to classes. Pay attention in band... Maybe. He could be a normal kid. Maybe flirt a bit with Serena, and even Melinda. It was all so fun and innocent.

He just needed to get home. That's all.

But there was some ground to cover. A few obstacles.

The fourth floor hallway was filled with a dark, dusty glow as if the light were old and struggling. The only sounds were muted, with music filtering in from one of the rooms and the city outside thrumming through the walls. The smell was cleaning compounds and old wood, dust and something metallic and harsh.

Jude stood where he was and waited. His eyes and ears slowly calibrating themselves to the long darknesses that lay down the hall in both directions.

But he saw and heard nothing.

He felt sure that Paulo would already have known where Penny's room was. And even if he hadn't, he would know by now. He would be lying in wait now. He would just knock on doors, like Jude did, and ask.

He considered his options. There were the elevator, the stairs and the fire escapes front and back. He suspected Paulo would either be waiting one flight down the stairs, or two floors down in the lobby, or worst of all, at Jude's bike.

Jude started to move toward the back of the hallway to the rear fire escape. He could at least test the door, see how easy it would be to open. And if he could open the door, then he could see if Paulo was waiting by his bike. But the squawk of the floorboards froze him in place.

He listened.

The building oozed a kind of weight and grayness. Colors and smells melded into a whole that was made of a past that had arrived here in the present unexpectedly.

But for a response to Jude's footfall, nothing.

He shifted to the side of the hall, and hugging the wall, he moved along. It was distinctly darker in the back of the building. Fewer windows, and the sun was striking the front of the building.

Jude cleared the landing, not daring to look down in case he was seen, and then slipped deeper down the hall, past one door after another. The lighter smell of sandalwood hit his nostrils outside one of the doors.

At the rear fire escape door, Jude wrapped a hand around the knob and tried it.

Locked.

He swore under his breath and tried again. Still locked. Duh.

He inspected the door. There was a keyed deadbolt in the door, high up, and Jude could see the steel shaft of the bolt in the crack between the door and the doorframe.

He swore again and turned back to face the dark hall.

He could knock on one of the last two doors on this floor. They would be able to access the fire escape from their rooms. But if he did try to involve anyone else, noise would be made and trouble could find him more quickly.

Jude returned to the landing and edged over until he could look down the stairs. He saw nothing.

He edged closer until he could see over the bannister. The view was of the narrow gap between the floor rails and the stair rails. It dropped three floors to the first floor where two mismatched chairs— one wooden with arms and wheels, and one metal without either but with a green faux-leather upholstered seat—sat on a worn red carpet. Next to the arm of the wooden chair, stood a single standing ashtray with a handful of cigarette butts poked into a small mound of shiny black sand.

He saw no one. And there was no movement or sound.

Jude did not imagine Paulo had given up, but he did hope Paulo was waiting somewhere where Jude could see him before he saw Jude.

Jude crept down two stairs. Then he stopped and leaned far forward to see if he could see Paulo, or anyone else, on the third floor below him. But he saw no one.

Holding the rail against the wall and moving on the balls of his feet, Jude stepped down two stairs and stopped again. He looked again. Then he repeated the process. Two quick, silent steps, and a quick look.

At the bottom of the flight of steps, he allowed himself a sigh of relief. He took a few quick steps into the lobby so he could look down the back hallway. The door down this hallway emitted not even a hint of light. It was barricaded shut. Jude turned back.

One flight down, three flights to go. And then there was whatever might be waiting for him outside. But making a flight of stairs gave Jude hope that Paulo was either gone or looking in the wrong place.

Jude took the next flight down to the lobby on the second floor. He moved slow and wobbly and wavering. His eyes strained against the musty, dank dankness. He sought shapes in corners, eyes down hallways. His ears strained to perk and twist like a dog's. His lips were painfully dry. His tongue fought against his patience with its sluggish misery, its clogged desire for water.

There was no one.

Jude went to rear of the hall and tested the door to the fire escape. Locked. Locked with an implacable, keyed deadbolt.

It seemed to him that his sample size—both doors on the fourth floor and this door on the second floor—was enough to establish the policy of the building. If you wanted out the back, you'd have to break a window. But the window here was painted black and covered with a steel mesh.

Jude returned to the head of the stairs and knelt to peer into the gloom below. He leaned far over to look down toward the front door. In the glimmers of reflected light, the hallway looked clear.

He took the first three steps and grasped the rail. Now he could look down the hall toward the back of the building.

But the second Jude's hand touched the sticky old, blackened wood of the rail, Paulo swung up into view on the landing below.

"There you are, you little shit," he growled out savagely. "You cost me an arm and a leg and maybe even a fucking fortune."

Jude's mind leapt and sparked like crazy. He dimly realized he was trying to identify someone, anyone he knew that he could at least imagine: What would he or she do? He needed some guidepost to follow, some intelligence.

But after a shattering instant of hesitation, the field was barren. His father? Mark? His mother? Greg? James? Kevin? Mr. Diaz? Each person was illuminated for an instant by his mind, and then, shrugging, each splayed their hands and retreated.

One thing was clear: Paulo's form blocked any exit path down.

Jude spun and shot back to the stairs and shot upward to the third floor. He took the treads two at a time and made his footsteps as light and easy as he could. He knew that if Paulo was going to give chase, Paulo's own lumbering weight would produce more noise than Jude's feet.

Now, Jude was in a game of hide-and-seek, the same as he and his brother used to play just a couple of years ago. And in those games, Jude had learned how to win. You used your opponent's size against them, you used your lead against them, you used misdirection, and you used patience.

Jude skittered up another flight to the fourth floor, and shot across to the elevator and punched the down button. The two mice, exasperated, bolted from the saltines box again. He waited at the elevator, eyes bugging, ears straining. Paulo was coming, but he was moving more slowly, methodically. Probably not wanting to miss Jude if he was hiding on the third floor hallway.

Behind him, the elevator doors opened and Jude rushed across the little lobby to catch the doors. He held them open, reached in and stabbed the 1. Then he ducked back out as the doors started to close. He crab-walked back to the stairs and flitted upward like a sprite.

When he was back on the fifth floor, Jude shrank back against the railing above, listening.

Paulo started back down and Jude began to feel a momentary relief. But then a door below opened and Jude heard Penny's voice, a demanding edge to it, "What the hell's going on out here?"

Paulo stopped and returned to the fourth floor. Jude could hear his dull steps rise up the stairs.

"You," Paulo snarled at Penny, "I'm gonna take care of. You're gonna tell me where to find her. And if you don't, well, we'll just have to find out what your price is. Won't we?"

"Fuck you, Paulo," she hissed at him. "You've always been all bark and no bite."

"Hey, bitch," Paulo almost whispered. "There's been no *need* for me to bite." He slammed a hand on the rail and dust jumped and stood in the still air around Jude's head a floor above them. "*Yet!*"

Now other doors were opening.

Jude used the distraction of other voices and noises to shoot down to the rear of the hall. He slid to a stop at the fire escape door, yanked off his left shoe and, holding the heel end with both hands, he slapped the sole against the glass, hard.

The glass shattered and crashed, the sound filling the space around him, filling the hall, the building, he felt, and echoing across the alley outside.

Jude reached through, but the door handle would not give. There was no way to unlock the door from outside.

His mind filled with two images that sat side-by-side in strange impossibility. One was Penny as he'd just seen her. Paulo was threatening her, and through her, Lacey.

The other image, oddly, was his brother's one-armed friend Emilio. What had he said when Jude had asked, how do know where to aim? Jude remembered Emilio had loomed over Jude, benign but with that thin, scary smile. "I just know."

Jude lifted the shoe again and quickly slapped out most of the remaining glass. He needed to make it look like he could have slipped out.

Then he leaned down, tugged his shoe back on, pulling hard because it was still laced. Then he turned back into the building.

One door was open on his left, one on his right. Heads poked out. He could hear the stairs creak and moan ahead. He could feel it in his body, precisely where Paulo was on those stairs. Jude knew he didn't have to hurry. He would get there at the right time.

He nodded at the first woman who was peering out. "Sorry about the racket. Some guy wants to kill me."

Her eyes popped open round and she pulled back inside.

He knew now who he needed to channel. He knew... A small man who had nothing on his side but his own conviction: Mr. Denny.

Jude rounded the corner where the landing opened on the stairwell. Ten steps down, Paulo stopped and glowered up at him. He was holding a long, ugly knife. "Yeah, I thought you'd be too chickenshit to take the fire escape. Besides, I've got guys watching the building front and back. You, you little piece of shit," he flashed the blade of the knife in the dull light, "are going to get cut down to size."

Penny was standing on the landing behind Paulo and Jude made a small gesture leftward with his chin. Penny eased back down.

Jude felt a calm spreading in him. Paulo's face, twisted and angry, was scary. But his eyes, Jude could see, were casting, seeking, gauging. The man did not know. He didn't know what to think, or how. He didn't know what to control. Who to threaten. Who to own. He just knew, like a shark, that he was hungry.

Paulo glanced over his shoulder to see who Jude was communicating with, and Jude felt the moment arrive. Jude leapt, and as Paulo's eyes swung back, Jude's feet struck him in the center of his chest.

Somehow, Jude had expected that time would slow down for him. He'd thought that there would be some sliver of time in which to think, to decide, to act.

But time collapsed on itself.

Jude and Paulo smashed down hard on the stairs and tumbled together like a pile of wood. Jude's head and shoulder were flung on past the center of their combined gravity, and he slammed into the rail and then, a breathless moment later, into the landing wall.

But Paulo was still toppling, and Jude, his feet caught in Paulo's folded form, was thrown again, headfirst, out into the hallway.

Jude sucked hard to catch his breath, but there was no room, no air. He curled in on himself and pulled again, but still no air would flow in. His chest felt like a stake was driven through it.

He rolled away from Paulo and lay on his back. He kept trying to fill his chest with air, but it would not take. He stared unseeing at the ceiling, a cloud of dust hovering over them.

"Jude?" Penny was over him. "You okay?"

Jude rocked his head back and forth slowly. His chest...

Penny thumped him high on the chest, hard, and it was as if she'd broken a wall somewhere inside him. Air pulsed in, sweet and thrilling, his body hungry for every molecule.

"Fuck!" Paulo roared and was stumbling to his feet. "You *fuck*!" he roared.

Penny, tugging at Jude's shirt, hissed, "Come on! Get *out* of here!"

But Paulo was on his hands and knees, getting up. And he was crouched between Jude and the stairs.

Jude swept the dingy carpet with his eyes. There, on the first step, lay Paulo's knife.

Jude rolled from his back and hopped to a crouch in a single deft motion. Before his feet were settled, his fingers were closed on the haft of the knife. Then he was in flight, slamming straight into Paulo, his voice urgent, lacerating, even, "Leave Penny alone!"

Paulo rose up like a wounded bear, his oily smell wrapping Jude's nostrils, and Jude falling away from him, desperately trying to hang on. But the man was slick as a seal and there was a terrible new smell, sweet and dark.

Jude was thrown to the floor, landing with a loud thump.

He scuttled quickly backward in a mad crab walk and looked up at Paulo.

Paulo was standing over Jude, pawing at himself, trying to get under his own arm, trying to see. He finally grasped the front of his jean vest and yanked it around.

Somewhere behind Jude a woman screamed.

Jude looked down at his hands. In his right hand was the knife, streaked with blood.

He looked up. Paulo's vest was black with blood. His lips had a thread of blood on them, too.

"Fuck!" the man spat blood at Jude. His hand flew free of his vest and he raised his hands, folding them into fists, attacking.

Jude fell backward, but the man was on him, flailing at him.

Blows were landing on his face and chest. Paulo's breath smelled of something toxic. His eyes were bleary, wild.

Jude felt himself engulfed in a sea of fear. His body was shocked to near paralysis. But his muscles, his feet, his hands… something kept working.

Paulo slapped him hard across the head and he tumbled backward.

A red-hot spark of fury pulsed suddenly and it shot through Jude. His mind cleared and his body began moving, and Jude experienced it with detached interest. He was driving right at the man. Paulo's big flat palms and balled fists were arcing down at Jude, but Jude somehow easily read and ducked each blow.

He stepped in and thrust forward. The tip of the knife snagged on the fabric of Paulo's jacket. He felt the tip catch and drag against something hard, but then it was past and driving into Paulo's clothing and then into his flesh, and Jude felt hot wet flowing over his hand.

He tried to back away, kicking. He could hear his voice. He was screaming.

Paulo, bellowing, was falling forward and Jude could not escape.

It seemed like an hour that he was under the man. Paulo's fists kept rising and falling, and his voice rattled out in anguished fury. Jude pulled the knife and stabbed again and again, having nothing else he could do.

At some point, Jude realized that there was a stillness inside the chaos. It started as a single, tiny pinpoint of awareness. But slowly, as Jude set his focus on it, it grew, and his experience separated out into pain in his face, the compression of his body beneath a great weight, and the stench of blood and dust.

There was a single small voice that called his name. It was Penny, far away, at the end of the impossibly long corridor of his senses.

Then someone rolled the mass off him and as reality swept over him like a cool breeze, he went black.

THINGS happened. Jude knew that much. But he only awoke to himself at the corner of Flower and Third, a half mile from the York-shire, and only then because two black-and-whites—the LAPD—shot past, their springs bottoming out and sparks flying as they bounced across the drains that crossed the intersection.

Jude took a deep breath and looked down at himself.

He was wearing a large men's shirt that he had never seen. He dimly remembered Penny pulling it over his head. Then what? She'd grasped him by the shoulders and said, "Get out of here. Go home. Get rid of these clothes. Clean up."

And then again, "Get the fuck *out* of here!"

Then she had kissed him on the forehead. Then she looked at his face a moment, pulled him closer again, and kissed his cheek. "Jude, you're insane. You're a maniac." She pulled him close, dug her knuckles roughly through his scalp, and held him tight. "Now, get out!"

The last thing she'd said… Jude pulled it into his memory and mentally caressed each word. She'd said, "I'll tell Lacey how to find you. How to get in touch."

Jude felt released then, and he had run down the stairs and pushed out through the front door. There had been no one out front, and no one in the back. The bike was exactly where he'd left it. But there were sirens on the air.

━

NO ONE noticed Jude come home. They were too busy. Down in the street, 37 steps down, it could have been the same truck that brought them to Los Angeles a few months earlier, the big orange-and-black Allied Van Lines logo stretched from one end to the other.

Jude slid into the house through the upstairs rear door. He shot through Mark's room and into the bathroom. In the pink-tiled room, he stripped his clothes, used the T-shirt to wipe all the blood he could off of himself, and rolled his bloody clothes into the oversized men's shirt.

He got dressed in his room and then was out the back again. He stuffed the bloodied clothes deep under the spent coals of the outdoor firepit, and then dropped back to the front of the house.

He sauntered up the front steps as though nothing was wrong.

"What's going on?" he asked. His mother was standing in the living room while two men were lifting the couch from either end. They set the couch in the center of a large moving blanket and began to wrap it up.

"Mom?"

"Oh," she turned and smiled broadly. "We're moving."

"What? Why?" Jude felt put out.

"It just turns out..." she lifted her hand and gestured at the men. "The cushions?"

"Oh, hey, look at that," one of the men grabbed the six cushions and began laying them in their places. The other man held the blanket open expectantly.

"Turns out what?" Jude asked.

"It turns out," she said in a voice meant to impart finality, "that Los Angeles is not a good place to raise children." She swung her head to meet his gaze. "And your father took a job at Loma Linda University Hospital."

"Where's that?" Jude asked.

"It's east of here. An hour or so."

"When..."

But his mother had turned to answer a question from one of the movers.

Jude did not sleep his last night in Los Angeles. He had no idea what had happened to Paulo. Alive? Enraged? Vengeful? Or maybe dead. By Jude's hand?

So Jude lay in bed watching the warmer, faster lights—the whitened car lights and the stinging yellow searchlights—slide over the top of the slow lights—the cool blue street lights, the pale green house lights, the amber glow of the city.

For many hours, he had tried to know what to feel. But any feeling he felt—fear, anger, hope, anything at all—was no more than a scrap in the wind. In just moments it would be overwhelmed, snapping and flashing, and then it would blow away.

So he tried to see what would be there if he tried to just feel without knowing.

This tipped him into a place of steely, dull awareness.

He could see where he stood with people. Like, he was not sure why his parents wanted him around, or even *if* they wanted him around, but he could see that his main function with his mother and father was to be respectable. He must not tarnish their name.

To that end, his father, and to an extent, his mother, would bully, punish, and insult him.

The people at school simply dealt with him because he was there, like a fish in a pond. They were, from Serena through Mr. Denny, and from Mr. Diaz through to Greg, interested in making him belong. Not belong in a welcome way, but belong by not questioning their rules and practices. Belong only as one of them.

The awareness of all this was dulled because it was a dark seeing he was experiencing. There was just a futility to things, as though everyone were drifting downstream to their deaths, and they could survive and ride their path only by grasping the line of the boat next to theirs.

To Penny and Frenchie, and to Russ, and to Paulo and Lance, Jude was an unwelcome intrusion. There were differences of degree, but if there were an erase button on Jude's time in Los Angeles, any one of those people would press it without a second thought.

It was Lacey alone who had seemed to just back up a little, to make space for him. No one really welcomed him. Not even Lacey. But she at least allowed him.

It was in this small, comforting pool of thought that Jude slipped into before he finally fell asleep.

THE NEXT DAY, Jude and Mark climbed into the back of their mother's Dodge Coronet 440 and rolled the windows down. It was the second of November, but the heat was still oppressive. She drove them up to Los Feliz Boulevard and across to Interstate 5. In a few short minutes they were slicing down through the heart of L.A. and Jude could feel Penny's presence a few blocks away.

Lacey.

Lacey floated inside him, improbably close and impossibly far away. Jude watched the towering city jump at the sky, fierce as clown's teeth. And then he looked up again and the skyline was receding into the baked brown smog.

He turned and faced forward.